WHATEVER IT WAS, IT WASN'T HUMAN . . .

"Master," she cried out.

At the sound of her voice, he turned toward her. Urgently he said, "Go child, hurry. This is not your battle."

As she spoke, a broad red slice appeared on his upraised arm as if drawn there by an invisible artist. Though she had caught a bare glimpse of something moving, it was gone before she could tell what it was . . .

Her mouth firmed as another wound appeared, weeping blood down the side of his crippled hand. She gestured, calling a simple spell of detection, hoping to locate the unseen attacker, but the magic in the room was thick and obscured her spell. The assailant seemed to be everywhere and nowhere at once.

She tried a spell that should allow her to discover the kind of magic the assailant used so that she could try un-working his spell. A cold chill rolled its way down her spine as her spell told her that whatever else it was, it was not human . . .

WHEN DEMONS WALK

PATRICIA BRIGGS

ACE BOOKS, NEW YORK

THE BERKLEY PUBLISHING GROUP
Published by the Penguin Group
Penguin Group (USA) Inc.
375 Hudson Street, New York, New York 10014, USA
Penguin Group (Canada), 90 Eglinton Avenue East, Suite 700, Toronto, Ontario M4P 2Y3, Canada
(a division of Pearson Penguin Canada Inc.)
Penguin Books Ltd., 80 Strand, London WC2R 0RL, England
Penguin Group Ireland, 25 St. Stephen's Green, Dublin 2, Ireland (a division of Penguin Books Ltd.)
Penguin Group (Australia), 250 Camberwell Road, Camberwell, Victoria 3124, Australia
(a division of Pearson Australia Group Pty. Ltd.)
Penguin Books India Pvt. Ltd., 11 Community Centre, Panchsheel Park, New Delhi—110 017, India
Penguin Group (NZ), Cnr. Airborne and Rosedale Roads, Albany, Auckland 1310, New Zealand
(a division of Pearson New Zealand Ltd.)
Penguin Books (South Africa) (Pty.) Ltd., 24 Sturdee Avenue, Rosebank, Johannesburg 2196,
South Africa

Penguin Books Ltd., Registered Offices: 80 Strand, London WC2R 0RL, England

This is a work of fiction. Names, characters, places, and incidents either are the product of the author's imagination or are used fictitiously, and any resemblance to actual persons, living or dead, business establishments, events, or locales is entirely coincidental. The publisher does not have any control over and does not assume any responsibility for author or third-party websites or their content.

WHEN DEMONS WALK

An Ace Book / published by arrangement with the author

PRINTING HISTORY
Ace edition / June 1998

Copyright © 1998 by Patricia Briggs.
Cover art by Royo.

ISBN: 0-441-00534-9

ACE
Ace Books are published by The Berkley Publishing Group,
a division of Penguin Group (USA) Inc.,
375 Hudson Street, New York, New York 10014.
ACE and the "A" design are trademarks belonging to Penguin Group (USA) Inc.

PRINTED IN THE UNITED STATES OF AMERICA

20   19   18   17   16   15   14   13   12   11

This one's for my siblings who've all contributed to my books:

Clyde Rowland who introduced me to Dick Francis and Louis L'amour;
Jean Matteucci who introduced me to Rice Krispies cookies, Mary Stewart and Barbara Michaels;
Ginny Mohl who introduced me to Andre Norton and Marion Zimmer Bradley;
and to my sisters' husbands Dan and Greg, for putting up with me all these years. Love ya all.

ACKNOWLEDGMENTS

This book owes debts to a number of people—

Dr. Virginia (Ginny) Mohl, MD, PhD—who put up with late-night phone calls concerning a variety of gruesome topics.

Donald J. LaRocca, Associate Curator, Arms and Armor, Metropolitan Museum of Art—who recommended a number of sources of information on swords, and answered a vital question concerning Kerim's sword.

Jess Roe, swordsman, swordsmaker, and martial artist—who lets me pick his brain at every con I see him at, and is largely responsible for all the authentic details for the fights in this and future books. Any mistakes are mine.

WHEN DEMONS WALK

ONE

Sham sat on a low stone fence in the shadows of an alley pulling on her boots. In the darkness that even the moonlight failed to reach, a sea breeze caressed her hair. She drew in a deep breath of the fresh air.

Even the sea smelled different here in the hilly area of Landsend. The Cybellian conquerors, like the Southwood nobles before them, had chosen to make their homes far from the wharves. In Purgatory, the westside slum where Sham lived, the ocean air smelled like dead fish, old garbage, and despair.

She stood up and ran her hands lightly over the silk of her courier's tunic to make sure that the black and gray material hung properly. She had to fluff the opaque sleeves twice to keep them from revealing odd bulges where she stored the tools of her trade.

It was still early in the winter season, so the silk was warm enough if she kept moving, but she was glad the trousers were made of heavier material. After bundling her other clothes, she tucked them out of sight in the lower limbs of a tree that graced the garden behind a wealthy merchant's house.

Messengers were common on the streets of Landsend, Southwood's capital, even in the darkness of early morning. Female messengers were not, but Sham was lightly built and, on the streets, could pass easily as a boy—as she had for the last twelve years. Even the long braid that hung down her back was not out of place. Only recently had the Southwood men begun to crop their hair like the Easterners who had conquered them.

As she strode through the empty, moonlit street, she noticed a guardsman standing near a cross street watching her.

The east-city guards were as different from the guards of Purgatory as the smell of sweetsalt was from rotting fish. Most of them were younger sons of Cybellian merchants and traders rather than the glorified street thugs who were supposed to keep order in the less prosperous areas of town.

The guard caught Sham's eye and she waved to him. He responded with a nod and waited for her path to bring her nearer.

"Late night," he commented.

She noticed with hidden amusement that he was even younger than she'd thought—and bored as well to talk to a mere messenger.

"Early morning, messire," she grumbled cheerfully in Cybellian, not bothering to hide her Southwood accent since her white-blond hair kept her from claiming Cybellian birth—as long as she chose to leave it uncovered.

He smiled agreeably and she continued past him, careful to keep a rapid straight path and looking neither to the left nor the right until she'd traveled several blocks.

The house she was looking for was on the end of a block, and she waited until she'd turned the corner before giving it more than a casual glance. The hedge was too high for her to see much of the building, but there were no signs of occupation in the upper story. First checking to see if anyone was watching her, Sham dropped to the ground and shimmied under the wall of greenery that enclosed her target for the evening.

The manicured lawn was tiny: Land was expensive in this part of the city. The tall greenery that surrounded it kept out the faint illumination provided by the street torches as well as the somewhat brighter light of the moon. Sham knelt where she was, watching the dark mansion intently for movement that might indicate someone was inside.

The three-storied edifice was newer than the hedge around it; the Eastern noble she was robbing had purchased an old manor and had it torn down and rebuilt in the Cybellian style as soon as the fighting had died down. Open-air windows on the second and third floor might have been useful in the hot, dry climate of Cybelle, but Landsend, despite its southern location, was wet and chilly in the winter months as the ocean currents brought cold waters from the other side of the world to the cliffs of Southwood.

She approved heartily of the new style of architecture, after all, *she* didn't intend to live in it. The open windows, even shuttered, made her job much easier than the closed, small-windowed native styles. As she studied the building, she warmed her hands against her body. The night air was cool and warm hands gripped better than cold ones.

According to her informant, the owners of this particular house were currently enjoying a se'nnight at the hot pools a day's ride from Landsend. Some entrepreneurial Cybellian had taken over the abandoned buildings there, turning them into a pilgrimage temple to Altis, the god of the Cybellians.

The Cybellians didn't believe in the restless spirits who were responsible for the abandonment of the old settlement. They called the native people "backward" and "superstitious." Sham wondered if the protection of Altis would keep the ghosts under control—and hoped that it wouldn't.

However, she wasn't going to wait for the Wraiths of the Medicine Pools to attack the Cybellians. In her own small way, she continued the war that had officially been lost twelve years ago to the god-driven Cybellians and their eastern allies who crossed the Great Swamp to conquer the world.

Using almost nonexistent hand-holds, she pulled herself

up the walls. Setting her calloused fingers and the hard, narrow soles of her knee-high boots in the slight ledges where mortar separated stone, she climbed carefully to a second-floor window and sat on the narrow ledge to inspect it closer. The lip of one shutter covered the opening where both met, making it more difficult for a thief to release the inner latch.

Her informant, the younger brother of the owner's former mistress, had said that the wooden shutters were held closed by a simple hook-latch. A common enough fastening, but not the only possibility, and it was necessary for her to know exactly what she was dealing with in order to open it.

Closing her eyes, she put a forefinger on the wooden panels and muttered a few words in a language that had been out of use for living memory. The shutter was too thick for her to hear the faint click of the latch hook falling against the wood, but she could tell it was done when they opened slightly.

She slid to one side of the window ledge and used her fingertips to open one of the shutters. Stealthily, she entered the building and pulled the panel closed, hooking the latch behind her. Magic was a useful tool for a thief, especially when her victims, for the most part, didn't believe in it.

She stood in a small sitting room that smelled of linseed oil and wax. With the shutters closed the room was awash in shadows. Without moving for fear of knocking something over, she drew magic from a place that was not quite a part of this world. She pushed aside the familiar barrier and tugged loose a small bit, just enough for her purpose. Holding it tightly she molded it into the shape she wanted, using gestures and words to guide her deft manipulation. In another place and time she would have worn the robes of a master wizard.

Magic had always felt to her as if she held some incredible substance that was ice-cold but warmed her hands anyway. With a pushing gesture she flung it away, watching its white-hot glow with a mage's talent. If there was someone here, she'd know shortly. When nothing happened after a count of twenty, she was satisfied she was the only person in the building.

The magelight that she called was dim, but it lit her way satisfactorily through the sparingly furnished halls. She wandered through the building until she found the room the boy had described as the lord's study.

Drawing a gold piece from one of her pockets, she murmured to it, then tossed it into the air. It spun lightly, and fell, clinking, to the hard floor. The coin spun on an edge before it came to rest—hopefully on top of the floor vault where the master of the house kept his gold.

Drawing her magelight near the floor, she inspected the parquet carefully. Under the cool glow she could just make out the subtle difference in fit where a group of tiles was slightly higher than the rest. *Predictable*, she chided the absent lord lightly. Satisfied she'd found the vault, she starting looking for the release lever to open it.

Under the mahogany desk one of the wooden tiles was noticeably higher than those around it. She tried pushing on it to no effect, but it pulled up easily with a click followed by a similar sound from the vault.

She pulled off the loosened section of flooring and peered below. In the small recess there were several leather bags in a neat row next to a stack of jewelry boxes. Lifting one of the sacks, she found it filled with gold coins. With a smile of satisfaction, she counted twenty-three into a pouch that she carried under her silk tunic. Finished, she replaced the bag among its fellows and arranged the sacks so that they looked much as they had before she'd taken her plunder.

She didn't even think of looking through the jewelry. It wasn't that she was opposed to robbery; after all, that was how she made her living—but tonight she sought retribution and ordinary thievery had no place in it. After shutting the vault she reset the tile under the desk.

She left his study to continue her explorations. The money was only a third of what she came to do here this night.

The house looked odd to her Southwood-bred eyes. The

rooms were too big and hard to heat, separated by curtains rather than doors. Floors had been left bare and polished rather than strewn with rushes. No wonder they left their houses to bask in steambaths, haunted or not: the chill air crept through this house as if this were a centuries-old, drafty castle rather than a newly built manor.

She climbed the back stairs to the third floor and found a nursery, the servant's quarters, and a store room. Returning to the second floor, she continued her search. This particular nobleman collected instruments of all kinds, and she'd heard from the Whisper that he'd lately purchased one that was more than it seemed.

She found the music room by the main stairway, a small room dominated by the great harp that sat in the middle of the floor. Several other large instruments were on their own stands, but the smaller ones were arranged on various tables and shelves that lined the walls.

The flute she was looking for rested casually on a shelf next to a lap-harp, as if it were nothing but the finely crafted, eight-holed instrument it appeared. Carved from a light-colored wood and inlaid with small bits of semiprecious blue stone, it looked as ancient as it was. It was more battered than she'd remembered it; several pieces of stone were missing and there was a deep scratch on one side. Even so, she knew it was the Old Man's: There was no mistaking the magic in it.

She shook her head at the ignorance that left such a thing within easy reach of every person who strolled past. It was part of the magic of the flute that it attracted anyone able to use its powers: That the house still stood was proof that the Easterners had no magic in their souls. Impulsively, she lifted it to her lips and blew once, smiling as the off-pitch note echoed weirdly through the house.

She wondered if the nobleman had yet tried to play the instrument and been disappointed by the flat, lifeless tones. She blew again, letting the single tone fill the empty house. The magic the flute summoned made her fingertips tingle, and the note lifted until it was true and bright.

Smiling, she pulled it away from her lips, holding the

magic a moment before letting it free, unformed. She felt a momentary warmth that brushed her face before it was swallowed by the cold room.

She'd once heard the Old Man play it with true skill, but he seldom had taken it out, preferring more mundane instruments for casual practice. Until she'd heard of its sale, she'd thought the flute had burned with the rest of his effects when the Cybellians had taken the Castle.

Respectfully, she slipped it into a hidden pocket on the inside of the arm of her undershirt, and inspected the blousy sleeve of her outer shirt to make certain the lump wasn't obvious. One task remained.

The temples to Altis (every Easterner's house had one) were usually built near the entrance where the all-seeing eyes could protect the inhabitants. So, she left the rest of the second floor unexplored and trotted down the staircase.

It took her much less time to find the altar than it had to find the music room. At the base of the stairs was a set of golden velvet curtains. Moving the heavy drapery dislodged a cloud of dust and left her coughing in the sanctuary of the Easterner's god.

It was no bigger than a large closet, and filled with a musty odor. Despite the obvious signs of disuse, the shrine more than made up anything it lacked in size by sheer gaudiness.

Gold and precious gems covered the back wall in a glittering mosaic, creating the feline symbol that represented the god Altis. The emeralds that formed the cat's glittering eyes watched indifferently as Sham palmed three of the coins she'd stolen earlier.

The first time she'd done this, the cat's eyes had frightened her. She'd waited for lightning to strike as she invoked her spell, but nothing had happened then, or since. Still, she couldn't help the chill that crept up her spine. As a warrior recognizes his enemy in battle, she gave a nod to the green eyes that watched her, then she turned to her work.

Gold was the easiest of all of the metals to work magic upon, so it didn't take her long to melt Altis's cat from the back of the coins. Two of them she left blank, but on the third she drew a rune that invited bad luck upon the house.

She held the third coin over the star on the cat's forehead and covered the green eyes with the other two, blinding the cat. Pressing her thumbs on the eyes and her index fingers on the star, she muttered softly to herself until the golden coins disappeared, leaving the cat mosaic apparently unchanged.

She stepped back and rubbed her hands unconsciously. The rune magic she used was not black; not quite—but it was not precisely *good* either and she never felt quite clean after working it. Not that it would do much harm: Ill luck took a particularly tricky rune. Still, the Old Man could have made it function for several years; the best that she had done was ten months—but she was getting better.

At the thought of the man who was her teacher, Sham reluctantly put her hands on the invisible coins and placed a limit to the physical harm the rune could work so that no one would be permanently injured as a result of the spell. Since she was doing this for him, she needed to follow his rules.

It had taken her years to discover who had been on the jury that had sentenced her mentor to darkness and pain for the remainder of his days. The records that were kept in the early days of occupation were skimpy and difficult for even the most innovative thief to get her hands on. The Old Man wouldn't tell her—he was a gentle man not given to vengeance.

One night though, he'd cried out a name as he thrashed in a nighttime reliving. Sham used that name to question an old court scribe. From him came three other names. She questioned others and offered money for information until she had the names of all fifteen members of the court who decided unanimously to cripple the sorcerer's hands and blind him. The Cybellians who had seen the King's Wizard fight had not been able to sustain their disbelief in magic's power, and they had struck back out of fear. Only later, after Southwood's mages had learned to hide themselves, could the Easterners dismiss it as superstition and delusion.

If she'd known the names of the Old Man's torturers at first, doubtless she would have destroyed them all, but the Old Man's gentleness had done its work. Certainly he would be upset about what little she'd managed to do—if he ever found out.

It was enough for her that she exacted a price from them, a price they might never miss. The bad luck that would haunt them for a while was nothing akin to the pain the Old Man would suffer for the rest of his life. They would shrug it off and go on with their lives, but she would know that they had paid.

The gold she took she kept safely hidden, and soon now she would have the resources needed to buy a small farm in the country. The Old Man had been born and raised in the fields of northern Southwood and he lived in the city perforce. He had given her a reason to live after her parents had been killed when the Castle fell: This was something that she, with the unknowing help of his destroyers, could give him back.

She exited the mansion by the front door, using her magic to trip the locks behind her. Squeezing under the hedge again, she made sure that the street was deserted before completely leaving the protection of the shadows. With luck it would be months before anyone discovered the theft. She hoped no one blamed some poor servant, but that was their business and none of hers.

This time she merely waved at the guard as she trotted past him, seemingly intent on the message she carried back to her employer. By the time a week was gone, he'd never remember her at all.

She retrieved her bundle of clothing and stopped in the alley that marked the edge of the unofficial but understood border of Purgatory. Quickly she exchanged the expensive silk for worn cotton pants, a baggy shirt, and a stained leather jerkin that disguised her sex much more reliably than the courier's garb. The undershirt, with its pockets, she left on.

For most people, walking at night in Purgatory was a dangerous proposition. But Sham's face was known and stealing from a mage was sure to bring ill luck to the thieves. That was protection enough from the Southwood natives, who already had more bad luck than they needed.

Like the rest of the Easterners who had come after the initial attack on Southwood, the Cybellian gutter-thugs generally did not believe in magic. But they were wary enough of her skill with the knife or dagger that they didn't attempt the well-known emptiness of her purse and pockets. If any of them had realized she was female, it might have been different.

Sham walked a while to make sure that no one followed her, casually nodding to one acquaintance and exchanging warm insults with another. As she came down the hill to the old docks, she used her magic to gather the shadows to her until they hid her from a casual glance.

It was strangely quiet at the docks without the constant murmurs that the waves usually made even in the calmest time. The sea was at Spirit Tide, leaving a mile-wide stretch of wet, debris-covered sand well below the lowest of the cliff tops.

The daily tides dropped the ocean level mere feet down the timbers of the docks and allowed only the tops of the cliffs to be exposed to the air. Only once each month did the Spirit Tide expose the pale stretch of beach for a tenth part of a day. One month it would fall during the night and the next during the day.

The support pillars of the docks rose high into the air, backlit by moonlight. The barnacles that covered them were drying for the few short hours that the tide was out. Years of salt water and tides had marred the thick wooden posts, and neglect had left the upper surface laced with missing and rotting boards.

The long expanse of beach was covered with the litter of the ocean; barrels and broken bits of refuse lay between the cracked shells and swollen remains of sea denizens. Once in a while, the broken timbers of a ship that the sea had taken would appear, only to be washed out with the next turn of the tide. Once, it was said, an ancient gold-laden vessel had washed up on the desolate weed-covered sands, and the king of Southwood had used the precious metal to form the great doors of the Castle.

Stories were told of the dead who walked the beach, searching for their loved ones to the creaking of the drying dock-timbers. There was enough truth in that to keep the beach clear of all but the most desperate slum-scavenger at night. By the light of day, the sands of Spirit Beach were fair hunting for all who were willing to fight with their fellow thugs for what treasures the sea had left behind.

When the western docks had been in use, the giant bell on the cliffs rang out as the waters began to recede, and the few ships that had chosen to race the tide would unfurl their sails and their masters would hope that they hadn't waited too long and stranded themselves on the land where they would be destroyed by the abnormally swift, crushing waves of the ocean that reclaimed the empty bay within moments of the turning tide.

Some claimed it was magic that caused the drastic tides that depleted a bay almost four fathoms deep, but the Old Man had explained it differently. Something about the converging of deep sea currents and the great sea wall that protected this bay of Landsend, as she recalled.

It had been a long time since the bell had been rung, as the Cybellian overlords preferred the shoaly bay on the eastern side of the peninsula upon which Landsend was built. They were uncomfortable with the dangers of the Spirit Tide, and Purgatory, once a small blight in the center of the city, had quickly spread its leprous mantle to encompass the abandoned western docks. Several years earlier the heavy bell had fallen from its mounting and landed in the sea to be swallowed by the shifting ocean sands, but the frame on which it had hung was still standing.

Near the docks, higher cliff peaks rose in the air, looking far larger than they did during normal tides. Sham made her way through the rocks of the cliffs, finally lying down on her belly to reach the undercut ledge below.

From the ledge, safely hidden from view, hung a rotted ladder that owed its continued existence more to her magic than any integrity left in the wood and rope. She used the ladder to climb most of the way down the slime-coated cliffs. At the last rung she hung by her arms and dropped two body-lengths to the soft sands below.

Warily she scanned the beaches for the predators that sometimes hunted here, though it was dark enough in the shadow of the cliffs that she wouldn't be able to see anything until it was upon her anyway. She had never discovered anything hunting here herself, but she'd come upon places where something had fed often enough that she remained cautious.

Pulling the shadows more tightly around her, she found the entrance to the cave system that riddled the ancient limestone cliffs, carved by the countless years of water pounding at the wall.

"WHAT IS THIS?" SHE ASKED, STRETCHING TO PLACE HER fingers on the edges of the runes that marked one of the openings.

Maur, his chestnut hair tinged with grey at his temples, smiled down at her. "Wards, child. To keep people out."

She thought about it for a moment. "They're not complete, are they?"

Pleased, the mage crouched beside her. "How would you finish them?"

She frowned at the patterns before her and traced a rune below the last one. As she finished, magic flared and she snatched her fingers back. The opening solidified until she faced a wall where a cave had been.

"Good girl," Maur laughed. Standing up, he ruffled her hair with one hand as he unworked the wardings with another.

"Who put them there, Master?" she asked.

"Now that's a story," he said, leading the way into the tunnel. "I first found this cave by chance when I was a young man. Have you ever heard the stories of Golden Jo?"

She tilted her head and grinned. "Who hasn't? There aren't many thieves with the—" she hastily dropped the word she'd picked up from her father's men and substituted something less shocking, "er—rashness to rob the king in his own chambers." She paused and thought about what she'd said. "*This* is where you found the king's lost crown?"

Maur smiled.

"I thought you did that with magic." For a moment she was disappointed; finding the crown was touted as proof of Maur's powers throughout Southwood.

"Magic," replied Maur, tapping on the runes, "—wit, and a little luck are always more powerful than magic alone. Remember that. I also found the remains of Golden Jo next to the crown; not much left of him after all these years. It looked like he took too much time storing the crown and got trapped in the cave. From the scorch marks in the cave and on the bones, I'd say that he tried to teleport and drew more magic than he could handle—the Spirit Tide's funny that way sometimes. All in all it's a better way to go than dying of thirst."

"He had luck and magic," said Sham slowly, "but his wits were lacking if he trapped himself here."

Maur nodded. "You remember that, child. Never trust to any one of the three: And don't stay in the caves too long."

ONCE THROUGH THE MOUTH AND SEVERAL STEPS INTO THE cave beyond, she called her magelight. By its illumination she worked her way upward through the damp tunnels until she passed the high-tide mark. The small grotto where she kept her treasures was well above the highest mark the water had made.

She stored the coins in the oiled-leather pouch with the considerable pile she had already amassed. There were other things in the cave, too. She knelt and loosened one of the oilcloths that protected her treasures from dampness. When she was finished, she held a small footstool.

LARGE FEET ENCASED IN NEATLY DARNED DAMP WOOLLEN socks rested on the battered footstool near the fire in her father's office. The warmth caused a faint mist to rise from the wool as her father wiggled his toes and set aside the crumb-covered wooden platter.

His blond hair, the same shade as her own, was caught back by a red ribbon from her mother's favorite gown. His chainmail shirt, which he had not taken off, was the best of its kind, as befitted the captain of the King's Own Guards. Over the metal links he wore a wine-colored velvet surcoat, one arm torn where a sword had parted the cloth. Beneath the tear, she could see the stained edge of a bandage.

"Thank you, my dear, though I didn't expect to see you. I thought the sorcerer had you tied up with his work."

Shamera grinned. "Maur released me from my apprentice duties today at the king's request as Mother is needed soothing and terrifying the ladies of the court into behaving."

Her father laughed and shook his head. "If anyone can keep those hens in line it's Talia. Nothing is worse during a siege than a bunch of helpless ladies twittering and—"

His words were interrupted by the call of a battle horn. Her father's face paled, and his mouth turned grim.

He grabbed her by the shoulders and said hoarsely, "You find someplace—one of the tunnels the children play in— someplace safe and you go there now! Do you understand?"

Terrified by the fear in her father's face, Shamera nodded. "What's wrong?"

"Do as I ask," he snapped, drawing on his boots and reaching for his weapons. "You go hide until I come for you."

He never came.

GENTLY, SHAM WRAPPED THE OILCLOTH AROUND THE footstool and set it aside. The next bundle she unwrapped was considerably larger—a small, crudely made chest. She lifted the lid and revealed its contents. She set aside a faded scarlet ribbon, miscellaneous bits of jewelry, a palm-sized ball of glass the Old Man had used to keep his hands lim-

ber, and a pillow embroidered neatly with stars and moon—
her last attempt at needlework.

Under the pillow was another wooden box. This she took
in her lap and unworked the magic that kept the lid closed.
Inside were several items that she'd found while thieving.
They weren't hers or the Old Man's, but like the flute they
were better stored well out of the reach of fools: a gold and
porcelain bowl that would gradually poison any who ate
from it, a worn silver bracelet that kept the wearer from
sleeping, and several like items. She started to put the flute
with them, then stopped.

The Old Man had nothing left from before—nothing but
the flute she held in her hand. The farm would have to wait
until she had the money, but the flute she would give to
him now. She returned it to her hidden pocket. As she did
so, she felt the surge of magic that preceded the return of
the tide.

She forced herself to set the seal on the larger chest carefully, but once that was done she rewrapped the oilcloth
with haste and left the grotto at a dead run. Slipping and
sliding she sped through the tunnels to the beach outside.
Far out on the sands she could see the white line of the
returning sea.

The sand was soft with water and sucked at her fleeing
feet, causing her to stumble and slow. The short distance
to the ladder seemed to stretch forever and the sands began
to vibrate. By the time she'd reached the cliff below the
ladder she could hear the roar of the ocean.

The cliffside was slick with moisture and without the
thread of magic that kept her fingers from slipping off the
rocks she would never have reached the ladder.

"Magic," she gasped as her fingers closed over the bottom rung of the ladder, "—and luck to make up for lack
of wits—I hope."

But there was no time to waste, if the wall of water hit
while she was still on the ladder she would be crushed
against the rocks. The ladder shook with the force of the
returning water and she increased her efforts, ignoring the
burning in the muscles of her arms and thighs.

The wind hit first, battering her against the hard rock cliff, and she spared a glance for the racing wall of water. As tall as the cliff she climbed, the foaming white mass covered the sands faster than a racing horse, the drumming of the surf echoing the beat of her heart. She couldn't help the wide grin that twisted her mouth as she fought to climb beyond the waves reach. The exhilaration of her race for survival helped add speed to her ascent.

Heart pounding, she threw herself on the top of the low cliff where her ladder attached, then turned to watch the tremendous waves that swept across the last few yards of sand. The noise was incredible, so strong that she could feel it thrumming in her chest, and she breathed in deeply to savor the feeling.

She jumped back involuntarily as the ocean crashed into the cliff with a hollow boom that shook the ground and sent spray high into the air. Laughing, she ducked her head to protect her eyes, and the salt water showered harmlessly onto her hair and shoulders as the waves retreated and pounded back again.

Magic poured over her, making her heart sing with the joy of it. It was shaped and called by the ocean itself, and no human mage could use its power to weave spells—but she could feel it and revel in its glory.

She wasn't certain what made her turn away from the waves, but she froze when she saw that someone else was watching the water hit the cliffs. He hadn't seen her where she crouched on her hidden ledge below him. The crashing waves were deafening, drowning any sound she had made. If she stayed where she was she could probably keep him from noticing her at all. But the water's magic made her reckless. She slid further toward the edge of her ledge, allowing herself to get a better look at the rider who dared Purgatory at night to see the Spirit Tide.

Unlike Sham, the man was in the open, clearly visible in the silver moonlight. A Cybellian warrior, she thought, outfitted with surcoat, sword, and war horse.

For a disorienting instant terror choked her as she stared at him from the shadows, seeing not a lone man but the bloody warriors who had taken the Castle. The past was too close to her this night. She swallowed the lump in her throat and ran her hands across various weapons hidden on her person. Thus reassured, she took a closer look at him.

The chainmail shirt that extended past his surcoat at wrists and throat was of the highest quality, the links so fine that it appeared to be fashioned of cloth rather than metal. The surcoat itself was of some dark color. He was facing slightly away from Sham, and she couldn't make out the device on its front. A wealthy warrior then, and a fool.

It had been a long time since she had been the daughter of the captain of the guards at the Castle, but not so long that she'd forgotten how to judge a horse. She ran an assessing eye over this one, an aristocrat from the flared nostrils to the long, dark hair that covered his legs from knees to hooves. Only a fool would take such an obviously valuable animal through Purgatory at night.

The stallion snorted and sidled as he caught her scent in the salt air. He rolled his eyes until the white showed and shook his wet mane fiercely. The impulse to stay hidden came and went unheeded. The warrior was the outsider here; she had no reason to avoid notice.

With a nearly invisible signal from his rider, the horse spun around on its haunches as the man looked for the cause of the horse's unease. The stallion blew spray of his own as he snorted impatiently and completed a full circle, giving Sham her first view of the man's coat-of-arms.

At the sight of the silver and gold leopard emblazoned on the silk she whistled soundlessly and altered her assessment of the man. Wealthy warrior he was indeed, but not a fool. Even the most formidable group of thugs would hesitate to attack the Leopard of Altis, Reeve of Southwood.

Lord Kerim, called the Leopard, ruled most of Southwood in the name of the Voice of Altis and the Cybellian Alliance that the Voice ruled. At the tender age of eighteen the Leopard had led an elite fighting unit to spearhead the invasion through the Great Swamp and across a fair portion of the lands between the Swamp and the Western Sea. Peo-

ple still talked in whispers at the cunning and skill that he'd
displayed.

Eight years ago, when the Cybellians had snuffed out all
but a hint of rebellion in Southwood, the Voice of Altis
had called upon Kerim to become his Reeve, answering
only to the prophet himself.

Kerim had been less than a quarter of a century old when
he'd taken control of Southwood, and turned it back into a
thriving country. With a mixture of bribery and coercion
he had made the Southwood nobles and the Cybellians cooperate with each other—resorting to force only once or
twice.

Whether as statesman or warrior, there were very few
people who would take on the Leopard without a great deal
of thought. She had just decided to try and escape unnot-
iced, when his eyes locked onto hers.

"I like to watch the neap tide come in," he said in
Southern. Nearly a decade of living in Southwood had softened the clipped accent Cybellians brought to the language
until he might have been mistaken for a native.

Sham waited where she was for a moment, caught by
surprise at the conversational tone the Reeve used—speaking as he was to a roughly garbed, wet street urchin. Deciding finally it was probably safe enough, she scrambled
up the rocks until she stood on a level with him. It struck
her as she did so that this was an opportunity to attack the
Cybellians that might never come again. She looked at the
Reeve and remembered the dead that littered the Castle
grounds after it had been taken by the invaders. Unobtrusively she slipped her hand toward the thin dagger strapped
to her forearm.

But it was more than just the suspicion that he was well
able to defend himself against such an attack that kept her
blade where it was. It was the sadness in his eyes and the
lines of pain that tightened his mouth, both revealed by the
bright moonlight.

Imagination, she told herself fiercely as the angle of his
head changed and shadows hid his features; but the impression remained. She shook her head with resignation: as

she'd noted earlier, the Old Man's gentleness was rubbing off on her. The Leopard had not been with the army that entered the Castle, and she didn't hate enough to kill someone who had never done her harm—even if he was an Altis-worshipping Cybellian.

"The Spirit Tide is impressive—" she agreed neutrally in the same language he'd addressed her, "—but hardly worth braving Purgatory alone." Her tone might have been neutral, but her words were hardly the respect he must be used to receiving.

The Reeve merely shrugged and turned to look at the foam-capped waves. "I get tired of people. I saw no real need to bring an escort; most of the occupants here are little threat to an armed rider."

She raised an eyebrow and snorted at his profile, feeling vaguely insulted. "Typical arrogant Cybellian," she commented, deciding to continue as she had begun. She didn't like to bow and scrape more than was absolutely necessary. "Just because you say something does not make it so. Jackals travel in packs and together can tear out the soft underbelly of prey many times their size and strength."

He turned his face back to her and shot her a grin that was surprisingly boyish. "Jackals are only scavengers."

She nodded. "And all the more vicious for it. Next time don't bring so much to tempt them. That horse of yours would feed every cutthroat in the city for a year."

He smiled and patted the thick neck of his mount affectionately. "Only if they managed to kill him and decided to eat him. Otherwise, they wouldn't be able to hold him long enough to sell him."

"Unfortunately for you, they won't know that until they try it." Despite herself, Sham wondered at the ruler of Southwood. She'd never met a nobleman, Cybellian or Southwoodsman, who would not have taken offense at being reproved by someone who was at the very least a commoner and more likely a criminal.

"Why are you so concerned about my fate, boy?" Kerim asked mildly.

"I'm not." Sham grinned cheerfully, shivering as a

breeze caught at her wet clothes. "I'm concerned about our reputation. If the word gets out that you came through Purgatory without a scratch, *everyone* will think they can do it. Although," she added thoughtfully, "that might not be such a bad thing. A few nobles to dine on might improve the economy around here."

The sound of another large wave hitting the rocks drew Kerim's attention back to the sea and Sham took the opportunity to study the Lord of Southwood, now that she knew who he was.

Though his nickname was the Leopard, there was little catlike about him. As he was sitting on his horse, it was hard to judge his height, but he was built like a bull: shoulders proportionally wide and thick with muscle. Even his hands were sturdy, one of his fingers larger than two of hers. As with his horse, the moonless night hid the true color of his hair, but she'd heard that it was dark brown—like that of most Cybellians. His features, mouth, nose and jaw were as broad as his body.

STARING AT THE ROILING WATER, KERIM WONDERED AT his openness with this Southwood boy who was so visibly unimpressed with the Reeve of Southwood. He hadn't conversed with anyone this freely since he gave up soldiering and took over the rule of Southwood for the prophet. The only one who dared to chastise him as freely as this boy was his mother, and the boy lacked her malice—though Kerim hadn't missed the lad's initial motion toward the armsheath. He hadn't missed the aristocratic accent the boy spoke with either, and wondered which of the Southwood noblemen had a son wandering about Purgatory in the night.

The novelty of the conversation distracted him momentarily from the familiar cramping of the muscles in his lower back. Soon, he feared, he would have to give up riding altogether. Scorch was becoming confused by the frequent, awkward shifting of his rider's weight.

The Leopard turned back from the sea, but the boy was gone. Kerim was left alone with an enemy that he feared

more than all the other foes he had ever battled; he knew
of no way to fight the debilitating cramps in his back or
the more disturbing numbness that was creeping up from
his feet.

SHAM TROTTED THROUGH THE NARROW STREETS BRISKLY
to keep warm. The cottage she'd found for the Old Man
was near the fringes of Purgatory in an area where the city
guardsmen still ventured. It was old and small, roughly cobbled together, but it served to keep out the rain and occasional snow.

She didn't live there with him, although she had used
her ill-gotten gains to buy the house. The Whisper kept him
safe with their protection, and Sham was well known as a
thief among the Purgatory guards. Her presence would have
caused them to disturb the Old Man's hard-won peace, so
she only visited him now and again.

The Old Man accepted that, just as he accepted her chosen work. Occupations in Purgatory were limited and
tended to shorten lives. Good thieves lived longer than
whores or gang members.

Sham dropped to a walk, as the lack of refuse in the
streets signaled her nearness to the Old Man's cottage. She
didn't want to come in out of breath—the Old Man worried
if he thought she'd been eluding pursuit.

It was the extra sensitivity necessary to survive in Purgatory that first alerted her that there was something wrong.
The street the Old Man lived on was empty of all the little
shadowy activities that characterized even the better areas.
Something had caused the tough little denizens to scuttle
back to their holes.

TWO

Sham began to run when she saw the door of the Old Man's cottage lying broken on the dirty cobbles of the street. She was still running, the dagger from her arm sheath in her hand, when she heard Maur scream in a mixture of rage and terror that echoed hoarsely in the night.

As she reached the dark entrance she stopped, ingrained wariness forcing her to enter cautiously when she wanted to rush in howling like a Uriah in full hunt. She listened for a moment, but other than the initial cry the cottage was still.

As she stepped across the threshold, the tangy smell of blood assailed her nose. Panicked at the thought of losing the old wizard as she had everyone else, she recklessly flooded the small front room with magelight. Blinking furiously, her eyes still accustomed to the dark, she noticed that there was blood everywhere, as if a cloud of the stuff had covered the walls.

The Old Man was on his knees in the corner, one arm raised over his face, bleeding from hundreds of small cuts that shredded clothes and skin alike. There was no one else in the room.

"Master!" she cried out.

At the sound of her voice, he turned toward her. Urgently he said, "Go child, hurry. This is not your battle."

As he spoke, a broad red slice appeared on his upraised arm as if drawn there by an invisible artist. Though she had caught a bare glimpse of something moving, it was gone before she could tell what it was.

His command was voiced so strongly that Sham took a step backward before she caught herself. The last magic her master had wrought was twelve years before. Blind and crippled, he was as helpless as a child—she wasn't about to leave him.

Her mouth firmed as another wound appeared, weeping blood down the side of his crippled hand. She gestured, calling a simple spell of detection, hoping to locate the unseen attacker, but the magic in the room was thick and obscured her spell. The assailant seemed to be everywhere and nowhere at once.

She tried a spell to discover the kind of magic the assailant used so that she could try unworking his magic. A cold chill rolled its way down her spine as her spell told her that whatever else it was, it was not human. It was also not one of the creatures who could use natural magic, for what she'd sensed had no connection to the forces stirred by the Spirit Tide. That left only a handful of creatures to choose from, none of them very encouraging.

She dropped the useless dagger to the ground. When the blade clattered to the floor, the flute slid into her hand, as if it had taken advantage of her inattention to slip out of the pocket in her sleeve.

As her fingers closed about its carved surface, it occurred to her that a thing did not have to be sharp to be a weapon. She set the mouthpiece against her lips for the second time that evening and blew softly through the instrument, letting the music fill the air. She would never be a bard-level musician, but she was thankful for the years the Old Man had sought to instill his love of music in her.

As the first notes sounded in the room, she could feel the magic gathering, far more than she would have been able to harness alone. It surrounded her, making her blood sing like rushing water with the heady vortex of power. She would pay for it later, of course—that was the secret of the flute. More than one mage had died after using it, not realizing until it was too late the cost of the power the flute called. Others had died when the magic grew too strong for them to control.

She fought to ignore the euphoria spawned by the rapidly mounting tide of magic. When she felt it push at the edge of her control, she took the flute from her lips.

Her body was numb from the forces she held, and it took more effort than it should have to raise her arms and begin a spell of warding. She watched her hands move, almost able to see the glow of the magic she wrought. She was so caught up in her weaving that when it began to unravel, Sham didn't immediately understand the cause.

The Old Man had come to his feet and moved close enough to touch her neck with one of his scarred and twisted hands.

"By your leave, my dear," said the old sorcerer softly as he drew the magic she had gathered.

For a moment she was startled by his action.

All apprentices were bound to their masters. It was necessary to mitigate the risk that the fledgling mages would lose control of the power they called and burn anything around them to cinders.

The bonds of apprenticeship had not been severed when she passed to journeyman as was the usual practice, since only the master can break such a bond, and the Old Man had been unable to summon magic since his crippling. Sham had never considered the possibility that he could work magic already gathered.

"Take as you will," she said, letting her hands fall to her side.

As the power she had drawn together gathered in the Master's hands, the old mage smiled. For a moment she saw him as she had the first time: power tempered with wisdom and kindness.

She watched with a keen appreciation the deft touch of the King's Sorcerer as he wove a warding spell similar to her own but infinitely more complex without resorting to any obvious motion to aid his work. The continued slashes failed to break his formidable concentration. When he finished his spell, the cottage vibrated from the force of his attacker's frustrated, keening wail. It tested the warding twice before Sham could no longer sense its magic.

The Old Man collapsed on the floor. Sham knelt almost as swiftly as he had fallen, running gentle hands over him. She found no wounds that could be bound, only a multitude of small, thin lines from which the old man's lifeblood drained to the floor. Her motions grew more frantic as she realized the inevitability of his death was spattered on the walls, on the floor, on her.

There was no magic she knew that could heal him. The runes of healing she drew on his chest would promote his body's own processes, but she knew that he would be dead long before his body could even begin to mend. She tried anyway. The effort of working magic so soon after she'd played the flute caused her hands to shake as she drew runes that blurred irritatingly in her vision as she cried.

"Enough, Shamera, enough." The Old Man's voice was very weak.

She pulled her hands away and clenched them, knowing he was right. Carefully, she drew his battered head into her lap. Ignoring the gore, she patted the weathered skin of his face tenderly.

"Master," she crooned softly, and the Old Man's lips twisted once more into a smile.

He would be sorry to leave his little, contrary apprentice. He always thought of her as he had last seen her, at that point where child turns to woman—though he knew she was long since grown, a master in her own right. She hadn't been a child since she'd rescued him from the dungeon where he lay blinded, crippled, and near death. He had to warn her before it was too late. With hard-won strength he reached up and caught her hand.

"Little one," he said. But his voice was too soft: It angered him to be so weak, and he drew strength from that anger.

"Daughter of my heart, Shamera." It was little more than a whisper, but he could tell by her stillness that she had heard. "It was the *Chen Laut* that was here. You must find it, child, or it will destroy..." He paused to grasp enough strength to finish. "It is...close this time or it wouldn't have chanced attacking me. Do you understand?"

"Yes, Master," she answered softly. "Chen Laut."

He relaxed in her embrace. As he did, a wondrous thing happened. The magic, his own magic, which had eluded him for so many years returned across the barrier of pain as if it had never been rift from him. As he stopped fighting for breath, the power surrounded him and comforted him as it always had. With a sigh of relief, of release, he gave himself to its caress.

Blank-faced, Shamera watched the old mage leave her, his body lax in her arms. As soon as he was gone, she set his head gently on the floor and began straightening his body, as if it mattered how the Old Man lay for his pyre. When she was finished, she knelt at his feet with her head bowed to show her respect. She let the magelight die down and sat in the darkness with the body of her master.

THE SOUND OF BOOTS ON THE FLOORBOARDS DREW HER from her reverie. She watched numbly as four of the city-guards flooded the small room with torchlight.

Belatedly, she realized she should have left when she could have. Her clothes were soaked with blood. Without witnesses, she was the most likely suspect. But this was Purgatory; she could buy her way out of it. Money was not a problem; the Old Man wouldn't need the gold in the cave.

Sham stood up warily and faced the intruders.

Three were Easterners and the fourth a Southwoodsman, easily distinguished from the rest by his long hair and beard. They all had familiar faces, though she'd be hard put to name any but the apparent leader—he answered to Scarf, named for the filthy rag he tied over his missing eye. She relaxed a little: The whisper was that he could be bought more easily than most.

Scarf and one of the other Easterners, tall for his race and cadaverously thin with large black eyes, looked at the blood that splattered almost every surface of the room with dawning respect. While the other two looked around, the Southwoodsman and the third Easterner kept their eyes on Sham. She carefully kept her arms well away from her body so she presented little threat.

Scarf put the torch he held in one of the empty wall brackets and motioned to the Southwoodsman to do the same with the second torch. Scratching at his forehead, Scarf turned in a full circle to assess the room again before letting his gaze come to rest on Sham.

"Altis's blood, Sham—when you decide to kill a bastard, you have a right pretty touch." He hawked and spat—a tribute of sorts, thought Sham once she'd deciphered his fragmented Southern.

Before she could answer, a fifth man walked into the room, this one dressed in the garb of a nobleman. She took a step back at the wide smile on his face.

Scarf looked up and spoke in his native Cybellian. "Lord Hirkin, sir, I think you'll find this one more helpful than the others. This is Sham the thief—I've heard the Shark watches out for him."

"Good, good," said Lord Hirkin, the man who ruled of the guardsmen of Purgatory.

He made a gesture toward Sham and Scarf stepped behind her, securing her by wrapping his massive hands around her upper arms.

Tide save her, Sham thought, this wasn't going to be easy after all. She set her grief aside for later, turning all her attention to the situation at hand.

"I have been looking for just such a murdering thief," Hirkin continued, switching to Southern for Sham's benefit. "This man who calls himself the Shark. You will tell me where to find him."

Sham raised her eyebrows. "I don't know where he stays; no one does. If you want him, leave a message with one of the Whisperers."

Actually she was probably the only person outside of the Shark's gang, the Whisper of the Street, who *did* know where the Shark was most of the time, but she had no intention of sharing that information with anyone. The Shark had his own ways of dealing with such problems: Methods bound to be much nastier than anything this man could dream up—besides, he was a friend.

Hirkin shook his head with mock sadness and turned away to address the three guardsmen behind him. "It always takes so *long*—" he spun on his heel and backhanded her across the mouth "—to get any truth out of Southwood scum—too stupid for their own good. Perhaps I ought to turn you over to my man here." He nodded at the cadaverous one who smiled evilly, revealing a missing tooth. "He likes boys about your size. The last one he got to play with I killed afterwards—out of mercy."

Sham looked suitably impressed by Hirkin's threats: that is, not at all. She snorted and smirked around her cut lip. She had learned early that the scent of fear only excited jackals and made them more vicious.

"I've heard about that one," she commented with a jerk of her chin toward the guard that Hirkin had indicated. "Whisper has it that he can't tie his own shoes without help. Throw me to him and you *might* find the pieces of him afterward."

She was expecting the next blow and turned her head with the strike, averting some of the force. They hadn't searched her for weapons. Her dagger lay where she had thrown it, but several of her thieving tools were almost as sharp. Scarf's grip wasn't as secure as he thought it was—not when he held a wizard. She just had to pick the best time to make her move.

Watching the proceedings, Talbot, the lone Southwoodsman guard, ground his teeth. This was the fourth such beating this night. The first two he'd only heard about. The third one he'd come upon after the victim was already dead.

It wasn't that he had trouble with a beating or two in the name of justice, but this interrogation had nothing to do with the body lying forgotten in the corner of the room—no way a lad that size could rip a door out of the frame that way. Then too, the sight of the Easterners hitting a Southwoodsman brought back an anger he thought long buried.

This was the first steady job he'd found in five years, but he wasn't going to watch Lord Hirkin beat a boy to death in order to keep it. With a silent apology to his wife, he turned and slipped out the door at a moment when the other's attention was focused on the little thief.

Once in the silent street, Talbot headed for the nearest thoroughfare at a brisk trot with the vague idea of finding a few other of the Southwoodsman guards. Hirkin's control wasn't as strong with them, and he knew of several who wouldn't mind a chance to kill a few Cybellians, be they guardsmen or nobles.

He toyed briefly with the idea of sending a message to the Shark, but dismissed it. The Shark generally avoided direct contact with the guardsmen; he would avenge the lad's death, but Talbot hoped to save it instead. Vengeance wasn't worth losing a steady job.

The nearest busy street was several blocks away. At this time of the night there were fewer people, but Purgatory was never quiet. Once on the busier thoroughfare, Talbot caught his breath and looked around for any of the guardsmen that he knew, but the only one he saw was Cybellian. He swore softly under his breath.

"Trouble?" asked a nearby voice in Southern.

Talbot whirled and found himself face to face with a war stallion. Prudently he backed out of range of the horse's eager teeth, and tipped his head back to meet the eyes of a man who, by his dress, could only be the Reeve of Southwood.

"Yes, sir." His voice was steady. He had been a hand on the ship that sailed under the old King's son. He was used to people of high rank, and the Whisper had it that Lord Kerim wasn't as high in the mouth as most of his breed. He'd even heard that the Reeve concerned himself with *all* of the people of Southwood, Easterners and natives alike.

For the first time Talbot felt some hope that he'd get through this night with his job intact. "If ye have a minute, messire, there's a crime that ye might be interested in."

"Indeed?" Lord Kerim sat back on his horse and waited for the other man to continue.

Talbot cleared his throat and took a chance. "There's been a murder, sir. When we came upon the body, there was a boy there with it. Normal procedure, sir, would be having us take him in for questioning and trial. But Lord Hirkin showed up an' is proceeding with the questioning. I don't think he intends to hold the lad for trial, if you get my meaning."

Kerim looked at him a moment before saying softly, "Lead on then, man, and I'll take care of it."

With Kerim at his back, Talbot made good speed back to the little cottage. At the entrance, Kerim kicked his feet free of the stirrups and swung one leg forward over the saddle before sliding off his horse. Dropping the reins on the ground to keep the stallion in place, he followed Talbot to the open doorway.

"IF YOU'RE A GOOD BOY, THERE WILL BE NO NEED TO meet the headsman just yet," purred Lord Hirkin.

He had begun alternating his threats with outright bribery. Sham wasn't sure why he was hunting the Shark, but it must be a matter of great importance to cause the urgency that he was demonstrating.

"I'd rather meet him than you," she returned somewhat thickly from her abused lips. "At least he'll smell of honest work. That's better than what you'll smell like when the Shark gets through with you. He doesn't like people who poke around in his business—they usually end up feeding his brothers in the sea."

Peripherally she was aware that someone had entered the room from the outside, but she assumed that it was only more guards.

This time the blow bloodied her nose. Eyes watering from the pain, Shamera knew that she needed to find a way to distract him soon. If she didn't make her move before the pain got too bad, she wouldn't be able to use her magic safely.

Obvious magic was out, unless her life was threatened. She wasn't eager to be responsible for one of the periodic witch hunts that even now swept through Purgatory. But there were things that she could do that would even the odds a little.

She glanced at the door and froze, not even listening to Lord Hirkin's verbal response to her insult. She was too busy staring at the Reeve of Southwood, standing inside the door just ahead of the Southwoodsman guard she'd seen leave a short time ago. When he noticed Sham's intent stare, Hirkin swung around to see what had caught her attention.

"So," said Lord Kerim, softly.

When he spoke the guards who had been looking at Sham turned to see the Reeve. She saw one of them take two quick steps forward and turn, standing shoulder to shoulder with the Southwoodsman just behind Lord Kerim—declaring silently where his loyalties lay.

"Lord Kerim, what brings you here?" asked Lord Hirkin.

"Did you *see* the boy kill this man?" The Reeve glanced casually down at the still form on the floor.

"No, my lord," answered Hirkin. "One of the neighbors heard screams and sent his son to the nearest guard station. I happened to be there and joined my men in the investigation of the disturbance. We arrived to find this boy next to the body of the old man."

Sham wondered at the lack of respect in the young lord's tones. She had heard that Kerim was more popular among the merchants and lower classes than he was among the nobles, but this was more than she'd expected.

Scarf released her and stepped away, his eyes on the conflict between Hirkin and the Reeve. Sham let herself collapse to her knees and wiped blood out of her right eye, using both movements to shift a sharp little prying tool into her hand. The tool was small, but heavy and relatively well-balanced—almost as good as a throwing knife.

The Reeve shook his head lightly at Hirkin and said in the same dangerously soft voice he had used previously, "I met the young lad out on the docks less than an hour ago. He could not have made it back here in time to inflict this kind of damage."

"I had no way of knowing that," defended Lord Hirkin. "It is my duty to question all obvious suspects in a crime. This may be a quieter section, but it is still Purgatory. They wouldn't tell the truth to their own mother, let alone guardsmen, without a little persuasion."

"Perhaps." Kerim nodded thoughtfully. "But from what I overheard just now, it sounds as if you are not overly concerned with the young man's guilt. Indeed a listener might be excused for believing you are not even concerned with this crime."

"My lord . . ." Hirkin's voiced died off when he met the Reeve's eyes.

"It *sounds* as if you are questioning him regarding an entirely different crime. The theft of a logbook perhaps?" Lord Kerim looked at Hirkin with gentle interest and smiled without humor. "I believe that I can help you with that crime as well. Someone left a very interesting present with my personal servant just after dinner this evening."

Hirkin whitened and slipped his hand down to grip the sword that hung from his belt.

Kerim shook his head with mock sadness. "I haven't had time to go all the way through it, but someone was most helpful and marked certain entries. The most damaging entry, as far as your fate is concerned, was the kidnapping of Lord Tyber's daughter and her subsequent sale to a slaver—he was not happy to hear that you were involved. I don't know that I would return to the Castle if I were you."

The Reeve's lips widened into a smile that never touched his eyes and his voice softened further as he continued. "Many of these things had already come to my attention, but I lacked the evidence that someone so generously provided. In light of the fact that Lord Tyber would make certain that you do not live to face a trial, I have already passed sentence with the consent of the council. You are banished from Southwood.''

Hirkin's face whitened with rage. ''*You* would banish me? I am the second son of the Lord of the Marshlands! Our oldest title goes back eight hundred years. You are *nothing*! Do you hear me? Nothing but the bastard son of a high-bred whore.''

Kerim shook his head, managing to look regretful as he drew his sword from the sheath on his back. His voice abruptly iced over as he said, ''High-bred whore she might be, but it is not your judgment to give. I cry challenge.''

The sight of the Reeve's sword distracted Sham momentarily. She had heard that the Leopard fought with a blue sword, but she had assumed that it was painted blue—a custom that was fairly prevalent among the Easterners.

Instead it was *blued* as was sometimes done with steel intended for decorative use. She'd never heard of true bluing done on the scale of the Reeve's massive blade. A lesser process was occasionally used to prevent rust on swords, but the blades came out more black than blue.

The Reeve's sword was a dark indigo that glittered evilly in the dim light of the little cottage. It was edged in silver where the bluing had been honed away. Thin marks where other blades had marred the finish bore mute testimony that this was no ceremonial tool but an instrument of death.

Hirkin smiled and drew his own sword. ''You make this too easy, my lord Reeve. Once you might have bested me, but I hear that two days out of three you can't even lift that sword. You have no one to help you here—these are my men.''

Apparently he didn't count Sham, who was definitely opposed to Hirkin—but she was surprised that he didn't notice that two of his guardsmen were also backing the Reeve, leaving only Scarf and the cadaver still loyal.

Kerim smiled gently. ''The order of banishment has already been listed in the temple and with the council. My death will not nullify that.'' He twisted the sword around in a shimmering curtain of lethal sharpness, then smiled ferally and said, "We are in luck, it also appears that this is the one day of three I am able to fight."

Apparently tiring of the posturing, Hirkin growled abruptly and sprang at Kerim, sweeping his sword low and hard. Without visible effort, Kerim caught the smaller blade on his own and turned it aside, destroying a table that stood against the wall.

As Sham winced away from the destruction, her attention was caught by a slight movement on her left. Without turning her head further from the flashing swords, she glimpsed Scarf edging slowly forward, a large, wicked knife in his hands. She frowned in disparagement at his choice of weapons—in the right hands a small dagger killed as surely and it was much easier to hide.

Knowing what little she did about Scarf, she would have thought he would wait to see who was winning before committing himself firmly to either side, but perhaps he had a greater interest in Lord Hirkin than she knew. She flinched again when Hirkin's sword crashed into one of the cheap little pots that lined the crude wooden shelf set into the wall.

Sham knew she should take advantage of the fight and leave. The back door of the cottage was behind her, and no one was watching.

She waited until Scarf chose his position before selecting her own. Judging the distance with an experienced eye, she took a two-fingered grip on the handle of her thieving tool, careful to keep it out of sight in the length of sleeve that dangled below her hand. Then she settled in to wait for Scarf to make his move.

She missed most of the fight, though she could hear. The clash of metal on metal was overshadowed by Hirkin's full-throated cries: Her father had done the same in battle. Kerim fought silently.

Slowly, Lord Hirkin backed to the corner where Scarf waited and for the first time since the initial strike, Sham got a clear view of the fight.

Time after time the blades struck and sparks flashed in

the flickering torchlight. Lord Kerim moved with the lethal grace of one of the great hunting cats—unusual in a man so large. Sham no longer wondered how such a burly man had won the title of Leopard. Though Hirkin was without a doubt a tremendous swordsman, it was obvious he was no match for the Reeve. Hirkin stumbled to his left and Kerim followed him, leaving the vulnerable side of his throat an easy target for Scarf's knife.

Sham waited until the guardsman pulled his arm back before sending her tool spinning through the air. It slid noiselessly into Scarf's good eye at the same time that a knife buried itself to its haft in his neck.

Startled, Sham raised her eyes to meet those of her fellow Southwoodsman, who raised his hand in formal salute. Near him the Cybellian who had supported Kerim was wrestling on the floor with Hirkin's remaining henchman. Satisfied that the situation was under control she turned to watch the sword fight.

Hirkin's sword moved with the same power that Kerim's did, but without the Reeve's fine control. Again and again, Hirkin's sword hit wood and plaster while the blue sword touched only Hirkin's blade.

Both men were breathing hard and the smell of sweat joined the smell of death that lingered cloyingly in the air. The blades moved more slowly now, with short resting periods breaking up the pace before the furious clash began again.

Abruptly, when it seemed that Hirkin was certain to lose, the tide of the fight changed. The Reeve stumbled over one of the old man's slippers, falling to one knee. Hirkin stepped in to take advantage of Lord Kerim's misfortune, bringing his sword down overhand angled to intersect the Reeve's vulnerable neck.

Kerim made no attempt to come to his feet. Instead, he braced himself on both knees and brought the silver-edged blade up with impossible speed. Hirkin's sword hit the Reeve's with the full weight of its wielder behind the blow.

With only the strength of his upper body, the Reeve took the force of Hirkin's blow and redirected it, slightly twisting as he did so. Hirkin's sword sliced a hole in the Reeve's surcoat before embedding itself in the floorboards.

Still on his knees, Kerim stabbed upward as if he held a knife rather than a sword. The tip hit Hirkin just below his rib cage and slid smoothly upward. Hirkin was dead before his body touched the floor.

The Reeve wiped the blade on Hirkin's velvet surcoat. Showing little of the litheness he had displayed in the battle, he slowly regained his feet.

"Thought you might be slowing down, Captain." The Eastern guard who'd supported Kerim spoke casually from his position on top of the man he'd been wrestling. He held the cadaver's twisted legs under one knee and used both hands to secure an arm he'd pulled up and back. The position looked uncomfortable for both men to Sham, but she seldom indulged in such sport.

Kerim narrowed his eyes at the man who addressed him and then grinned. "It's good to see you again, Lirn. What is an archer of your caliber doing working in Purgatory?"

The guardsman shrugged. "Have to take what work's offered, Captain."

"I could use you, training the Castle guards," offered the Reeve, "but I have to warn you that the last man to hold the post of captain quit."

The guard's eyebrows rose. "I wouldn't have thought that Castle guards would be that difficult."

"They're not," returned Kerim. "My lady mother, however *is.*"

The guard laughed and shook his head. "I'll do it. What do you want me to do with this one?" He gave the captive's wrist a twitch and the man beneath him yelped.

"What was he doing when you caught him?" asked Kerim.

"Running."

The Reeve shrugged. "Let him go. There is no law against running, and he is no worse than most of the guards around here."

The Easterner untangled himself, letting his prisoner scramble out the door.

"What is your name, sir?" asked the Reeve turning to the Southwoodsman guard.

"Talbot, messire." Sham saw the older man straighten a little at the respect that Lord Kerim had shown him.

"How long have you been a guard in Purgatory?" Kerim asked.

"Five years, sir. I was a seaman on the ship that served the son of the last king. Since then I've worked as a mate on several cargo ships, but the merchants like to change crew after each voyage. I have a wife and family and needed steady work."

"Hmm," said Kerim, and smiled with sudden mischief that animated his broad features to surprising attractiveness. "That will mean that you are used to proving yourself to those that you command. Good. My health problems have kept me from attending to Lord Hirkin as he should have been. I have need of someone who can keep an eye on such as he, without being subject to the consideration of politics. I would be pleased if you would accept the post of Master of Security—Hirkin's recently vacated post plus a few extra duties."

Lord Kerim raised his hand to forestall what Talbot would have said. "I warn you that it will mean traveling to the outlying area and keeping an eye on the way that the nobles are running their estates as well as managing the city guards. You'll will be the target of a lot of hostility—both because of your nationality and your common birth. I will outfit you with horse, clothing, and arms, provide living quarters for you and your family, and pay you five gold pieces each quarter. I tell you now that you will earn every copper."

Talbot looked at the Cybellian and smiled slowly. "I'd like that."

The Reeve turned to speak to Sham and then took two steps forward until he could peer into the windowless bedroom. "Did you see where the boy went?"

The newly appointed Captain of the Guard shook his head.

"Nay," said Talbot, "but that one's a wee bit canny."

At the Reeve's puzzled look, he explained further. "I mean he has the reputation of being a magician. I've seen him here and there, and asked around. Most of the folk in Purgatory leave him alone because he's a right hand with magic—that includes the guardsmen." Talbot hesitated then nodded his head at the old man's slight form. "He seemed pretty upset by the old man's death. Wouldn't want to be in the killer's shoes right now. I'd rather face a crazed boar than anger a sorcerer."

Sham watched from a corner of the room that the three men had ignored, thanks to her magic. She wished they would hurry and go; she wasn't certain how much longer she could hold the spell.

The Reeve knelt to examine Hirkin's body. "After the way he threw this thing at Hirkin, I'd be more worried about his knife."

Talbot shook his head and muttered something that sounded like "Easterners."

LONG AFTER THE THREE MEN HAD LEFT, SHAM HUDDLED on a nearby rooftop and watched the old man's cottage burn to ashes without scorching either of the buildings next to it. She closed her eyes wearily and shivered in the warmth of her magical flames.

THREE

For the past several days Sham had been following the new Master of Security as he haunted the back streets of Purgatory looking, according to the Whisper, for her. The contrariness of it pleased her, and she'd had little enough else to do.

Neither she nor the Whisper had been able to find out who or what had killed Maur, though they'd found several other victims, ranging from nobleman to thief. Four days ago one of the Whisperers told her that Talbot was looking for her and that she might be interested in what he had to say. It could be something about the Chen Laut, or perhaps something more sinister.

With Maur gone, she hadn't continued her attempt to exact vengeance; somehow there was no point in it. The last thieving she'd done was the night Maur died almost three months before. Even so, if Talbot wanted to he could tie her to any number of her past crimes and have her hung. She didn't *think* the Whisper would help him do that, but the Shark was unpredictable.

She watched Talbot from an abandoned building near the

docks as he spoke to an old woman who shook her head. The Southwoodsman was greatly changed. It wasn't his clothing—brown and grey look pretty much the same no matter how good the fabric. He hadn't changed the way his grizzled, light-brown hair was pulled back and tied, though she thought his beard might be closer clipped than before. His features were still arranged in a good-natured fashion that made her want to like him despite her suspicious nature.

The difference, she decided, was that he'd lost the perpetual fear that haunted everyone forced to live in Purgatory: fear of hunger, fear of death, fear of living—and the hopelessness that traveled hand in hand with the fear. Like the Shark, Talbot had become a shaping force rather than another of the helpless vermin who infested Purgatory.

All her fears of hanging aside, would someone of his current rank spend three days looking for her just to arrest her? She was a good thief, but she was careful too. She never took anything irreplaceable, and never really hurt anyone if she could help it—she avoided anything that would lend urgency to her capture.

With sudden decision, she stopped following him and climbed easily to the roof of one of the buildings nearby. She skittered cautiously across the moldering rooftop and down into the alley behind it, startling several raggedly clothed youths. Before they decided if she was worth attacking, she was up and over the next building and dropping to the street beyond.

From the paths Talbot had followed the previous days, she surmised he was headed for one of the taverns she occasionally frequented. She took a path through vacant buildings and twisted thoroughfares, saving several blocks over the distance Talbot would have to cover. Near the tavern, she found an alley he should pass by and settled in to wait.

When Talbot walked by her, oblivious to her presence, some sense of reluctant caution almost kept her silent. In direct defiance of her instincts of self-preservation, Sham spoke.

"Master Talbot."

She was pleased when her theatrical whisper caused the old sailor to crouch defensively. There was a smile on her face as she assumed a relaxed pose against the brick wall of an abandoned building.

He straightened and looked at her. Her father had used the same look when she had done something that displeased him. At ten it had made her squirm; now it only widened her smile.

"The Whisper has it that you have been looking for me," she said.

He nodded in response to her question. "That I have, Sham. I was told ye might be interested in doing some work for me."

"You *do* know what I do?" she asked, raising her eyebrows incredulously.

Again he nodded. "Aye. That's why I've sought ye out. We're needing someone to sneak in and out of the houses. The Whisper gave us a number of folk who might do. Yer name was particularly recommended—" then he smirked at her, "*Shamera.*"

She laughed and leaned more comfortably against the wall. "I hope that you didn't spend too long looking for a thief called Shamera."

The Shark wouldn't have told Talbot, if he'd thought the sailor would spread her identity around. But, she wasn't certain she cared either way; with the Old Man dead, only his promise kept her in Landsend. In Reth there were no Easterners and a wizard could make a fair living.

"No." Easy humor lit his blue-gray eyes. "But I've got to admit the purse was sadly lightened by the time I found out exactly who I'd be looking for. I'd never have thought that Sham the thief was a girl."

She grinned. "Thanks. I've had a few years of practice, but it's good to know I'm convincing in my role. I take it you got your information from the Shark—he enjoys making people pay twice for the same goods."

Talbot nodded. "Dealing with the Shark directly is more expensive than buying the same information from his men, but it's faster and more complete. 'Tisn't my gold I'm spending, and the Reeve's more interested in quality than price.''

"I've heard that the Reeve has been confined to a chair," said Sham impulsively. She'd liked the Reeve despite his heritage, and was half-hoping the rumor had it wrong.

Talbot nodded; a shadow of sorrow chased his usual cheerful expression off his face. "Right after the fight with Lord Hirkin. Says he's got an old injury that's been worsening since it happened. He'll stay steady on for weeks and then he'll have an attack that'll cripple him up something bad. After a few days it'll ease off, but he's never as good as he was when it started.''

Daughter of a soldier, she knew what confinement in a chair meant. They were used mainly for the old, who had difficulty moving, but occasionally a fighter would have the ill luck to survive a back injury. One of her father's men had.

He'd been slammed in the lower back by a mace that crushed his spine. For a summer he'd sat in his chair and told stories to Sham; sometimes even years later she'd call up that soft tenor voice and the visions of great heroes.

She'd overheard the apothecary tell her father that when a man lost the movement of his legs it interfered with the flow of his vital essences. Anyone who stayed confined to a chair was headed for an early pyre. Some died quickly, but for others it was a slow and unpleasant death. The autumn winds had brought an infection that her father's man was too weak and dispirited to fight off and he was gone.

She remembered the Reeve's lithe strength as he wielded the blue sword and decided that she didn't like the thought of him crippled in a chair—it was like the wanton destruction of a beautiful piece of art.

"I'm sorry to hear that," she said.

"His health is one of the reasons that we need ye, girl," said Talbot gruffly.

"You'll have to tell me more of what you want of me before I decide to take on your job."

Talbot nodded his head. "I'll do that. We've a killer here at Landsend."

Sham said dryly, "I know several dozen; would you like to meet one?" Not by a twitch did she reveal her sudden alertness.

"Ah, but ye don't know one like this, I'm thinking," replied Talbot, shifting toward her. "The first victims seemed random—a spit boy at a tavern near the new port, a cooper, the Sandman. It started, as nearly as I can figure, from Hirkin's books, seven or eight months ago."

"The Sandman?" said Sham, surprised. "I'd heard he'd ruffled some feathers when he took out a contract the assassins' guild hadn't approved."

"That's as it may be, but I don't think the guild had anything to do with his death. He died without a sigh or a squeak while his mistress was sleeping beside him. She woke up to find her man cut to ribbons." Talbot waited.

"Like the Old Man," said Sham, since he'd already drawn the parallel himself.

"I thought that would snare yer interest," said Talbot with satisfaction. "The last five victims have been nobles, and the Court is beginning to fret. Himself thinks it might be a noble doing it, and he wants someone to search houses for evidence. If his health were better, the Reeve would have done the investigating himself; instead he sent me to find a thief who would do the job without robbing the nobles blind. Someone who could blend in with them." Talbot met Sham's eye. "Ye might as well be knowing that I added to the requirement 'cause I don't think, myself, that our killer is a noble—though I believe he's very much at home among the nobles. And we have a source"—there was an odd emphasis on the word "source"—"that says it's in the Castle at least sometimes and it isn't human. Himself, being Eastern, dismissed the last part, but is almost convinced of the first."

"What *do* you think the killer is?" asked Sham, lowering her eyes so he couldn't read her thoughts in them.

"I think it's a demon," he said.

Sham looked up, and repeated softly, "A demon."

"Aye," he nodded slowly. "A demon."

"Why would you think that?" smiled Sham, as if she'd never heard of the demon called Chen Laut.

"Sailor's superstition," he answered readily enough. "I know the stories, and the killings fit. The last noble was killed in his locked room. They had to take an axe to the door to get to him and there were no passages that anyone could find. *If* it is a man, all ye have to do is search the houses. If it isn't, I'd rather have a wizard around to deal with it."

"You overestimate my abilities," she commented. "Officially, I've not been released from my apprenticeship."

"Maur," said the sailor softly, "was a man who left an impression wherever he went. He came to the ship I served on from time to time—saw to it that I learned to read and write. I'd rather have his apprentice than any master wizard I could name. Besides, the Shark assures me that ye are as capable as any wizard left here in Landsend."

"Ah." Sham wondered how many other people had known who the Old Man had once been.

"Ye owe the Reeve for yer rescue," said Talbot softly. "Wizard or not, there were too many people for ye to handle on yer own. Himself pays well, but if that is not enough, add the satisfaction of finding yer master's killer."

Sham's eyebrows rose and she shrugged, as if it were no great matter—never let them know what bait you'll jump for or how high. "Maybe you're right. In any case, I certainly owe *you*. When do you want me at the Castle?"

The former sailor narrowed his eyes at the early morning sun that was creeping slowly to lighten the sky against the rooftops of Purgatory. "His words were, I believe, 'as soon as you find her.' I'd be thinking then, *now* would be a good time."

THE CYBELLIANS HAD A TASTE FOR COLOR THAT WAS ALmost offensive to Southwood eyes. The servants of the Castle, Easterner and Southwoodsmen alike, were arrayed in jewel tones of sapphire, ruby, topaz, emerald, and amethyst. Talbot appeared underdressed in his brown and grey.

One of the blank-faced servants snickered behind them as Sham followed Talbot through the entrance hall. Still walking, she rubbed conspicuously at one of the smaller stains on the front of her leather jerkin. Then she spat loudly on it and rubbed some more while she looked for a better means of retaliation. The carefully placed, bejeweled trinkets that littered every available surface caught her eye.

Walking slightly behind Talbot, she picked up a gold-and-ruby candlestick from the entrance of a long formal meeting hall and carried it with her the length of the room. She set it down casually on a small table inside the far door, smiling inwardly as a footman sighed with relief—not noticing that the small figurine than had occupied the table was now in a pocket of the full sleeve that covered her left arm.

The figurine was encrusted with green gemstones that Sham thought might be diamond rather than emerald in the quick glimpse she'd managed before secreting it away. If so, the statuette of the dancing girl was worth far more than the candlestick that she could hear someone rushing to re-store to its former position.

The foolery distracted her from the fact that the last time she'd walked through this hall it had been strewn with bodies, many of whom she'd known. As they passed by the doorway she could still picture the young guardsman who had lain there in a limp heap, blind eyes staring at her. Only a little older than she had been, he'd asked her to dance one evening and talked about his dreams of adventure and travel.

Sham winked at a timid maidservant who was staring at the lad in the ragged clothes. The maid blushed, then winked back, smoothing her bright yellow gown with cal-loused hands.

Talbot led Sham into the private wings. The difference was immediately apparent from the lack of servants standing ostentatiously in the corridors. This was an area of the Castle she wasn't familiar with, and she felt some of her tension dissolve.

There were none of the richly woven rugs that were scattered around the floors in the public rooms, but she thought that it might be a recent modification to accommodate a wheeled chair. No small tables littered the halls as they had elsewhere; there was nothing the wheels of the Reeve's chair would catch on.

She bit her lip and the little statuette in her sleeve made her increasingly uncomfortable: the Old Man would not have approved. The Reeve had enough things to deal with; he didn't need to worry that the thief he'd been forced to ask for help was untrustworthy enough to steal from him. She looked for an innocuous little table to set the stupid thing on, but Talbot's path seemed to be confined to the denuded corridors that twisted and snaked back and forth.

Finally they came to a narrow hall that bordered the outside of the Castle. On one side was the finished marble that pervaded the castle but the other side was rough-hewn white granite from an earlier age. The hall ended abruptly in a wall with a plain door; Talbot stopped and tentatively rapped on it with his knuckles.

He raised his hand to knock a second time, but stopped when the door opened smoothly to reveal another one of the bland-faced servants that Sham was developing a hearty dislike for—a dislike that was compounded by the dancer in her sleeve. If it hadn't been for that bland I-am-a-servant expression she wouldn't have taken the blasted thing in the first place. She glowered at the wiry man who held the door.

"The Reeve was expecting you, Master Talbot. Come in." His voice was as expressionless as his face.

Giving in to the impulses that had often brought her grief in the past, Sham slipped the statuette into her hand and gave the valet the little dancer with her glittering green eyes and begemmed costume.

"Someone is bound to have missed this by now." Her tone was nonchalant. "You might take it to the first long room to the right of the main entrance and give it to one of the footmen."

A brief snort of masculine laughter emerged from a dark-ened corner of the room. "Dickon, take the stupid thing to the emerald meeting room and give it to one of my mother's servants before they shrivel with terror.''

With no more than a slight nod of disapproval, the man-servant left the room holding the statuette in two fingers as though it might bite him.

Sham looked at the expansive room that managed somehow to appear cluttered. Part of the effect was caused by the way the furniture had been arranged to be easily accessible by a wheeled chair, but most of it was the result of the wide variety of weaponry and armament scattered on walls, benches, and shelves.

"Thank you, Talbot, I see you found her." As he spoke, the Reeve wheeled into the light that drifted into the room through colored glass panels of the three large windows high on the outer wall. Although the original builders of the Castle had planned on the building being fortified, later Southwood Kings had added a second curtain wall and traded safety for comfort and light.

Sham was surprised at how unaltered the Reeve seemed. Though confined to the chair, the silk of his thin tunic revealed the heavy muscles in his upper arms and shoulders. Even without the bulk of the chainmail he'd been wearing the night of the Spirit Tide, he was a big man. She couldn't tell anything about his lower body because it was wrapped in a thick blanket.

"Have you satisfied your curiosity?" There was bitterness in his voice, though the man's innate courtesy kept him speaking Southern rather than his native tongue.

Sham looked up into his face and saw there the changes she hadn't seen in his body. Pain darkened his eyes to black and made his skin grey rather than the warm brown it had been. Lines she didn't remember seeing before were etched deeply around his eyes and from nose to lips.

Remembering the young soldier who sought the company of a child too young to hide her curiosity rather than endure the sympathetic pity of his former comrades, her reply was different than courtesy demanded.

"No." Her voice was neutral. "Do you cover your legs because they are deformed or because you are cold?"

She knew that she'd chosen correctly when his crack of laughter covered Talbot's gasp at her temerity.

"A bit of both, I suppose," Kerim answered with a surprising amount of humor considering his former bitterness. "The wretched things have started to twist up. Since it bothers me to look at them, I wouldn't want to inflict the sight on anyone else."

Sham observed him shifting slightly uncomfortably in the chair and said, "You ought to have more padding in the seat. And if you asked your wheelwright, he'd tell you that a lighter, larger wheel would turn more easily. You might try something like the ones on the racing sulkies—" she shrugged and found a seat on the wide arm of an expensive chair, "—if more padding and bigger wheels work for horses, they should work for you."

The Reeve smiled. "I'll take that under consideration. I trust that Talbot explained what we need you for?"

She grinned at him. "He said that I get to rummage through the houses of the aristocrats with your permission. It will certainly make life easier, if not as much fun."

Talbot cleared his throat warningly, but Kerim shook his head and said, "Don't encourage her, she's just baiting you."

"Who else is going to know about me?" she questioned, realizing that she was enjoying herself for the first time in a long time.

"Just Talbot and myself," answered the Reeve. "I don't know who else to trust."

"What about your source?"

The Reeve's eyebrows rose.

"You know, the one who told you the killer is here?"

"Elsic," said Talbot. "He doesn't know about ye, and we won't be telling him."

Sham looked at the Reeve's discomforted face and Talbot's bland one and thought that the first thing she would look for was this Elsic.

"Do you have any particular house that you want me to . . . explore first?" She asked.

Kerim shook his head and gave a frustrated grunt. "I

don't have any idea where to start. If you've robbed the manors of Landsend as frequently as the Whisper claimed, you probably have a better idea than I.''

Sham shook her head. ''No. I've been fairly selective in my targets. I haven't stolen anything from anyone with close connections to the Castle for . . . hmm . . . at least a year.'' So she lied—did they really expect her to give them something solid enough to hang her with?

The Reeve grunted; she almost hoped he knew how much her answer was worth. ''Talbot and I have talked about it. We thought it might help you to meet the people of the court before you decide which residences to . . . *explore*. I tire too easily of late to keep abreast of the latest gossip, and Talbot has no entrance to the court proper, as he not only is a stranger and a peasant, but also a South-woodsman.''

''So am I,'' she commented, ''stranger, peasant, and Southwoods native as well.''

Talbot grunted. ''But you're not the Master of Security either.''

She allowed her lips to twist with amusement. ''How are you going to introduce me to your court? 'Excuse me, but I'd like to introduce you to the thief who has been relieving you of your gold. She's going to look around and see if she can figure out which of you is killing people, so be sure that you tell her who it is.' ''

Kerim smiled sweetly with such innocence in his expression she knew immediately that she wasn't going to like what he was about to propose. ''The original idea was that you could become one of my household.''

Sham raised both of her eyebrows in disbelief. ''Half the servants know who I am, and the rest of them will know before I leave here this morning. The only reason the thief-takers haven't hauled me in is because they can't prove what I do, and you have the reputation of punishing thief-takers who work with more zeal than evidence. A reputation, I might add, that I am extremely grateful you deserve.''

Kerim's smile widened, and the innocence was replaced

with sudden mischief and a certain predatory intentness that made her realize again how well the title of Leopard suited him. "When we found out just who and what you were, lady, Talbot and I came up with a much better solution. They know Sham the Thief—a boy. You are going to be Lady Shamera, my mistress."

Talbot put his hand to his mouth and coughed when Sham spit out a surprised curse she'd learned from one of the more creative of her father's men.

"Ye won't have to go quite that far, lassie," commented the Reeve blandly, in a fine imitation of Talbot, complete with seaman's accent. "I don't demand anything so . . . strenuous from my mistresses."

Sham gave Kerim an evil glare, but she held her tongue. He was almost as good at teasing as she was, and she refused to present him with any more easy targets. She took a deep, even breath, and thought about what he'd proposed, her foot tapping on the floor with irritation.

"I expect—" she said finally, biting off the end of each word as if it hurt her, "—that you mean I am to play the role of mistress, not fulfill it. *If* that is the case, I am inclined to agree that the role would have its uses."

A short silence greeted her, as if neither Kerim nor Talbot had expected her to give in so easily. Before either man had a chance to speak, the door opened and Dickon returned from replacing the statuette. Sham shot him a look of dislike which he returned with interest and doubtless more cause.

Clearing his throat, Dickon addressed the Reeve. "When I arrived at the emerald meeting room, Her Ladyship had already been summoned. She questioned my custody of her statuette. I had no choice but to inform her where it came from. She instructed me to tell you that she will be here momentarily."

"Dickon, wait outside the door to welcome her in," snapped the Reeve, and the servant responded to his tone and jumped to do his bidding.

"Hellfire," swore Kerim. "If she sees you, she'll recognize you when you reappear as a woman. My mother has eyes that would rival a cat's for sharpness." He wheeled rapidly to the fireplace that all but spanned one of the inner walls and pressed a carving. A panel of wood on the wall next to the fireplace slid silently inwards and rolled neatly behind the panel next to it, revealing a passageway.

"Ah," commented Sham, tongue in cheek. "The fireplace secret-passageway; how original."

"As the passage floor is mopped every other week, I would hardly call it 'secret,' " replied the Reeve sardonically. "It will, however, allow you to avoid meeting my mother in the halls. Talbot, get her outfitted, cleaned up and back here as soon as you can."

Sham bowed to the Reeve and then followed Talbot into the passageway, sliding the door in place behind her.

"WE NEED TO GET YE CLOTHES BEFITTING A MISTRESS OF the Reeve," commented Talbot.

"Of course," replied Sham in a casual tone without reducing the speed of her walk.

"Lord Kerim told me to take ye t'home. My wife can find something for ye to wear until a seamstress can whip something up." He cleared his throat. "He also thought we ought to take a week and ah . . . work on your court manners."

"Wouldn't do to have the Reeve's mistress tagging valuable statuettes?" ask Sham in court-clear Cybellian as she stopped and looked at Talbot. "I should think not, my good man. Must not tarnish Lord Kerim's reputation with this little farce."

"Well now," he said, rubbing his jaw. "I suspect that clothing might be all we have to worry about."

She nodded and started off again. After a mile or so Talbot cleared his throat. "Ah, lassie, there is no place in Purgatory that carries the sorts of silks and velvet that ye need."

She sent him a sly grin. "Don't bet on it. If there is something that people will buy, Purgatory sells it."

He laughed and followed her deeper into Purgatory.

• • •

"THE PROBLEM WE FACE—" SHE EXPLAINED AS SHE LED him through the debris-covered floor of a small, abandoned shop near the waterfront, "—is that a mistress of a high court official must always wear clothes built by a known dressmaker. Most of them wouldn't let someone dressed like me through the door. If we managed to find one that would, it'd be the talk of the town by morning."

She stooped and pulled up a section of loose floorboard out of the way, leaving a narrow opening into a crawlspace that the original owner of the building had used for storage. She had several such storage areas here and there around Purgatory and she was careful never to sleep near any of them. She had found she lost less of her belongings if she didn't keep them with her.

"You're too big to fit in here, Talbot. Wait just a moment."

Sham slipped through the crack with the ease of long practice and slithered through the narrow crawlway until she came to the hollow that someone else had widened into a fair-sized space underneath the next building over. No one mopped the floor twice weekly here, and the dust made her eyes water.

She called a magelight and found the large wooden crate that held most of her clothing. Lifting the lid, she sorted through the costumes she had stored there until she came to a bundle carefully wrapped in an old sheet to protect it from the dust. As an afterthought, she also took her second-best thieving clothes and added them to her bundle.

In darkness again she crawled back out the small passage. She put the floorboard back and scuffed around with her feet until the dust by the loose floorboard was no more trampled than it was in the rest of the room.

"If you'll turn your back for a bit, I'll change into something that the dressmakers will find acceptable."

Talbot nodded and walked a few paces away, staring through the dirt-encrusted window at the vague shapes of the people walking on the cobbled street outside, commenting, "For a Purgatory thief, ye know a lot about the court."

Sham removed her belt and set it aside, after freeing the small belt pouch that carried the few coppers that she traveled the streets with. It gave her time to think about her answer.

"My mother was a lady in the king's court, my father a minor noble," implying that her parents were court parasites, poor gentry with aspirations and little else who hung on at court for the free boarding. Not flattering to them, but somehow she didn't want to tarnish her father's name by making it common knowledge that his daughter was a thief. Sham set the money aside and pulled out a comb, a few hairpins, and a clean cloth, before stripping out of her clothes.

"Didn't ye have a place to go? Purgatory is not where I'd like to see a young court miss forced to live." Like the gentleman he was, Talbot kept his back firmly toward her.

"After the Castle fell? No. My parents died when the gates were opened. They had no relatives who survived the invasion." There had been no one to turn to, just a blind old man who had been her teacher. He had wanted to die as well, but she wouldn't let him. Perhaps he would rather have gone then, than survive these last twelve years blind and magicless.

"How did you survive?"

"Not by selling my body," she said dryly, finding the sympathy in his voice oddly disturbing. She used a touch of magic to dampen the cloth and cleaned her hands and face as well as she could. The rest of her was cleaner than most people in Purgatory were, but clean hands and face would have made her stand out. "I knew a little magic. Thieving is not a bad way to make a living, not after the first time—though I know a whore who says the same thing about her line of business. My choice has a longer career span."

"If ye don't get caught," added Talbot, matching her dry tones.

"There is that," agreed Sham politely.

She unfolded the sheet and took out the blue muslin underdress, shaking it out as best she could. The rest of the wrinkles were swiftly eliminated by another breath of magic. Usually she wouldn't waste her energies on something so trivial, but she didn't have time to heat a flatiron.

Once the dress was on, she slipped the knife that usually resided in her boot into the thigh sheath, and slipped her hand through the hole in the skirt to see if she could reach the handle. It was a little awkward, so she pulled the sheath over the narrow strips of leather that she'd tied around her thigh until the knife came more naturally to hand.

She had to leave off her arm sheath and dagger, but the long, sharp hairpin was almost as good. The yellow overdress covered the small slit in the skirt, but as it was open on the sides it didn't hamper her access to the knife. A pair of yellow slippers completed the outfit.

"You can look, now," she said, rolling the clothes she'd been wearing into the bundle she'd brought from the cubbyhole. She pulled her hair out of its braid and tugged the small wooden comb ruthlessly through the thick stuff until she was able to twist it neatly on the top of her head, securing it with the wicked hair pin.

"Now," she said, "we are ready to visit the dressmakers and acquire a wardrobe."

SHAMERA SWEPT INTO THE CASTLE, LEAVING TALBOT TO direct the disposal of her purchases. Looking neither left nor right she followed the path that she'd taken earlier in the day.

She'd scorned Talbot's suggestion that the Reeve wouldn't take a woman of questionable taste as his mistress. Everyone knew that the Reeve had never taken a mistress, so she had to be extraordinary. With her angular features and slender body, that left her wardrobe.

The dress she wore was black, a color that the Cybellians used only for mourning. She'd had the seamstress lower the bodice and take off the sleeves, leaving most of her upper body exposed. Small sapphire-blue flowers, torn hastily from another dress at Shamera's request, were sewn here and there on the satin skirt of her gown.

Her hair, free of its usual restraints, hung in thick soft

waves past her shoulders and halfway down her back. She'd colored her lips a soft rose and lined her large eyes and darkened her lashes with kohl. Her face she'd powdered until it was even whiter than usual, a shocking contrast to the darker-skinned Cybellians. She had even changed her movements, exchanging her usual boyish stride for a sultry swaying walk that covered the same amount of ground in a completely different way.

When she'd emerged from the dressing room at the dressmaker's, Talbot had started laughing.

"No one, but no one, is going to confuse ye wi' Sham the thief." Even the outrageous bill that she'd run up hadn't been enough to take the wide grin off his face.

SHAMERA DIDN'T BOTHER TO KNOCK AT THE REEVE'S door, but thrust it open hard enough that it hit the wall behind it with a hollow thud.

"*Darling*," she gushed in heavily accented Cybellian. "I couldn't believe it when I heard that you were ill. Is *this* why you broke off with me?"

After a dramatic pause at the door, Shamera rushed over to his side trailing expensive perfume behind her and ignoring the stunned looks on the faces of the man and woman who were sitting in chairs next to Kerim. As she crossed the floor she looked at them from the corner of her eye.

The woman was small and beautiful despite the fine lines around her mouth and nose. Her coloring was the same as the Reeve's: thick dark hair, warm brown skin, and rich dark eyes. She must have been extraordinarily beautiful as a young girl; even now, with strands of silver and a slight softening of the skin of her neck, she would have brought a pretty penny at any of the higher-class brothels in Purgatory.

The man sitting next to her was similarly beautiful; his features were fine-boned and mobile, a refined version of the Reeve's. The dark eyes were large and long-lashed. A warm, approving smile dawned on his lips at her appearance, revealing a single dimple.

Shamera reached the Reeve's chair and leaned over, pressing a passionate kiss on his mouth, lingering longer than she'd really intended when he responded with matching theatrics. Breathing a little harder, she pulled back before she ended up sitting on his lap in front of the woman who, judging by the look of moral outrage on her face, could only be his mother.

"But sweetheart, *what* is it they are feeding you?" Sham looked with honest horror at the mush on the tray that sat on a table beside Kerim's chair. She picked up the tray and sought out the servant standing in the shadows, where a good servant learned to make himself at home.

"You, sir, what is your name?"

"Dickon, my Lady."

"Dickon, take this back to the kitchens and get something fit for a man to eat." She thickened her vowels deliberately when she said "a man"; it *might* have been her accent.

The servant came forward to take the tray, stiffening slightly as he got a good look at her face. But he took the gold inlaid wooden slat without commenting and left the room before anyone had a chance to object to Shamera's order. She turned back to the remaining three occupants in the room and noticed that Kerim had lost control of his laughter.

She widened her eyes at him and gestured dramatically, saying, "Horrid man, I come here to rescue you, and all that you do is laugh at me. I think I shall leave." With that she turned on one foot and took two steps toward the door.

"Shamera," Kerim's voice darkened and Sham felt as if he'd run a caressing hand down her back. "Come here."

She turned back with a pout and crossed her arms under her breasts. The effect caused the other man in the room to swear softly in admiration and the immaculately garbed woman's eyebrows rose as Shamera's gown slid lower. Slender she might be, but not everywhere.

"Shamera." There was a soft warning note in the Reeve's voice, but Sham was glad that no one but she was looking at him. No one could have missed the inner amusement that danced in his eyes. She felt her lips slide out of their pout and into an honest smile in response.

"I'm sorry," she offered softly, obediently traversing the floor between them, "but you *know* I don't like being laughed at."

He took the hands she offered him and brought them to his lips in apology. "Dear heart, your presence is like a breath of summer in these dark chambers." He spoke in the sultry voice that would have made a young maiden swoon.

"*Our* presence is obviously unnecessary," commented the other man. "Come Mother." The older woman took his arm and allowed him to assist her to rise.

"Wait," ordered the Reeve raising a hand imperiously. "I would like to introduce you to the Lady Shamera, widow of Lord Ervan of Escarpment Keep. Lady Shamera, my mother the Lady Tirra and my brother, Lord Ven."

Shamera's shallow curtsy was hampered by the fact that Kerim hadn't released her hand. She smiled at them and then turned back to Kerim, without waiting to see if they would return the greeting. With her free hand she smoothed the hair out of Kerim's amused face.

Shamera heard the Lady Tirra draw her breath in to speak as Kerim's servant came in with a new tray from the kitchen. Sham straightened, took the tray, and gifted the servant with a warm smile for his timely interruption; she wasn't sure how far she could push Lady Tirra without offending Kerim. Balancing the meal easily on one hand, she lifted the warming covers to reveal a nicely roasted chicken with an assortment of greens.

"Ah, that's *much* better. Thank you, Dickon."

The servant bowed and retreated to the corner he'd occupied from the beginning as Sham set the richly carved wooden tray on Kerim's lap rather than on the nearby table. She knelt in front of him, ignoring the damage to the material the dressmaker had so carefully pressed.

"Eat, my Leopard; then we will talk," she purred in the sultriest tone she could manage; it must have worked because she heard the rustle of crisp fabric as Kerim's mother stiffened with further outrage.

Without taking his eyes off Shamera, Kerim spoke. "My thanks, Mother, for your concern. It seems that I will not be dining alone tonight after all. The gentlemen of the court are doubtless awaiting your late arrival."

Lady Tirra left the room without another word, leaving her youngest son to trail after her.

FOUR

As the door closed, Kerim turned to his servant. "Dickon, I believe Talbot will be nearby. Find him and send him in, will you?"

"Very good, my lord." Dickon bowed and left the room.

As soon as the soft click of the latch reached Sham's ears, she relaxed and sat back in a more comfortable cross-legged position on the floor.

The Reeve looked at her for an instant and then began laughing softly, his shoulders shaking. "I was wondering how we'd pull this off. You'll forgive me, but when Talbot proposed this, I thought he was insane."

"Thievery requires a certain amount of boldness, and a touch of theatrics," she answered, batting her lashes at him. "I have it on good authority that being a mistress has similar requirements."

He nodded. "No doubt it does, but I've seen warriors quake at the sight of my mother."

She started to reply, but a soft sound from the corridor caught her attention. A moment later there was a gentle tapping on the door. She stood without tangling her feet in the yards of material that formed her skirt, and strode across the room to open the door for Talbot.

The former sailor entered with his usual rolling gait, aiming a wide grin at the Reeve. "Impressive, isn't she?" Talbot nodded at Sham with the expression of a doting hen viewing her egg. "Told her that black was for when folks were dead. She raised her brows and looked down her nose and said black was erotic. When she came out looking like that I bought a nice black nightdress for the missus."

"I didn't expect her this soon."

"Mmm, well now, it seems that she'll not be needing tutoring in court ways—she was brought up here under the old king."

Kerim turned to her, and Sham nodded, quipping, " 'Fraid I'm not much credit to my upbringing."

The Reeve gave her a thoughtful glance, then turned his attention back to Talbot. "No word tonight?"

Talbot looked grim. "Nay, sir, but it'll come." Looking at Sham, he explained, "Our killer likes to hunt every eight or nine days: 'tis the only real pattern the thing has. Yesterday was the eighth day and no one died, so tonight's it."

She frowned, trying to remember what little she knew about demons. "Is there any pattern to the numbers? Like three times it feeds on the eighth day and then twice on the ninth?"

"I don't know," answered Talbot, intrigued, "I hadn't thought it might be a fixed pattern rather than whimsy. I'll go through the deaths again and see."

"Is it important?" asked the Reeve.

"It depends," she said, helping herself to a roll that was sitting ignored on Kerim's plate. She found a comfortable chair and tugged it around until it faced the Reeve. Talbot took up a seat on the nearest couch.

"On what?" The Reeve picked up his eating knife and began to carve the chicken.

"On whether or not you believe in demons," she replied—though she didn't recall any pattern to demon killings. She waited smugly for his reaction. Intelligent, educated Cybellians did not believe in demons.

"I've seen a few," said the presumably intelligent, educated Cybellian Reeve thoughtfully, "but never anywhere near the city."

Sham choked and then coughed when she inhaled a crumb.

Kerim ignored her outwardly, though she thought there might be a hint of amusement in the lines around his mouth as he continued, "There is no way that these murders are the work of demons. The last victim died in his room in the middle of the day. He kept thirty-odd servants; if it had been a demon, the thing would have been spotted long before it found Abet's room."

"Abet's locked room," added Talbot meaningfully, looking at Shamera.

"In any case," continued the Reeve, "I can't imagine one of the swamp demons dragging its carcass through the whole of Abet's mansion without someone noticing. Not only are they loud, but they stink like a week-old fish."

"Ah," said Sham, enlightened. "These demons of yours, are they strong and devilishly hard to kill? Roughly human in shape?"

The Reeve nodded, "Sounds like all the ones I've met."

"Uriah," she said firmly. "I've never met one—not that I'm complaining. But I'll tell you this much, I'd rather face a hundred of the things than take on a demon. Uriah are monsters, abominations created by magic. Demons *are* magic."

"*Magic*," barked the Reeve, at last giving her the reaction she'd been waiting for. "Every time you Southwoodsmen hear about something that is not easily explained, you sit around nodding sagely and say 'magic'—as if the whole pox-ridden world turns on it."

She laughed, "It does, of course. Only self-blinded Easterners can't see it."

Kerim shook his head at her, and resumed his speechmaking. "I've lived here for almost ten years and I've never seen someone work magic. Sleight-of-hand, yes—but nothing that can't be explained by fast hands and a faster mouth."

"The wizard-born aren't stupid, messire," said Talbot mildly. "Ye weren't here for the blood that followed the conquest of the city—the witch hunts we have now are nothing in comparison. Proper terrified of magic, yer armies were, an' they slaughtered any mage they could find. The wizards who survived would prefer ye kept on thinking magic's what the streetcorner busker uses to pull a coin from behind yer ear."

"And it's easier for me this way," added Shamera, to stir up the Reeve again, who'd begun to let Talbot's calm voice soothe him. "It gives a thief a decided advantage to be able to use magic where no one believes in it. Who am I to ruin the fun?"

"Do ye remember how long the Castle stood against the Prophet's armies after Landsend itself had fallen?" asked Talbot, ignoring Sham.

"Nine months," said Kerim reluctantly.

Talbot nodded. "Nine months on what little food they had stored here. Did ye ever find a water source other than the well that was dry long decades before the siege?"

"No."

Shamera noticed that the Reeve was beginning to sound huffy, as if he didn't like the direction that this conversation was taking. She had thought that Talbot was only trying to calm Kerim down, not change his mind.

In a spirit of general perversity she said, "The weekly mopping of the secret passages aside—"

"Every other week," corrected Kerim.

She ignored him. "—I would wager there are still ways out of the Castle that no one knows about. Master Talbot, if the Reeve is determined not to believe in magic it's a waste of time to try and prove otherwise."

"If his ignorance is a threat to his life it needs to be altered," countered Talbot with a touch of heat. "This killer is attacking in the Castle, it might choose the Reeve next."

"Who could stop it if it did?" replied Shamera, becoming serious. "If *I* don't know what to do with a demon, how could a magicless Cybellian—whether he believed in demons or not?"

"Others have tried to educate me concerning magic," said Kerim neutrally. "Why don't you educate me about demons instead?"

"Very well," agreed Sham. Adopting her best "mysterious sorceress" manner she said, "Demons are creatures of magic, called to this world by death and dying." She grinned at the expression on the Reeve's face and switched to more matter-of-fact tones as she continued. "Actually, they are summoned here by black magic."

"What makes you think that it is a demon we're hunting, not a man?"

"Because my friend—the one Hirkin said I murdered— was killed by a demon."

Sham looked at the Reeve carefully, trying to see what he was thinking, but his face was as neutral as his voice. "What makes you so certain?"

She shrugged. "He told me as much before he died."

Talbot stepped in to keep the Reeve from offering the offense disbelief would be. "I doubt ye ever met him, sir, ye came later to Landsend; but the old man who died was Maur, the last king's advisor."

Kerim frowned thoughtfully. "The King's Sorcerer was tortured before he disappeared from the Castle dungeons, but I didn't think he was as old as the man who died looked."

"Wizards," said Sham, striving to keep the bitterness out of her voice, "—especially those as powerful as Maur, can live longer than mundane people. When he could no longer access his magic, he aged rapidly."

Kerim looked her in the eye. "I was not here when he was tortured, and I would not have countenanced such an action. Magic or no magic, if the records of his words in the King's council meetings are accurate, he was a man of rare insight."

Sham allowed herself to be mollified by his answer. "He was attacked by a demon called Chen Laut. He drove it away, but was mortally wounded before it fled."

"How did he drive it away?" asked Kerim with obvious patience for her Southwood-barbaric beliefs.

She smiled sweetly. "Magic."

"I thought Maur couldn't work magic," said Talbot, frowning.

Sham shrugged, seeing no need to explain the difference between calling magic and working magic.

"So what does a demon look like?" said Kerim. He ignored her attempt to bait him and finished the last of his food.

Sham smiled in anticipation of his reaction. "I don't know. I couldn't see it."

Kerim paused briefly, then shook his head with an air of long-suffering patience. "Demons are invisible. What else can you tell me about them?"

She shrugged, enjoying herself. "Even in Southwood, most people believe in them the way that you believe in magicians—stories told to keep children in at night. You know—" she switched to a sing-song voice and recited,

> *"The evening comes, the sun is fled.*
> *Shadows chase the fleeing light.*
> *Let fear inspire your silent tread*
> *When demons walk the world of night."*

"I've never heard it." The Reeve bared his teeth at her. "So tell me a story."

She returned his smile, such as it was. "Demons, like dragons, are creatures of magic rather than mere users of it. They are almost always evil, though there are tales of some that have offered aid or shelter. Demons never appear unsummoned, and are difficult to get rid of. The Wizard's Council has forbidden the use of sacrifice or human remains while working magic since just after the Wizard Wars about a thousand years ago. Apparently such things are necessary to get rid of demons as well as to summon them."

She had meant to stop there. She really had. If only he hadn't gotten that self-righteous, see-what-an-ignorant-savage-you-are expression on his face.

She leaned forward and lowered her voice dramatically. "The wizards would find a likely young man and kidnap him. Demons have no form here on our world. They must be given one. The ceremony is long and brutal, culminating in the young man's death as the demon takes his body." That was true enough, as far as she knew. She decided to add a few of the choicer rumors to go along with it. "Sometimes though, the first victim's body was not usable, due to the brutal rites that summon the demon. You see, the death spells set to keep the demon's host body from procreating have a tendency to kill the person, or in this case, body they are set upon if the subject is too weak." She grinned cheerfully and saw that even Talbot looked grim. "If everything is successfully completed, the wizard had a demon enslaved to his will until the wizard's death."

"What happens after the wizard died?" asked Kerim, who had resumed an impartial expression soon after she'd began her last speech. How entertaining to find someone who could resist her baiting.

"The demon was destroyed by a contingency of the original binding—" she replied, "—unless the demon was the one who killed the wizard, in which case the demon controls itself."

"Ah," said Kerim, "now, the stories."

"Tybokk—" she said, nodding at Kerim's remark, "—is probably the most famous of these. The name of his summoner is lost to time, but for four hundred years, more or less, he would join a Trader Clan as it crossed a certain mountain pass—"

"And kill them all?" offered Kerim blandly.

Shamera shook her head, "No, Tybokk was more creative than that. The travelers would arrive at their destination, every one of them, chanting a simple rhyme, day and night; until, one by one, they killed themselves."

"The rhyme held the clue that destroyed the demon?" suggested Kerim.

Again she shook her head. "That would make a good story, but no. As far as I have heard the rhyme was something like this:

'Winds may blow,
  To and fro.
But we'll ne'er more
  A roaming go.
Tybokk, Tybokk, Tybokk-O!'

He would probably still be destroying Traders if he
hadn't killed the family clan of the man who was then the
ae'Magi.''

''The who?'' asked the Reeve.

''The ae'Magi,'' replied Talbot, sotto voice. ''It's an old
title given to the archmage. He's the wizard who presides
over the Wizard's Council, the appointed leader of all of
the magicians—usually he's the most powerful, but not always.''

Sham waited until they were through talking before she
began again. ''The ae'Magi was born to the Trader Clans.
When news came to him of the deaths of his family, the
ae'Magi went hunting. For three years he traveled over the
mountain pass that the demon frequented, accompanying
various clans as none seemed to be favored over the other.
When a stranger joined the party, not an uncommon oc-
currence, the ae'Magi would test him, to see if he were a
demon.''

''How did he do that?'' asked the Reeve.

Sham shrugged. ''I don't know. Since the proscription
on demon summoning, many of the magics associated with
demons have been lost as well.''

She cleared her throat and continued. ''One day, or so
the story goes, the clan that the ae'Magi was traveling with
came upon a skinny young lad, placing the last stone on a
newly dug grave. There was a wagon overturned nearby
with both of the horses that pulled it lying dead in their
traces. The boy had a few scratches, but was otherwise
unhurt by the wolves that killed his family while he
watched from a perch in a tree.

''The boy was accepted with no questions: children are
treasured by the Trader Clans. He was a solemn child, but
that might have been because of the death of his father. The

ae'Magi, like most of the Traders, would sooner have suspected himself of being a demon than he would have suspected a child.

"One night the ae'Magi sat brooding in front of a small fire while his fellow Traders danced and exchanged stories. Gradually the stories changed from acts of heroism to more fearful topics, as is the case with most such story-exchanges. Someone, of course, told the story of Tybokk.

"The ae'Magi turned to leave and caught an unusual expression on the strange boy's face. The boy was smiling, but not as boys do—his smile was predatory.

"A chill crawled up the ae'Magi's spine as he realized how well the demon had been disguised by its summoner, and how close the mage had come to being defeated by the creature he hunted.

"A great battle followed, one that is yet spoken of with awe by the descendants of the Traders who witnessed it. In the end, the demon's body was destroyed. The demon was left without form, unable to do more than watch as the Clan traveled out of the mountains in safety.

"Still today, the pass is called the Demon's Pass or Tybokk's Reach, and some say that there is an unnatural mist that occasionally follows those that walk that path at night."

A small silence followed her story, then the Reeve said, "You should have been a storyteller rather than a thief. You would make more money at it."

She smiled blandly. "You obviously don't know how much I make thieving."

"So you think we have another Tybokk?" asked the Reeve.

She shrugged. "If Maur was right when he named it Chen Laut, then we do."

"Chen Laut is the monster who eats children who don't do their chores," explained Talbot. "My mother used to threaten us with him."

"If the King's Sorcerer was mistaken?" Kerim asked.

"Then perhaps we have a man who enjoys killing," she replied. "He works seven or eight days in a row with the

eighth or ninth day off, or perhaps his wife visits her
mother every eighth or ninth day. He travels freely among
the upper classes—a servant of some kind, or perhaps a
noble himself. He can pick locks and skulk in shadows so
skilfully, I didn't see him when I entered the old man's
cottage.''

There was a slight pause, then Kerim nodded his head.
''As long as you are willing to continue to look for a human
culprit, I will listen to anything you have to say concerning
demons.''

''Agreed. Now may I ask you a question?''

''Certainly,'' said Kerim agreeably.

''Just who is Lord Ervan, and how did I become his
widow?''

IT WAS LATE IN THE EVENING WHEN THEY FINISHED IRON-
ing out their respective stories, and Sham was led, yawning,
to the chamber that the Reeve had given her. As she shut
the door behind the Reeve's manservant, she stretched
wearily and looked around.

It was smaller than Kerim's chamber, but the lack of
clutter made it seem much the same size. Unlike the
Reeve's room, thick rugs adorned the floor to keep the chill
stone separated from vulnerable bare toes. Sham took off
her shoes and let her feet sink into the pile of a particularly
thick rug.

Experimentally she peered into the surface of the nightstand near the bed; the reflection that stared back at her was
less blurred than the one in the little polished bronze mirror
she habitually carried. The candles that lit her chamber
were of the highest quality, and left the room smelling
faintly of roses. In the Reeve's chambers the lighting had
been augmented by several large silver mirrors. Without the
mirrors or the windows, the corners of this room were very
dark.

She had never slept amid such extravagance even when
she'd lived here with her Father—she couldn't even remember when she'd last slept in a bed. The widow of Lord
Ervan would have taken it as no more than her due, but

without someone to perform for she was only a peasant-thief in a place she didn't belong.

Like the one in Kerim's room, the fireplace stonework covered most of one wall with tapestries hung on either side. As she walked closer, she noticed a door tucked discreetly behind one of the elaborately woven wall hangings on the small part of the wall not occupied by the fireplace.

The sight of the discreet opening cheered her, reminding her why she was here. Dickon had taken her through several halls that twisted and turned, but thieving had gifted Sham with a very good sense of direction. She suspected that the door connected to a similar one in the inner wall of the Reeve's chambers—fitting for the Reeve's mistress, of course.

Returning to the bed, Sham kicked off the slippers that matched her black dress. The fastenings were on the front, so she had refused the offer of a maid. She left the gown lying on the floor where it had fallen, knowing that only someone used to such costly apparel would be so careless. Snuffing out the candles, she climbed into bed and tucked her knife under the pillow, successfully resisting the urge to lie on the floor until she fell asleep.

BLOOD DRIP-DROPPED FROM THE MAN'S HAND ONTO THE smooth granite floor, making a dark viscous puddle. This one had been very satisfactory; his surprise, his terror was sweetening for the meal he'd so generously provided. The demon smiled as it contemplated its handiwork.

THE PLAIN-FACED MAID WHO ENTERED THE ROOM THE next morning and began to light the candles never saw the knife Sham reflexively seized at the sound of the door opening.

"Good morning, Lady Shamera. My name is Jenli and my Uncle Dickon told me you would need a maid. If I am not satisfactory, you are to let him know and he will find someone else." This speech was said to the bed tick as the girl folded it neatly back; it was also said in Southern that was so thickly accented as to be virtually indecipherable.

Sham belatedly remembered her role as the Reeve's mistress and responded accordingly—in accented Cybellian. "As long as you keep your tongue still about my personal business and listen to what I say, a replacement will not be necessary."

"No, Lady . . . I mean, yes, Lady."

Sham gave the maid an assessing glance. Jenli didn't resemble Lord Kerim's personal servant in the slightest. Where he was tall and spare, she was short and round. Every thought that crossed her mind crossed her face first. It would be a long time, if ever, before she matched the perfect-servant expression favored by Dickon—thank the tides.

Sham palmed her knife to keep it out of the maid's sight and got out of bed, wandering languidly to the trunk at the foot. When she casually dropped the soft lace nightdress on the floor, Jenli blushed and paid even closer attention to the bed tick.

Sham opened the trunk, newly purchased to hold Lady Shamera's necessities and inspected its contents—the few items of clothing the dressmaker could make ready immediately, her bundle of Purgatory garb, the flute she'd taken the night the Old Man died, and several canvas bags full of sand to make the trunk weigh what it should. She supposed that she really should have stored the flute in her cave, but it was tied to Maur and she hadn't had the will to set it aside.

When Jenli stepped forward to help, Sham tossed a neatly folded dress across the room where it graced the floor like a dying butterfly. Jenli brought her hands to her cheeks and rushed to save the expensive material.

"Oh, Lady, these should have been hung up and . . . here, let me take that."

The shy, soft-spoken maid snatched the cloth-of-gold overdress out of her hands with the swiftness of a pickpocket. When the maid turned her back to hang the garment the wardrobe, Sham took the dress she wanted out of the trunk, closing and locking the lid with a touch of magic.

The gown she chose was a blue so deep it was almost

black, complementing her eyes perfectly, and trimmed in a light yellow the same color as her hair. The sleeves covered her arms and shoulders entirely. The back was high cut and the collar fastened tightly around her throat. Jenli stood behind her and fastened the myriad of buttons that ran up the back of the dress. When Sham turned around the maid's eyes widened a little.

"Where is the underdress, Lady?" questioned the maid uncertainly.

"What underdress?"

Jenli cleared her throat. "Some packages arrived from the dressmakers this morning, madam; shall I have them brought up?"

Sham nodded absently, adjusting the gown for maximum effect. "Thank you. Where is the Reeve this morning?"

"I don't know, Lady, I am sorry. Would you like me to do your hair this morning?"

"Just brush it out," said Sham, then added in a fretful tone, "I need to find Kerim."

The maid led her over to the delicate bench that sat in front of a small bronze mirror. While she brushed the heavy blond mane, Shamera examined the dress with satisfaction.

It *had* been intended to be worn with an underdress. The silk stopped just below the peak of her breasts, offering a tantalizing view of their undersides as she moved. It managed to push her breasts in such a manner as to make her look far more endowed than she was. Material draped from the sides gracefully, exposing her navel before gathering together at her hips.

It wasn't as if the dress were indecent by Southwood standards. Away from the cool ocean air of Landsend, one of the traditional styles of dress was an embroidered bodice and skirt that left the midriff bare. It was the contrast of the modest style and color of the dress with the bare skin that made the dress shocking.

When the maid was finished with her hair, Shamera applied her own cosmetics, shading her eyelids with grey powder and staining her lips red. Face powder was something that she'd never been able to abide for long periods of time, so she left it off. Finished with her toilet, Sham drifted gracefully to the inner door, ignoring the one leading to the hall.

"My Lord?" she said softly, cracking the door open so the Reeve would hear her address.

"Enter."

She ducked daintily under the heavy material and advanced into the room. Kerim was talking with several noblemen. As Shamera sauntered across the soft carpeting, conversation ground to a halt.

"Lady."

Shamera looked behind her to see the maid ducking through the door. In her hands were a pair of satin slippers that matched the blue dress.

"How silly of me, to forget my slippers. Thank you." She took the shoes and slipped them on.

"Good morning, Lady." There was amusement in the Reeve's voice. "I will be only a few moments, then we can break our fast."

"Thank you, Kerim . . . My Lord."

Shamera approached him and kissed him on the cheek before sinking to the floor beside him, and gazing up at his face. A slight flush rose on his cheekbone. She wasn't sure whether it was suppressed amusement, embarrassment, or something else. The silence echoed in the room for an uncomfortably long time before one of the men began speaking. When the others left the room at last, Shamera was thankful that none of them looked back to see Kerim dissolve into laughter.

"That *dress* . . ." he gasped when he could.

She widened her eyes at him in mock innocence. "Whatever do you mean? Is there something wrong?"

He was still laughing too hard to make speech easy. "Did you *see* Corad's face when you came into the room? He's a Kerlaner. They keep their women confined to their houses and veiled. I thought that his eyes were going to join his feet on the floor." He relaxed into his chair, his shoulders still shaking and pointed a finger at her. "And you were no help at all, Mistress Adoration. Every time I looked away from Corad's sweating face, I had to look at you.''

"Self-control—" Shamera smirked, "—is good for you."

FIVE

"It might be more circumspect to wait until the next evening session," he explained as he led her rapidly through the corridors, "but then there will be so many people that you can't hear yourself think. Besides I wouldn't want to waste the effect of that dress."

Sham didn't have to look at him to know that he was smiling. "I hope you'll remember how much you like it when you get the dressmaker's bill."

He laughed. "Usually there's some form of entertainment at the court—music for dancing, a minstrel, or something." He paused, and his chair slowed briefly as he cast her a wicked glance. "I was told there was a magic act this afternoon."

"I'll look forward to it," replied Sham dryly, and Kerim laughed again.

As they neared the public area, the halls widened and became more expensively furbished. Kerim nodded at the footmen who opened a set of wide doors. When Sham and Kerim entered the room, people began to converge on him. Keeping a steady forward progress, he acknowledged each person who approached, introducing them to Sham. She nodded and smiled blindingly as her eye found the place where she'd found her mother's dead body.

Shamera placed her hand on the Reeve's strong shoulder and gripped it tightly against the tide of memories, hoping he would ascribe it to stage fright. After a moment, the immediacy of her memories faded and the hall became merely a highly polished room full of brightly clad people.

As the Reeve's mistress, she represented an unknown force in politics of the court, one that threatened to upset the established influences. She was careful to act stupid, and concentrate on Kerim—which did much to add to the amusement that lingered in his eyes.

"Kerim," announced Lady Tirra, coming upon them from behind. "You told me that you would see to it that the Lady Sky's lands and property would be released to her. She tells me that her husband's brother still refuses her the right to the manor house at Fahill."

Kerim nodded. Much of the enjoyment left his face as he turned to look at his mother, though his expression was carefully pleasant. "I have been negotiating with him. It would have helped matters greatly if you hadn't sent a message to Johar yourself. He is so irate now it may take a full-scale siege to get him to relinquish the estate. He's even trumped up a charge that Lady Sky murdered Fahill."

"Ridiculous," Lady Tirra responded immediately. "He is merely being greedy, and you are too worried about upsetting his cronies to curtail him properly."

The Reeve leaned back against his chair. "I agree that Lady Sky had nothing to do with Fahill's death, Mother—it's an obvious attempt to hold the lands. We are not going to get her all the land, but if you quit 'helping' me I can come up with a reasonable compromise."

"With her estates and yours joined, you would have the wealth to make your position unassailable," suggested Lady Tirra aggressively, leading Sham to the conclusion that this was something she'd proposed before.

The Reeve bridled visibly. "The only one who can relieve me of my duties is the Prophet of Altis, Mother. He is not affected by the wealth and power of those who object to my rule. Moreover, I am not marrying Lady Sky. She was the wife of my dearest friend—''

"Who has been dead these eight months," she pointed out briskly. "It is time that I have grandchildren. I would not mind accepting Lady Sky's child as my first."

"Then marry her to my brother," he snapped impatiently. "She and he have been lovers for some time. If he'd offered for her, she'd have married him three months ago." Taking a deep breath, he dropped his voice so he wouldn't be overheard by anyone not concerned. "You know Ven and Johar have always gotten on well. Ven asked me to seek a settlement based on his marriage to Sky."

The level of noise in the room had dropped as the conversation progressed. Sham had the impression that everyone in the room was intent on overhearing the exchange between the Reeve and his mother—an impression that was confirmed as silence abruptly descended in the room when a young woman entered through a nearby door. From the reactions of the courtiers, she could only be the Lady Sky that the Reeve had been discussing with his mother.

Like Sham, the woman had typical Southwoodsman coloration, but where Shamera owed her attractiveness to dress and cosmetics, this woman was beautiful. She was tiny, fragile, and *very* pregnant.

Ah, thought Sham, that explained the "first grandchild" remark. Ven hadn't struck her as the type of man who would find a pregnant woman attractive; his involvement with her hinted at depths she had not expected from her first meeting. Or, more probably, he was a fortune hunter after her estates.

Lady Sky kept a pleasant smile on her face as she made her way to where the Reeve sat. Ignoring Sham, the Lady kissed the Reeve's cheek and said, in unaccented Cybellian, "Good morning, Kerim. I take it you and Tirra were discussing Fahill again?"

The Reeve smiled, but there was a subtle reserve in his expression. It was odd considering that Lady Sky was the only one beside Lady Tirra who she'd heard address the

Reeve by his first name. She wondered if there had been something between Kerim and his friend's widow.

"We were discussing Fahill," he replied, not untruthfully. "My mother has taken it upon herself to berate your brother-by-marriage for his unnatural hatred of womankind."

Lady Tirra's lips tightened with anger. "I merely implied that if he had any respect for the woman who bore him, he would not turn an expectant mother out of her own house."

Lady Sky laughed and shook her head. "Thank you for that, Lady, but my brother-in-law knows I can always depend upon your generosity for a place to stay. He is only claiming property, not harming me." She turned back to the Reeve and said in a gently chiding voice, "But, we are being impolite. Would you introduce me to your companion, Lord Kerim?"

Kerim had enjoyed shocking the court and his mother, but Sham could hear the reluctance in his voice when he introduced her to Lady Sky. Sham nodded at the other woman and began toying with a seam in the tunic that Kerim wore.

"I heard of Lord Ervan's death, several years ago," said Lady Sky, obviously trying to make Sham feel welcome. "I knew him only by name, but he was reputed to be a kind man. I had not heard that he was married."

Sham lowered her gaze modestly, but spoiled it by moving her hand off the material of Kerim's velvet tunic and onto the skin over his collarbone. She could almost hear Kerim's mother, who had been steadfastly ignoring her, tremble in outrage. Kerim took her hand firmly in his, bringing it to his lips before he set it safely on the back of his chair.

"Indeed, we married shortly before his death," allowed Sham, absently. Then in a much more animated voice she continued, "Kerim, this tunic doesn't hang right in the shoulders. Leave it with me tonight and I'll fit it for you."

He reached up and patted her hand, "As you wish, my dear."

"You are looking tired, Kerim." Lady Sky's concern

was obvious, and Sham felt herself warming to her. "If you would like, I can introduce Lady Shamera to the members of your court and you can rest."

Kerim shook his head. "Actually, I find that I feel better today than I have for some time. Otherwise, I would have waited to bring Shamera into this viper pit—she doesn't have the experience to protect herself. Ervan was a hermit, even he admitted it, and he kept her secluded with him."

Kerim turned to Lady Tirra, and changed the subject to less personal matters. "Dickon informs me you have quite a spectacle planned for today."

"Would you stop repeating servant's gossip? It is unfitting." Lady Tirra's rebuke was absent; obviously this was an old battle she had long since lost. "However, in this case it is correct. He comes with the strongest recommendations from no less than three of my ladies."

"I look forward to it. You will have to excuse us, ladies, while Lady Shamera and I continue through this mob." Kerim set his chair in motion.

As they proceeded from one small group of people to another, Sham felt the eyes follow her: outraged female and intrigued male glances took in her dress, her company, and her probable position, before turning to the Reeve.

She noticed that Kerim was not beloved by most of the Eastern members of the court. Their manners hid their feelings, almost as well as Sham's bare-midriff dress hid her lack of beauty—but, there was little warmth in the voices that spewed forth the flowery phrases of welcome. Kerim, she thought, was paying for his attempts at uniting the country.

If the Easterners were unsupportive, the few Southwood nobles in the room made up for it. They stood together in a loose-knit cluster on one end of the hall. At Kerim's approach, they broke off talking, and one noble stepped forward with a low bow.

There was a slight wariness in his manner that did not detract from the warmth of his greeting. "My Lord, we were discussing the merits of burning the fields in the spring versus burning them in the autumn. As it has turned into mere speech-making without meritorious debate, we welcome the distraction.''

Kerim smiled, and Sham saw an answering affection in his face. ''It sounds as if you were losing the debate, Halvok.''

Several of the Southwoodsmen had drifted away, but at Kerim's remark the others relaxed and exchanged lazy insults with the man Kerim had addressed as Halvok.

''Allow me to introduce my companion, Lady Shamera, widow of Lord Ervan,'' said Kerim. ''Lady Shamera, these are the Lords Halvok, Levrin, Shanlinger, and Chanford.''

Sham smiled vaguely at them all. All of the names sounded familiar, and Chanford she recognized, though he was much older now. He had been with the defenders of the Castle in the final days of the invasion—she doubted that he would remember the Captain of the Guard's sorcerous daughter, or associate Lady Shamera with her if he did.

Lord Halvok was the obvious leader, from his placement in Kerim's introduction as well as the deference the other lords gave him. He was younger than Chanford, but a good decade older than Kerim. Being short for a Southwoodsman, he was about the same height as most of the Cybellians. His fair hair was more silver than gold, and the clipped beard he wore was completely white. As he took her hand and bowed over it, she caught a speculative look in his eye, as if he were assessing a new hunting hound.

Kerim spoke with them on several small concerns before moving on with Sham drifting beside him. They hadn't gone far when someone began ringing chimes, drawing the crowd's attention to a portion of the hall where a platform had been built. On top of the platform, where he was easily viewed from the floor, stood a man clad in a black robe and hood, his face veiled.

He raised both hands in a dramatic gesture, and from either end of the stage, blue smoke began to emerge from silver urns on the floor. A second gesture, and flames shot forth accompanied by an approving murmur from the crowd. His bid for attention done, the magician waited patiently for the audience to assemble. Kerim found a place near the front, giving Sham a clear view of the proceedings.

"Ah, bold lords and gentle ladies, welcome." The magician's voice was dark and mysterious; Sham saw several ladies shudder eagerly. "I thank you for the opportunity to—"

"Tabby? Tab-*by*!" interrupted a woman's shrill voice from the nearest doorway.

Sham, like most of the audience looked over to see one of the serving women staring incredulously at the magician, who stared back with equal astonishment. The flaming urns began to sputter and die down.

"Tabby, what *are* you doing? Does Master Royce know what you are up to?" The woman put her hands on her hips and shook her head at him as he jumped off the stage and scurried toward her making frantic shushing gestures. As he ran, his hood fell back to reveal the round and freckled face of a young man.

"Hush, Bess," he said in a stage whisper, darting a nervous glance at the crowd. "Master Royce is . . ." He looked again at the rapt audience and leaned closer to the woman and whispered something.

"What did you say?"

The magician cleared his throat and whispered again.

She laughed, and turned to the crowd. "He says Master Royce had a few too many last night. You'll have to make do with his apprentice."

The audience roared with appreciation, as they realized this had been part of the act. The magician shuffled back to the stage, looking embarrassed, and frowned at the silver urn. The one nearest him gave an apologetic burp of flame.

"I'm really not as bad as all that," explained the apprentice earnestly. "I even brought Master Royce's familiar along to help me if I forget the spells." He motioned to a table set discreetly behind him, covered by a black cloth. One of the various bumps under the cloth seemed to move toward the front of the table, rising briefly to a greater height before settling down again.

The crowd laughed, which seemed to cheer the magician.

Sham watched in appreciative silence as the sleight-of-hand master used a façade of incompetence to distract his audience.

He pulled a small rabbit from underneath a nobleman's tunic and examined it sorrowfully. "This was supposed to be a gold coin. Let me try one more time."

He put the rabbit back under the clothing of the discomfited noble, whose comrades were beginning to tease him, but it wasn't a gold coin this time either. The crowd roared, and the Cybellian nobleman flushed, though he was laughing too. The magician mutely held up a wispy bit of muslin, easily recognizable as a lady's undergarment.

The nobleman snatched it back and bellowed in the tones of a field commander, "Now how did *that* get there?" He opened his leather purse, stuffed the lacy thing in, and produced a coin saying, "Here's your gold coin, lad."

The magician took it and shook his head, "So that's how Master Royce does it."

While the audience cheered, the magician stepped back to the stage and drew away the cloth that covered the table. The audience grew quiet as he began to work wonders with the props he'd brought with him. Without using a spark of genuine magic, he had his jaded crowd gasping in awe and wonder—most of them anyway.

Although he seemed to enjoy the spectacle with the rest, Lord Kerim kept up a steady stream of enlightenment directed at Sham that usually began "Dickon says."

"Dickon says that there are two glasses, one within the other," he explained softly as the magician made water appear and disappear by moving a glass through a wide tube of leather. "There are hooks in the tube to catch the inner glass filled with water, and the outer glass that he is displaying for us now is empty. Notice how careful he is to hold the tube upright."

If Sham hadn't been certain that it was a direct attack on her claims of magic, she would have been interested in the methods the magician was using with a smooth competence that put the lie to his claims of being "merely an apprentice."

"There's a false base in the lid of the pot," said Kerim, nodding at the empty pot the magician held up for all to view.

The entertainer took a small twig from the table behind him and set it on fire with a breath. He placed the flaming bit of wood into the pot.

"He shows us the empty pot," continued Kerim, "puts the lid on and the spring-loaded base is pressed into the pot, snuffing the fire between the twin plates of metal. Dickon says that between the second base and the top of the lid there is room for a small animal or two—maybe a couple of doves. They take up less room than you'd think when you see them fluttering their wings."

Sham smiled, and, having had enough of Kerim's lecture, began to work her magic. The performance proceeded as Kerim predicted. When the pot was opened, the fire was gone—replaced by two ring-necked doves . . . and an osprey.

The predator mantled, displaying its wingspan to good advantage as it surveyed the crowded hall with hostile eyes while the doves fled in terror.

The audience, oblivious to the look of dumbfounded amazement on the magician's face, began to clap; the osprey screamed and took to the air. It circled the room twice before it flew at the central panel of the stained-glass window that spanned half the distance from the arched ceilings to the polished floor.

A gasp arose from the crowd as the bird hit the glass, flying through it without damaging the valuable window. As the applause rose, the "magician" recovered his aplomb and bowed deeply.

Sham shook her head, "It was incredible the way that man fit the osprey into the lid of the pot. How do you suppose he worked the trick with the window?"

She widened her eyes at Kerim who scowled at her, making her illusion well worth her effort.

The entertainer wisely chose to end his performance, though there were several props he hadn't yet used. He threw up his hands and blue smoke filled the air; when it cleared he was gone. The fraudulent servingwoman collected coins from the assemblage while several dark-clad men packed away the magician's belongings.

As they were moving away from the stage, Sham felt Kerim's shoulder stiffen slightly. She looked up to see a tall, thin man in clerical robes of red and gold weave his way purposefully through the tangle of people that stood between him and Kerim. Like many of the Cybellians, this man had dark skin, though his hair was a golden color rare for an Easterner. His hawk-like features and his coloring gave him an arresting quality that was heightened by the peaceful assurance with which only zealots or madmen are blessed.

Beside him and to the left was a short, slender man clad in robes of white so brilliant Sham's hands ached in sympathy for his laundrywoman. He kept his head down and had a determinedly peaceful expression. His hands were folded calmly over the green belt that wrapped twice around his waist.

Sham stopped behind Kerim's chair. She recognized the foremost man by his robes of office; he was Lord Brath, High Priest of Altis. She narrowed her eyes at him, before dropping them to the floor—this man had been among those to condemn her Master. She hadn't gotten around to him with her thieving; perhaps she should resume her efforts.

"Lord Kerim," he announced in a rich voice made for singing hymns of praise, "I understand you have declined my request for additional monies for the building of the new temple."

"Yes," said Kerim baldly in such regal tones that Sham looked at him with respect.

"That is unacceptable. The glass-artisans' guild has presented a design for the entry hall that is perfect, but it will require the funding I requested to begin the work. The ruby glass is particularly dear, and the supply of it is barely adequate."

"Then the work will not commence. There are other matters more urgent to the treasury than another stained-glass window. If you have a grievance with my decision, you may take it up with the Prophet in your next letter.'' Kerim propelled his chair forward.

The high priest stepped into the chair's path. ''I already have. He's sent a letter for your perusal.''

Behind his back, the smaller priest rolled his eyes and shrugged helplessly.

''Very well,'' said Kerim. ''Come to my room after dinner has been served and removed.''

''Be certain that I shall, Lord Kerim,'' replied the high priest darkly.

''THAT ONE BEARS YOU NO GOOD WILL,'' COMMENTED Sham when the churchmen were safely left behind.

''Him, I don't worry about.'' Kerim's voice lost the haughty tones as easily as it had gained them. ''Brath is too occupied with windows and altars to be a real threat. His assistant, Fykall—the little priest in white and green, is another matter. I have found him invaluable, but I suspect it is only because he shares my understanding of the needs of Southwood, so we haven't had to battle each other— yet. If we do, I'm not certain who will come out on top.''

Sham nodded, and noticed a man standing by one of the doorways, looking like a hen who had wandered into a fox's den. In contrast to the silks and satins of the nobles, he wore dark homespun and the boots of a horseman who was not above mucking stalls.

She nudged Kerim lightly with the hand she rested on his shoulder and the Reeve turned his head. When he saw what she was looking at, he held up a hand to signal the other man to wait while he worked his way to the door.

Kerim didn't stop to converse, but simply pushed himself through the arching entrance and out into the hall beyond. The other man followed Shamera, pulling the door closed behind him.

''Elsic, again?'' asked the Reeve in a resigned voice.

''Aye, my lord,'' replied the stableman.

Elsic, thought Sham, the ''source'' of Talbot's theory about demons. She wondered how much he knew about it.

The hallway, in marked contrast to the other halls in the castle, was straight. There were no other openings until they reached the end of the hall, where a rough-hewn door hung open. A massive bar leaned against the wall where it could be used to hold the door shut in times of need. Stepping through the doorway, Sham squinted against the bright sunlight.

Large stone walled runs held fat-bellied mares and their sleek foals. The narrow path running between the pasture wall and the castle was newly paved with wooden slats. Since the area did not look well traveled, Shamera assumed that the boardwalk had been built to facilitate the Reeve's wheeled chair.

The path followed the walls of the castle as they bent and turned with a pattern known only to a collection of long-dead builders and ended, after an abrupt turn, in the stableyard.

Sham's attention was immediately drawn to a high-roofed structure filled with heaping mounds of hay where a small, milling crowd gathered. There was a man on the roof, which puzzled her slightly as he didn't seem to be doing anything useful.

"I fetched him, Stablemaster!" bellowed the man who had brought them from the public hall.

A wiry old man broke away from the crowd of stablemen, most of whom had turned their attention to the approaching Reeve and away from the cause of the tumult.

As Kerim led Sham nearer to the hay barn, she realized the person on the roof was not a man at all, but a young boy apparently ten or eleven summers old. His skin and hair were so fair that they appeared white. He sat, seemingly oblivious to the noises from below. His feet dangled over the edge of the roof and he held his chin on his hands—the epitome of dejection.

"Thank you for coming, Lord," said the Stablemaster in Cybellian. His voice was so thick with an odd Eastern accent, Sham had difficulty understanding him.

"What caused this?" asked Kerim with a frown.

The man frowned in return. "Me, sir. I caught the lad in with your stallion again."

"After I talked to him last time?" asked the Reeve.

The Stablemaster nodded. "The stallion's been in a foul temper lately; he kicked his groom yesterday. Scorch has never been an easy horse, and he hasn't been getting as much work as he's used to. None of us would see the lad hurt, and I suppose I was harder on him than I should have been."

Kerim nodded and began moving again. The stableyard wasn't smooth, and the tires of the chair caught in the rough dirt. Sham moved behind it and added her weight to the struggle. Kerim waited until he was directly below the boy before speaking.

"Unless you can grow wings, Elsic, your seat is a bit too high for my comfort," commented the Reeve in a casual tone.

The boy started, "Sir?"

"Come down, lad." Kerim's voice was soft, but held enough steel that the boy reached down and grabbed a large beam under the roof and somersaulted off the edge.

Someone near Sham swore. She watched with a connoisseur's appreciation the lithe, comfortable way the boy descended. She'd had enough experience at similar activities to know that he was making it look a lot easier than it was. He swung easily from one horizontal beam to another until he reached a vertical support that he shinnied down.

As he dropped lightly to his feet, Sham noticed for the first time that boy wasn't the albino he first appeared—his eyes were so dark they appeared almost black. She also revised his age upward. Like the street children that she was familiar with, he was merely small for his years. His odd coloration caused her to frown thoughtfully.

"Come here," said the Reeve.

Sham slanted him a glance: The boy had come down readily enough, he didn't need another reminder. It wasn't until Elsic reached out to touch the Reeve's chair before crouching down on his heels that Sham realized that

Kerim's words had been directions rather than commands.
Like the Old Man, the boy was blind.

"I hear that you have been getting into trouble again,"
said Kerim in a reasonable tone.

Elsic's face looked even sadder then before. "He won't
hurt me. He's lonely and he likes me."

The Reeve sat quietly a moment, rubbing his jaw. Finally
he said, "Under most circumstances I would agree with
you, but since I've been stuck in this chair he's not been
worked as he ought to be. The Stablemaster does what he
can, but Scorch is a war horse. He kicked his groom yesterday."

Elsic frowned, hesitated, and then said, "His groom
chews beggarsblessing when the Stablemaster isn't looking.
Horses don't like it when people act odd."

"The groom is lucky Scorch didn't take off his head if
he was on 'blessing," agreed Kerim. "Did you hear that,
Stablemaster?"

The old man grunted. "I caught him at it once. If he's
still doing it, he can do it at someone else's stables."

That coloring . . . Sham reached out and touched the boy
lightly on the shoulder. Her hands almost hurt with the
force of his magic.

He straightened and cocked his head. "Who are you?"

Sham glanced around at the crowded stableyard. "I am
a friend of the Reeve," she answered finally, and then in
a soft tone that went no further than Elsic and the Reeve
she said, "I am a wizard."

Elsic smiled gravely.

"My lord," she said, "I think he's safe enough with
your warhorse. I doubt that it will hurt him."

The Reeve looked at her carefully, frowning, and then
turned his gaze to the boy. Slowly he nodded his head. "Be
careful, then, boy."

Elsic grinned widely. "Yes, lord." He swallowed and
then said in a soft voice, "Sometimes it's good to be with
something so arrogant and sure of himself. It makes me
feel safe."

The Reeve sat forward, "Has anyone been bothering you?"

"No one, Lord," said Elsic quickly. "It's just . . . there's something wrong here, something very old and evil." The boy's face lost all expression as he spoke, and he turned to Sham and met her eyes with uncanny accuracy.

His voice quieted so that Sham was fairly certain that no one but she and the Reeve could hear him. "It knows who you are, mage, and the threat that you represent to its intentions. It wants the Reeve more than it has desired anything in a thousand years. Be very careful."

"I will," she agreed, as a chill crept up her spine. She wondered, having heard him speak, how the Reeve could dismiss any warning Elsic chose to give him—but then Easterners were like that.

The boy nodded his head and turned away, disappearing without another word into the enclosed stables. The Reeve looked at Sham for a moment, then he turned his chair around, and she hurriedly moved behind it to help push. Neither spoke until they were alone on the narrow walk.

"I found him, a little more than a year ago, washed up on the sands exposed by the Spirit Tide." Kerim paused. "He was sitting quietly, humming a little, wearing nothing but a finely woven kilt."

He fell silent momentarily, stopping his chair and gazing at a mare and her spotted filly. "I suspect that someone left him there to die because he is blind. The people here have an unnatural fear of blindness—they see it as a sign of evil magic." Kerim smiled without humor. "He didn't speak for a long time. I don't think his native language is Cybellian or Southern, but he learned both very quickly. Elsic tells me that he cannot remember anything before he woke up here."

"I kept him with me in the Castle at first, but I was distracted by the business of running Southwood. I didn't notice some of the nobles were tormenting the boy until Dickon pointed it out to me." Kerim sighed, and shook his head. "Elsic has a way with animals, and the Stablemaster is a kind man who holds absolute control over his lads, so

I gave Elsic into his keeping. I hope that he's become enough of a fixture around the stables that when . . .'' The Reeve's hands tightened involuntarily on the arms of his chair, but he continued calmly enough, ''—when I'm no longer here, no one will hurt him for being the way he is.''

''I'll keep an eye on him,'' promised Sham softly. ''If there is a problem, there are places that he can be made safe. Wizards are used to strange creatures and would do him no harm.''

''How do you know he'll be safe with Scorch?'' Kerim asked.

Sham shrugged. ''Selkies have a way with animals.''

He gave her a narrow glance.

Sham smiled and continued amiably. ''Selkies are one of the seafolk. They generally appear in the shape of white seals with dark eyes—a better form for swimming than a man's body, I imagine. No seaman who wants to live long would dream of spearing a white seal—ask Talbot. They are said to be a race of warriors, as harsh to their own kind as they are to others. When one is too old or wounded, they attack him, driving him away or killing him upon a whim. I would not think they would allow a blind child to live past his first hours unless his mother was very clever.''

He seemed to be taking this calmly enough, so she continued. ''His people don't use human magics. They have access to knowledge I do not. I would take any warning he chooses to give you very seriously.''

Kerim's lips quirked into a smile and he shook his head, ''I don't think that I should ask this question; if Dickon were here, he'd disown me. What did Elsic mean when he said the demon wanted me?''

''Assuming magic is real?'' asked Sham with raised brows.

Kerim sighed theatrically, and nodded.

Sham shook her head. ''I don't know. Was anything specifically happening to you when the killing started?''

''Hmm . . . that would be about eight months ago. It was about that time that I moved Elsic to the stables. A good friend of mine died of the wasting sickness.'' He

closed his eyes briefly and leaned back, "My mother dismissed the cook. My favorite mare foaled. My back started
hurting."

"That was when your back trouble started?"

Kerim nodded. "I wrenched it on the way back from
Fahill's funeral."

"Lady Sky's husband?"

The Reeve nodded shortly, and then began to push himself forward again. "Come. If we hurry we'll have time to
eat before Brath and his entourage invade my chambers."

INDEED, DICKON HAD JUST FINISHED TAKING THE DINNER
trays out when someone knocked on the Reeve's door.

"I'll get it," said Sham.

The high priest waited in the hall with the aesthetic-
looking Fykall a step behind him. Brath nodded at her as
he entered. "You may leave us, Lady Shamera."

She glanced at Kerim who made a negative motion with
his hand. Shutting the door after Fykall was inside, Shamera said pleasantly, "I *am* sorry, Lord Brath, but my lord
has a headache and I promised to do something about it as
soon as you're gone." She bushed by both churchmen and
sat down gracefully in the chair nearest Kerim, leaving the
visitors to occupy the chairs opposite him.

"You said you have a letter for me?" asked Kerim.

Lord Brath gestured to Fykall who pulled a sealed courier's envelope out of his purse and handed it to Kerim. "As
you see, I have not broken the seals."

Kerim looked up and raised an eyebrow. "I doubt that
you could have done so, Lord Brath. The Voice has methods to prevent his letters from straying." With a finger, he
touched the seal and it opened readily without use of a letter
opener.

Sham leaned sideways, shamelessly reading over the
Reeve's shoulder. There were two sheets of paper in the
courier's pouch. The first was a plain sheet of paper with
a quick scrawl that said merely:

*Sorry I inflicted him on you, but the old fool's a fa-
vorite with Altis. I didn't know anyone else who could
deal with him better than you. Hope this helps.*

Terran

The second paper was embossed and official. The
scribe's art had been practiced so heavily that Sham had to
stand up and walk directly behind Kerim in order to read
it. It was folded so she couldn't see the top third, but the
meat of the letter was decipherable.

*Be it known that the first desire of Altis is that all of
his subjects live in peace. To those ends, the Reeve of
Southwood is to make such judgments as seem him
mete. All who live in Southwood shall abide by his
decisions.*
Signed this day by
Terran, the Voice and the Eyes of Altis

As Sham was connecting Terran of the first letter to the
Voice of Altis, Kerim began to read the official letter out
loud. When he was finished, he looked up at the high priest.

His voice softened from the official tones in which he'd
read the letter. "I will, of course, keep the original. If you
would have a copy, Fykall is welcome to stay and render
it for you."

The high priest stood stiffly, looking much older than he
had coming into the chambers. "That won't be necessary,
Lord Kerim. Come Fykall, there are things to be done at
the temple."

The little priest nodded, but before following his retreat-
ing superior he reached out and patted Kerim's shoulder
twice in gentle sympathy.

Sham waited until the door closed and said, "Trust a
churchman to take all the joy out of putting him in his
place."

Kerim eyed her unfavorably. "Don't make light of any man's pain."

She tossed her head. "That was not pain you saw, but thwarted ambition. I have no sympathy to spare for Lord Brath—he has no mercy for those in his power."

Kerim watched her face; he'd known too many people consumed by hatred to watch while it consumed another victim. "Perhaps you are right; he doesn't deserve our sympathy. But, Shamera, if we do not feel it—how are we better than he is?"

She snorted and strode to a small table that held a pitcher of water and several cups.

As she filled a cup with water she said, in an apparent change of subject, "You know, I have always wondered why there was never an official injunction against magic since Altis dislikes it so."

"And you accuse me of gross ignorance," he mused.

She turned toward him, cup in hand, and said, "Excuse me?"

"Even *if* magic were real, there would be no injunction against it. As far as I know Altis has never handed down a directive one way or the other."

She frowned. "After the Castle fell, Lord Brath declared magic an anathema to Altis and incited the soldiers to kill anyone who might be a mage."

"Fear makes idiots of us all, at some time or the other. Brath was officially reprimanded for his part in the deaths after Landsend was taken."

She set the cup down without drinking from it and wandered aimlessly around the room. "I don't like him."

"Brath? Neither do I. He's an arrogant, self-righteous, self-interested worm," he agreed lightly.

She tilted her chin up. "If he were drowning I wouldn't throw him a rope."

"The question is—" said Kerim slowly, "—would he throw you one?"

SIX

Sham entered her room with a tired sigh. Without calling for the maid, as she knew was customary, she rapidly stripped off the blue dress and left it where it dropped. Tonight she was too tired to play Lady Shamera for the maid's benefit. A nightdress had been left on the bed, and she slipped it on.

Something nagged for her attention and she frowned, staring at the mantel over the fireplace. She had a very good eye for detail and a memory that seldom failed her: The ornaments on the mantle had been moved. Someone had been in her room while she was gone.

Alert now, she noticed that the keys were in the lock of the trunk, as if someone had tried to open it. Sham stretched and deliberately relaxed her muscles. This was not Purgatory, she reminded herself—she was the only thief here.

The servants had been in to dust the mantel and moved a few of the figurines and the ornamental dagger. Jenli had probably tried to open the trunk to put the rest of the clothes in the wardrobe—not that she would have had any luck.

Sham knew without looking that the fastening spell had not been broken.

Still, she opened the lid and dug through the remaining clothes to make sure nothing had been disturbed. The flute lay awaiting her touch, its call so strong she had to force herself to cover it again with her tunic.

Her knife and dagger were there, slim-bladed and honed to deadly sharpness. Her thieving tools were there too, neatly tucked inside a small kit. She felt naked without them, but they were hardly necessary in the rarefied atmosphere of court. Tomorrow she would begin searching the courtier's houses, then she could wear them.

Sham closed the trunk and locked it again, first with the key and then with magic. She picked up a long-handled brass snuffer that was leaning against the wall, and started to put the candles out one by one.

She could have used magic, of course, but she always used it sparingly. A wizard who used her magic for little things was likely to have nothing left in time of need. With a demon on the loose in the Castle she was likely to need it—and she was convinced it was in the Castle. One of the talents said to be strongest in the seal-people was sensitivity to danger. If Kerim's selkie said it was here, it was so.

As Sham stood on her toes to reach the small candelabra that hung from the center of the room, a strange shiver ran down her spine. It was similar to the sensation the shifted ornaments on the mantel had given her, but this had no such mundane cause. Casually she circled the fixture, scanning the shadows that cloaked the corners of the room. She saw nothing, but she was certain something was here with her.

Slowly, Sham continued darkening the room. Moving to the fireplace, she extinguished the three large candles placed on the far end of the mantel. As she moved, she forced herself to keep her hands steady.

Warding spells were effective against magical beings like demons and dragons only if the warding was around the spellcaster's home and cast by someone who understood the exact nature of the creature. Even if she had been better-versed in demonology, she was caught fairly on the demon's hunting grounds—and she was beginning to feel like dinner.

After she'd extinguished the last candle, Sham casually set the snuffer against the fireplace and stared at the polished floor as if in deep thought—the sea could freeze before she'd crawl into that bed with its hampering blankets while there was a plaguing demon in the room. It wasn't the best time to remember that the demon was overdue for a kill.

Sham caught a bare glimpse of something as a light touch stroked her shoulder. She didn't realize it had been an attack until she felt the warmth of her blood sliding down her arm. Whatever it used to cut her with was so sharp that she did not hurt initially—an oversight soon corrected.

Deciding that staying in character might have its advantages, she screamed for help. She hoped the walls were thinner than they looked, so Kerim might hear her. The demon had been avoiding a public display, for reasons of its own; Sham hoped that it would continue the pattern. She didn't have the knowledge she needed to destroy the demon yet, though she had the Whisper looking for any wizard that might. Without intervention, there was a better than even chance that she wouldn't survive the night.

Hand to her shoulder, she spun around, looking frantically for her attacker while carefully maintaining the mannerisms she'd adopted in her role as the Reeve's mistress. The room was quiet and appeared as empty as it had before the attack. All she could hear was the harshness of her own breathing.

Just as in the Old Man's cottage, the intruder wasn't using conventional methods of invisibility. No matter how powerful a sight aversion spell was, a wizard who was aware of the spellcaster could overcome it—as he could any other illusion. Sham couldn't see anything out of place. Warm fluid dripped off her fingers, but she didn't look down at the growing stain on the floor.

•   •   •

IT HAD FED ITS HUNGER ONLY LAST NIGHT; SO IT HAD ONLY come to watch the newcomer—although it had placed the dagger on the mantel for possible use. Weapons were difficult to carry in its own insubstantial form.

The Chen Laut breathed deeply. The scent of the woman's terror-inspired sweat was titillating—much too arousing to resist. She was so vulnerable, pitiful really. A millennia of evading human detection told it that it was taking unnecessary risks. Even a decade ago, it would have resisted hurting the human for fear of betraying itself.

But the Castle was held by fools who didn't believe in magic or demons: And this woman played where she didn't belong. It considered the crippled human that it could hear struggling to the wheeled chair on the other side of the door, and dismissed him with the last of its caution.

Upon entering the room, the demon had changed into its secondary form, calling upon magic to hide its body from the woman. As a noncorporeal entity, the demon needed a physical form to affect things in this world. The Summoner had provided two. The first form must be protected; without it the demon would be powerless, cut adrift here forever. But the second form, though infinitely more useful, was not necessary to survival.

SLOWLY SHAM BACKED AGAINST THE STONEWORK AND stretched a hand behind her, fumbling amid the implements that hung on hooks near the hearth. Her magic was unlikely to hurt it until she understood better what she was fighting—so she decided to try something else. The most obvious tool for a frightened woman to grasp was the poker. She had no intention of getting close enough to the demon to use such an ineffective weapon. Deliberately Sham knocked the poker loudly to the ground and snatched the small shovel instead, as if she had missed her target. She held the iron handle with an awkwardness that was not completely feigned; her shoulder *hurt*.

There was a soft sound to her right as if something hard scraped across an expanse of floor that the rugs didn't cover. She was certain that the demon was as capable of masking sounds as Sham herself was: It was goading her.

The next sound was louder, and to her right again. She turned toward the fire and dipped the shovel in the hot coals. Continuing her turn, she cast the fiery lumps in the general direction of the second sound.

When she faced it, Sham saw the vague form of her attacker. Though magic concealed its face, it appeared to be a man. She must have hit it with some of the coals, because it shrieked in an inhumanly high tone. As the sound died down, she could hear someone rattle the catch on the door to Kerim's room.

As Sham turned to the door, the intruder grabbed her by the shoulders and threw her towards the far wall. She landed on the polished nightstand, an improvement to the well-being of neither her nor the small, formerly sturdy piece of furniture. Used to street fighting, though no one had actually thrown her across a room before, she managed to roll to her feet, shaking off bits and pieces of wood as she did so.

The demon had summoned the shadows around itself, using the same spell that Sham favored in the dark streets of Purgatory. In the dark room, the unnatural shadows covered the whole area until the only thing Sham could see were the coals that had landed on the bedclothes and started to ignite the cloth.

As she peered into the darkness, the demon surprised a cry out of her when it cut her bared calf. She looked down before it had completed its stroke, and she caught a glimpse of something metallic in the darkness: the pox-eaten thing was using a knife!

For some reason that turned her fear into fury. She was being attacked by a demon, a legendary creature of song and story—and it was using a knife like a common thief.

She crouched with a snarl, but the entire room was encased in the peculiar shroud of shadow and the demon's presence was too strong to pinpoint. Smoke from the small fires amid the bedding and the rugs began to fill the room, making her eyes water, and she acquired another wound, this one on her thigh. Sham growled with frustrated anger.

A deafening crack echoed in the room, followed by an assortment of sounds, including the opening and closing of the outer door as the intruder escaped into the anonymity of the hall.

THE DEMON RAN CAUTIOUSLY THROUGH THE HALLS UNTIL it was far from possible pursuit. The Reeve would be more interested in protecting his woman than finding her attacker. In the shadows of an unused room, it examined the body it wore. The damage the coals had inflicted was minor, though it would require a fair amount of power to return the golem to wholeness. The mild irritation it felt toward the Reeve's mistress flamed to momentary rage. It calmed itself by deciding the woman would be its next meal, seven days hence. Until then, she could do little harm.

AS THE UNNATURAL SHADOWS DISSOLVED, SHAMERA could see that the door by the fireplace had been split down the center. The half with the latch lay on the floor, tangled in the tapestries that had covered the doorway; the other half hung awkwardly from the lower hinge. The upper hinge clung tenaciously to the door, pale splinters of wood attesting to the force that had ripped it from the door frame.

She turned her gaze from the door to the Reeve, who was dressed in night robes with a wicked-looking war axe in one hand; his chair was placed sideways to the door frame to allow him to strike effectively. She gave him a grin of sheer relief.

"I'm glad you could make it," she quipped, her voice not quite as steady as she wished.

"When you issue an invitation to your bedroom, it's common practice to make sure the door is unlocked," he returned without a pause. He looked beyond her and said, "It's also common to wait until your partner's here before you start getting the sheets hot."

She turned and noticed that the smoldering blankets had begun to flame. Fires were the second magic that an apprentice learned, since fire is the easiest element to call into being. The *first* magic was how to extinguish them. She jerked the covers to the floor beside her. Given Kerim's disbelief in magic, she assumed that he would think that she smothered the fire with the weight of the blankets.

To her continued astonishment, Sham liked the Reeve, Cybellian that he was—but she didn't know if she could trust him. Twelve years ago she'd learned that fear was a brutal enemy, and she decided not to give him proof of magic's existence for a little while longer.

"Sorry," she quipped lightly, "I'm not familiar with the etiquette required of a mistress. Next time I'll make sure that you're in the bed before I throw hot coals at it."

Kerim grunted in approval and swung the axe in a short arc that connected with the remaining hinge. The second half of the door dropped to the ground. By the simple expedient of grabbing both sides of the doorway and heaving, he pushed the awkward chair through the cleared opening and into her room.

"What happened?" he asked.

"You remember the demon that Talbot and I keep talking about?"

"The hypothetical one that's the reason you're here?" he said, rolling his chair slowly up to her.

She nodded. "That's the one. It decided to check me out. It didn't seem to care for more company, and so it left as soon as it became obvious that you were coming in."

When he was close enough to see the blood in the shadows of the room, he said, "How badly are you hurt?"

"Not much, unless the cut on my shoulder is worse than it looks."

He reached up and pulled her hair aside so that he could get a good look at her shoulder. "I've seen worse, but it's deep enough to warrant stitching. Dickon's pretty good at it."

"Dickon?"

He laughed at the disbelief in her tone. "He was a soldier before he was a valet, and he sews torn skin better than most of the healers." He looked again at her shoulder and his brows lowered in thought. "It looks like a knife wound."

Sham nodded her head. "A plaguing sharp knife at that."

Kerim laughed. "From your disgruntlement I assume that you were hoping for claws and fangs?"

She smiled, closing her eyes to relieve the dizziness brought on by loss of blood. "Guess I was at that."

"Come with me and tell me what happened." He wheeled back to the doorway and pulled his chair back over the door sill.

"Have you talked to your stablemaster about modifying that thing yet?" asked Shamera, following him into his room.

"He and one of the carpenters are working on a new chair," answered the Reeve. He gestured toward a seat. "Sit before you fall down. I'll go get Dickon and you can tell me what happened after he has taken care of you."

She complied gratefully and lowered her head to her knees. Dickon must have been sleeping nearby, because the Reeve returned with him shortly. She didn't know how Kerim had explained the wounds, but Dickon was as contained as ever as he cleaned and mended the cut on her shoulder with small, even stitches. Determining the slice on her thigh was superficial, the servant bent down to get a closer look at the gash on her calf.

"My Lord says the magician last night was skilled in alchemy," said Dickon as he pulled the skin of her calf closed.

"There's a white rock, mined north of the glass desert. If it is mixed with water, an open flame held near it will ignite the surface of the water," said Sham, trying to ignore the tug of the needle. "I didn't get a clear view of the urns, but it seemed to be the kind of fire the white rock produces. I don't know what the purple smoke was."

Dickon paused briefly in his sewing to look at her in surprise, then a slight smile crossed his lips at her peace offering. "I've heard of the pigeons in the pot, but I've never seen one large enough to house an osprey."

"There must have been some magic at work," offered Sham, tongue in cheek.

Dickon snorted in disbelief, tying off the thread tidily. He produced bandages from the kit he'd brought in and began wrapping her calf.

"I've yet to see any magic that cannot be duplicated with a little work," said the valet as he wiped his hands fastidiously clean.

Sham nodded congenially. "I'm sure that's true."

Dickon shot her a suspicious look, and she smiled.

"Will that be all, my lord?" he asked Kerim.

"Please see that the covering for Lady Shamera's bed is discreetly replaced and the burned covering destroyed."

"Very good, sir."

"Dickon?" said Shamera. "Thank you."

"Very good, my lady." Dickon bowed himself out of the room and shut the door.

"How did you explain the fact that your mistress needed stitches in the middle of the night?" asked Shamera, pushing her hair out of her eyes with a hand that shook slightly.

"I didn't. Are you steady enough to tell me what happened?"

She shrugged and immediately regretted it as the stitches in her shoulder pulled. "It's more painful than damaging, I'm fine. I was snuffing the candles when something attacked me from behind."

"You're still sure that it was a demon? One that used a knife?" He sounded as if he were willing her to answer rationally.

Shamera sighed with more exasperation than she really felt. It would have been unfair to expect him to accept her view without allowing him evidence that true magic existed.

"I *told* you," she said, "I don't know enough. It looked like a man, but I didn't get a glimpse of his face."

"Why are you discounting the possibility that the killer is human?" He sounded honestly curious.

She felt guilty for deliberately misleading him with the truth, but she had never let a little guilt alter her course. "Because it picked me up and threw me across the room. I've been in a lot of fights, some of them with men bigger than you are. This thing was *much* stronger, and faster. I couldn't see it.''

''It was dark,'' he said patiently.

''So it was,'' she agreed with equal patience.

''You said that it looked like a man—'' he paused significantly, ''—in the dark.''

''It did.''

''But it was a demon.''

''Yes.'' Sham closed her eyes and yawned.

She could hear the squeak of the chair's wheels as the Reeve moved around, but she was suddenly too weary to see what he was doing. He had a substantial presence that relegated demons to the realm of stories, despite the throbbing in her shoulder. She smiled to herself and started to drift off to sleep when a flash of memory caused her to sit up and open her eyes.

''The knife was in the room when I entered this evening.''

Kerim had been balancing the broken pieces of door against the wall. At her speech, he paused and looked up. ''What knife?''

''The one the demon used. It was lying on the mantel next to the silver and porcelain dog. I noticed the ornaments on the mantel were altered from this morning, but I didn't realize the dagger was new.''

Kerim pushed his way back into her room. He came back shaking his head. ''There's no knife there now. What did it look like?''

Shamera closed her eyes, trying to visualize it clearly. ''It was ornate, like the swords on display in the hall—not inconsistent with its use as an ornament. The hilt was wooden. There was a dark stone set in one end. Ruby . . . no, sapphire. A dark blue sapphire as big around as my thumb.''

''With etching on the blade?''

''You know the knife?'' she asked, startled. ''Who does it belong to?''

''My half-brother,'' he answered with a tired sigh. ''I don't think that your attacker was a demon.''

Sham felt her eyebrow rise at his acceptance of his brother's guilt. "It wasn't Lord Ven," she snapped before she thought.

Kerim turned to her. "Oh?"

"Look—" she said finally, rubbing her hands briskly on her cheeks in an effort to wake up, "—whatever it was that came into my room did it without opening the door. The hinges on the door creak and I would have heard it if someone opened them."

"There is a 'secret' passage into that room, similar to the passage in this one."

Sham shook her head, "I was next to the fireplace when it came in. All of the doors were closed."

"You think that something used *magic* to enter your room."

She hadn't realized just how easy it was to make such a small word sound like something obscene. "Yes, I do. There is no way that the thing that attacked me was your brother."

The Reeve closed his eyes briefly. "It's too late at night for this."

Shamera yawned and started to stretch before she remembered the skimpy silk shift that she was wearing and cursed her pale skin as it heated, though she hadn't seen any sign that Kerim had noticed her state of undress. "I'm going to sleep. Do you need any help getting back to bed?"

"I can manage," he replied. "I think that we ought to keep tonight's attack quiet. I don't want to spread panic any faster than it is already propagating."

Shamera nodded and started back to her room, giving the disabled door a wry glance as she passed it. As much as she hated to admit it, she was glad to give up her privacy in return for the security of Kerim's presence. Crippled or not, the man was a warrior.

"Good night, Shamera," said the Reeve behind her.

"What's left of it," she replied, trudging on to her bed.

SHAMERA WOKE THE NEXT MORNING TO THE SOUND OF A gentle tapping on the door.

"A moment," she called as she threw the covers back and sat up.

If she'd been in any doubt of the events of the night, the soreness of her various wounds would have eliminated it. A moment of thought had her cloaking her wounds with illusion. Dickon's niece might very well be trustworthy, but if Kerim wanted to keep the attack quiet, the fewer people who knew about her bruises the better. She glanced in the little mirror to make certain that she'd gotten all of the blood washed off last night. Only when she was satisfied that she looked no worse than usual did she bid the maid to enter.

When Jenli came in, she was not alone. Three husky footmen carried a trunk and two baskets into the room, keeping their eyes carefully averted as they set their burdens near the door and left. The last one was blushing furiously.

It wasn't her state of undress that had done that, for the boys had not so much as glanced at the bed. Sham frowned thoughtfully and glanced at the fireplace implements scattered around the rugs that, like the floor, were covered with bits of porcelain and splinters of wood. A tapestry had been rehung over the opening to the Reeve's chambers. While it provided privacy, it didn't hide the fact that there was no door there anymore.

This little investigation was really going to have an interesting effect on the Reeve's reputation, thought Sham with amusement.

"Delivery from your dressmaker, lady," said Jenli, indicating the luggage. A smile fought to make itself seen, as the maid took in the damage done to the room with wide eyes.

"Good," said Sham assessing the new arrivals thoughtfully. "I told Kerim I didn't have a wardrobe suitable for court and he generously provided the means to acquire one." She didn't want Jenli questioning why her wardrobe consisted only of new items.

She chose a dark green velvet dress heavily encrusted with glass gems and pearls. It was an old dress from several decades past that she had glimpsed hanging in the dress-maker's storage area waiting to be stripped of the reusable finery.

The velvet had been worn threadbare where the sleeves and side of the dress had rubbed together; she'd directed the fabric removed and the edges finished in gold braid. The dress left her sides bare from underarm to halfway down her hip, relying only on the weight of the fabric to keep from revealing more than was acceptable. The skirt was artfully sliced in a similar manner.

She ducked cautiously under the tapestry and into Kerim's chamber, more worried about how much the dress revealed as she bent down than she was about who would be there. She made it through without displaying anything untoward and smiled at Dickon who waited alone in the room with a covered warming plate containing her breakfast.

"Good morning, Lady Shamera," said the servant, with no sign that he had sewn her shoulder for her the night before. "The Reeve instructed me to tell you he will be meeting with various claimants on his time today, and regrets he will be unable to entertain you. He thought you might be interested in visiting with the courtiers, and he will join you for your evening meal."

"Good morning, Dickon. Thank you."

After Dickon left, Sham ate then ventured into the wandering halls alone. Her sense of direction served her in good stead, and she had no difficulty finding the public room on her own. These Eastern nobles were an idle lot if all they did from dawn to dusk was practice at court intrigue. With a mental shrug, Sham fixed a bright smile on her face and ventured into the room.

Lord Ven, Kerim's brother was the first to approach her, bowing low and kissing her fingers. "Ah Lady, you put the stars to shame."

Shamera fixed a puzzled expression on her face and shook her head. "I didn't mean to. I like stars."

He paused briefly before straightening. "I meant only than your beauty is brighter than the stars."

"Oh," she said, then smiled in comprehension. "You like my dress. Isn't it beautiful? And it only cost ten gold pieces. Kerim didn't mind. He likes my dresses."

Lord Ven was looking slightly distressed. Sham supposed it was the public mention of the cost of her dress.

"Did you eat something that disagrees with you?" asked Sham, thoroughly enjoying herself. "I find that wintergreen oil makes me feel better if I eat something that makes me sick."

Lord Ven was saved from further babble by the advent of a young man whose blond coloring proclaimed him a Southwood native. He was, Sham estimated, a good decade younger than she.

"Ah, fair lady, do me the honor of walking with me. My Lord Halvok asked me to entertain you, since he has been forced to rob you of the Reeve's company this day."

Sham treated him to a bright smile. "Of course. Did I meet you yesterday?"

The young man shook his head. "No. I am Siven, Lord Halvok's fosterling, Lord Chanford's youngest son."

Sham let the boy led her away, noticing that Lord Ven left the room unobtrusively behind her. She set her arm through Siven's, chatting with him about inconsequential things.

He left her speaking with Lady Sky on the nature of fashion, but when the pregnant lady excused herself to retire to her rooms, a second fosterling attached himself to Sham. Lord Halvok and his cronies had apparently decided to keep her out of trouble when she wasn't under the eye of the Reeve. Only good could come of having a Southwood lady as the Reeve's mistress.

THERE WAS A NOTE WAITING FOR SHAM IN HER ROOMS when she returned to them before supper. It was sealed with wax to prevent any of the servants who happened to be able to read from peeking. She smiled with satisfaction as she read the information the Whisper gave her on the nobles of the Court. Tonight she would visit three or four dwellings and see what she could discover.

SEVEN

Sham smothered a yawn, and glanced around at the group of men who surrounded her. Several of Lord Halvok's fledglings mingled with the older crowd. Kerim was right—the evening gatherings were more crowded than the daily press.

He had intended to come with her to her first night event, but had felt too ill. Without his formidable presence the men gathered around her like locusts on a wheat field, which she found both annoying and amusing. True to the character she portrayed, Sham flirted with them gently, but made it clear she was faithful to the Reeve.

She was beginning to think that attending court was less than useless. The Whisper had more detailed knowledge of the less public lives of the courtiers than the court gossip did. So far though, she had found out nothing about the demon.

This night the entertainment was a minstrel of indifferent skill—at music. From the heated glances he exchanged with several of the ladies of the court, Sham assumed that his skills in other areas were more than adequate.

She yawned again and scratched her thigh discreetly. The wounds the demon had given her were at that stage in healing where they itched like wet wool. She gave serious consideration to retiring to her rooms early.

She opened her mouth to make her excuses to her current escort, when she saw Lady Sky sitting alone, with a pair of Eastern women tittering nearby. One of the things that Sham had discovered during her tours of court was that although the Southwood lords were tolerated by the Eastern lords, the Eastern women had no such tolerance for the Southwood ladies—who numbered two: Shamera and Sky.

They stayed away from Shamera, who was protected by Kerim's presence or Halvok's fledglings, but Sky was fair game as long as Lady Tirra wasn't in the room. That the Eastern men didn't share their ladies' abhorrence for Lady Sky made things worse.

Shaking her head silently at herself, Sham began making her way through the throng to Lady Sky. The Shark swore her weakness for defenseless waifs was going to be the death of her.

Sky looked up, startled, as Shamera sat next to her—or perhaps it was her purple and yellow dress; it was certainly startling enough. Halvok's appointed guardian took one of Sky's hands and kissed it lightly before moving smoothly into the background, ensuring that the pair of Eastern ladies would have to find other prey.

"So tell me," Shamera said, settling her skirts around her, "how a Southwoods lady managed to snare an Eastern warrior."

Sky looked at her cautiously, but she must have taken heart from Sham's artless stare. "I met him at Fahill's pilgrimage gate."

Sham widened her eyes, "How romantic! Ervan bought me from my father. I assure you it wasn't romantic at all. I made him work hard to make it up to me—that's how he died." Ervan, an elderly, bitter man had died in his bed by all reports. Kerim had assured her that he was the only one at court who'd ever met him.

Sky couldn't help a sputter of laughter. "I'm not certain

my situation was any more romantic." She rested her hands gently on her swollen belly. When she looked back at Sham her eyes were haunted. "My father had held onto our manor by swearing fealty to an Easterner, but when the plague claimed him our overlord claimed the manor for his second son. My brother gathered us together and left for the court here at Landsend, where he'd heard the Reeve was receiving homeless nobles. Bandits overtook us just outside of Fahill. I was washing in the stream when I heard them. I was not armed, so I had to wait until they left before leaving my hiding place. The raiders killed everyone but me."

Shamera leaned forward and took Sky's hand. "I am sorry."

Sky shook her head, forcing the old pain away. "No. It was a long time ago, and some good came of it. I continued toward Landsend, for lack of any better choice and came upon Fahill close to nightfall. Fahill himself answered my knock." She smiled then, lost in the moment. "Fahill was bigger than life. He was as red-headed as any trader child and larger than Kerim. When I had him, it seemed that nothing could go wrong."

Sham remembered the security the Reeve had given her the night she'd been attacked by the demon and nodded. "At least you have his child."

Encouraged by Sham's sympathy, Sky continued. "I lost our first child two months before Fahill died. This one is an unexpected miracle."

She looked up and quit talking as Lady Tirra came upon them.

"Lady Sky," exclaimed Tirra, ignoring Shamera. "I've been looking for you; stand up, child."

Kerim's mother pulled Sky to her feet and into an open space on the floor. Clapping her hands loudly she caught the attention of the minstrel who stopped playing. She raised a graceful hand and gradually the attention of everyone present was drawn to her small figure.

"Lords and Ladies, I beg your indulgence for a moment." Her voice, low and rich as it was, carried clearly

to the farthest corners of the room. At her side, Sky looked
like a rabbit caught in a hunter's snare. "You have all been
aware of the problems we've had settling Fahill's estate.
The dilemma has been a conflict between Southwood law
and Cybellian custom. By Southwood law the lands should
go to Lady Sky; by custom they should go to Lord Johar
of Fahill. Most of his objection was that the lands, which
were in Eastern hands, would be given to a Southwood's
lady. We responded by proposing a marriage between my
son, Lord Ven, and Lady Sky. He has most graciously accepted."

Sham wondered if Lady Tirra was deliberately antago-
nizing the Southwood lords or if she was blind to the damage she was doing to the Reeve's attempts to bind Easterner
and Southwoodsmen together.

"The estates of Lord Fahill," continued Lady Tirra tri-
umphantly, "—long held in contention, have been settled.
The estates of Fahill, Oran, and Tiber will be given into
the hands of the late Lord Fahill's brother and convey such
title to him—from this day forth Lord Johar will be Lord
Fahill. The estates of Kerhill and Tourn, as well as the title
of Lord Kerhill will be settled on my son, Lord Ven, upon
his marriage to Lady Sky. I ask you all for your congrat-
ulations."

Lady Sky was frozen where she stood; all trace of color
had left her face. She obviously had been told none of this.
To have such an announcement made in front of the
court—for the first time Sham was thankful for her life in
Purgatory. At least there were some choices she could make
for herself.

Lady Tirra continued as the room quieted. "I am sorry
that Lord Ven was not here to help receive the well-wishes
of the Court. He had urgent business and left early this
morning: I shall inform him of the good news as soon as
he returns."

Sky stayed for a few minutes before leaving the room,
leaning tiredly on Lady Tirra. As soon as the pair of them
left, the court exploded into wild speculation and venomous

whispers. Shamera drifted from group to group with her escort trailing politely behind.

"Lady Shamera, a word with you," said Lord Ven's smooth tones from behind her.

Sham glanced around. The room was still quite full, and she was able to catch the eyes of several men with whom she'd become sociable. Only after they began to approach her did she turn to Lord Ven. He'd tried to corner her several times, mostly, she thought, to see if he could find a way to spoil Kerim's enjoyment of her. Poor Lady Sky. Sham wondered if he'd been told of his betrothal—surely there was some fun to be had here.

She looked back at the handsome noble and frowned, tapping her chin in a puzzled fashion before she exclaimed, "Kerim's brother!" She paused again, before saying, "Lord . . . Van? I thought you were gone."

There were a few smothered laughs from the group forming around them. Kerim's brother was not well liked among any but the most radical groups of the court. It was not lost on these men that the pushier Lord Ven became, the less impression he seemed to make on her.

His handsome face reddened slightly, but he said easily enough, "Lord Ven, Kerim's legitimate half-brother. I just returned."

Shamera nodded wisely; his sly reminder of Kerim's bastard origins had removed her few remaining scruples about humiliating the Reeve's brother. "Now, I remember. What can I do for you? Does Kerim want me? He said he was going to rest this evening and I should amuse myself, but if he wants me now I'll be happy to leave."

There was another round of smothered amusement.

"No, Lady," answered Lord Ven, managing, with an effort, to keep his voice soft. "I haven't spoken with Kerim since I left this morning. I just wanted to speak with you in private."

"Oh," Sham said, in obvious disappointment. "I suppose that as long as you are certain that Kerim doesn't need me, I can talk to you. What did you want?"

Before he got a chance to speak again there was a tentative touch on her shoulder. Sham turned to see Kerim's valet standing behind her.

"Dickon!" she exclaimed, then she said to the gathering in general, "Dickon is Kerim's servant."

Dickon cleared his throat, but otherwise maintained his usual equanimity as he nodded to the cheerful greetings.

Sham regained his attention by tapping Dickon's arm. "Is Kerim awake yet?"

Dickon, looking uncomfortable with all the attention, said, "Yes, Lady. Lady Tirra—"

"His mother," interrupted Sham, as if she were announcing a new discovery to a group of the uninitiated.

"Yes, Lady," said Dickon patiently. "His mother has discovered a new healer who has a reputation of working miracles. He is with him now."

Sham considered that briefly. It was obvious that Dickon had come to her to save the Reeve from a charlatan. Naturally the servant thought she would care—she was, after all, his mistress. Although she'd dropped her false mannerisms in front of Dickon since the night of the demon attack, he didn't know everything—or perhaps he did. The strength of the anger she felt frightened her.

When Sham spoke, she carefully displayed nothing more than the possessiveness of a mistress whose position was threatened. "His *mother's* healer? How long has this man been with Kerim?"

Dickon shuffled his feet and said, "Since dinner."

Sham smiled blindingly. "Gentlemen, I pray that you will excuse me. Lord Van . . . er, Ven, we shall have to have our talk at another time. Dickon—"

"—Lord Kerim's servant," supplied Halvok's fosterling, Siven, with amusement.

Shamera nodded and continued with dramatic flare, "—has come to get me. Lord Kerim has need of me, and I must go."

With a quick curtsey, she followed Dickon out the door. As soon as they were alone in the maze of hallways, she dropped her facade and broke into a less than decorous trot.

"How bad is he?" she asked grimly.

"Bad enough. I didn't know what was happening until I brought in some of his lordship's clothing from the mending rooms. It seems that one of her ladyship's cronies discovered this *miracle worker* who has the reputation of making the lame walk. Lady Tirra has found several such; most of them are harmless, but this one . . ."

"I'm a miracle worker too," said Sham direly. "Watch me make the healer disappear. Is her Ladyship there?"

"Kerim's mother?" asked Dickon in an innocent tone.

Sham snickered, despite the urgency that kept her pace only nominally under an outright sprint. "Liked that one did you? Yes, the Reeve's mother."

He shook his head. "And be in the same room with a partially clad man? Never."

"How did someone like Lady Tirra conceive an illegitimate son?" questioned Shamera with a touch of wonder.

Dickon shook his head. "Things happen in life that are so strange not even the most daring bard would relate them for fear of being ridiculed."

Sham glanced at the servant's face.

"Dickon!" she exclaimed in surprise, "you *can* smile!"

IN TRUE LADY SHAMERA FASHION, SHE THREW KERIM'S door open so hard it almost hit the wall. She rushed to the wooden table where Kerim lay face down. He was oblivious to her entrance, as his face was buried in his arms—but the dirty little man standing beside him certainly was not.

His mouth dropped open unattractively, revealing several blackened teeth. He began a protest of her entrance, but he widened it into a smile as he took in the sensual being that was the Reeve's mistress.

"Kerim!" she exclaimed, touching of the Reeve's bare shoulders gently. "Dickon said that you couldn't be bothered, but I *knew* that you wouldn't mind if I told you that Lady Sky had the most *interesting* little hat . . ." Kerim turned his face toward her and Sham was enraged at his stoic expression, though she was careful not to show it.

She looked at the "healer" and frowned. "You need to

leave now. I *have* to talk to Kerim, and I don't like strang-
ers listening to my private conversations.''

The man drew himself up in outrage that outweighed his
lust. "Do you know who you are talking to?"

"No," she replied, putting her hands on her hips. "I
don't care, just as long as you leave now."

"Her Ladyship . . ." began the man.

"Dickon," called Sham, knowing that he was waiting
anxiously in the hall to assess the damage done.

The door opened and the bland-faced servant entered,
showing no sign of his recent dash through the Castle.

"Take him away," Sham ordered airily. "You may
come back and dispose of his belongings later."

"Yes, Lady," agreed the servant with remarkable com-
posure as he seized the protesting man in a grip that spoke
of the soldier he had been. "I shall return directly."

When he left, Sham hurried over to shut the door behind
him.

"Dirty, filthy, little leper," she muttered in an evil voice,
though she was intimidated enough by her surroundings not
to use stronger language.

Turning back to the hard wooden table where the Reeve
was still lying, she saw that he had turned his face into his
arms. Careful not to touch him, she inspected his back carefully for damage. "Why did you let him do this?"

Kerim started to shrug then grunted. "It can't do any
harm, and it makes Mother happy."

Sham muttered something suitable about the stupidity of
males, Cybellian males in particular, under her breath. Beneath the beautiful brown skin, his muscles, heavy from
years of battle, were twitching and knotted. Dark mottled
bruises told her that Tirra's healer had used the small
wooden clubs that were set carefully on a nearby table, but
there were no blisters from the iron rod that was being
heated over a large candle.

Taking one of the set of clubs in her hands, she traced
the misfortune rune she'd used to avenge Maur. She wished
she were powerful enough to add an extra year to her curse,
and had to argue with herself before she added the mark

that limited the amount of damage that the spell could cause.

"What are you doing?" asked the Reeve, his voice only slightly hoarser than normal.

Shamera looked up to see that he had turned his head to watch her. She also noticed he was being very careful not to move anything else. She was tempted to alter the limits of the spell again.

"It's just a little spell," she said in her best mistress style. "About that hat—"

He smiled, tiredly, but it was a smile. "About that spell."

"I thought that you had your doubts about magic."

"I do, but I have made it a policy never to dismiss any possibility completely—one of the reasons you are here now. About that spell," he repeated firmly, his smile becoming a little less strained.

"Just something to occupy that little worm . . ." Sham paused as an intriguing possibility occurred to her. "I wonder if the Shark knows about him. I'll have to ask."

Kerim started to laugh, and then stopped abruptly and gritted his teeth.

Dickon entered the room quietly. Judging by the air of satisfaction that he wore as well as a slight redness on the knuckles of his right hand, Shamera assumed that he'd gotten a little of his own version of vengeance.

He cleared his throat quietly so that Kerim would know that he was there before he said, "The healer has chosen to wait in the kitchens until we retrieve his items. If you wish to rest a while on the table before we try to move you, Lord, the man didn't seem to be in a great hurry."

"No," Kerim said, levering himself up with his hands until he was sitting.

Dickon brought a light robe. It wasn't warm enough to wear outside, but in a room with a fire burning merrily and tapestries to keep out the draft, it was more than adequate. The Reeve's face appeared more grey than brown against the dark blue satin of his robe and the lines around his mouth were more pronounced than usual.

Shamera worked hard at being solitary; she'd learned at an early age that people died, and if you let yourself care for them it only hurt worse. She'd become adept at hiding herself behind the roles that she played, whether she was mistress or streetwise thief. There were only two people Sham considered friends, and one of them had been killed by a demon. In less than a week, the Reeve of Southwood had joined that select group, and Sham was very much afraid he had become something more.

"If everything's taken care of here, I think that I'll run around and do a little snooping while people are still gossiping at court," she said, suddenly anxious to leave the room.

The Reeve settled into his chair and nodded, as if conversation were beyond him. Sham worked the lever that opened the "secret" panel and stepped through. She started to close the aperture behind her when she noticed Dickon packing the healer's belongings.

"Dickon," she said. "Be careful how long you hold those wooden clubs—and make doubly sure that the healer gets them back."

Dickon eyed the clubs, flexing his right hand slightly, as if he were envisioning returning the clubs in a less than gentle fashion. "You may be certain I will."

THOUGH THE PASSAGE WAS KEPT DIMLY LIT BY CANDLES during the day, most of them had burned out. Sham called a magelight to follow her as she was highly unlikely to meet anyone here. The steady blue-white light glistened cheerfully off the polished floor as she walked. There was a brief passage that ran back along the Reeve's room and ended in a stone wall. She didn't bother to travel that way but took a step to where the main passage branched to the right. Straight ahead was a narrow tunnel that ran the length of her rooms; she decided to go there first.

Since the only people living in this area were she, Dickon, and the Reeve, she'd only been this way once, though she'd learned the passages elsewhere in the Castle thoroughly.

Next to the hinged panel that opened into her bedroom was a set of brackets that held a board against the wall. In all the passages Sham had found such brackets marking spy holes into most of the rooms of the Castle. The boards were originally placed in front of the hole so light from the tunnel wouldn't alert the person being spied upon. As the passageways were no longer secret, most of the peep holes in personal rooms had been permanently sealed.

Experimentally, Sham shifted the board, and it slid easily into her hand. Frowning, because she should have thought of it before, she set the wood back into the brackets and used a fastening rune to hold the board against the hole. If she stayed longer than a few weeks she would have to remember to renew the spell. Satisfied, she returned to the wider passage and continued her explorations.

The spy hole opening into the room next to the Reeve's chambers revealed a meeting room of some sort when Sham sent her magelight through the opening to illuminate it. There were a number of uncomfortable-looking chairs surrounding a large, dark oak table. A space was left empty, the more visible for the uniformity of the spacing between the other chairs—a space just wide enough for the wheeled chair that the Reeve used. Finding nothing of interest, Sham turned away and crossed the passage to look into the room next to hers.

White sheets covered the furniture in the room, protecting the valuable embroidery on the chairs from the dust that accumulated with disuse no matter how good the housekeeping was. She could tell from the shapes of the shrouds that the muslin-covered furniture was arranged in fashion similar to the last room she'd seen.

Her nose wrinkled as a whiff of air came through the little hole and she frowned at the stench.

"By the tides . . ." she swore softly, forcing herself to take a deep breath near the spy hole.

The Castle had been occupied for a long time, and all the rooms had their own smell. The Reeve's room had the musty-salt smell of leather, horses, and metal; her room smelled faintly of roses and smoke—this room smelled like a charnel house.

Increasing the power of the magelight, she sent it up near the chandelier so she could get a better look. There was a large table surrounded by fifteen high-backed chairs, all draped in white fabric. With better lighting, Sham could tell that the chair just opposite the oaken door had been pulled out of place. The dust covers made it difficult to tell, but it looked as if the chair faced the door rather than the table.

From the position of the spy hole, she couldn't see anything else. She walked to the passage door. The levers worked smoothly and the panel slipped back onto a track and slid easily out of the way, just as the door to the Reeve's room did. The full effect of the stench hit her when she opened the door, and she had to swallow hard before she entered.

She increased the intensity of her light again, as much for reassurance as for the increased visibility. The oddness in the placement of the chair seemed suggestive, and she remembered that the demon's pattern should have led it to kill again several days ago—though no body had been found.

She took a step into the room and noticed for the first time that the polished granite floor near the oaken door was stained with dried blood. Breathing shallowly, Sham rounded the chair until she stood in front of it. From there she could see more blood stains on the floor, washing up in splatters against other furnishings and disappearing under the chair's covering. Between the door and the chair was a larger stain where there had been so much blood that it had formed a puddle. The rank smell of the rotting blood made her cough.

Oddly enough, the sheet covering the chair was virginally white, as if it had been kept clean purposefully. A shroud, she thought, not to hide the body it clearly outlined, but to frighten the poor maid who found it the next time the room was cleaned.

She forced herself to step forward onto the dark-stained

floor near the chair. Not wanting to disturb the body any more than she could help, she was careful as she tugged the sheet off and tossed it on top of the table.

Sham had lived in Purgatory for a long time. The sight of a body, no matter how gruesome, did not bother her . . . much. It didn't require an intimate examination of the dead man before she deduced that whatever had killed her old master had also killed this man. Thin cuts covered his skin, just as they had Maur's.

His head had fallen forward, obscuring his features. The chances were slim that she would know who this man was; from the condition of the body, he had been killed near the time when she had moved into the Castle, but she had to look. Rather than moving the body, Sham crouched low so that she could look up into his face.

When she saw the bruised and battered death-greyed features, she swallowed hard against the terror that chilled her blood. This man had been dead at least three days, perhaps longer. Dead, Lord Ven wasn't nearly as handsome as he had been when she last spoke with him—less than an hour ago.

THE REEVE SAT IN HIS CHAIR IN FRONT OF THE FIRE WHERE she had left him; Dickon was nowhere to be seen. At Sham's abrupt entrance he looked up. He appeared so tired and worn that she wondered if she shouldn't find Talbot instead.

"What's wrong?" he said, turning his chair slightly and pushing it closer to her.

She bit her lip. "I found a body in the room next to mine."

The tiredness disappeared from his face to be replaced with animation, and Sham realized that it was depression as much as fatigue and pain that was bothering him. She wasn't sure that the discovery of his half-brother's body was going to help his melancholy much. Without a word he passed her on the way to the opening that led to the passageway.

"Kerim?" Her voice cracked with strain.

He stopped and looked at her inquiringly. Shamera bowed her head a brief moment before meeting his eyes. "It's Lord Ven."

She caught a flash of something in his eyes, before his expression flattened unreadably into that of a battle-hardened warrior. He nodded and continued through the passage door. Sham took a lighted candle from a nearby table, since she'd doused the magelight before entering Kerim's chambers, and followed the Reeve.

She'd left the door to the room ajar and the stench had traveled into the passage. She brought the scented candle closer to her nose; it didn't help. Kerim's chair didn't fit easily through the narrow doorway; the hubs left deep mars in the wood as he forced it through. He stopped just inside the opening.

"Hold your candle higher," he said, the tone of his voice making it a request rather than an order.

Sham raised her hand and let the flickering light illuminate the room. She noticed the eerie shadows that jumped as the flame moved on the wick and was exceedingly grateful that she hadn't found the body by candlelight. Kerim looked over the scene carefully before he moved forward, stopping again to look at the places where Sham's feet had cracked the dried blood.

"Me," she replied in answer to his unvoiced question. "There was no sign that anyone had been here before I came in."

He nodded and circled the chair with its macabre occupant. She watched his face and knew that he noticed the pattern of the blood on the floor—the pool had been evenly distributed. Lord Ven had been killed standing and brought to the chair after he was dead, as evidenced by the trail of blood his heels had made. It was the large pool of blood that the Reeve would find most troubling. There was no disturbed area where a killer would have stood, absorbing blood that would otherwise have fallen on the floor, no bloody footprints where the killer had run away.

Sham pulled the white cloth off the table and held it so

Kerim could see its pristine condition. "This was covering him when I came in."

Kerim frowned and touched the cloth without taking it, rubbing it lightly between his fingers. He looked again at the stains on the floor and frowned.

"Someone went to a lot of work to make this murder look odd," he commented; Shamera didn't reply.

Finally he pushed himself over the stained floor and touched his half-brother's face, tipping it up. Shamera's candle revealed the high-carved cheekbones and the wide, straight nose that both men shared before he gently let the head fall back down.

Silently, Kerim wiped his hands on his thighs, not to clean them but as an outlet for his excess energy. Without looking at her, he spoke. "My brother has been dead for three or possibly four days. This room is cool, so it is hard to be certain."

"Yes," agreed Sham without inflection.

"I talked with him this morning."

"He spoke to me an hour ago," she replied evenly. "He said that he had something to tell me in private, but Dickon came to fetch me before I went with him."

"The demon." Kerim stared at the body without seeing it. There was belief in his tone.

"I think so," she agreed.

"I thought that it could only take the form that was given to it by its summoner." His voice was neutral once more: she couldn't tell what he was thinking.

Sham shrugged. "So I was told—apparently wrongly."

"It could be anyone, then. Taking one person's shape then another as it chooses."

She shook her head helplessly. "I don't know."

"Come." He spoke curtly as he wheeled out of the room, ignoring the grating sound of metal on wood as his chair caught the frame a second time. "Shut the panel behind you."

Back in his room, she waited for him to speak. She had the feeling that he would be pacing if he could. Instead, chained to the chair, he shifted restlessly and stared into the fire.

Abruptly he wheeled back and around, so that he faced her directly. "Magic . . . Could you do this? Take the form of someone else?"

Sham swallowed, not finding the Reeve's impassive face reassuring. "No. Wizards, with very few exceptions, are not capable of doing that. Illusion, yes, but to maintain an illusion of a specific person well enough to fool people who know him, no. My master was once the greatest wizard in Southwood, fourth or fifth most powerful in the world; he could not have done this. Perhaps the Archmage could, but I doubt that he could do it for so long."

"You think the demon can alter its form?"

"There may be another possibility," said Sham slowly.

"Tell me." It was not a request, and she shot him a nasty look.

"Please remember that, despite appearances to the contrary, I am *not* your mistress," she snapped.

There was a touch of a smile warming Kerim's eyes as he restated his order. "I beg you, Lady, please touch these unworthy ears with the alternative explanation."

Sham rubbed her chin and sighed, murmuring as if to herself, "I suppose that's good enough." She cleared her throat and then resumed speaking. "I have never heard that the demons could change their appearance at will. Granted that demonology hasn't a great part in a wizard's education, but I would think that such an ability would have made it into the folktales."

Kerim broke in softly, "Whatever it is that has worn my brother's appearance sounds like him, moves like him, and uses the same idioms of speech. This morning I spoke to him concerning an incident in our childhood, and he added details I had forgotten."

"There is always the possibility that the demon is capable of such a thing," she said, "—but I hope not. The second possibility is not much better. The killer, be he demon or human, might have access to a rare golem—called a simulacrum." Sham had been speaking Cybellian, but used the Southern words for golem and simulacrum as there was no Cybellian translation.

"What is a golem?" Kerim switched to Southern so smoothly, Sham wondered if he noticed.

"A golem is any nonliving thing animated by magic," replied Sham in the same language. "Puppets are often used for such purposes as they are well suited to it, but anything will do."

She glanced around the room and pointed at a hauberk that was carefully laid out on a table. For effect she said dramatically, "*Ivek meharr votra, evahncey callenahar-dren!*"

The chainmail rustled, and the hauberk filled out as if there were a person inside the mail. With a discreet brush of Sham's magic, it rose to stand on the end links. This hauberk wasn't the one Kerim had worn the night of the Spirit Tide; its links were heavier, less likely to part under the force of a blow. Over the right shoulder the metal was a slightly different color where it had been repaired.

"Golems are largely useless for anything other than amusement now," said Sham, making the mail shirt bow once, before it resettled itself on the table with a sound that might have been a sigh of relief. "It is too difficult to create one big or complex enough to do anything useful. For one thing, they don't have a brain so the wizard has to direct every move."

Kerim was still looking at the hauberk. "I'm not sure I'll ever be able to wear that again."

She grinned. "That's what it's made for. If you don't use it, you'll hurt its feelings."

He gave her a black look, spoiling the effect with the twinkle of laughter in his eyes. "Back to the golem."

"I told you about the forbidden black arts that have to be used to summon a demon," continued Sham soberly. "Golems weren't always so useless. There are several kinds that may be created, if the wizard is willing to resort to black magic."

"Black magic requires the use of sacrifices," said Kerim.

"Or human body parts," she agreed. "When creating

golems though, human sacrifice is generally required—sometimes more than one, which is the case of the simulacrum. It can take on the aspect of anyone it slays for a certain period of time. It is my understanding that when not under the direct control of its master the golem functions like the person it has slain would."

She folded her arms and tapped her biceps with a finger, thinking for a moment. "I seem to remember reading that some wizards created golems for their demons to use when they carried out their master's pleasures. I believe the purpose was to save the host body—which was much more difficult to create than the golem."

"I would have sworn that the man I talked to this morning was my brother," said Kerim softly, some minutes after she finished speaking. "Is it possible that it is the body we found that is not my brother's, but a careful copy?"

"To what purpose?" responded Sham. "I can think of many reasons for a demon to assume your brother's shape; but none for anyone to kill someone and make it look like Lord Ven. If you would like, though, I could examine the body more closely."

Kerim shook his head and turned back to the fire. The light playing across his face revealed the sorrow that lived there. Briefly he closed his eyes.

"You don't have any idea how to stop it?" He spoke in Cybellian, as if it were easier to hide his emotions in his own tongue.

Sham shook her head. "I'm sorry. I have a word in with the Whisper, but that is the best I can do. Even if I could find a mage who knows anything about demonology, he won't be anxious to admit to it—it is forbidden magic. Any mage caught using it would be put to death by the wizard's guild if a mob didn't find him first. The Shark has a few wizards who work for him upon occasion who might know something, but no one keeps secrets better than a mage."

"Can you kill the demon once you find it?"

"I don't know," she answered honestly.

"So," he said heavily. "We have a creature that we can't detect, killing people for an unknown reason, and, if by some chance we stumble onto this thing, we don't know what to do with it."

"There is this—" she offered hesitantly, "—the demon doesn't know we are aware Lord Ven is dead."

"If we hide my brother's body for a while longer, we might be able to trap it," agreed the Reeve so readily that Shamera knew he'd already had the same thought. "But what good does that do us if we have no way to kill the demon?"

"I don't know," replied Shamera. "I don't know."

Eight

Sham sat up abruptly as a low sound echoed through her darkened room. The bed was too soft and hampered her movements; she rolled off and crouched on the floor with her knife in hand. She didn't feel the presence of the demon, but lit the candles with a breath of magic anyway. The light revealed nothing out of place.

Once again the moan traveled through the room. The soft illumination of the candles dispelled the darkness and allowed her to put aside her initial fears. The sound was coming from the Reeve's chambers.

The frame had been badly damaged when the Reeve destroyed the door. His carpenters were having a difficult time replacing it, so the tapestry was still the only barrier to the Reeve's rooms. If the door had still been there, she would never have heard anything.

She lay down on the floor by the tapestried opening and remembered to extinguish the candles in her room before she rolled under the bottom of the heavy wool.

Flames crackled merrily in the Reeve's fireplace. It was Kerim's custom to keep the fire well fueled throughout the

night to keep the room warm; poor circulation left him
easily chilled. The fire provided enough light to allow Sham
to see inside the large chamber. When she discovered nothing out of place, she came to her feet and saw what her
lowly position near the floor had hidden from her.

Kerim lay stiffly on his bed. As she watched, his back
arched and he gasped soundlessly, his face grimaced in
pain. Apparently the miracle-worker his mother had found
had done more damage than they had realized.

She thought briefly of allowing Kerim his privacy. When
she was hurt, she always sought some dark corner to wait
it out. She'd even taken a step or two back toward her room
when another soft moan came from the bed. Enough, she
thought, was enough.

The surface of the Reeve's bed was waist high, and she
couldn't reach him from the floor. She put her knife on the
corner of the bed and levered herself up—gently so she
wouldn't jostle him more than she had to. Leaving the knife
where it was, she crawled up on the bed until she sat near
him.

Magic was incapable of doing much more than concentrating the effects of herbal medication, speeding healing
and setting bones—and even in that, Sham had little experience. Armed with nothing more than a rune that pro-
moted health, a vague recollection of rubbing down her
father's warhorse, and a bottle left on the dresser that
smelled suspiciously like horse liniment, Sham set to work.

Kerim helped as Sham rolled him over until he lay face
down on the bed. With three quick slices of her knife she
rid him of the soft robe he wore. She was tossing the scraps
to one side when another spasm twisted the still-impressive
muscles of his lower back. The flesh strained and knotted
beneath his skin, forcing his spine to twist unnaturally to
the side.

She put a few drops of the liquid in the bottle on her
hands and rubbed it into her skin. When she felt the familiar
warmth begin to seep into her hand, indicating that it was
indeed a liniment of some sort, she splattered it liberally
on Kerim's back and set to work.

"Remind me to recommend you to the Stablemaster," said Kerim, his voice tight with pain. "You need to find more honest work than thievery."

"*Honest*?" questioned Sham, pressing deeply into his back with her thumbs. "I'm the most honest thief in Purgatory, just ask the Shark. I pay him a copper a week to say so."

Kerim's laughter was broken by a gasp as another muscle spasmed. Sham moved up where it seemed the worst and poured more liniment onto her hands.

She'd heard somewhere that it sometimes helped to distract a person in pain. "I've answered some of your questions, would you mind if I ask you a question or two?"

Taking his grunt as consent, Sham set the liniment aside for fear of burning his skin with it and rubbed the back of his neck. "Do you really believe Altis has awakened? That this religion of yours wasn't just created by men to fulfill their own purposes?"

Kerim drew a deep breath and shifted his head. "Once," he said, as if he were a storyteller, "there was a young boy, the bastard son of a great lady. He was born a year after the Lady's husband left on his never-ending pursuit of the perfect battle—nine months after a warrior, traveling to another land, stayed briefly at the manor where she lived. Bastard son of the Lady, but no kin to the Lord, the boy learned early to keep himself out of everyone's way. He was no one and less than nothing."

"One day a young man came to the village near the estate where the boy lived. He spoke of a wondrous vision he had been given by an ancient god; a vision that foretold how the small war-torn country that was the boy's homeland would be powerful, as it had been in the distant past. At last the boy's life took on a purpose. He would become a great warlord, and his family would honor him for his skills.

"That night he dreamed he was visited by Altis, who told the boy he would indeed grow to become a warrior of legends, that he would lead an invasionary force such as had not been seen on the face of the earth for many generations. Altis bestowed on the boy the gifts of agility and strength, but told him that he must win skill on his own. A man would come, capable of teaching the art of war.'' Kerim's voice gave out briefly as Sham put pressure on a particularly tight area.

''Two days later a man came looking for work. He was a soldier, he said, but willing to work in the stables if that were all an old man was good for. As it happened the stable had need of workers, and the man was given the job. He wasn't big, this man sent by Altis, but perhaps because of that he had spent much time studying fighting skills. He taught the boy—me—how to battle and, more importantly, when. When the Prophet of Altis called upon the people of Cybelle, I went to him and followed where he led. I fought for Altis with the zeal only a boy is capable of; for him I became the Leopard. As you believe that magic is real, so I believe that Altis is real.''

''You don't have any of the trappings that most of the followers of Altis have,'' she commented. ''There are no altars in this wing. I have seen how you revere the High Priest Brath.''

Kerim snorted with what might have been a laugh. ''Altis is real, but he is not my god anymore. A man learns things with age, if he is lucky. I woke up one morning and saw a field laden with bodies, and listened to His prophet dedicate that bloody field to Altis. I asked myself what Altis had done to deserve the lives of so many and whether he had done me a favor by creating the Leopard who had wrought such carnage. But I finished what I had started, fought to the last battle.

''After it was over—as over as war ever is—the prophet called me to him and told me to ask for a reward. It is not wise to refuse such an offer. Refusing a reward makes the ruler wonder if you are not looking for greater things—like his position.''

Her massage seemed to be having some effect; he wasn't tensing against the pain and his voice had recovered its normal tone. ''I told him to send me somewhere a warrior would be of use. Hurt that I didn't ask for a position at his

side, he sent me here, among the barbarians, if you will
forgive the designation, while he rules the glorious Empire
from Cybelle.'' Kerim turned his head and granted Shamera
a wry smile. "Why are you interested in Altis?''

"It occurred to me to wonder if Altis would permit a
demon to worship in his temple," said Sham slowly—
though she hadn't thought of that until he'd been almost
finished.

The Reeve considered her words briefly before shaking
his head. "I don't know. I *can* tell you that there are any
number of people who do *not* worship Altis: the Southwood
nobles, like Halvok, Chanford, or even Lady Sky. For that
matter most of the servants are Southwoodsmen and there
are even a few Easterners, like Dickon, who decided that
worshiping gods is a thankless task even before I . . ."

Kerim broke off speaking as a wracking spasm took his
breath. Horrified, Sham saw the muscles tighten and cramp,
worse than it had been before. His back bowed impossibly;
she expected to hear the crack of bone.

Discarding mundane methods, Sham traced the lines of
the rune of health on his back where the turmoil seemed to
be focused. She closed her eyes, seeking to visualize each
muscle relaxing, forcing herself to draw the rune slowly so
she would make no mistakes. Finished, she straightened,
looking with magic-heightened senses at the rune she'd
completed.

The symbol glittered in orange and then began to fade,
just as it ought. Kerim sighed and relaxed gradually. When
only a faint visible trace of the rune left, it flared brightly,
fading to a sullen red glow.

"By the winds of the seven sea gods . . ." muttered
Sham with true perplexity. The rune should have faded
completely . . . unless the cause was unnatural.

*It wants the Reeve more than it has wanted anything in
a thousand years.* The words of the blind stableboy echoed
in her thoughts. The Reeve had begun losing his health near
the time that the first slaying started.

Sham watched, thinking furiously, as the symbol darkened to black and Kerim's back began to spasm once more.

Urgency lending cleverness to her fingers and power to her work, she traced another rune: a warding against magic. As she toiled, she could feel the rune touch a spell of binding that was beyond her ability to sense otherwise. Startled, she worked another spell.

Slowly, as if it were reluctant to show itself, thin yellow lines appeared. A rune drawn on living flesh had more power than was usual for such things, and this one was drawn by a demon. As the curls and line of the rune became clearer, she was able discern a rune of binding—source of the spell she'd detected—though much of it she didn't recognize.

A harsh sound was driven out of Kerim as the muscles in his back tightened further. She set her hand tentatively on the demon's rune and began unweaving it. After several attempts, she realized it wasn't going to work. But there was another way, if she was fast enough and if the demon was slow enough.

Quickly, she began retracing the demon's rune, displacing the demon's power with her own and binding the rune to her. She had completed half the pattern, not nearly as much as she needed, when the demon began to steal back its work. It surprised her at first; she hadn't known that anything could work runes without being present. After only an instant's hesitation she started adding touches to the pattern, small things, nonsense things, parts of the rune that were wholly hers. Things the demon couldn't see.

Sweat beaded on her forehead as Sham struggled to break the demon's hold. For only an instant the demon became caught up in one of Sham's useless twists, but it gave her time to finish the rough outline of the main rune. The master pattern hers; she was able to dissolve the complications that blurred the simplicity of the rune, small additions belonging to her weaving and the demon's, destroying the demon's hold on the binding rune completely.

The moment the demon's hold broke, Kerim relaxed limply on the sheets. The hand Sham used to push her hair out of her face shook with fatigue. Taking a deep breath, she unworked the last of the rune, leaving Kerim free of any binding. That done, she stared at the room assessingly.

She had expected the demon to come to the chamber, but it had not needed to do so. Magic didn't work that way. Magic—all magic—was subject to a few laws, one of which was that a mage could only work magic where he was physically present—*unless* . . . the demon had a focus rune in the room.

"Shamera?" questioned Kerim softly, without moving from his prone position.

"Ssst." She hushed him, staring out at the room.

The rune mark would be somewhere hidden from view, she thought, somewhere a mage wouldn't be likely to glance at casually. Her gaze fell on Kerim's wheeled chair. She rolled off the bed and tipped the chair over.

Kerim turned his head at the clatter of the chair hitting the floor. "Shamera? What are you doing?"

"I'll tell you in a minute," she muttered staring at the underside of the chair's seat.

The focus was easy to find. It was not drawn with chalk or cut into the bottom of the seat as she would have done it, but scribed deeply with magic, invisible to anyone not mageborn.

With a foul comment, Sham pulled aside the fire screen and rolled the chair into the huge fireplace. The flames drew back, as if the very nature of the mark repelled them.

She raised her arms over her head, chanting a lyrical incantation to aid the fire with the force of her magic. The flames grew suddenly brighter, licking with fierce hunger at the chair. Neither the theatrical gesture nor the chant had been necessary, but it suited her mood.

How *stupid* of her not to consider such an explanation of Kerim's "illness" especially after the selkie, Elsic, had practically *told* her that Kerim was the focus of the demon's attack. Human magic was not suited for such use, but she had known that she was dealing with a demon. She knew there were creatures that fed upon pain and despair; certainly the demon had not consumed its other victims in a physical sense.

As she watched the orange tongues flick at the chair, she thought again of the selkie's warning: . . . *more than it has wanted anything in a thousand years.*

She spoke a spell that would expose any more runes such as she had found on Kerim, but there were no more in the room. A focus rune, though was much less powerful than an active rune unless it was being used and would not reveal itself easily to her spelling, nor would any other simple rune.

There was no real reason to suspect a second focus rune. They were uncommonly used, for the same reason familiars were avoided—if destroyed they could seriously hurt the mage whose creatures they were. All the same, if the Reeve's selkie was right, Kerim was important to the demon. She turned on her heel and strode back to the bed.

"Shamera, why did you throw my chair into the fireplace?" Kerim's voice was abnormally reasonable.

Ignoring him, Sham yanked on the heavy down-filled tick that had settled at the foot of the bed. She searched it thoroughly before throwing it onto the floor. Muttering nastily, she started to tear away the sheets, and her hand touched a section of the robe Kerim had been wearing. With her heightened senses she could almost see the magic imbued in the fabric.

The rune on the robe was a lesser one, not a focus rune but another binding rune—far simpler than the one Kerim had worn. It was the sort of thing one would put on a animal so that it would not wander away. Far easier, she thought, to turn such a simple rune into a stronger, more powerful sign than to try it from scratch. The great mages, she knew, used to transfer a rune from one surface to another. The means had been lost to time, but perhaps the demon still knew the method. Kerim could have been ensorcelled again by morning.

As she stepped through the assorted bedding on the way to the fireplace with the remnants of Kerim's robe, Sham's foot knocked her knife from the folds of the tick and sent it clattering across the floor. She scooped it up and continued on her way.

The flames were still spitting high with the magic she'd fed them earlier. With the addition of the bedrobe, they turned purple and shot up through the chimney with such force that it dislodged months of old ashes. As the soot fell into the fireplace, it was consumed in the superheated flames, creating a shower of bright sparkles like a thousand falling stars.

Sham started back toward the bed when she heard the slight scuff of the "secret" panel sliding open behind her. She jumped sideways with reflexive speed, holding her knife in a fighter's grip as she turned to face the gaping opening in the wall.

For a moment nothing happened, and she took a cautious step toward the dark passage doorway. The dim glint of light on metal was her only warning as a sword swept through the air.

Frantically, she threw herself to one side, rolling over the top of a waist-high table to put it between her and the sword wielder. As her attacker stepped toward her, the firelight threw his face into high relief.

"Ven?" said Kerim, incredulously.

Even knowing that this could not possibly be the Reeve's brother, Sham couldn't detect anything about the man that appeared unnatural, not even the aura of magic that she'd felt when the demon had attacked her before.

"What do you want?" she asked, snatching a heavy, leather-covered shield from the wall and heaving it at the golem as she tried to get some distance between herself and the creature. The knife she held was balanced for throwing, but she didn't want to use it and lose her only weapon.

"*Mine. He is mine*," hissed the thing that wore Lord Ven's body, knocking the shield aside easily as he slid over the table that blocked his path.

"No," answered Sham as the creature started toward her in a trained warrior's rush.

She took three steps back and rumpled the rug under his feet with a touch of magic. He stumbled heavily, but recovered faster than she'd hoped: many automatons were clumsy things. Twisting and scrambling, she evaded him,

managing to nick his arm with her knife as she slipped past
him. She saw the blood on his arm, but knew it had been
chance more than skill on her part.

He held the advantage of reach and strength. Sham's
lowborn knife-fighting skills meant nothing unless she
risked breaking through his guard and closing in with him.
She was deterred by the recollection that one of the attrib-
utes the golem enjoyed was disproportionate strength. As
if to confirm her thoughts, a blow of his sword reduced a
sturdy oaken chair to a broken shadow of itself and she
decided to try magic instead.

She began to weave a spell to cause the cloth on his
body to stiffen and imprison him in its hold, but she was
just an instant too slow. Lord Ven closed in and swung his
sword at her throat. She managed to deflect his blow with
her knife, but the force of his strike wrenched her wrist
painfully.

Sham lost control of the magic she'd gathered and the
embroidered chair that sat by the fireplace burst into sudden
flame. She took a quick step back and hit her elbow painfully against the wall—there was no more room to retreat.

Breathing hard, Sham ducked under Lord Ven's second
strike. As she ran under the blade he reversed his stroke,
catching her brutally on the back of her wounded thigh with
the pommel. The blow drove her to the ground where she
hit her chin on the floor with stunning force.

Face down, she missed exactly what happened next, but
there was a shrill cry and the sound of sharp metal imbed-
ding itself in flesh. Frantically, Sham scrabbled forward and
then twisted to her feet.

Lord Ven stood facing her with an oddly blank look and
something dark pushed out of his chest; Kerim swayed unsteadily behind him—though he stood without aid. Sham
jumped to her feet as the Reeve collapsed to his knees,
sweat beading his forehead as a tribute to the effort it had
cost him to stay on his feet so long.

The demon's creature fell limply forward, and the great
blue sword slipped out of its back and sang out as it hit

the floor. Sham stared at the motionless body, gasping hollowly for breath.

"You're not hurt?" rasped Kerim.

She shook her head. "No, and I have you to thank for it. I wouldn't have lasted much longer against it." She chose the neuter pronoun deliberately in order to remind Kerim, if he needed reminding, that the thing he'd just killed had not been his brother.

Nodding, the Reeve collapsed backward until he was seated on the ground with his back supported by a heavy chest. He tilted his head back and closed his eyes.

"Shamera, would you get Dickon? His rooms are down the hall. I think we could use his help to take care of the body."

"Right," she replied, frowning with worry as she looked at Kerim's pale face.

She didn't realize until she was halfway to the door that she still held her knife in her right hand. Shaking her head at herself, she started to set it on a table. It wouldn't do for the Reeve's mistress to run about the Castle at night with a knife.

"Shamera!"

The urgency in the Reeve's tone caused her to spin around.

Kerim's blue sword in one hand, Lord Ven's simulacrum advanced with a stealthy gait that changed to an awkward run as she finished her turn. Almost without thought she ducked under his swing and imbedded her knife deeply into the creature's eye.

"Plague's spawn!" spat out Sham in revulsion as she was carried to the floor in the thing's embrace. She scrambled frantically until she was free of its convulsive movements, jerking her knife out of the body so she'd still have a weapon if it came at her again. "Tide take it! Why can't this thing just stay dead?"

As she spoke the body, still writhing, vanished with a loud cracking sound, leaving the blue sword behind. She lunged to her feet and spat a filthy word, wiping her forehead with the back of the hand that held her knife.

"Is it coming back?" inquired Kerim in a suspiciously mild tone.

Sham shook her head, but there wasn't a lot of assurance in her voice as she said, "I don't think so. I'll go get Dickon."

"No, wait," said Kerim. "I think . . . I need an explanation of this night's events before you go. I feel like I have been thrown blindfolded into a pack of wolves. You might start with what it was you did to me that allowed me use of my legs."

Sham sank wearily to the floor opposite Kerim's position. "I think I need to ask you a few questions before I understand enough of it to tell you what's happened."

He inclined his head, managing to look regal in spite of being clothed only in sweat and the light cotton knee-length trousers that served as Cybellian undergarments. He wouldn't have been wearing that much if the trousers had been rune-marked like his robe.

"Something amuses you?" asked Kerim.

Hastily Sham rearranged her face and cleared her throat. "When exactly did your back begin bothering you?"

His eyebrows rose briefly at her question, but he answered her without hesitation. "I was traveling and my horse slipped off a bank while we were crossing a river. I wrenched my back. Perhaps eight or nine months ago."

"Talbot told me that it has gotten worse in fits and starts, not a steady progression."

Kerim nodded. "I have a bad spell, like tonight's, and when it's over I'm worse than before. The muscles in my back ache constantly with occasional shooting pangs. My legs are . . ." he paused and for an instant there was a wild hope in his face that he quickly repressed. "My legs *were* numb from mid-thigh on down. It felt like they were encased in ice. I was cold all the time." He looked at Sham intensely. "I didn't realize how cold until now."

"Now that it's gone," commented Sham with the dawn of an impish grin.

"Now that it's gone," he agreed hoarsely. He closed his eyes and swallowed, clenching his hands.

She took pity on him and, looking away, she began to piece together the story out loud. "Somehow, you must have attracted the demon's attention. I don't know why it chose to attack you differently than the other victims, or what it was gaining from you, but I *can* tell you that the demon caused your disability."

"How can you be certain?"

Shamera glanced at the Reeve and saw that he was still fighting not to hope too much.

She sighed loudly. "I suppose, since you are a *Cybellian*—" she let her tongue linger over the term as if it were an insult of the highest order, much the same way Kerim habitually said "magic" "—I shall have to begin with a basic lesson on magic. I generally use rune magic rather than casting by voice, gesture, and component. The runes are more subtle and they last longer."

There was a bare hint of amusement in Kerim's voice when he interrupted her, "What is a rune?"

Sham sighed a second time and began to speak very slowly, as one might to someone who was very young and uninformed. "Runes are . . ." She stopped and swore. "I'm going to have to go simpler than that. I always knew that there was a reason that wizards don't talk about magic to nonwizards . . . hmmm. Magic is a force in the world—like the sun or the wind. There are two ways a mage can harness the magic: spellcasting or runes. Spellcasting uses hand gestures, voice commands, and material components to shape the magic. As a mage gets better he can reduce what he uses."

"And a rune is?"

"Runes are patterns that do the same thing. They take skill, precision, and time—but last longer than spells. Unless a limit is placed upon them, runes will absorb magic from other sources so that the ending spell is more powerful than it started out to be unless the rune is triggered. When you were hurting, I drew the rune of health on your back. It showed me that there was another rune already there. The demon managed somehow to bind you to it. I broke that rune, but there was another on your robe and a focus rune on your chair.''

Kerim rubbed his temples. "What is a focus rune?''

"Wizards cannot cast magic over long distances without aid. Some mages use an animal that is connected to them— a familiar. But the more common means is the use of a focus rune, a wizard's mark. It allows the wizard to work magic someplace without being there. Both the rune and the familiar are dangerous to use, because their destruction hurts the spellcaster.''

"So you hurt the demon, and it sent my brother.''

Tiredly she shifted her weight off of one bruise and onto another one. "The demon probably sent the golem when it sensed that I was meddling with the rune on your back. As it happens my talents lay in the making and unmaking of runes, so I was able to destroy the rune before the golem came.''

Kerim swallowed, but he didn't ask the question that was on his face; instead he said, "Is it dead?''

"The golem? It was never alive, remember? I suspect it's still functioning—otherwise the demon would never have risked transporting it out of this room.''

Kerim's eyes closed again; his mouth was set in grim lines and his hands lay forcibly lax on the ground as he said quietly, "I can feel my feet for the first time in months, and the coldness is gone. But I still don't have much control over my legs, and I still ache. Am I going to get worse again?''

Sham rubbed weary hands over her eyes like a tired child, then managed to find the magic to cast a quick spell that would allow her to see any magical ties that still bound Kerim to the demon.

"It has no hold on you now," she said finally. "Tomorrow I'll clear your rooms of its meddling. Until then you should find someplace else to sleep. As for the rest . . .'' she shrugged, "I am no healer, but I'd be surprised if you were able to get up and walk right now. I am absolutely amazed that you were able to attack the golem. You should know as well as I that lying around waiting for a wound to heal is almost as incapacitating as the wound itself.''

Kerim nodded once, abruptly. "Lady, would you get Dickon and send him for Talbot? There is much to be done tonight—and I think the four of us need to develop a plan of action.''

Sham nodded and struggled to her feet. She started for the door, but belatedly remembered she was still in her nightgown. Snagging the tick off the floor where she'd left it, she wrapped it around her like a robe before leaving the room.

As she trotted through the hall it occurred to her that Dickon could be the demon. He was very much at home in the Castle. Hadn't he been one of the ones that Kerim had said did not worship Altis? She stopped in front of his door, and hesitated before knocking.

The hall floor felt cold on the soles of bare feet, and Sham shivered. Deciding that she would drive herself insane trying to discover who the demon was if she resorted to random guessing, she forced herself to knock on the door. Wearing a dressing robe, Dickon opened his door soon after the first knock.

"Lady?" he asked politely, giving no outward sign that it was unusual to be awoke at that hour by a woman splattered liberally with blood and wearing a rather large bedtick.

Sham drew the thick covering tighter, as if that would warm her feet or ward away demons. "Lord Kerim wants you to collect Talbot from his lodgings and come with him to the Reeve's private chambers.''

"Is something wrong?" asked Dickon, losing some of his professional demeanor.

She shook her head, "Not at the moment. But . . . you might bring a bedrobe for Kerim.''

Dickon looked at her face closely a moment, before nodding and closing the door, presumably to dress.

WHEN SHAM ENTERED THE REEVE'S CHAMBERS AGAIN, Kerim had managed to pull himself into a chair. Balancing his chin on his fists, he looked up when she came in.

"Go get dressed," he said waving a hand toward the covered doorway to her room. "I expect this is going to be a long night and you might as well be warm."

Sham ducked under the tapestry again and opened her trunk. She saw no need to wear a dress, so she pulled out her second-best working clothes and put them on. She pulled a brush through her hair and washed her hands.

Just before she splashed water on her face, she got a glimpse of herself in the mirror and laughed. She must have run her hand across her cheek after stabbing the golem—a swipe of blood as wide as her palm covered her from ear to chin. She was impressed anew by the mildness of Dickon's reaction when she had knocked at his door.

Clean and dressed, Sham reentered Kerim's room carrying his tick to find Kerim asleep. She set the bedding on the floor and quietly found another chair near the wardrobes. She slid her rump to the edge of the seat, propped her feet on a convenient bit of furniture, and settled into a comfortable doze.

A soft knock on the door aroused her, but before she could get up, Kerim called out, "Enter!"

Dickon came in, followed by an anxious-looking Talbot. They stopped just inside the door and took in the chaos that neither Kerim nor Sham had taken the time to clean up. Chairs, tables, and broken glass lay scattered across the floor. Talbot knelt by a dark stain and ran a finger through it.

"Blood," he commented thoughtfully, rubbing his fingers on his pant leg.

"Pull up some chairs, both of you," ordered Kerim shortly. "Dickon, I would look upon it as a favor if you would clean my sword and set it back in its sheath. I'd clean it myself, but I doubt that I'd do a good job at this point."

"Of course, Lord," replied Dickon.

He handed Kerim a neatly folded bedrobe before picking up the sword and wiping it down with a square of cloth he removed from a drawer. Talbot pulled a pair of chairs near

Kerim's and sat in one, while Kerim struggled into Dickon's robe.

"I hate to admit it, Talbot," began Kerim heavily, once everyone was seated, "but you were right; we needed a mage."

Dickon stopped polishing the sword and gave the Reeve an appalled look before turning his accusing gaze to Sham. She grinned at him and motioned to herself to indicate that she was the mage in question.

Kerim turned to his valet. "Dickon, have you noticed any change in my brother's behavior in the last few days?"

"No, sir," came the immediate reply.

Kerim nodded, and rubbed wearily at his temples. "I thought not, but couldn't be sure. I haven't been as attentive since I found myself confined to that chair."

Talbot and Dickon followed Kerim's gaze to the fireplace where the metal remains of his wheeled chair sat forlornly in the middle of the flames.

Kerim cleared his throat, "Yes, well, that doesn't seem to be a problem at the moment, does it? Let me start from the beginning so that Dickon knows as much as everyone else. You all know that I've been concerned with the random murders that have taken place over the past months. Once the killer began to concentrate on the courtiers, it became obvious that he was comfortable in the court—otherwise someone would have noticed him wandering through the halls."

"I thought your selkie stable lad had more to do with that determination than the killer's habits," commented Sham.

Kerim smiled tiredly. "Yes, I suppose it was good we listened to him, don't you? Talbot suggested it might be beneficial if we could search the nobles' houses as well as the apartments in the Castle itself. Although I could have done so in an official manner, it would have caused needless panic and resentment. Talbot suggested that we bring in a thief. I agreed, and he went to the Whisper of the Street to find a skillful thief who could be trusted to do no more than look."

Sham stood and bowed solemnly.

The Reeve smiled tiredly and continued. "According to the Whisper, Shamera had a personal grudge against the killer. One of the victims was a close friend and she was looking for him on her own. We decided to give her the role of my mistress to allow her easy access to me as well as the court. Both Shamera and Talbot were of the opinion the killer was a demon. Not the things we fought in the Swamp, Dickon—but a magical creature."

Dickon snorted and shook his head sadly.

Kerim smiled, "That was my thought as well. The second night we were here she was attacked by the killer, but she didn't get a good look at him."

"The cuts I sewed up were caused by a knife or a sword; there was nothing magical about them," commented Dickon briefly.

Sham lowered her voice dramatically. "Demons are wholly evil, highly intelligent, and better magic users than most wizards. They do not age. They hunt humans for sustenance and pleasure, though they have been known to kill other animals as well. They come from another world, akin to the one the gods inhabit, and can come here only if summoned by a mage—and the pox-eaten thing attacked me with a knife."

"Thank you," said Kerim with a touch of sarcasm. "I'm sure you're trying to be helpful, but Dickon might find this more palatable if you keep the dramatics to a minimum."

Sham tried to look repentant.

"At the time of the first attack," continued the Reeve, "I also thought it was a human that attacked Shamera. I saw only knife wounds and surmised that the killer had chosen his victim—it fit the pattern of one killing every eight or nine days."

"Tonight, however, Shamera found proof that convinced me that she and Talbot were right." Kerim paused, but other than that, there was no emotion in his voice as he continued. "She found the body of my brother, Lord Ven. I examined him myself, and he has clearly been dead for several days."

"But that's impossible," Dickon broke in. "I saw him this evening when I retrieved Lady Shamera."

"Nonetheless," replied Kerim, "his body is in the meeting room next to Shamera's room. Dickon, you and Talbot have both seen enough battle to know how long a body has been dead; after we are through here you are welcome to examine it yourselves."

He drew in a breath. "After I saw Ven, I thought that Sham and Talbot might be closer to the truth than I thought. When the man who wore my brother's face attacked later this evening, I was convinced. Sham thinks the thing that attacked us is a simulacrum—a creature animated by the demon that can assume the identity of its victims. Between us, Sham and I managed to drive it off.

"Regardless of the nature of the killer, we are left with several problems. The first of these is my brother's body. We are not the only ones who have recently spoken to Lord Ven. If we turn his body over to the priests as he is, they will certainly discover the discrepancy between the time of his death and his last appearance. Last year's riots in Purgatory will be a faint echo of the witch-slaying that will take place if word gets out that there is a killer loose who can look like anyone."

"Can the priests be reasoned with or bribed to keep the secret?" asked Sham.

Kerim shook his head, but it was Talbot that explained. "Our little priest, Brother Fykall, could keep it a secret if it were anyone but the Reeve's brother who slipped his rope . . . er died. As it is the High Priest himself will want to prepare the body, and he has bilge to bail with Lord Kerim. It would please him immensely to get the Prophet to remove Lord Kerim from office and replace him with someone more devoted to Altis. A large riot might just put wind in his sails."

Kerim leaned forward in his chair. "We need some way to conceal how long Ven has been dead."

"We could stage a fire," offered Dickon.

Kerim shook his head. "Where? My brother seldom went into the city and I doubt that there is a place inside the castle that can burn hot enough to destroy his body without hurting someone else.''

"We could leave him for a few days," offered Talbot.

"No," said Shamera. "In this climate, the body will start to rot soon. It will still be too obvious how long Lord Ven has been dead."

"But it might work, if no one remembers exactly when the last time they saw Lord Ven was," said Kerim with obvious reluctance at the thought of leaving his brother's body untended for so long.

"No," said Dickon, but he was unable to come up with more of an objection. Sham knew that he was more concerned with Kerim than with the state of Lord Ven's body.

"I won't be able to sleep in a room next to a dead man's rotting body," lied Sham firmly.

Dickon nodded approvingly at such ladylike sentiments.

Kerim, for his part, shot her an impatient look. "You were willing enough to leave Ven there when we thought that we could use the knowledge of his death to trap the demon."

Sham dismissed that with an airy gesture. "That was different," she said.

"What about magic?" said Talbot. "Is there some way that you can make Lord Ven's body stiffen with rigor mortis again?"

Sham tilted her head in consideration. "Yes, and mask the smell of the blood as well. I'll need an hour of rest first."

Dickon looked at her. "Do you really have some way of changing the appearance of the body?"

Sham grinned cheerfully at him and responded as she usually did to someone who so obviously didn't believe in magic, "I have a few tricks up my sleeve that I wouldn't expect a Cybellian barbarian to understand."

"Parlor tricks," commented Dickon in thoughtful tones.

Sometime during the past hour, Dickon had lost most of the mannerisms of a servant. Sham looked at him narrowly. Maybe she wasn't the only one here who was good at playing roles.

After a moment, Dickon shrugged. "If it works, then it doesn't matter if it's chicanery or not. But—" he added with honest offense, "—if you ever call me a Cybellian again, girl, I'll wash your mouth out with soap. I am Jarnese—" He named another Eastern country. "Cybellians are uncultured, bark-eating barbarians."

Sham lowered her head in submission, saying in a sweet voice, "If you call me 'girl' again, I'll turn you into a minnow."

"Children!" said Kerim sharply, as Sham and Dickon exchanged mutually satisfied looks. The hint of amusement in his tone faded as he continued to speak. "Back to the issue at hand. Shamera, go rest. We'll wake you in an hour to see about my brother's body. I'll fill in the details of what we know, for Dickon and Talbot."

Sham nodded and came to her feet. As she started to duck under the tapestry, Kerim's voice followed her, "I thought that it bothered you to sleep in a room next to my brother's body."

She gave him a sly look and continued into her room.

NINE

Alone in the putrid-smelling room, Sham surveyed Lord Ven's body. Filthy work this and nothing she relished, but it had to be done. She'd told Kerim she worked best alone, but the truth was she feared his grief would distract her. He tried to hide it, but in the short time that she'd known him, she had learned how to read deeper than his public presentation. She rubbed her eyes and put such thoughts aside.

The blood first, she decided after surveying the task before her.

She could clean up the old stuff, but couldn't create new blood to replace it without exhausting her magic well before she'd finished. Creating matter was extremely inefficient, and true alchemy, changing one kind of material into another, was almost as fatiguing. Sham had briefly considered visiting the kitchens and bringing in the blood of a slaughtered pig or some such, but the risk of someone noticing her was too great.

She knelt at the edge of the dark stain, ignoring the faint queasiness resulting from the rancid smell. She pulled her dagger from her arm sheath, which she had donned with the rest of her thieving garb, and opened a shallow cut on her thumb. Three drops of fresh blood joined the old.

Sympathetic magic was one of the easiest kinds of spells to work: like called to like. Using blood, though, was very close to black magic. There were many mages who would call it that even if the blood she used was her own. Even Sham felt vaguely unclean doing it—but didn't allow that to hinder her.

Bending near the floor, she blew gently on the fresh blood, then murmured a spell. Lord Ven's blood began to change, slowly, to the pattern lent by hers. Sweat gathered irritatingly on Sham's forehead as she fought to work the magic and watch the results at the same time. It was important that the blood not appear too fresh.

She stopped her spell while the edges of the largest pool were still dry. She cooled the blood to match the temperature of the room and surveyed the results. The smell of new blood added to the unpleasant mix of aromas already in the room. Rising somewhat unsteadily, Sham walked around the newly wet pool until she could view Lord Ven's body.

She did not risk stepping in the mess; what she had done to the blood destroyed the traces where she, Kerim, and later Talbot and Dickon, had disturbed it. It would be disturbed again, but the mistress of the Reeve would have no business in the room with a corpse, and she wanted no questions about a woman's footprint.

What she needed to do to Lord Ven's body could be done from a distance, and she had no real desire to touch the corpse anyway. It was easier than the blood, since she only had to emulate the stiffness of joints rather than duplicate it.

When she was finished with her spell, she stepped away from the scene. Wiping her hands on her clean shirt as if they were stained—though she'd touched nothing with them—she turned and picked her way across the floor to the panel that opened into the passages and left the room.

● ● ●

THE THREE MEN LOOKED UP WHEN SHE ENTERED THE Reeve's chambers.

"It is done," she said, her voice sounding as raw to her ears as she felt, "but if his laying out takes too long, someone could discover that I've been meddling: Lord Ven's rigor will not loosen for a week or more."

Kerim nodded. "I'll take care of it."

Talbot called in several men to travel to the Temple of Altis for priests to attend to Lord Ven. Until they arrived, Talbot guarded the hall door of Ven's final resting place while Dickon stood watch at the panel.

Sham retreated to her room to change, carefully locking the trunk after she put her thieving clothes away. After an extensive search of the closet she found a dress she could don without help.

In her guise of the Reeve's mistress, she rejoined Kerim in his room where they waited for the priests without speaking. Sham didn't know what caused Kerim's muteness, but she kept quiet because she was too tired to do otherwise. It would be a long day before the fatigue of her magic use would leave her.

Dickon entered the room and nodded at Kerim.

"Tell the priests to step in here a moment before carrying out their duties." Kerim's normal baritone had deepened to a bass rasp, either from exhaustion or from sorrow.

Dickon nodded, returning with five men in the brown robes of the lesser minions of Altis. Four of the robes were belted with blue ties and the fifth wore yellow.

Kerim addressed the man in yellow. "Blessings upon you, brothers."

"Upon you also, Lord Kerim," responded the yellow-belted one.

"The dead man is my brother."

"So we were informed by Master Talbot."

Kerim nodded impatiently. "My brother's affianced wife is heavy with child, and already bears the death of her first husband this past year. I would spare her further grief, and Ven's body is not fit for viewing in any case. It is my command that his body be shrouded immediately and a

funeral pyre laid and ready for burning in the Castle court-
yard at sunset.''

''It shall be done, Lord Kerim,'' agreed the solemn-faced
priest.

Kerim watched as they left the room. Sham turned her
eyes away from the expression on his face. When she
looked back he was sending Dickon to find some of the
court pages to deliver messages.

He busied himself writing short notes at his desk. When
Dickon returned with a small herd of young boys who
looked as if they had been roused out of their sleep without
a chance to do more than scramble into their clothes, the
Reeve sent them to Lord Ven's closest friends, to Lady
Sky, and to his mother.

When the last messenger left, Dickon frowned at Kerim.
''Shouldn't you break the news to Lady Tirra yourself?''

Kerim shrugged. ''Lord Ven is my brother, but he is also
the latest in a number of bodies that are appearing among
the courtiers. Sham may have been able to disguise the time
of his death, but the mere fact of it will increase the city's
unrest. I need to meet with the Advisory Council immediately to forestall as many of the adverse effects as possible.''

Sham, watching forgotten from a seat in the far corner
of the room, thought the Reeve was using the meeting as
an excuse to avoid taking the news of his brother's death
to Lady Tirra. Not that she blamed him; she wouldn't want
to be the one to tell the Lady that her favorite son was dead
either.

''Dickon, I need you to send messengers with the news
that the Council has been called in the Meeting Room to
the counselors who live outside the Castle walls. When you
are finished, go to the rooms of those who live here and
tell them the same.''

''Yes, sir.'' Dickon slipped back out.

''Do you want me to go?'' asked Sham.

Kerim shrugged tiredly. ''It doesn't matter. If you stay,
you'll reinforce your status. Be warned, it might make you
a target for bribery or threats if the court believes you are

close enough to me to influence my decisions."

Sham smiled. "If you think that I haven't been receiving bribes, you are sadly mistaken. Lord Halvok's fledglings are skilled at interfering with the courtier's attempts to corner me, but your nobles have become quite devious. Gifts and notes appear in my laundry, under my pillow, and on the food trays. I've gotten several very fine pieces of jewelry that way; they usually come with very subtle notes. My favorite was one implying that certain grateful parties would gift me generously if I would just slip an innocent-looking powder in your drink."

"Poison?" questioned Kerim, though he didn't seem alarmed.

Sham grinned. "No. Someone has access to a real wizard; it was a love-philter."

"A *what*?"

Sham laughed at his outrage—outrage that had been absent when he thought it was poison. "Don't worry. Love-philters are very temporary and are simple to resist—not that the person who sent it would necessarily know that. To be safe, if you find yourself suddenly lusting after someone, just wait a few days to approach the lady. If it persists, it isn't magic."

Kerim raised his eyebrows. "What did you do with the powder?"

Sham looked at him innocently and smiled.

"Shamera."

"Calm yourself," she advised. "I threw it in the fire, though I was tempted to find the biggest, nastiest man in your personal guards and give it to him. I thought finding out who you were supposed to fall in lust with could be useful, but Talbot wasn't certain you would approve."

Kerim brought one hand up to his face, and bowed his head, his shoulders shaking with weary laughter. "You would have, wouldn't you. I can just see it. Karson, all fifteen stone of him, chasing after some noble's daughter."

"Is Karson the one missing his front teeth?"

"That's he."

"Nah," Sham said, "I wouldn't have picked him: he's

married. I talked to Talbot about the first few treasures that
I found in my water glass.'' She displayed the diamond
solitaires in her ears. ''He said to keep them, and eventually
they'd give up. He said that's what Dickon did, and
Dickon's long since ceased to receive gifts from anonymous sources.''

Kerim raised an eyebrow and asked again, ''Have you
had any threats?''

She shook her head. ''Not yet. I suspect it will come in
due time.'' When he looked worried, she laughed. ''My
lord Reeve, I have lived half my life in Purgatory. I assure
you it is much more dangerous than court.'' After a moment's thought she added, ''Even with a demon hunting
here.''

WHEN DICKON RETURNED, HE BEGAN SORTING THROUGH
Kerim's wardrobe for clothing. When he brought them to
the Reeve, Sham stopped him and examined each garment
closely. When she was finished, she tossed the tunic into
the fire.

''My lord,'' protested Dickon.

Kerim shook his head. ''Find another tunic.''

Dickon frowned, but he found a second tunic and presented it to Shamera with a bow. When she handed it back
to him, he mutely pointed to the covered doorway. With a
faint smile, Sham left while Dickon saw to the Reeve's
dressing.

BECAUSE THE WHEELED CHAIR WAS IN THE FIREPLACE,
Talbot and Dickon carried Kerim to the meeting room next
to his chambers. It was undignified, but only Sham was
there to see. By the time the council members began to
filter in, Kerim was settled in a high-back chair facing the
door with Sham standing behind him.

Except for Halvok, the lone Southwoodsman counselor,
the Advisory Council ignored Sham's presence. It might
have been because the rather plain cotton gown she wore
was remarkable only for being ordinary. More probably the
death of the Reeve's brother was of more moment than his

unorthodox mistress. Lord Halvok smiled when he saw her.

Kerim waited until all the counselors were seated before speaking. Tired and grieving, he was very much the Leopard.

"Gentlemen," he began, "we have a problem. As you have already been informed, my brother's body was discovered this evening. He was killed in much the same manner as Lord Abet and the other nobles these past months. As his body is in no fit state for viewing, I have ordered him shrouded, and set the pyre for sunset. I need your suggestions, my lords, as how to best stem the fear yet another such death will cause. To make sure you are all thoroughly aware of the entirety of the matter, Master Talbot will tell you what we know."

Sham approved the smooth delivery that directed the inquiry away from the unseemly need for haste.

The Reeve nodded at Talbot who stood up and gave a brief summary of who had been killed by similar means and a partially fictitious account of what was being done to catch the murderer. By the time that a carefully worded eulogy and public announcement were drafted, to be delivered by the High Priest to the court at large, the skylights overhead were beginning to lighten.

After the others had left, Talbot and Dickon carried the Reeve to Dickon's room for a few hours of sleep. Sham wouldn't let him occupy his own room until she had a chance to search it more carefully.

She retreated to her bed and dreamed fitfully of dead bodies and blood before she lapsed into a deeper slumber that lasted until just before dinner. Her sleeping schedule had never been particularly regular, and she woke up refreshed when Jenli knocked at the door. She hastily covered up the new bruises and old wounds with an illusion before she called out an invitation.

"I am sorry to disturb you, Lady," said the maid, "but the Reeve sent me to make sure that you are ready for the state dinner that precedes Lord Ven's pyre."

Sham gave the woman a sharp glance. Exposure to Jenli's uncle had given her a healthy respect for the intelligence that could be hidden under a bland facade. Jenli's large, brown, cow-like eyes blinked back at her and Sham turned back to her wardrobe, shaking her head.

She rummaged, ignoring Jenli's moans as she shoved dresses left and right, and pulled out another black gown. She hadn't chosen it for mourning, but it would work well for that as well.

As Jenli began working on the myriad tiny buttons that closed the narrow sleeve, her brows twisted in puzzlement. "Lady," she said hesitantly.

"Yes?" Sham preened before the mirror.

"This is a dress that my grandmother would find overly modest, Lady."

Sham smiled slyly and said, "I think it will contrast nicely with the more daring gowns that have become the style recently, don't you?"

SHAM MIGHT HAVE GOTTEN A DECENT AMOUNT OF SLEEP, but it required only a glance at the Reeve's face when he welcomed her to the state dining area to tell her that he'd managed far less.

He brought her hand to his mouth and greeted her with the solemnness required on such an occasion. Someone had finished the new wheeled chair, though they hadn't had enough time to stain it or cover the wheels with leather to provide traction—instead the metal had been crudely scored.

"Your timing is impeccable," Kerim commented as she sat in the cushioned chair next to him. "You missed the vultures gathering for the bones."

Sham nodded gracefully, "I have found timing to be an extremely useful skill in my work."

His mouth quirked upward in something not quite a smile, "I expect you have."

The time for personal conversation ended as Lady Tirra took up her post on Kerim's other side. Her skin was too dark to be truly pale, and her features were composed— but she looked ten years older. Sham sat quietly in her seat, feeling no desire to antagonize the matriarch in her grief.

Around the room the buzz of gossip was loud enough to be deafening, but at the high table silence reigned.

At last, the High Priest stood before Kerim's table, facing the rest of the room. When the roar died to a sullen murmur, he began to speak.

"High Ones, we come here to mourn the passing of a bright star. He leaves us one less light to steer by, and we are bereaved by his falling. Tonight we will witness the last, faint reflection of his light as his mortal form is reduced to ashes. Let us remember the illumination he brought to our dark world. Let us remember the untimely method by which he was stolen."

Beside her, Kerim stiffened and muttered something nasty. Sham touched her rouged lips lightly in thought—this was not the speech he and his counselors had prepared.

"This is a dark and troubled time," continued the High Priest, playing the crowd. "Lord Ven's life is not the first of our brethren to be so rudely extinguished, yet they go unavenged and the killer still stalks among us."

In tones that carried no further than Shamera's ear, Kerim muttered, "If he keeps this up, we'll have a riot, and my brother's will not be the only body on the pyre."

It was his grim tone that made Sham glance around the room and see the emotions that were rapidly increasing: flames of terror and outrage, fanned by the High Priest's speech.

Sham did the first thing that came to mind. Though never formally taught, there were a few cantrips that every apprentice learned from an older one: simple tricks like making milk go sour—they didn't require much magic, which was good as she was still tired from her earlier battles.

". . . someone or something killing—" the High Priest's eyes began to water and the beautifully trained voice faltered as Sham's cantrip took effect.

He cleared his throat and began again. "Killing . . ."

She added more power to the spell.

The High Priest began to cough. A brown robbed man ran up to him with a goblet of water. It seemed to help until the High Priest attempted to speak again.

Kerim frowned and glanced at Sham. Whatever he saw in her face made him relax slightly; he folded his hands loosely and rested them on the table.

When it was apparent the High Priest would not be able to complete his speech, the High Priest's slender assistant, Fykall, took his place, head bowed as if with heavy mourning.

"High ones," he began, "—we share our sorrow, and yet we must glory for him who has gone before us as so many others have done. It is the best part of being mortal that we may throw off the robes of this life for the next." He too, diverted from the approved text, but even Sham, inexperienced as she was with demagoguery, saw it was necessary to control the people first.

The little priest raised his head and surveyed the crowd. Shamera could almost hear the High Priest grit his teeth as the Fykall continued. "This night we must put our fears aside; only by doing so can we properly mourn and celebrate the passing of Lord Ven. We are aided by the trust we hold for the wisdom of a man who has served Altis so well in the past. As the Prophet has spoken: *What need we fear when the Leopard is on the field? Altis calls, and Lord Kerim answers with a roar to snatch victory out of the gaping maw of defeat. Let the murdering jackals howl as they will, when the battle is over, the Leopard of Altis will stand alone on the field of his enemies!*"

Right now the Leopard of Altis was muttering under his breath about firepits and cooking pots, noted Sham with well-hidden amusement. He straightened, though, when the priest's words were met with a roar of approval. As the people quieted the priest took a step back and to the side, clearly leaving the floor to Kerim.

The Reeve rolled his chair back slightly and used the table to lever himself to his feet; at this there was a second cheer.

"My brother has been taken from me," he said, when the noise had quieted in a voice as carrying as the priests' had been. He spoke slowly, so he could be heard by every person in the room. "I will find the one who has done this and force them to suffer justice if I must take him to the very throne of Altis myself to see it done." He could not have said another word if he had wanted to, such was the response he won.

The priest's blessing on the food was decidedly anticlimactic.

SHAM WAITED UNTIL MOST OF THE ROOM HAD TURNED their attention from the Reeve to their plates before saying softly, "Fykall did a good job of calming the waves."

Kerim growled, but when he spoke it was equally soft. "I have worked to pull away from Altis's priests since I became Reeve; some of the people have embraced Him, but none of the Southwood nobles. If they think I've become a puppet of the priests, they'll run back to their estates and stay there until they rot. In one speech, Fykall ruined a decade's work. I'll be lucky if a third of the Southwood nobles I've managed to coax into Court are here tomorrow."

"I wouldn't be too sure of that," replied Sham, remembering Lord Halvok's pleasure at discovering that the Reeve's mistress was a Southwood native. "I suspect the need to believe you can help them will outweigh their distrust. You bring them hope: it will take more than a single speech to destroy it."

He didn't look reassured.

"In any case—" she said, taking a bite of fish, "—that boat has left the docks, and the tides will see its journey's end."

AT DUSK, LORD VEN'S BODY WAS LIFTED TO THE PYRE and his soul given to Altis in an elaborate ceremony presided over by the High Priest. Kerim touched a torch to the base of the pyre, stepping back as the oil-soaked wood began eagerly to burn.

Long before the flames died down, most of the court retired, to leave only Lord Ven's family to mourn him. Lady Sky would have been there, but she had taken the news of her betrothed's death badly. The castle healer had confined her to bed for fear that she would lose her child. Sham waited until everyone else was gone before leaving the Reeve and his mother staring silently at the orange flames.

EARLY THE NEXT MORNING, SHAM OPENED HER TRUNK and took out her dagger. It was a moment's work to pull the itching stitches out of her wounds and toss the pieces of thread into the fire.

She put her second-best working clothes on again. The baggy breeches and the black cotton shirt, patched roughly on the left sleeve where she had once caught her arm on a wooden casement, would serve her better than any of her dresses and she wouldn't have to keep the illusion over the cut on her arm.

She caught up a candle and lit it with a breath of magic before pulling the tapestry aside and peering into Kerim's room. With no reason to maintain the fire or to light candles and the sun on the wrong side of the sky to light Kerim's windows, the room was hidden in shadows. Sham's instincts told her there was no one in the room.

With a gesture, Sham lit every candle in the chamber as well as the wood laid in the fireplace. Setting her candlestick on a convenient table, she contemplated the wardrobe. It seemed a fit place to start looking for more of the demon's runes.

WHEN DICKON AND THE REEVE ENTERED THE ROOM SOME time later, the fire was roaring merrily as it consumed the majority of the Reeve's clothing, and Sham was tugging one of the large woven rugs across the floor with the obvious intention of sending it to join the clothing.

Dickon cleared his throat and spoke quickly, "Sir, that is a three-hundred-year-old rug, a bridal gift from the King of Reth to his sister on her wedding to the King of Southwood."

Sham straightened and gave both men an annoyed look as she wiped the sweat off the back of her neck. "It also contains one of the demon's runes—I don't have the strength to remove them all. If the Reeve would like to stay in that chair for the rest of his shortened lifespan, I'll be glad to leave it here.''

"Sir," Dickon's voice was almost a moan. ''. . . *demon runes* . . . that rug is irreplaceable. There are ways of making one man look like another. To destroy such a rug on mere superstition . . .''

"We could put the rug in a store room somewhere, if you like," offered Sham. "If we get rid of the demon there's no need to destroy it and until then it will do no harm in storage."

"But that has to go in the fire." She nodded at a large, ornate bench sitting against one wall. "There's more than one rune on it, and two of them I haven't seen before." They looked to her like the strange bits and pieces that had been on the binding rune she'd taken off Kerim. ''—I'm not certain how to deal with it—it won't fit in the hearth. You must be very important to this demon, Kerim. It has expended a tremendous amount of energy to ensure that you were vulnerable to it. I've found its runes on your shoes, your clothes, your armor—''

"What!" exclaimed Kerim, noticing the heavy war hauberk crumpled into a pile on the floor for the first time. It had taken a master armorer nearly a year to complete the shirt and ten years of battle to make it fit like a second skin.

Sham shook her head, "The metal is fine, it was on the leather padding. For some reason, none of the marks are on metal—maybe the nature of the demon's magic."

Dickon shook his head and muttered softly.

"Over a lifetime of dealing with difficult women, I have learned it is often better to give into their demands immediately," said Kerim approaching the bench Sham had condemned. "See if you can find my axe somewhere in this mess, Dickon, and I'll follow my orders and reduce this defenseless work of art to kindling. Then track down a couple of strong men to cart the more valuable pieces to the nearest storeroom."

Once Sham knew what she was looking for, she couldn't believe that she hadn't seen the magic that touched almost everything in the chamber. The fire roared higher and higher and the room began to look as if a mischievous giant had decided to toss furniture around.

At some point in time, Talbot entered the room to join the effort, and his help was invaluable as they moved several especially heavy items. Shamera suspected that the wardrobe in particular hadn't been moved in several hundred years: judging by the effort required to shift the thing it wouldn't be moved again for another hundred.

Once he'd resigned himself to the destruction, Kerim seemed surprisingly lighthearted. It struck Shamera he'd lost the air of quiet acceptance that had formerly characterized him. Not even the death of his half-brother tempered the energy with which he attacked the room.

He chopped not only the bench, but a room divider of six panels into pieces small enough to fit in the fire—as the divider bore one of the strange runes as well. He insisted on helping when Shamera directed the complete disassembly of the large state bed, the last place left untouched in the room. It was there she found the second of the demon's focus runes.

The hall door opened quietly.

Sham, whose black trousers and shirt were the same grey as the dust that had been stirred up by the tumult, crouched where the center of the bed had been, muttering hoarsely in a long-dead language. Kerim watched her intently, immobilized because the various pieces of the bed were scattered helter-skelter around his chair. Talbot leaned with half-assumed weariness against one of the imposing bedposts that leaned in its turn against the wall. Dickon had left to see what could be done to replace the furnishings and rugs Sham relegated to storage. It wasn't until the intruder spoke that anyone looked toward the door.

"It seems meet that, after ruining your brother's funeral with political theatrics, you would spend the next day rearranging your room," Lady Tirra's tones could have frozen molten rock.

Although Sham registered the sound of Lady Tirra's voice, she didn't pause in her chanting. The mark she'd found on the floor under Kerim's bed was older than the rest, and the demon had spent time since reinforcing the spell. As the option of burning the stone floor seemed as doubtful as removing it to storage, Sham had to unwork the spell. This was the third time she'd tried and it finally looked as if she might succeed—if she could concentrate on her work.

Tracing the rune backwards (or so she hoped, since like several others the demon used, this rune was somewhat different from the one she knew) and calling upon parts of several spells, Sham felt the rune fade, but not completely. As long as a portion remained, it could be reinvoked. She tried again, varying the pattern of the spells and feeling them begin to unravel the rune at last.

When she finally looked up from her task, the first thing she noticed was Talbot attempting to be invisible. For a man without the ability to call upon magic, he was doing a fair job at it.

". . . could expect little more than that from you."

"Mother, I am sorry that Lady Sky lost her child, but I don't know how my actions could have altered that one way or the other." Kerim faced his mother across the pile of boards and leather straps that had been his bed, his voice dangerously soft.

Lady Tirra ignored the warning tone and continued to attack him, "You could have broken the news more gently to her—a note delivered in the middle of the night is hardly considerate. If you had even arranged a proper laying out . . . instead you had him burned with less dignity accorded the son of a gutter-thug."

"I did as I thought best at the time. Since I am not responsible for Ven's murder—whatever you may feel to the contrary—I was unable to choose a more convenient moment to announce his death. As for laying him out for public mourning: his body was not fit for viewing, certainly not by a lady in the advanced stages of pregnancy. I suppose I might have allowed my brother's body to rot for a month or so to give Lady Sky time to have her child safely." Kerim said the last sentence with bitter sarcasm reflecting, thought Sham, a fair portion of the hurt he was feeling.

"You have always resented him, haven't you?" said Lady Tirra in the tone of soft discovery. "Why would you give him honor in death when you granted him none in life? We came here five years ago in the hope that you would find Ven an estate worthy of the Reeve's brother, but instead you kept him here at your beck and call. You wouldn't even make him heir to your office. Then, just when he might have come into wealth by marriage to Lady Sky, he is killed. I find it interesting that the other nobles killed by this . . . unknown killer opposed your policies."

Kerim had regained control of his temper, and there was only sadness in his voice when he replied. "Lady, almost *all* the Eastern noblemen oppose most of my policies regarding the Southwood Lords. It would be difficult to find one who didn't."

"With the wealth of Lady Sky's dowry, Ven would have been a problem for you," commented Lady Tirra icily.

Sham looked at the bitter woman and saw, unexpectedly, the same strength in Lady Tirra that characterized her son. It might have been the resemblance that made Sham stop her; it might have been the white-knuckled grip Kerim's hands had on the arms of his chair.

"Lady Tirra." Sham watched as the other woman hesitated, as if she wanted to ignore her son's mistress.

Stiffly, Tirra turned to her. "I see you have continued in your attempt to win attention by the strangeness of your attire."

Sham looked at the black shirt and pants, grey with dust and smiled, but when she spoke, it was not a reply to the lady's challenge. "Kerim has reasons for his actions, Lady Tirra. He has chosen to keep them from the rest of the Court, but I think you have the right to know the whole," *or*, Sham thought, *as much of the whole as I choose to reveal.*

Without giving Kerim the opportunity to stop her, she continued. "As you said, there have been a number of murders of which your son was but the most recent victim. My lord has been utilizing some of my—" she cleared her throat gently, "—unusual talents, to trap the killer. In the last several days, we have become convinced that the killer was not what he appeared. The discovery of Lord Ven's body last night merely confirmed those suspicions."

Sham carefully met Lady Tirra's eyes. For some inexplicable reason, people always thought that meant you were being honest with them. "Lady, Lord Ven was not killed last night; he has been dead for several days."

The Lady stiffened and her eyes flashed and when she spoke her voice shook with a repressed emotion Shamera couldn't put a name to. "You are mistaken. I talked to my son yesterday."

"As did we all, Lady," agreed Shamera, not ungently. "But all of us in this room saw Lord Ven's body when it was found last night. He had been dead for several days."

The Lady's hands clenched, but her face remained cold. "Master Talbot, saw you this as well?"

Talbot bowed. "Yes, Lady. It is as Lady Shamera has spoken. I am passably familiar with death."

"How do you purport to explain this?" Lady Tirra asked, finally addressing her son. The flare of anger had dissolved, leaving only a very tired woman who was no longer young.

He rubbed his hands on the smooth-sanded armrests of his chair and said bluntly, "Demons."

His mother stared silently at him.

"Lady Tirra," said Sham, "I assure you that there are such; ask any Southwoodsman of your acquaintance—perhaps the magician who keeps shop on the Street of Bakers and supplies your maid with the cream she rubs into your hair. Demons live among people and prey upon them. We have reason to believe that this one is living among the courtiers, looking as human as you or I. It has killed more people than just your son, but we are hopeful that Lord Ven's death may lead us to it."

Lady Tirra whitened a touch further. "Just what are your special talents that Lord Kerim would call upon you for aid?"

"Magic," said Sham softly, and, with a gesture, snuffed all the candles and the fire in the fireplace, bringing shadows to the room, now lit only by skylights.

She waited a long breath then raised her hand and pulled a ball of magelight out of the shadows. Small at first, she manipulated the ball of light until pale illumination seeped from an oval source as tall as she was and twice as wide.

From the items Sham had found littering Kerim's mother's private rooms when she'd searched them several days previously, Lady Tirra was fascinated by the possibilities of magic. If Sham was convincing enough, Lady Tirra would leave here with the belief that Ven had been killed by a demon and Kerim was doing his best to find it. For Kerim's sake it was important that Lady Tirra didn't think he had killed his brother.

"I have heard that there is no magic in the East," she said softly, "but here there is magic aplenty, and other things beyond the common ken. Selkies dance in waves of the sea, howlaas wail in the northern winds, Uriah skulk in the Great Swamp and here, in this Castle a demon walks the night." As she spoke, she caused the surface of her magelight to flatten and shimmer with illusions to illustrate her words.

Sham had never actually seen any of the creatures that she spoke of, except possibly the selkie, but she'd heard stories since she was a child. From these childish images she drew lifelike pictures that filled the illusionetic mirror. The demon was particularly impressive. Sham let its image hang in the air for a moment, allowing the full impact of silver-edged claws and six eerie yellow eyes before calling the illusion back into the simple magelight as big around as a man's fist.

She waved, and the candles relit themselves. The fireplace was harder, as some of the fodder still contained remnants of magic and didn't want to burn, but it caught finally and sputtered to life. Sham dismissed the magelight.

Kerim's mother swayed and would have fallen, but for Talbot's quick support. Kerim tried to push his chair over the mound of disassembled bed that trapped him, but one wheel caught in a hole and the chair tipped precariously.

"Talbot's got her, plague it. If you don't stop it, you and the chair are going to be on top of me," grunted Sham as she grabbed at the corner of his chair and braced herself against it until it stabilized.

"She's fine, Lord," said Talbot promptly, as he carried his burden to the couch and arranged her comfortably. "She's a delicate Lady, unlike some here. The sight of that demon was enough to cause a grown man to faint, much less a gentlewoman."

Reassured, Kerim helped Sham back his chair into the cleared space.

"I'm sorry," apologized Sham. "I guess I got carried away with the demon."

"You were able to remove the rune beneath the bed?" asked Kerim, bending to heave one of the dark boards aside to clear a path through to the couch where his mother rested, deliberately refraining from commenting on her decision to tell Lady Tirra about the demon.

Sham nodded and took one end of a heavy bedpost and rolled it aside. "That should be the last of them. I'm afraid that it has left you rather short of clothing . . ."

The Reeve grunted as he managed to collapse the rest of the boards into a relatively flat pile that he muscled the chair over. Sham winced at the scratches the sharp edges of the narrow metal wheels left in the finely polished wood.

Talbot stepped away from the couch as Kerim rolled near his mother and hovered over her, holding her hand. In a voice designed to carry no further than Sham's ears, Talbot commented, "Considering the poison she's always spewing at him, he's very concerned with her well-being."

Sham glanced at the Kerim near the prone figure of Lady Tirra. "She's all the family he has," she said finally and turned to begin the task of rebuilding the bed.

Without a word Talbot helped her to lift the heavy baseboard and shift it into position. The bed was an old one, slotted and carved so it was held together like one of the intricately carved puzzles that were sold in the fairs. Sweating and straining, the sailor and Sham managed to slide the first of the four, heavy bedposts into position. Long before they were half-finished rebuilding the bed, Lady Tirra opened her eyes and struggled to sit up, pushing Kerim's restraining hands away impatiently.

"You believe that demons killed my son?" Lady Tirra's gaze was focused on the ground so that she might have been addressing anyone.

It was Kerim who chose to answer. "Yes, Mother. Furthermore, I believe that it is still here, waiting to kill someone else. I don't know what it looks like, or how to destroy it—but it must be done before it kills again."

Lady Tirra raised her dry eyes to meet Sham's. "Why did you tell me this? I assume Kerim would have kept it to himself."

Sham shrugged, falling back into her thief persona. "It was becoming clear that you held Lord Kerim responsible for Lord Ven's death. I thought that was unnecessarily harsh for the both of you."

Lady Tirra nodded and started to speak, but her voice was overridden by the sound of someone pounding frantically on the door. Talbot, who was the closest, opened it. Sham recognized the stableman who'd come to get Kerim before, but this time he had obviously been running.

"My Lord, there's a man murdered in the stables. There's a riot brewing with Elsic in the middle. The Stablemaster sent me to fetch you 'fore things get out of hand."

Kerim nodded and started for the door, pausing briefly to snatch the war horn that hung on the wall. "Talbot, stay with Mother. When she feels well enough, escort her to her rooms and then join us in the stables. Shamera, come with me."

She started after him then realized she still had her thieving garb on. Stepping to a mirror on the wall near the door, she set a brief spell, not really an illusion, since her talents didn't run that way, but something akin to an invisibility spell—almost as good as Dickon's don't-look-at-me-I'm-only-a-servant demeanor.

She caught up with Kerim halfway down the corridor.

TEN

Elsic tucked his head against the silky-soft shoulder of the Reeve's warhorse. He held the brush in one hand as he absorbed the warm scent of horse and fresh straw.

The stallion had a long name in the Eastern tongue, but Kerim called the horse Scorch because he was blackened on all ends like a scorched bit of wood. Elsic liked to curl his tongue around the odd name when he talked to the stallion.

Since Kerim had granted him leave to work with the horse, Elsic had been given the task of grooming him and keeping his stall clean. Relying on touch rather than sight, it took him longer than the other grooms; but the Stablemaster said he did as good a job as Jab, who had groomed the Reeve's stallion previously. The praise hadn't made Elsic any more popular with Jab or any of his cronies, especially after Jab was dismissed for using beggarsblessing. He really didn't mind the other stablemen's antagonism. He didn't like to talk much anyway, except to Scorch and occasionally with the Stablemaster or Kerim.

Elsic spent most of his time in the quarantine barn where Kerim's stallion had been banished after breaking out of his stall and savaging one of the other stallions. There were four stalls in the barn, stout-walled with barred windows, but Scorch was the only occupant.

When the stallion shifted restlessly, Elsic returned to grooming the last bit of sweat that remained from the long-line exercise the Stablemaster gave Scorch twice daily to keep him fit. Usually the big animal relished the attention and stood motionless as long as Elsic kept the brush moving, but today Scorch took a half-step away from the brush and began making huff-huff noises as he expelled air forcefully through his nostrils.

Elsic put a hand out and touched the horse's shoulder. The velvet texture was damp with nervous sweat, and the muscles underneath were taut with battle-readiness. The boy tried to smell what disturbed the animal—he'd long ago found that his nose was almost as keen as the horse's. As he drew in a deep breath, he heard something brush against wood as it entered the barn. Instinctively, Elsic stood as still as he could trying not to draw attention to himself.

Like Elsic, the warhorse was quiet, issuing no challenges to the invader of his territory. Elsic wrapped a hand in the horse's mane for reassurance as he heard rustles and bumps in the stall across the aisle.

It was gone as suddenly as it had come. He didn't hear it leave, but it was gone all the same. Scorch whistled piercingly, half-rearing until Elsic's feet were lifted off the floor. The boy smelled it too—blood.

Reluctantly, he loosened his grip and stepped out of the stall, shutting the door but not latching it behind him. He thought about seeking out the Stablemaster, but a strange sense of dread drew him across the aisle to the next stall instead.

The door was latched; it took him a moment of fumbling to open it. When his left boot touched something, he knelt and stretched out a reluctant hand, though he knew the man was dead.

• • •

AS THEY NEARED THE STABLES, SHAM COULD HEAR ANGRY muttering and the shrill scream of an enraged stallion. There was a small barn to the side of the main buildings where most of the disturbance seemed to be concentrated. She felt a bit of smug satisfaction when the Reeve's new chair traveled easily over the ruts and rocks of the stableyard.

A group of angrily muttering stablemen were gathered at the east end of the barn, near the entrance. The Stablemaster stood in front of them, a long, wicked whip held readily in one hand as he struggled to be heard over the growl of the crowd.

Sham had seen enough mobs to know when one was brewing; a thread of uneasiness had her palming her dagger.

When the Stablemaster noticed them approaching, he quit trying to address the crowd and contented himself with keeping them back. His eyes passed over Sham without pause, dismissing her as he would a servant. Distracted by her spell's success, it wasn't until they were quite close that Sham realized it was more than just the stablemaster's whip that kept the mob from entering the building.

Snorting and tossing its head, a large dark-bay stallion paced restlessly back and forth, occasionally striking at the air with a quick foreleg. White foam lathered his wide chest and flanks. His ears were flattened, giving him a wicked look not lessened by his rolling eyes. He looked like the horse Kerim had been riding the night she'd met him, but Sham wasn't certain.

When they were within several paces of the crowd, Kerim stopped and blew the war horn he'd brought from his room. The mournful wail cut easily through the lower rumbling of the crowd. When the last echoes of it died down the stableyard was quiet; even the stallion had stilled.

Satisfied that he had their attention, Kerim continued forward. A path opened in the crowd and Sham, anonymously androgynous in her dusty clothes, followed him until he stood next to the Stablemaster.

Kerim turned to the crowd and addressed them in South-

ern first, repeating himself in Cybellian. "I believe you all
have duties elsewhere."

At his cool look, most of the small crowd dissolved until
only a handful of stubborn men remained.

Kerim's eyebrows raised in mock surprise. "Am I to
understand that none of you work in my stables?"

The men shifted uneasily, but one stepped forward. Doff-
ing his cap, he looked at the ground. "Begging your pardon, sire, but the man what died is my brother, Jab. He
asked me to meet him in the barn when I finished with my
horses, said he had somewhat to show me. When I comes
in, I sees that weirdie . . ." He cleared his throat, perhaps
remembering that the Reeve was known to take an interest
in Elsic. " 'Cuse me, sire. I sees Elsic kneeling down next
to the body of my brother. There weren't no head on the
body, sire. I only know'd it was Jab 'cus of his boots."

Kerim eyed the sharp-bladed scythe the stableman was
carrying and said blandly, "So you decided to carry out a
little justice of your own, did you?"

The ruddy stableman blanched, and his friends began
quietly to drift away.

"It were for my own protection, sire. That demon horse
opened its stall and drove me out of the barn 'fore I could
catch Elsic and hold him for the guards."

Kerim shook his head in disgust. "Enough. Take the
scythe back to where it belongs. You have the rest of the
day off. Your brother will be seen to by the priests of the
Temple. If you desire other arrangements for him, talk to
one of them." He waved his hand in dismissal.

When the last of them were gone, Kerim turned his attention to the barn. The big stallion snorted and raised both
front legs in a slow, controlled rear that he held for a long
moment before dropping to all fours.

"Ye'd better see to the horse first," suggested Talbot,
who'd arrived just as the mob dispersed.

Kerim nodded and propelled himself forward. As he
passed the entrance, the stallion snorted at him but never
took its attention off of Sham, the Stablemaster, and Talbot.
When Kerim gave a sharp, short whistle from the shadows

of the barn, Scorch reluctantly followed him.

"Come," said Kerim after a moment.

Inside the barn it was dim and cool. By the time Sham's eyes had adjusted from the brightness of the late afternoon sun, Kerim was backing his chair out of a stall opposite the one he'd put his horse into. Mutely he gestured Talbot into it. The shadows hid whatever reaction Talbot had, and after a moment he came out and shut the stall behind him.

"Did you notice anything strange?" asked Kerim.

The former seaman nodded grimly. "Not enough blood. 'Tis gory enough I grant ye, but if he were kilt here there'd be quite a bit more. Someone brought the body here after he was dead."

"Elsic," Kerim called softly.

The stallion's stall opened and closed behind the thin, pale boy. There were smears of blood on his hands and on his clothes where he'd wiped them off.

"Stablemaster," said Kerim softly, his eyes still on Elsic. "Send a rider to the Temple and inform the priest there is another body to retrieve. I also need someone to find Lirn— the Captain of the Guards—and let him know I need a pair of guardsmen here to keep people out until the priests come."

"Yes, sir," the man left, patting Elsic's shoulder as he passed.

Kerim waited until he was sure the Stablemaster was gone before approaching Elsic.

"It was Jab, wasn't it?" Elsic asked quietly.

"Yes," replied Kerim. "Do you know who brought him here?"

Elsic shook his head, leaning against the stall door as if it was the only thing holding him up. The stallion put its head over the door and began to lip Elsic's hair.

"It came in very quietly," said Elsic, rubbing the animal's prominent cheekbone with one hand.

"*It*?" asked Talbot intently.

"It scared Scorch too," added Elsic.

Kerim nodded, understanding what Elsic meant by the

remark. "Scorch wouldn't have been afraid if it had been human."

"It needed another shape," commented Sham.

"What?" asked Talbot, looking at her in surprise as if he'd just noticed her presence. She smiled grimly, removing the concealment spell. "The golem needed another shape. It couldn't use Lord Ven's again, so it found someone else."

Kerim shook his head. "That doesn't make any sense. It must suspect we know it has a golem. Why display the stableman's body so prominently? In less than an hour everyone in the castle will know Jab is dead. He's been here longer than I have, everyone knows him."

"He's anonymous enough for all of that," commented Talbot. "He looks not a whit different from any number of lads running about Landsend. If the demon didn't want to stay in the Castle, Jab would give him anonymity."

Sham had continued to puzzle it out. "I bet it's killed someone else by now—then it made certain Jab would be found. Found moreover, somewhere that would cast suspicion on an obvious suspect for the mysterious deaths. Talbot, look at Elsic and tell the Reeve what any Southwoodsman sees."

Talbot nodded his understanding, and to Sham's surprise began, softly, to sing.

> "... Frail she stood, and fair of face,
>   Her eyes as black as the fathomless sea,
> And long pale hair as all her race,
>   She sang her song to me, to me ..."

Talbot hesitated, looking embarrassed although his tenor was in key and rich in tone. "It's an old chantey. I thought of it the first time I saw him. I've never seen a selkie before, not even a white seal like they're said to turn into: but Elsic looks too much like the stories for any sea-bred Southwoodsman to think he was anything else. I imagine that's why ye've had such a hard time settling him in here."

"Selkies," explained Shamera, to Kerim, "have a rep-

utation of being ruthless and bloodthirsty.'' She noticed that
Elsic was looking even more distressed so she added,
''Bear in mind that their reputation comes from people who
fish and hunt the mammals of the sea for a living—people
unlikely to be popular with a race that changes into seals.
I'm surprised you haven't been asked to try him for the
killings just because he is a selkie.''

''Selkie?'' Elsic mouthed the word softly. ''I dream of
the sea, sometimes.'' Although his face did not change,
there was a melancholy note in his voice that touched even
Sham's Purgatory-hardened heart.

''I tell ye what, lad,'' said Talbot slowly. ''Not even the
Leopard of Altis is going to make the stable a friendly place
until we catch the demon. My wife and I have eight girls,
and she always wanted a boy—the reason we have eight
rather than six. She would enjoy yer company for a few
days if ye would be pleased to stay with us until this blows
over.''

Kerim gave Talbot a look of thanks. ''I think it would
be best, Elsic.''

The boy nodded, and gave the horse a final pat before
allowing Talbot to lead him away.

''Now that's just what the boy needed,'' rumbled a deep
voice from behind Sham in Southern. ''A house full of
women always makes me happier.''

Sham turned to see a man sitting casually on a barrel
against the back wall of the barn. He was well above av-
erage height, with a build that would credit any lady's play-
thing. The velvet and silk he wore suggested he was
moderately wealthy. His waving blond hair made him
Southwoodsman and his large, heavy-lidded, vacant eyes
hinted at a correspondingly vacant mind—an image already
fostered by his size. The only thing that was really out of
place was the well-worn hilt of the heavy cutlass he wore
at his hip.

Kerim was probably wondering how he sneaked past
them in the little barn without anyone noticing him. Sham
didn't wonder, she'd taught him that little trick and several
others as well.

"My Lord Reeve," she said in overly formal tones, "if you have not met him already, I pray you allow me to present the Shark."

The Shark drew himself to his extraordinary height and made a courtier's bow. Sham noticed that he was looking even more stupid than usual, and she wondered what he was up to. "We've dealt only through others 'til now. Greetings, my lord."

Kerim nodded, giving the Lord of the Whisper an assessing look. "Well met, sir. You will forgive me if I ask you why you are here." Kerim indicated the stable with a broad sweep of his hand.

The Shark raised his weaponless hands to signify his harmlessness. "I? I am simply honoring an agreement that Sham and I had concerning a tidbit of information. That I found her in your august company is simply a matter of happy chance."

Though the words and phrases the Shark used were High Court, his accent was steeped in the vowels of Purgatory, in marked contrast to the rich clothing he wore. As Sham knew he could speak with any accent he chose, switching from one to another as easily as fox could change directions, his show of coarseness could only be for the Reeve's benefit.

"You found something on the Chen Laut?" Sham asked abruptly, irritated with his attitude.

The Shark bowed to her, without taking his gaze from the Reeve. "I found someone who says that he knows something about it, but he won't talk unless the Reeve is there."

"Why would he think that the Reeve is interested in the matter?" Sham kept her eyes on the Shark's face until he finally met her gaze.

"I have no idea. The associate who found him swears the wizard introduced the condition without prompting."

She couldn't see any sign that the Shark was lying, but she knew he could cover a lot with the stupid expression he cultivated. She frowned at him, until he shrugged and lifted his hands to protest his innocence.

"On my mother's grave, Sham, I don't know why he decided that the Reeve had to accompany you. The word of your current whereabouts is not on the street, and none of my people has been asked about you. The wizard approached one of my associates yesterday. The Whisper occasionally uses the mage; we questioned him several times about the Chen Laut, but he claimed ignorance. Now, he wants to meet you this afternoon in his workshop in Purgatory . . . with the Reeve."

Sham shook her head. "How did he expect us to get the Reeve into Purgatory in that chair without attracting every would-be thief and ransom taker for a hundred leagues? Does he want an audience of several hundred thieves? Even if we make it in and out without getting killed in the process, every man in the city will wonder what the Reeve was doing traveling to Purgatory."

The Shark's lips quirked at her attack, "I haven't talked to the man to ask him what he was thinking. I suppose that part of it will be up to you. I can only guarantee that the Whisper will not pass it in the winds."

"I can ride," Kerim pointed out mildly. Sham had almost forgotten him in the heated exchange. "Since the feeling is back in my legs and the muscle cramps have abated I should be able to stay in the saddle. Once we're there, Dickon can assist me into the wizard's dwelling."

Sham aimed an assessing glance at him. "The risk is too great. You might as well have a target painted on your back as ride through Purgatory on a Castle-bred horse."

"This demon of yours killed my brother," Kerim reminded her. "If my presence will help to catch it or figure out what to do with it when we have it, by all means let us travel on to Purgatory. There are cart horses here, as well as the highbred animals. I am sure that we can find mounts to suit."

Sham turned to the Shark. "What time this afternoon?"

"Now."

"I'll get Dickon."

The two men waited until she was hidden by the Castle walls before speaking.

"So—" commented the Shark, rocking back on his heels, "—she found another one."

Kerim waited politely, well used to the fighting of many kinds of battles.

"Another puppy to mother," clarified the Shark with a casualness that roused Kerim's mistrust. "I wondered how long it would be after the sorcerer died before she found someone else to coddle."

"I don't see any milk teeth, here," replied Kerim, baring his own in a white flash. "As for whom is taking care of whom, I think that the honors are about even so far."

The Shark turned away, watching the shadows gather in the corner of the barn. "Be careful what you do, Cat-lover. Those of us who live in Purgatory are good haters and we eat our foes. Sham no less than I."

"Whom does she hate?" Kerim said softly.

"Ah, my Sham hates many people, but she channels and controls it. She follows rules, picking and choosing her victims. Those rules keep her sane, while the rest of us rot in our own well of hatred and despair." When the Shark turned back to Kerim, old anger robbed his eyes of the blandness that created the illusion of stupidity. "But I owe her my protection—and there are no rules to my hatred. If you hurt her, I will find you." Kerim noticed that the thick accent had disappeared as well and the Shark's Cybellian speech was as refined as any at court.

Kerim nodded his head wisely. "Your protection includes suggesting her to us, knowing—I assume—that this investigation would lead her to confront a demon?"

The Shark shrugged, resuming his don't-ask-me-I'm-an-idiot expression. "She asked me to help her find the demon. Since it appeared the creature was tied to the Court in some way—it seemed the best way to fulfill both of your requests."

THE WIZARD KEPT HIS WORKROOM IN A REMOTE PART OF Purgatory where only the most miserably poor people lived. The land was littered with the cardhouse remnants of ware-

houses that a generation of the salt sea air had rotted virtually to the ground. Here and there, a few boards had been
scavenged and erected into crude shelters.

A heavy sea mist hung in the air, clinging to the low
places and robbing any hint of color from the area. It was
a mist thick with despair and untold tragedy; Sham had
never seen this place without it.

She shivered and wrapped the ragged cloak she'd bor-
rowed from the stables more tightly around her. This area
was controlled by one of the most ruthless ganglords of
Purgatory and she knew that in a few days his gang would
sweep through here and knock the shelters down, taking
the few possessions the occupants still had. On the ground,
a human femur lay forsaken, a mute warning for those who
cared to heed it.

It was odd, she thought, with a touch of bitterness, that
people could create horrors greater than any presented by
demons or ghouls. The Old Man had said that the same
atmosphere prevailed in old battlegrounds even after centuries had passed. Places that absorbed too much violence
had a propensity for collecting ghosts. When she let herself
listen, she could hear the dead moaning in the winds. The
horse she was riding tucked its head and scooted closer to
the other animals from the Reeve's stable, as if it, too, could
hear the echo of misery in this place.

They were a strange-looking band, but they blended
nicely with the few ragged souls who scurried in the shadows. The Shark's brilliantly colored velvets were as much
a warning as clothes. Only a fool or a very dangerous man
wore clothing like that here, and a fool would never have
made it this far. Sham spared a thought to wonder where
he'd learned to ride; as far as she knew he lacked the benefit
being the offspring of the Captain of the Guard.

Kerim rode easily, looking every inch a warrior. The
comfortable way his hand rested on the hilt of his sheathed
sword would not escape someone looking for an easy mark.
Most surprising to Sham was the ease with which Dickon
had shed his civilized mannerisms with his civilized cloth-

ing; he looked as dangerous as either of the others. With a faint breath of amusement, she realized that she was the least imposing member of the party.

As they rode on, the buildings began to rise again, built of reclaimed lumber and brick and stuck together with slabs of mud, bits of rope, and a few rusty nails. A whore gazed at them with dull eyes, knowing that such a well-dressed party would wait until nightfall before indulging in the product she sold.

The Shark stopped the horse he rode in front of a hastily cobbled building with blankets draping the windows and a few of the larger holes. Sham felt a momentary twinge of surprise that no one had stolen the blankets before she noticed the magical warding that surrounded the building.

As the Shark swung out of the saddle, a small group of urchins broke from the safety of the shadows to hold the horses. They weren't as skinny as the rest of the children in this area, so Shamera felt it safe to assume the Shark had imported them. If he had thought that far ahead, he probably had other, more lethal minions in hidden nearby. Feeling more optimistic of their chances to make it back to the Castle without incident, Shamera dismounted.

Getting the Reeve off the horse was easier than getting him on had been. Watching his face, Sham thought that he would pay for the unaccustomed riding. With Dickon on one side and the Shark on the other, the Reeve managed the trip from the horse to the building supporting much of his own weight.

Once inside they found themselves in an earth-floored room, empty except for two chairs and a clear crystal globe that hovered waist-high in the center of the room without visible support. Shamera frowned momentarily at the chairs; she had expected nothing more than a bench—chairs were for nobles who could afford the woodcrafter's high prices and lived where such things wouldn't be stolen.

The Reeve settled comfortably in one of the chairs, and Dickon and the Shark stood next to him. The other chair faced the Reeve's and was obviously meant for the wizard. Shamera took a step back to lean against the wall, but before she got to it, the back of her head hit something with an audible crack.

Rubbing the sore area, she turned and examined the apparently empty space behind her suspiciously. As she frowned at the wall, she noticed a subtle blurring around the edges of the room—she whispered a few arcane words.

The illusion of emptiness slid to the floor like so much water, leaving behind several bookcases packed with a few books and obscure paraphernalia, a bench set against one wall, and a wizard wearing a hooded robe watching them from the far corner of the room. She bowed to him and took up a seat on the bench. The hooded figure cackled merrily and shuffled out of the corner. Sham felt a brief tingle of his power as the hovering globe rose to the ceiling and began to emit light.

She snorted. "We are not all barbarian Easterners to be impressed by a magelight trick that I could do before I could talk."

"Oh," croaked the mage hoarsely, leaning heavily on his black staff as he shambled further into the light. "A sorceress. I'd heard that one was looking for the demon."

"*I* told you so, wizard. I don't lie," answered the Shark in a cold voice.

"Aieh." The old man's shoulders shook with mirth and he turned to Kerim. "You see, you see how easy it is to annoy a prideful man. Beware pride, boy, it will bring you down."

"Foretelling or conversing, ancient?" questioned Sham.

The wizard moved to her; the smell of the rich-but-filthy fur robe he wore was enough to make her eyes water. "Conversation, child. I get paid for foretelling. Is that why you came here? I thought you were looking for a demon."

"Foretelling is a double-edged sword—" replied Sham, "—while trying to avoid a bad fate, it's easy to create a worse one. We have come to you for your knowledge, not your magic. I need to know what you can tell me about the Chen Laut."

"And you—" the hunched figure turned to Dickon, "—what do you come here for?"

Sham thought that she caught a glimpse of confusion on Dickon's usually impassive visage, but it was gone too swiftly to be sure.

"I am the Reeve's man."

"I see." The old one rocked back on his heels. Sham took a step forward fearing that he was going to over-balance himself and fall over backwards, but he recovered.

The wizard limped slowly to the unoccupied chair and fell back into it. He shook his head. "Demons are not pleasant company, my dear."

Sham assumed that he was speaking to her, though his gaze was focused on the wall slightly to her left. "It chose us, we didn't choose it—it has been using Landsend as a hunting ground. It killed the Reeve's brother as well as my master, the former king's wizard, Maur."

"The old king's wizard?" The time-ravaged mage drew himself up and whispered as if to himself, "And you were his apprentice? I thought he had died long ago—I haven't felt the touch of his magic since the Castle was taken."

"He is gone now," said Sham, though her tone wasn't as sharp as she'd intended. "The last words from his lips were a warning against a demon called Chen Laut. I need to find the demon and destroy it."

The wizard nodded, rocking a little in his seat. "The Chen Laut is the demon of the Castle. Long before the present castle stood on its hill, the demon came from time to time—feeding itself before wandering away for decades or centuries. The story of its origin is shrouded in the veil of time, and I know for certain only bits and pieces."

"We are listening," said the Shark.

"Aieh, so you are," agreed the wizard. "Well then, long and long ago, well before the wizard wars, there was a wizard, Harrod the Grey—strong in magic and weak in wisdom—for only a foolish man would bind a demon to him as his servant, no matter what his strength. The spells are difficult and too easily lost in moments of passion or pain."

"The demon he bound was patient, with the patience of all immortal things. It served its master well, until the man thought of it as a friend as well as a slave. When it had its chance, it killed him—trapping itself here, away from its own kind forever. The wizard called it 'Chen Laut'—which means 'gifted servant' in the old tongue.''

''Do you know how to find it?'' asked Sham

''Aieh.'' The old man stared vaguely at the carved handle of his staff for a moment. ''I think perhaps it may find you as it did Maur.''

''Are there any other stories?'' asked Kerim. ''Every Southwoodsman I've ever met has stories about some sort of magical creature or the other.''

The wizard snorted with surprised laughter. ''Have you heard of the demon of the Castle? No? It is an obscure tale in truth; more because of the efforts of the rulers of Landsend than any lack of evidence or interest, hmm. He'd have nobles leaving in droves—unless they were Easterners, too sophisticated to believe in such errant nonsense.'' He chortled to himself for a while.

''Would there be records?'' asked Sham. ''If this is something that has happened before, maybe someone has come closer than we have to solving it.''

Kerim shook his head. ''I don't know. When I got here, a lot of things had been destroyed. I sent what was left to the temple for safekeeping—Talbot can have some of his people go through them and see.''

''If we find the demon,'' said Sham slowly, ''what can be done with it?''

''Those wizards who know of demons and such are hunted down by their own kind. I have told you what I can about the demon.'' With a wave of his staff, the room filled with greasy, odoriferous smoke.

Coughing, Sham ran for the door and tugged it open, allowing the smelly fog to escape the malformed little cottage. When it had cleared, the mage was gone and illusion once more cloaked the interior of his workshop.

''WELL,'' SAID SHAMERA, AS DICKON AND THE SHARK helped Kerim onto his horse, ''the good news is that we know something of the Chen Laut. Unfortunately, if the mage was correct, it has survived at least a thousand years during times when mages of my strength were as common as church mice in Landsend. We still don't know how to find the thing—or kill it when we do.''

"Do you think he told us all he knew?" asked Kerim.

It was the Shark that answered with a wry grin. "Haven't been around Sham long, have you? Getting a straight answer out of a wizard is like waiting for a fish to blink—it won't happen. He probably knows quite a bit more that he's not telling you—but you'd need a rack to get it out of him.''

Dickon had been riding quietly behind the Reeve, staring at the ground. He cleared his throat and said, "Isn't anyone else surprised to find that Lord Halvok fancies himself a wizard?''

"What?" asked Kerim sharply.

"I said—" repeated Dickon slowly, as if to someone who was extremely slow of thought, "—don't you think it's odd that Halvok thinks he's a wizard?''

"You believe the old wizard was Halvok?" asked Shamera.

The servant frowned at her. "I admit that his impersonation of an old man was good, but under the hood of his cloak he was clearly Lord Halvok.''

Kerim looked at Sham. "I didn't see Lord Halvok.''

The Shark had begun to smile, looking at Dickon. "An Easterner? How strange, I thought that the magic had been bred out of you all.''

Sham, ignoring the Shark, muttered a few words and held out her hand, "What am I holding, Dickon?''

The servant frowned at her, but he answered. "A stone.''

She looked at the frog resting on her hand, it blinked lazily twice and then disappeared, leaving a small rounded stone in its wake.

"What does that mean?" asked Kerim thoughtfully.

Sham shrugged, putting the stone back in her pocket and urging her horse back toward the Castle. "I suppose that it means that Lord Halvok is a wizard—a clever one.''

"And?" asked Kerim, while Dickon looked uneasy.

The Shark chortled. When Sham cast a stern look at him, he straightened his face, but his shoulders still shook with mirth.

"Who would have thought it," he said. "An Eastern-born wizard."

"Maur," said Sham softly, "—always maintained that Easterners or Southwoodsmen, all are the same beneath the skin. It seems he was right. Dickon is mageborn, my lord, and it seems he has a talent for illusions."

ELEVEN

Sham opened the door to her room cautiously, but it was empty. Breathing a sigh of relief she stepped in and shut the door behind her; she had not been looking forward to explaining her dusty tunic and trousers to Jenli.

She stripped rapidly out of the filthy garments, stuffing them in the trunk. The ever-present ewer of water near the bedside took care of the grime on her hands and face, then she searched unsuccessfully for another dress she could don without help. After the second time through the wardrobe, she pulled one out randomly and tugged it over her head.

Struggling and contorting she managed to button all but the top few buttons. Sham surveyed the result in the polished bronze mirror dubiously. Made of pale yellow silk, the gown resembled a shift rather than a dress. Fine lace, made for a child's gown edged the neckline and shoulder straps. It wasn't the gown that bothered her, but the body it covered.

She set an illusion to cover the healing wound on her shoulder and several bruises she didn't remember receiving.

After twisting around for a minute or so, she decided she'd covered the worst of the contusions and any left were bound to be attributed to rough play rather than disassembling furniture and chasing wizards through Purgatory. Dickon had promised to bring dinner to the Reeve's room, and since she had missed breakfast and lunch, she wasn't about to miss dinner.

As she was running a brush through her hair, her gaze fell on the trunk lid, and she realized she'd forgotten to lock it. Frowning, because securing her possessions was second nature, Sham quickly took care of it before entering Kerim's room. Still puzzling over her unusual oversight, she forgot to make certain Kerim was alone.

The Reeve had also taken the time to change his garments, and he bore little resemblance to the rough warrior who dared cross the heart of Purgatory. He sat regally imprisoned in his chair, staring coldly at the Eastern nobleman who confronted him. Neither of them seemed to notice Sham's presence.

"Do you always listen to gossiping stableboys, my lord?" Kerim sounded irate.

"Of course not," replied the noble in fussy tones, "but my man reports that there was indeed a body discovered in the stables with that weird, blind boy of yours."

"The stableman's body was in several pieces—not something a boy of Elsic's age would be capable of doing." Kerim's voice lowered to a warning purr that caused the nobleman to take a step backwards. "I suggest you be careful what you repeat in public; lest you find yourself looking a fool—or worse. It might, for instance, become known that your coffers aren't as golden as they appear. Odd how tradesmen attend to such rumors so closely."

Without looking away from the other man, Kerim held out his hand toward Sham. "Come here, my dear, Lord Arnson was just taking his leave."

She hadn't been aware he'd noticed her, but she recovered quickly, stepping forward with a bright smile. "Kerim, would you finish buttoning this for me? Jenli wasn't there, and you ripped the shoulder of the dress I was wearing—

it's positively indecent.'' She shrugged slightly so the unbuttoned gown hung even lower, giving the flustered nobleman a wide, empty smile.

She didn't bother looking at Kerim for his reaction to her lie. After the servants had discovered the mess the demon had made of her room in its first attack, Kerim had begun to enjoy his newly enhanced reputation; she had no doubt that he'd follow her lead.

''Of course,'' answered Kerim in a voice that made Shamera shiver involuntarily, and not from fear. That man wielded his voice as well as he did his sword. ''Come here and I'll take care of that. You *were* leaving, my lord?''

The nobleman started, and took his eyes off the neckline of Shamera's dress that was sagging even further as she knelt before the Reeve. ''Yes, of course.''

Kerim finished the buttons and waited until the door shut behind the nobleman before dropping his loverlike manner.

''I cannot abide fools,'' Kerim growled. ''I can't fathom how an idiot like that managed to win as many battles as he did.''

''Being ruthlessly brutal can sometimes be as effective as intelligence,'' commented Sham, idly staring at the closed door. She hadn't recognized his face, but Lord Arnson was well known in Southwood for ordering the slaughter of children in several northern villages. Perhaps she could arrange to meet him in a dark corner somewhere. One more victim of the demon . . .

Kerim eyed her speculatively. ''I think Lord Arnson will be called back to his estates. He has a large holding in Cybelle and the return might be beneficial to his health.''

Sham wasn't used to being so easily read and found it disconcerting. She batted her eyes at him, and with artificially thick accents said, ''Does the poor man find our climate unhealthy?''

Before Kerim could reply, Dickon opened the door for a pair of servants bearing a large and aromatic tray, covered to keep the food hot, as well as an assortment of diningware. Dickon looked around and found a table that had survived Sham's cleansing of the room. He pulled it forward, and directed the servants to set it for dining.

Sham rose to her feet and gathered a pair of chairs while Dickon ushered the kitchen helpers out the door. She set the tray cover on the floor and snatched a thick, crusty slice of bread. She buttered it and took a large, satisfying bite, ignoring Kerim's amused glance with the same insouciance she accorded Dickon's disapproval.

Kerim pushed his chair forward to one of the place settings and cut a slice of the roast off with his eating knife and placed it on his plate opposite Sham's.

"Lady," said Dickon hesitantly, taking a seat after he made certain all the plates were set properly.

Sham smiled at him and continued chewing as she sliced some meat.

"What did you mean when you said I was mageborn?" He spoke in Southern, and mispronounced the last word— as if that would make it mean something other than what he thought it meant.

"Well—" she said, when she was sure she wouldn't laugh, "—only a mageborn person could have broken through an illusion as strong as the old wizard had. Nine-tenths of the magic most wizards work are illusionary— like this frog." She held out the little frog again.

"What frog?" asked Dickon.

Kerim frowned warningly. "Don't play games with him."

Sham shook her head. "I'm not. Look at it closely, Dickon." She muttered a few words, increasing the power of her spell. "Tell me when you see a frog instead of a rock."

She was perspiring with the effort of her spell weaving before Dickon sat forward and drew in a swift breath. "I see it."

Sham closed her empty hand. "Illusion—" she managed finally, with only a hint of amusement, "takes on the appearance of something that it is not. There are three ways to penetrate the spell. One is by magic. The second is by touch; there are very few mages who can create illusions that are real to more than one sense at a time. The third method is simple disbelief. Anyone can break an illusion that way, you don't have to be a wizard to do it. But most illusions set by a wizard of any power are miserably hard to dispel by disbelief—unless you are a wizard yourself." She glanced at Dickon's discomfited expression, feeling a surprising amount of sympathy for him; it wasn't easy to find your long-held beliefs crumpling at your feet. "Your disbelief in magic is so strong that when you walked into the magician's cottage you didn't even see the illusions. I have never heard of such a case before; the only possible explanation is that you are mageborn."

Dickon muttered a foul word that indicated his disbelief in graphic terms.

Sham's eyebrows climbed at the vocabulary the fastidious servant had used, and she commented with interest, "I've never heard of it done that way before, I wouldn't think it possible."

Dickon looked at her with the expression of a cornered boar.

Deciding he was still too shaken for teasing, she sobered and touched his sleeve lightly. "There is sleight-of-hand, Dickon, but magic is real, too. Illusion is only part of it. Here—I'll demonstrate."

There was a fingerbowl full of water near her plate. She pushed the plate aside and pulled the bowl in front of her.

"Water is a common means of scrying, because it's easy to use. The important thing to remember is that water is a liar, easily influenced by thought. If I expected the demon to look like a giant butterfly and I asked the water to show me the demon, I might see a giant butterfly, possibly I would see something really related to the demon, or I might see a kitchen maid cleaning vegetables. It isn't illusion though, so you should be able to see something."

Sham looked into the bowl and muttered a soft spell, waving her hand three times over the water.

When she was done, she set the fingerbowl before Kerim and said, "We'll let Kerim try it first. I have called the water to show the person you hold most dear—probably, it will only show you the face of the person you think you care about most. Don't take it too seriously."

Kerim leaned forward until he looked directly into the bowl; he nodded thoughtfully and shifted it across the table to Dickon. With a doubtful look at Sham, Dickon leaned forward in his turn. He looked in the bowl, then tensed. A white line rose on his cheeks as he clenched his teeth, staring into the pool of water.

"Remember," she cautioned him, because he seemed so distressed, "what you see is what you expect to see."

Dickon shook his head and said softly, "It's not that. My wife was killed in a bandit raid shortly after we were married. I haven't seen her face for ten years; I'd forgotten how beautiful she was." Dickon drew in a swift breath through his nose and looked away from the water as if with great effort.

"This is magic?" he questioned warily.

"Yes." Sham pulled the table back to its original position and dipped her fingers in the water—cleaning them and dispelling the magic.

Dickon eyed her cautiously, but he seemed to be considering the matter, which was the best that she could hope for under the circumstances.

"With that done," said Kerim, cutting the meat on his plate with his eating knife. "I need your thoughts on the wizard we met this afternoon, Shamera."

He had plainly decided that Dickon needed some time to think about magic alone. Well, enough, she didn't mind changing topics.

She frowned thoughtfully. "Yes, Lord Halvok. That was . . . interesting."

"Why would he work so hard to keep his identity a secret?" asked Kerim.

She raised her eyebrows. "How would the Eastern lords react if they knew they were negotiating with a wizard? It would destroy his credibility with those who do not believe in magic. Those who *do* believe in magic would distrust him even more, fearing his power."

"Halvok's personal ambitions aside," she continued, "—I imagine it would be difficult to find another noble

who was not consumed with bitterness toward you Easterners and still commanded the respect of the other Southwood nobles. It is only his singlehanded defense of the
northern reaches at the end of the war that allows him to
negotiate at all without being named a traitor and losing
the support of the Southwood factions.''

"So you think Halvok was trying to help?'' Kerim
sounded as if that were the answer he was hoping for.

Sham shrugged. "I don't know. I don't know him very
well—I only know what I have seen and heard. Although
he apparently likes you, his first loyalties seemed to be
given to Southwood. I don't think he would jeopardize his
position to help you, but as long as you are no threat to his
goals he shouldn't go out of his way to harm you either.''

"So he was just trying to give us information? Couldn't
he have sent word through the Whisper?'' asked Dickon.

Sham sighed and brushed her hair back from her face.
"I don't know.''

"What else would he be doing?'' asked Kerim.

"I can think of one other reason Halvok could have
called us there,'' she said reluctantly. "The quality of Lord
Halvok's illusions make him a master sorcerer—perhaps
better than I am. Black magic is proscribed and punishable
by the most dire consequences if the Wizard's Council finds
out. In the last two decades I've heard of only three wizards
discovered using it anyway.''

"Meaning?'' asked Kerim when she hesitated.

"Meaning there are almost certainly more black mages,''
Sham answered. "If Lord Halvok is such a one and summoned the demon himself he might have told us the story
to concentrate our efforts on the demon, rather than looking
for a human summoner. Lady Tirra said the men who died
all opposed your protection of the native Southwood lords—
certainly Lord Halvok would have seen them as a threat.''

Kerim sat for a moment, before shaking his head. "The
wrong men died, Shamera. The men who died were petty
lords for the most part; none of them, my brother included,
had much power.''

"Maybe Halvok's purpose was just what it appears,''

said Shamera. "I'll visit his house tonight and see what I can find."

Kerim nodded, saying, "I'm not all that anxious to find out that one of the few Southwood lords willing to consider the good of the whole country rather than trying to recapture the past is involved with a demon—but I'd rather know as soon as possible either way."

"Wouldn't it be better to wait until tomorrow, when you know he'll be at court?" asked Dickon.

Sham shook her head. "This is the night he spends with Lady Fullbright, to get information about her husband's business. The servants have the night off." She grinned at them. "I see that hasn't made it to the rumor mill yet—it's nice to know the Shark hasn't lost his touch."

THE NIGHT WAS DARK, THE MOON HIDDEN BY DRIZZLING clouds. Sham hoped the rain would take care of the dust that Purgatory and Kerim's room had left on her working clothes.

Lord Halvok's mansion was in a quiet area of town some distance from the Castle. The shortest way there brought her past the Temple of Altis. Although it was still under construction—and would be for several more decades—it was already an impressive edifice.

Dickon was not the only one finding his beliefs altered abruptly. Since she had taken up her role as the Reeve's mistress, Sham had found herself in danger of forgetting her hatred of Easterners. It felt odd not to be angry all the time—she felt naked and defenseless. That vulnerability made her resent Altis all the more. Things were changing, and very few changes in Shamera's life had been for the better.

"You do not belong here," she said to the god.

Great windows on either side of the massive entrance glistened darkly against the light-colored stone like two large eyes. As she resumed walking, she could almost feel someone watching her until she was well away from the temple.

Lord Halvok's residence was a modest manor to be the

home of an influential noble, but Sham was suitably impressed by the amount of gold he must have spent to buy two hundred rods of land in the middle of the city. She had plenty of time to view the lawn as she walked completely around the building to make certain there was no light that would suggest a servant was up and about.

As she stepped onto the grass, the hair on the back of her neck stood on end: if she'd had any doubts that Halvok was a wizard they were clearly resolved. She hadn't tripped any obvious warding, but the tingling sensation strongly suggested there was one nearby.

She inched forward until she found it. It was a simple spell, designed to warn Lord Halvok if a thief was about, but not to keep out wizards—such a spell would be too taxing to sustain, even with runes. Carefully, gently, Sham stepped across leaving the spell undisturbed.

The lower floor windows were shuttered, but those on the second floor were open. Scrambling up the native rock face and through a parlor window gave her little trouble. She stood in the darkness in the small room and pulled a sliver from her thumb with her teeth.

Places where magic was worked frequently began to collect a certain aura about them. Even people who couldn't normally sense magic would begin to feel uneasy, as if they were being watched or followed. Such places tended to get the reputation of being haunted. Chances were good that Halvok's workroom was in an isolated area of the house to avoid driving off the servants.

Sham closed her eyes and whispered a scrying spell to find where the workroom was. The return information was immediate and strong. Hastily she pulled the shutters on the window and lit a dim magelight to look around.

"Plague take him," she muttered irritably.

The darkness had hidden the exact nature of the room she was in. The dark forms she'd assumed were bookcases were filled with a wide variety of antiques, each neatly labeled by a piece of parchment tied by wire to the artifacts. At another time, she would have been fascinated and covetous—particularly of the fine dagger display.

Unfortunately, there were several items radiating magic, a few as strongly as her flute. She was going to have to sneak through the dark house hoping no one heard her until she could get far enough away to find any other magic.

Sham called her magelight, restored the shutters to their former position, and opened the only door in the room. Rather than a hall, she found herself in a large bedroom. The bed was neatly turned back and a bed warmer was set near the banked coals of the fireplace.

She walked through the room and opened a door into a dimly lit hall, deserted except for a yellow-eyed tomcat. The cat stared at her indifferently from its perch on an open window sill before returning its gaze to the night.

A dark stairway broke off from the hall, too narrow to be anything but the servant's staircase. Sham crouched low and listened for any sound that might indicate that it was in use.

She counted slowly to twenty before creeping quietly down the wooden stairs, walking as close to the edge as she could so the stair wouldn't flex and squeak. Pausing briefly on the first floor, Sham decided to continue to the basement before trying to scry magic again. The further she was from the little collection room the better her chances of making the spell work would be.

She traveled down several steps when something both soft and sharp touched her gently on the back of the neck.

Stifling a scream, Sham jumped down two more stairs and turned, knife in hand to confront her attacker. She stared into the darkness, but saw nothing. Holding absolutely still, she listened for the sound of breathing.

The cat, sitting on a narrow shelf in the wall of the stairwell, purred smugly. She could hear it lick its foot in the darkness. Sham had passed by the animal without seeing it, and it had batted her gently with its paw.

Biting back her relieved laughter, she continued into the cellar. The temperature dropped noticeably as the last faint light faded behind her. She stopped and scried for the fragmented magic of the workroom again, though she didn't close her eyes this time—it would have been pointless in the utter blackness of the cellar. She could still sense the spells tangled in the collection of antiques, but this time the stronger pull by far lay ahead of her, slightly to the left.

She decided the risk of someone seeing her light was less than the risk of someone hearing her as she tripped over the cat in the darkness, so she called her magelight once more. She kept it dim, so it wouldn't spoil her night vision. The cat, with typical contrariness, was nowhere to be seen.

The first door that she came to opened into a storage area filled with foodstuffs. The second room was obviously a workshop—the wrong kind. Bits and pieces of broken or unfinished furniture were set in an organized fashion around the room. There was no third door, though she could feel the pulse of magic quite strongly when she tried.

Frowning, she tapped one foot with silent impatience and stared into the workroom. She inhaled and detected, underneath the smell of the lemon oil and varnish, the tang of herbs and the acrid scent of burned hair. Mentally she compared the size of the food storage room and the woodshop. The storage room had been significantly narrower.

Back in the storage room, behind a shelf of dried parsley and fresh vegetables, she found a plain door that opened into Lord Halvok's workshop—this one scented with magic rather than varnish. Stepping into the room gave her an odd feeling of going back in time. This was what the old man's workshop in the Castle had looked like.

There was no trace of black magic here, as there had been none in the hut in Purgatory; but she hadn't expected to find any. A magician who practiced the forbidden arts would hardly have done so in his own house. She began to search his books.

All magic had a certain signature that identified itself to a wizard. Because of that signature it was possible to tell what a spell would do, even if it were unfamiliar to the magician looking at it. Rather than waste time looking through each book, Sham touched the books in turn using her magic to search out the tomes that might contain black magic.

After twenty minutes of work, she laid three books on the smooth surface of a marble table. The first was an old copy of an even older text. It had several spells that called for the use of various body parts . . . "the forefinger of a man hanged on the vernal equinox," "the eye of a man who died in his sleep." Enough for the spells to be black magic, but a farseeing spell was not what Sham was looking for. She set it aside.

The second book, bound in butter-soft leather, was embossed with the enlightening title, *Majik Boke*. Unlike the first one, it was spelled shut so no unsuspecting person could casually open it. It took Sham some time to dismantle the protection spells, as they were old and powerful—also vaguely familiar. As soon as the spells lost their hold, the book fluttered open and the signature of evil increased tenfold.

"I found that in the ashes of the bonfire where they burnt the library of the King's Sorcerer," Lord Halvok spoke quietly from behind her.

Sham turned to him and nodded, with a casualness she didn't feel. Never show fear or let them know they've surprised you. "I thought that I recognized the Old Man's work in the warding. You haven't opened this?"

Lord Halvok's blunt fingers stroked behind the ears of the yellow-eyed cat that was draped limply over his shoulders. The cat purred. "No, I have one just like it—though I believe Maur's copy is somewhat older than mine."

He strode casually to the table where the books rested and picked up the one she hadn't had time to examine. He unworked the spells that kept it closed and opened it to display essentially the same text as the page her book was opened to—although written in a different hand. "This is my copy. As Maur's apprentice, I suspect the one you opened should be yours. I advise you to keep it somewhere no one will find it. Texts that deal with black magic are forbidden, Lady Shamera."

He snapped the book shut and met her gaze. "Tell me, how did you know that I was the wizard this afternoon? The illusion of the old wizard has fooled many mages who, forgive me, were more powerful than you are.''

She shrugged. ''How long have you known I was a sorcerer searching for a demon rather than just the Reeve's mistress?''

''After all these years Lord Kerim chooses a mistress—not just any mistress, but a native.'' He closed his eyes briefly. ''We have been without hope for so long. Holding on to our lands by the thread of Lord Kerim's honor.'' He opened his Southwood blue eyes and met hers. ''When I realized something was going on, it was easy to connect it with you. Why would he choose an unknown Southwood lady of, you'll forgive me, more style than beauty, when he could have his pick of court ladies—including Southwood women like Lady Sky if his tastes were so inclined?''

''My scintillating intellect, of course,'' she offered in Lady Shamera's vacuous style.

He laughed involuntarily. ''Right. I had already begun to rethink your intelligence, based on the reports of my fosterlings. Siven said he thought you used your stupidity with great skill and shrewdness.'' Halvok shook his head. ''All that aside, you had to be a wizard helping the Reeve track down the demon—he would never have risked taking up with a Southwood lady in this political climate for anything less. Now, you answer my question, how did you recognize me?''

''Maur always said that illusions are an unreliable spell—they are one of the few spells that can lose effect without the spellcaster being aware of it.''

''You aren't going to tell me.''

''No. It's not my secret to tell.''

He stared at her for a moment, then nodded his head. ''Fair enough.''

Sham pursed her lips and tapped her fingers lightly on the table. ''You sound as if you value Lord Kerim.''

He frowned sharply. ''Of course I do. Why do you ask?''

She looked up from the table and narrowed her eyes at him. ''Because some idiot summoned the Reeve through the worst corner of Purgatory just to recite an old story that could have been told to the Whisper.''

Halvok's eyebrows flew up at the tone of her voice. "It was an opportunity I could not resist. Purgatory is a black hole where our people disappear. The Easterners like to forget that it exists—or they pretend that it is nothing more than a slum like most cities of any size have. You were safe with the Shark beside you, no one would risk his wrath—"

"—To kill the Cybellian Lord who is given primary credit for putting down any hope that Southwood had of shaking off Altis' yoke? You are the one who needs to visit Purgatory, if that's what you think," snarled Sham. "The Shark, despite his own belief, is neither omnipotent nor omniscient and there are any number of people in Purgatory who would be happy to give their miserable lives to prove it."

"Are you—" said Halvok softly, obviously keeping a firm hold on his temper, "—speaking as a concerned citizen or as the Reeve's mistress?"

"Does it matter?" she returned roundly. "What you did was stupid and unnecessary. The Reeve knows all he needs to about Purgatory; where do you think he found me?"

Halvok stilled. "You were in Purgatory?"

Sham nodded. "The Reeve saved my life. Why do you think I am working for him, an Altis-worshipping Cybellian?" Twisting the truth was one of her many talents.

"Lord Ervan was hardly so poor that his widow—" he hesitated, then said in the manner of one stating an obvious fact he had overlooked, "You're not his widow."

"I," said Shamera, losing enough of her annoyance to grin at him. "—am a thief, and have lived in Purgatory since the Castle fell. Look, I need to know everything you can tell me about demons."

Suddenly he grinned as well. "Now that I'm feeling guilty enough to risk talking about them? All right, I admit, it was a stupid impulse to insist that the Reeve come to my workshop—especially as weak as he is. Although he's been getting better ever since Ven died, hasn't he?"

"Actually," she said, "not quite. He's been getting better since we discovered Ven's body, though one had little to do with the other. That night I found a number of runes on and about the Reeve's person that tied him to the demon. Apparently the demon was responsible for Lord Kerim's illness—I'm not sure why, or even exactly what it was doing. The runes it was using are odd forms of the masterpatterns.''

Lord Halvok looked around until he found a pair of stools. He gave one to Sham and sat upon the other. ''Why don't you tell me what you know about this demon, and I'll tell you anything I can.''

''Very well.'' She perched on the proffered seat. ''The demon is killing people every seven to eight days and has been for the past . . . oh three quarters of a year or so. It didn't start concentrating its kills at the Castle until several months ago. As I told you, it killed Maur—which is how I first got involved.''

''So the killings started about the same time as the Reeve's illness?'' said Halvok.

''Yes.''

Lord Halvok frowned. ''From what I know of demons, it is killing far more frequently than it needs to. Demons need to feed on death—but supposedly only once every several months.''

''Right,'' agreed Sham, ''but in order to keep its simulacrum working, I believe it needs to kill much more often.''

''A simulacrum?'' Halvok sounded intrigued.

''Lord Ven had been dead several days before we discovered his body. I . . . freshened it to avoid frightening everyone who had seen him in court while his body was rotting in a little-used room in the Castle. The last form it had to wear that I know of belonged to a dead stableman.''

''The stableman who was found dead in the company of the Reeve's pet selkie?''

She nodded. ''It killed him to get rid of Ven's form and used Elsic—the selkie—to throw as much sand over its trail as it could.''

Halvok shook his head. ''By the tides,'' he swore, ''no wonder it has been so hard to catch.''

"Can you tell me how to find the demon?"

"No."

"All right, then. Do you know how to kill it?"

Halvok shrugged. "Find out who it is and kill the body that houses it—after you destroy the simulacrum. It should take the demon a decade or so to find a person whose body it can steal. They are capable of that, you know, if they are not already tied to a host. The demon itself cannot be killed . . . unless—." He stiffened as if a new thought had occurred to him, "—if you can find the demon, and enslave it the way the old magicians used to, it will die when you do."

Sham thought about that and shook her head. "It's free now because it killed the mage who called it and he knew far more about demons than I do. Is there a way I can send it back where it came from?"

Lord Halvok nodded and elaborated, "You'll need to find a virgin, cut out his tongue, put out his eyes, chant a few lines, cut out his heart and feed it to the demon after taking a bite yourself. Death is capable of generating great power if you use it right. I have a young cousin who might work, though I'm not certain about his virginity, you understand."

Sham snorted. "I think I'll pass—if nothing else works I'll settle on killing its host. What about the Archmage who destroyed Tybokk? How did he do it?"

"He managed to bind it to the dead body it had occupied so it was unable to seek another host. He used a spell that has been lost with most other demon lore—it's not in Maur's book. Perhaps there is something in the ae'Magi's library. I won't stop you if you want to ask the ae'Magi if he has a book of demonology in his possession—although such an admission would require him to present himself to the council for execution. Maybe it would help if you told him that you had a book on demon lore, but needed a specific reference."

Sham laughed despite herself and held up a hand in surrender. "Would it be acceptable if I talk with you again after I have had a chance to read this?" She tapped the book he'd given her.

The nobleman bowed his assent. "Lady, you have whatever aid I can offer. I will contact my old master and see if he has any suggestions."

"I would appreciate that." Sham rose from the stool and walked to the door. Before she opened it, however, she turned back to him. "Lord Halvok, would you happen to have any books on runes? Something that might have the forms that the demon is using?"

"Old runes?" He thought a moment. "I might have one that would help."

Kneeling, he drew a thin volume from the bottom shelf and brought it to her. "This is something I picked up in the market a number of years ago. It's quite a bit older than it looks, and it has runes in it I had never seen before."

"Thanks," she said taking it.

"You may leave by the front door if you wish."

She turned to bat her eyelashes at him. "And have the Reeve's mistress be seen leaving your manor at night? I can find my own way out, sir."

"SO HALVOK ISN'T CALLING DEMONS?" ASKED KERIM, pulling another pillow behind his back to prop himself up higher.

Sham, so tired that her very bones ached, struggled to think clearly. She had come directly here after leaving Lord Halvok's chambers, without stopping to find a safe place for her newly acquired books—not that there ever was a really safe place for a black grimoire.

"I don't think so," she answered finally. "If he is summoning demons, he is a better actor than I think he is, and he's not doing it from his home."

Kerim nodded. "Good enough for me. Why don't you go to sleep and we'll see what the morning brings."

Sham gave him a mock salute and exited under the tapestry.

• • •

ALONE IN HER ROOM, SHAM STOOD FOR A MOMENT IN THE darkness. The rune book was no trouble, but she wasn't sure what to do with the other one. Even though she had replaced the spell-warding on the book, the signature of black magic leaked from it.

Sighing, she set the book on the nearest flat surface she came to and set the second, more innocuous one on top of it. She could deal with it in the morning. She stripped out of her filthy clothing—the rain had turned the thick layer of dust to mud—and tossed her clothes in the trunk. As she shut the lid, the thought of the mildew the damp clothing invited crossed her mind, but she was too tired to deal with it.

TWELVE

The thunderous pounding on Kerim's door was loud enough to force Sham to sit up in her bed and curse under her breath. From the weight of her eyelids, she estimated she'd been asleep less than an hour. She thought seriously about ignoring the noise and going back to sleep, but anything worth waking up the Reeve at such an obscene hour of the night was worth investigating.

Knowing her intrusion might not be welcomed, she stretched out on the floor and raised the bottom of the tapestry until she could see into Kerim's room.

Kerim had already thrown on his bedrobe and was using his quarterstaff for balance as he hobbled painfully across the room.

"Yes?" he called out, before he opened the door.

"My Lord, Lady Tirra sent me to tell you that Lady Sky is in danger."

Sham heard Kerim throwing the bolt on his door and the hinges squeaked once. A chest obscured her view, so she had to rely on her ears.

"I don't know the exact circumstances, but Lady Tirra

seems to feel it may be due to the Lady's recent miscarriage.'' From his voice the messenger was painfully young.

Kerim reappeared in Sham's sight. He grunted as he settled himself in his wheeled chair and tossed the quarterstaff on his bed. Wasting no time he left the room.

As soon as the door shut behind him, Sham leapt to her feet and opened her trunk, shuffling through the assorted mess until her hand closed on damp cloth. She preferred her wet thieving clothes to court dress. As she wrestled with recalcitrant fabric, she realized she hadn't had to unlock her trunk. Once decently clothed, she slammed a hand on the leather and wood top and spelled it closed without bothering with the latch.

Quickly she opened the panel into the passages and slipped through. By this time, she knew the passages of the Castle better than she knew the halls where more conventional people traveled from place to place in the Castle. There were only three short sections of main thoroughfare she had to cross. Either luck or the lateness of the hour blessed her with empty halls, and there was no one to see when she cautiously scurried from one passage to the next on her way to Lady Sky's quarters.

Like most of the occupied rooms, the spyhole to Lady Sky's bedchamber had been sealed. It took Sham less than a wisp of magic to pull the board off the wall. Before she pulled the board completely away, Sham doused the magelight. Luckily, Lady Sky lived on the third floor where all the unmarried ladies of the court stayed, so there were several windows to let moonlight into the room.

Lady Sky might almost have been posed for an artist. The silvery light of the moon played upon her fair hair and caressed her graceful figure, which was as slender as if her pregnancy had never been. The white muslin gown that she wore made her appear younger than she was. She sat crosslegged on her bed, staring down at a dagger she held in both hands.

Sham couldn't see her face except for the corner of her jaw, but she had a clear view of Lady Sky's fine-boned hands turning the dagger over and over, as if she were examining the knife at a marketplace, looking for flaws.

Sham began searching for a hidden door that would let her enter the room. Purgatory had eliminated any sympathy she might have had for people who took the easy way out, but the lady had the excuse of her recent miscarriage: It was common knowledge that such women were overly emotional. Sky had become as close to a friend as she had among the women at court, and Sham didn't want anything to happen to her. She was exploring a likely looking area when she heard Kerim's voice. Quickly she darted back to her spyhole and set her eye against it.

"Give me the dagger, Sky."

The bolt must not have been thrown on the door, for Kerim's chair had stopped just inside the threshold. Lady Sky held the dagger up until the moonlight danced on the blade.

"This was my husband's," she said in conversational tones. "He was very careful that all his weapons were kept sharp."

"Sky, do you know how hard it is to kill yourself with a dagger? Unless you know what you're doing, it can take days to die of such a wound. Despite Fahill's axioms, dagger wounds are very painful . . . and messy." Kerim matched her conversational tones exactly, as, with an easy push, he sent his chair rolling toward her bed.

A fresh breeze blew in from the window, causing the modest white muslin of Lady Sky's nightgown to flutter softly against her skin. Wheels touching the edge of her bed, Kerim waited patiently for her reply.

"They all die," Lady Sky said finally, in a child's soft bewildered voice. "My babies, my parents, my husband, Ven—everyone. I think perhaps I'm cursed. There are so many people dying here—if I am dead too, maybe it will stop."

"Sky, dying never stops." Kerim's voice was gentle but implacable. "The only certainty life contains is death. Would your parents, Fahill, or Ven want you to die for no reason? Should there be one less person mourning their deaths and one more person to mourn? Fahill loved you. I fought side by side with the man, and he was a withdrawn, embittered warrior until you came to him. During the few months he had you, he was happier than he had ever been. He would not like it if you used his death as a reason to destroy something he loved so.''

In the passage, Sham backed away from the spyhole. There was no threat to Kerim here, and somewhere along the line she'd developed faith in the Leopard's abilities— he would talk Sky out of her foolishness without her help.

Shamera needed to get away from Sky's voice. It wasn't death that was hard, or the dying, though the tides knew it could be bad enough: it was finding a reason to keep on living. She wished Sky luck.

From the lady's room, Sham heard the sound of a dagger flung to the floor, followed by sobs muffled against a man's shoulder. Sham stopped, and turned back to the spyhole.

Kerim held Sky in his lap, petting her hair gently as her shoulders trembled with grief. Sham bit her lip and turned away. There, in the dark passage listening to the sounds of another woman's sorrow, she admitted what she would not admit in the light of day: Sham the Thief loved the Reeve of Southwood.

Tiredly, she walked back to her room. She threw her clothes back in the trunk, and found her nightgown. Then she climbed into her bed, pulled the covers over her head, and waited for sleep to come.

THE DOOR TO SHAM'S ROOM HIT THE WALL WITH A LOUD bang. She awoke abruptly to find herself in an unladylike crouch on the edge of her bed, her dagger clutched in one hand. Frowning blearily, she peered at the intruders.

Talbot's raised eyebrows caused her to remember just what the Reeve's mistress wore for nightgowns, and she dove back under the covers. Elsic, of course, was immune to the sight.

"Sorry to trouble ye, Lady," said Talbot, smothering a laugh, "but the Reeve is in a meeting, and I have work to do sorting through records that the temple sent down. I waited as long as I could, as Kerim said ye were out until the wee hours. It's now past luncheon and someone needs to see the lad here—'' Talbot clapped the boy's shoulder with a heavy hand, ''—doesn't get himself mob-eaten.''

Sham scowled at Talbot. ''It is customary to knock, before throwing open a door.''

He grinned at her. ''Worry about knocking do ye, thief? First I ever heard of it.''

Laughing, Shamera raised her hands in defeat. ''Welcome, Elsic. Shove off, Talbot. We'll keep each other out of trouble. I'll fight off mobs and Elsic can handle the nobles.''

Elsic grinned. ''For you, Lady, anything.''

Sham shook her head at Talbot. ''From stableboy to courtier in one night. Shame on you for corrupting youth.''

''Me?'' answered Talbot indignantly, ''It was the womenfolk. Cursed I am with a pack of daughters who look upon any unrelated male as fair game, especially a lad as fair and mysterious as this one.''

''Ah,'' said Sham knowingly, ''—the real reason to move Elsic into the Castle for the day.''

Talbot grinned at her and left. Sham started to get out of bed, then hesitated, glancing at Elsic.

''I really can't see you,'' he assured her with a wicked smile. Obviously an evening spent with Talbot's family had been good for him—he looked a good deal less lost than he had in the stables yesterday.

''I think you can wait in Kerim's room until I'm dressed, my lad. If you walk straight about four paces—'' she waited as he complied, ''—left a step, then six paces to the wall. Turn right and walk until you find the tapestry. Under the tapestry is a doorway to Kerim's bedroom.''

When he was safely out of her room, she threw back the covers and pulled out a dress at random. It was a flowered silk in flaming orange golds and deep indigo, with slits on either side of the skirt to the top of her hips. She had to rummage further to find the slip—little more than colored silk strips hung on a string. It was based on some of the dresses the Trading Clan women wore, but far more provocative—it also had relatively few buttons, and the ones

Sham couldn't work didn't make the dress any more revealing than it already was.

As she started toward Kerim's room, her gaze fell on the pair of books that waited patiently on the nightstand that had mysteriously appeared to replace the one she'd destroyed. She was going to have to find some way to occupy Elsic while she worked through the black grimoire, as well as a better place to keep it when she wasn't in the room. Her trunk would work to keep the book out of innocent hands, but that wouldn't disguise what it held from any magic user.

Sham heard the soft sounds of someone tuning a harp. She ducked under the tapestry to find that Elsic had located a small bard's harp amidst the weaponry that littered the room and was sitting at the foot of the Reeve's bed tuning it. There was a smudge on the bedclothes that looked suspiciously as if he'd used it to dust off the harp.

Elsic looked up when she came into the room and left off touching the strings. "Kerim lets me play this when I am here. It's a fine instrument."

Sham looked at the harp doubtfully. It wouldn't bring more than three coppers at the market, and that only if someone cleaned and polished it; the wood was old, and the finish marred as if it had indeed been carried by a bard through several lifetimes of wandering.

"Did he teach you to play?" she asked, unwilling to comment on the harp's quality.

Elsic shook his head and began running his hands over the strings again. "No. I already knew how to play, though I didn't remember it until I held the harp. Lord Kerim says his fingers are too cumbersome for the strings, but he'll sing with me sometimes."

The tune that he played was unfamiliar, but its haunting tone caused a shiver to run up her unsentimental spine. She had always accounted the Old Man a master of music, but he'd never approached the skill that Elsic displayed as he called the music from the old, worn harp. The strings wept with the sorrow of his song.

Unable to find any words that didn't sound trite, Sham

found a seat and closed her eyes, letting the music wash over her. After few refrains, Elsic traded the melancholy air for the more familiar melody of a feast-day song. He played the lilting verse through once before adding his voice to the harp's.

Sham smiled in contentment, pulling her bare feet to the velvet seat of her chair. The skirt she was wearing made the position less than modest, but Elsic and she were the only ones in the room. At the end of the last chorus, he set the harp aside, flexing his fingers and laughing self-consciously when Sham applauded him.

"It's the harp—" he explained, "—anyone could make such an instrument sound good."

"Not I," replied Sham, "nor my master who was a talented musician by all accounts. I have some reading to do. If you would like to continue playing, I'll bring my book in here where the chairs are more comfortable."

Rather than answering her with words, Elsic took up the harp again. Sham ducked back into her room, and got the book Lord Halvok had given her. Returning to Kerim's room, she settled comfortably in a chair and started to un-work the binding spells on the book.

Elsic stopped playing and cocked his head to one side. "What are you doing?"

She released the first of the spells and stopped to answer him. "Magic."

He frowned. "It feels . . . odd somehow . . . not like the magic I know."

Sham thought about that for a moment, trying to decide just how the magic the Spirit Tide generated was different from the magic she used.

"It is different than what you do," she said finally. "I don't understand your kind of magic very well; I don't know if any human does. I can sense it sometimes if it's strong enough, the way you can sense what I do. The magic that you use is already shaped by the forces of nature—like the ocean tides. The magic I use is unformed. I impose it on the book, or whatever I want to affect."

"There's something else," said Elsic after a pause, his voice tentative. "Something I don't like."

"Ah, that," she said. "The book I'm reading has a rather large section of demonology. There is magic that feeds—"

"—upon death," he interrupted, having come to alert like a fine hunting hound.

"Even so. I'm not working the spells, but even writing about such things taints the pages."

"Ah," said Elsic in a fine imitation of her tones earlier. He nodded once, and resumed playing. He didn't appear unhappy, just thoughtful, so she left him to his music.

IT WAS INTERESTING TO READ THE DETAILED EXPLANATION of the proper ceremony for summoning the dead accompanied by "How the Cow Ate the Roof" and "The Maiden's Caress." There were worse choices, she supposed, but somehow the simple country songs made the sacrifice of three piglets in a particularly cruel manner even more distressing in comparison. It was a relief when someone knocked on her door, and gave her an excuse to quit reading.

She ducked under the tapestry, tossing the book in the trunk, which was unaccountably unlocked again, as she passed it to reach her door. She looked at the trunk and frowned, but the knocking resumed.

"Coming," she called, opening the door.

Talbot ran his eye over her outlandish costume and shook his head. "And here, I've heard ye've become an old maid in your choice of clothing. First time I've seen an old maid wearing orange."

Sham batted her eyelashes at him and cooed, "Oh, but sir, a woman never likes to be predictable."

Talbot laughed, stepping in the room at her motion of invitation. "And where have ye stowed the lad, eh? Under the bed?"

"Actually we were taking advantage of the more comfortable furnishings in Kerim's rooms."

Talbot's eyebrows climbed. "If a man weren't to know

better, I'd say ye were sleeping with him the way you make so free of his rooms.''

Sham flashed the Reeve's Mistress's most enigmatic smile at him without answering the real question in his eyes. Elsic ducked under the tapestry and negotiated the room as if he'd been in it a hundred times rather than one.

"Through with business, Master Talbot?" he asked.

"For the nonce, lad." Talbot turned back to Shamera. "There's enough evidence of the story the old mage told ye to warrant a closer look, though I haven't found anything interesting yet. I have a few meetings tomorrow as well, I don't dare leave Elsic to my lassies—they'll eat him alive."

"By all means bring him here. All I'm doing now is reading. Given my material, it's good to have another person here so I don't scare myself silly," she invited truthfully.

Talbot laughed. "Right. Now if I don't get us home soon, the missus will have thrown the last of supper to the neighbor's dog. Come along, Elsic."

Talbot tucked Elsic's hand in the crook of his arm and took his leave. Before she shut the door Sham heard Talbot say in a fatherly voice, "Now the missus said she had a nice fat duck to roast. Ye'll want to avoid the gravy if ye can, but ye'll not find better stuffing in all of . . .''

THE OUTSIDE AIR WAS CRISP AND FRESH SO SHAM PULLED her hood lower over her face. The stablemen had seen her in both her guises so she hoped the hooded cloak, aided by the darkness of late evening, would allow her to look like a lady meeting her lover in secret. She'd received the Whisperer's message on her dinner tray, but because it had taken her time to get out of the house unseen she wasn't certain the messenger would still be waiting.

"Ah, such fair countenance should never be hidden away like lost treasure." The Shark's voice rumbled out of the darkness of the hay barn.

Sham dodged into the shadows where the Shark waited and watched the stableyard warily until she was sure no one was taking undue notice of her actions before snapping impatiently, "Leave off with the manure; the stable has more than enough as it is. Why didn't you just send another letter?"

He sank into a stack of hay and pulled a strand loose to chew on. "I thought I'd better check on you and see that you don't grow too attached to your feathers—" he nodded at her clothes, "—and forget you are not a peacock, but a fox."

Sham folded her arms and frowned at him. "What do you have for me, Sir Fox?"

"Halvok studied magic under Cauldehel of Reth for twelve years. I don't know why that little fact escaped all the other times I've asked for information on him, but I got this one from Halvok's half-sister myself."

Sham raised her brows. "You've been masquerading as nobility again? That's a hanging offense."

The Shark gave her one of his dangerous smiles. "Ah, but I have some influence with the Reeve. I happen to be very close friends with his mistress."

"And who was cautioning me a moment ago to remember that the Reeve really doesn't have a mistress?" asked Sham with a grin.

"Guilty," he replied with a flourishing bow. "I also asked around about the story of the Castle's demon. It seems that there is indeed such a tale, though nothing I heard connects it with the name Chen Laut. I've gotten two or three versions of the story, but most of the particulars fit with the wizard's account."

Sham nodded. "Good. Talbot's been looking through the old records. It looks like there's enough information to confirm the story Halvok told us."

The Shark spat the hay strand on the ground. "The third bit of interest that I picked up might be the reason the demon attacked the Old Man. It seems Maur had a run-in with a demon before he became the King's Sorcerer. He'd been called to help a village, where a series of odd murders took place. He discovered a demon, hiding among a group of players who had stopped to winter at the village. He was able to drive it away, but couldn't destroy it."

"The Chen Laut?" she asked.

"My source didn't know. If it was, Maur might have been able to identify it."

"The old man was blind," Sham reminded him.

"If he knew what the demon's human form looked like, he could have described him well enough to identify who it is. It would explain why the demon attacked him."

"I can feel this pattern coming together," she said ruefully, "but I feel as if I am looking at the whole picture from the wrong side."

"I hope you find that demon before it can kill again. I have a feeling that you're not high on its list of favorite people."

Sham laughed, "I've had that thought several times lately. I'll be careful."

The Shark snorted, "And *I'll* be a fisherman. Just be smarter than it is."

WITH ELSIC'S MUSIC IN HER EARS, SHAM READ THE SPELL to return the demon to its origins for the fifth time. Somewhere beneath the neatly laid out recipe was a philosophy that dictated it. There seemed to be some special significance to the death of the sacrifice beyond the power of death magic.

As she read the spell again, goosebumps crawled up her arms. She ignored it at first, as a natural reaction to the nature of the spell she was exploring. Only gradually did she realize that her nerves were tingling from very real presence of magic. She looked up from her book and noticed Elsic wasn't in the room with her. His music was coming from her room—and it wasn't a harp he was playing.

A chill crept up her spine as she heard the clear tones of Maur's flute. She must have left the trunk unlocked again . . . it wasn't like her to forget to lock her trunk. Yet at least on two occasions and now apparently a third, she'd done just that. Plaguing flute . . .

She tucked her book under her arm and ducked under the tapestry. In her room the magic was so thick, she felt she might choke on it. She'd known the flute had a nasty habit of calling to someone who could use it. With his magic and musical ability, Elsic would have been especially sensitive to its call.

He played the flute softly, perched on the edge of her bed with a dreamy expression on his face, so absorbed by the music, that Sham thought he probably had no idea of the mounting storm of magic. On the principle that it was dangerous to interrupt someone working magic, Sham sat on the bed next to Elsic, with the intention of breaking his focus on the music slowly.

Unfortunately, he stopped playing immediately.

"I'm sorry . . ." He didn't get the chance to finish before the gathering magic broke free of the fetters of the flute's music and began to shape itself to fire—as all wild magic did. Smoke curled up from the bottom of the tapestry and little flames flickered here and there on the carpets, the upholstery, and anything else marginally flammable.

Instinctively Sham reached for control before her reason told her there was no chance she could work green magic. She started to pull back and look for another way to undo the damage the magic was causing before the smoke in the room became dangerous when two things occurred to her.

The first was that it was only human magic that tended to turn to fire when loosed unshaped; by its very nature, green magic was already shaped before it was called. The second was that when she'd reached for control of the magic, it had responded to her. She didn't waste time wondering why Elsic had called human magic with the flute. The smoke burning acridly in her lungs was reminder enough of the lack of time.

She sought control again. It was difficult to contain magic she hadn't summoned—Elsic was not her bound apprentice—and this was more power than she'd ever used at one time. As she wrestled with it, she was peripherally aware that flames leapt from the bedclothes sparked by the magic escaping her hold.

It struck her that it might be easier to channel the magic into a spell, rather than try to contain it. Deciding a fire in the fireplace was as likely a candidate for dispersing it as any, she fed the magic into the logs that were prepared for lighting.

This time her effort was much more successful. The wood burst into flame and erupted into glorious fury, burning to ash in an instant. She used the last touch of magic to dispel the random fires and the smoke. In a moment it was quiet in the room—though a good deal warmer than it had been.

"What happened?" asked Elsic in a subdued voice.

Sham laughed a bit shakily. "That is a very good question. The flute is a device designed to allow a magician to gather magic easier and faster than he normally could. Apparently it works for green magic as well as human—but the magic it gathers is still the raw stuff human mages like me use. Human magic disperses itself in flame if the person who draws it can't control it."

"I suppose that means I shouldn't play it." The regret in his voice was reflected in his face.

"I suppose not," she agreed firmly, tucking the flute back inside the trunk and keying the lock-spell into place. The next Spirit Tide she was going to put the stupid flute in the caves where it wouldn't be a problem—she hoped.

RUBBING HER EYES TIREDLY, SHAM SPELLED THE BOOK closed. Talbot had collected Elsic and left several hours ago. Sometime after that Dickon had brought her dinner with a message from the Reeve. Kerim would stop by after he was through with his meetings, but it would be very late.

Sham was contemplating trying for some sleep when someone knocked gently on her door. It was the outer door so it probably wasn't Kerim, and the knock was too soft for Dickon.

"Who is it?" she called, in the heavily accented Cybellian the Reeve's mistress affected.

"A message for you, Lady," replied an unfamiliar male voice.

She hesitated, then opened her trunk and set the book

inside. With the trunk carefully relocked, she fluttered, "A moment . . ."

Briefly, she checked her appearance in the mirror. Satisfied that she looked as she should, Sham opened the door.

The man who stood outside the door wore the colors of a Castle servant. In his gloved hands he held a small wooden box that he extended to her. A gift then, she thought, like the others left for her in attempts to curry favor.

She took the box and examined it, as any greedy woman would. The dark wood was covered with a multitude of carved birds, no two alike. She wondered briefly if this was the gift, but as she turned it something rattled in the box.

"You may go now," she commanded haughtily, deciding she didn't need an audience.

"I am sorry, Lady, but I was told to wait until you had opened the box."

Shrugging, Sham worked the small catch. Nestled in black cloth was a polished star-ruby set in a gold ring. Her experienced eye calculated how much such a ring was worth: more than the small treasure of gold coins in her sea cave. The man who sent was either a fool or he had a specific favor in mind. There was no note in the box.

"Who sent this?" she asked.

"It was sent in confidence, Lady. I am to see that the gift fits before returning."

Sham frowned at him, but it was one of Kerim's mistress's frowns: lightweight and frivolous. She didn't really expect that it would affect a servant used to dealing with Lady Tirra. Deciding it was the easiest way to get rid of the man, she slipped the ring in place.

The sleep-spell took effect so fast she didn't have time to berate herself for stupidity. Her frantic attempt to counter the spell ended stillborn.

IMPASSIVELY THE SERVANT CAUGHT THE WOMAN BEFORE she fell and threw her over his shoulder. He stepped inside her room and shut the door, throwing the bolt. He set the Reeve's mistress temporarily on her bed while he pulled off the servant's tunic and trousers. Under these he wore a plain brown shirt and loose, dark pants.

Hefting the woman over his shoulder again, he worked the panel opening near the fireplace and stepped into the passage.

THIRTEEN

Fykall sighed with more weariness than the end of the day required. He was finding himself more and more discontent in his position as the High Priest's assistant. Even the euphoria of outmaneuvering the Reeve at Lord Ven's funeral had not lasted long.

As a boy he had heard the call of Altis, serving Him faithfully with all the strength in his wiry little peasant's body. Through the years his devotion had paid off, and the little priest had risen quickly through the ranks of Altis's servants. Once, and he remembered the occasion as the most inspiring of his life, he had been allowed to kiss the Voice of Altis's hand. The prophet had smiled at him, spoke briefly of Fykall's service, and sent him to Landsend.

The little man sighed again. Moving the temple cat that had made his rooms its personal domain from the prayer stool, Fykall knelt and bowed his head.

He had come to Landsend with such high hopes—not just because the Voice had sent him here personally. Back in Cybelle, the priests used to tell stories about the Leopard and the miracles he performed in the name of Altis. He'd been prepared to be awed by a legend and had met, instead, a man—one who displayed very little liking for the temple priests. Although, thought Fykall, dealing with Brath for a decade might give anyone a distaste for the priesthood. Even so, sometimes the little priest wondered if Kerim worshiped Altis at all.

If the Leopard was a disappointment, the High Priest was a tribulation of a different magnitude. How could a man of his position in the church lose the light of Altis's guidance? The High Priest was greedy for wealth and glory—less concerned about the spirit of the temple than he was the gold in the door of his office.

Fykall closed his eyes, uttering a prayer that was so familiar to his tongue that he didn't have to think about it. "Blessed One, grant me the understanding of thy wisdom and the patience to wait for the outcome of thy desire. I thank thee for thy understanding of my imperfections. Amen."

A warm tingle swept through him, and he knew that if he opened his eyes he would see the glow of Altis' marks upon his hands. But he waited, listening as he'd been taught. Only when the tingle of power had left completely did he open his eyes.

He rose to his feet with a sigh and straightened his white robes fussily until they hung in perfect folds to the midpoint of his calf. Tightening his green belt, he stepped away from the small altar, reaching for the glass of orange juice he habitually drank before sleeping.

Fykall, clean my house.

Shaken, the little priest fell to his knees, not noticing the pain of falling to the hard floor. He hadn't heard Altis' voice since his conversion as a boy, but the deep rumble was just as he remembered. It took a moment for the awe he felt to allow him the meaning of the words.

Clean house? How could this be? Certainly his current assignment seemed to point to Fykall's loss of favor in the eyes of his god, but never would he have thought he would face such a rebuke. The temple servants did the cleaning, leaving the priests to more important labor.

Fykall, clean my house.

Fykall left his room. If he slept first, he was afraid his determination would fail in the night. Perhaps Altis had found the kernel of pride in his heart that had grown as his duties had risen from the mundane. If Altis would have him sweep floors, he would find a broom and begin.

After a moment's thought, he decided the most likely place to find such an instrument was near the kitchens, currently located on the other side of the temple. With his head meekly bowed to the will of his god, the priest took a torch off the wall and began traversing the long, dark corridors.

He took a shortcut through the sanctuary, where workmen had left off for the day. The marble tiles sat in neat piles, and Fykall, momentarily distracted from his mission, noticed with some satisfaction that work was progressing rapidly here.

The flickering torchlight caught a rough broom leaning against the far wall of the sanctuary near one of the doors. Fykall crossed the dark room and picked up the disreputable object doubtfully. The straw end was white and clogged with an accumulation of grout from the tile, and he beat it against the wall in an attempt to dislodge the powdery substance.

Looking at the resultant mess in dismay, Fykall became aware of an unusual amount of noise in the hall bordering the sanctuary. Moved to secrecy by some primal instinct, he snuffed the torch on the floor where the tile was not yet laid. Broom in hand, he walked quietly to the doorway and looked down the long hall that was dimly lit by several torches in wall sconces.

From his position Fykall could see the entrance to the eating chamber where two men stood: members of the High Priest's personal guards in their blue-belted grey robes. The guardsmen were well-trained mercenaries, paid from the High Priest's own pocket because they were an affectation of the Priest rather than a necessity of his office.

Fykall frowned at their presence. He had heard of no official meeting that would require them here at this late hour.

Someone in the eating chamber grunted then swore, and the little priest's carefully plucked eyebrows lowered even further, partially with distaste and partially with puzzlement. The grunt sounded involuntary, as if someone had been hit in the stomach.

Clean my house.

Fykall waited for the guards to look up at the sound of the voice that rang through him. If they turned in his direction, they would see him, but they stared straight ahead. He took a firmer grip on his broom.

The sound of unhurried footsteps came from the far end of the hall, the same way Fykall would have come had he not impulsively taken a shorter way through the construction area. Somehow he was not surprised that the footsteps belonged to the High Priest. The older man's hawklike visage was composed in peaceful pleasantness, one of the expressions he habitually used to impress the masses with his wisdom and faithfulness.

As Fykall watched the High Priest, something changed. For a moment he felt dizzy, and another picture superimposed itself over the High Priest's features when he stopped to speak with the guard. Fykall blinked, and the vision gradually faded, but he retained the feeling of wrongness, of evil that shadowed the representative of Altis in Southwood.

Fykall, clean my house.

Though the voice had not lost its power, it had lost some of its urgency, and Fykall knew what his task was.

"Did you get her?" asked the High Priest.

One of the guards nodded. "She was alone as you said she would be, lord. She awaits you as you'd ordered."

"Excellently well done. You may go, and take your men with you." As he spoke, the High Priest walked past the guard and entered the eating chamber.

"Yes, lord," the guard bowed briefly and summoned his men with a short whistle.

Fykall could have tripped the nearest man as they walked down the hall to the unfinished public access, but none of them noticed him in the sanctuary doorway. Altis, it seemed, had other battles for him to fight this night.

As soon as the guards turned the first corner, Fykall walked boldly into the hall.

SHAM TWISTED AND THRUST, MANAGING TO LAND HER bound feet into one man's stomach with satisfying force before the men were able to attach her to the sturdy chair with their ropes. She wasn't sure where she was, having awakened from the sleep spell slung over a hard shoulder and in the middle of an unfamiliar hall.

The bonds that she wore were made of something that swallowed magic. Struggle as she might, she could find no way of working around them. She took in a deep breath, her body shaking with the force of her fury. A sharp whistle from the hallway drew the guards away as the High Priest entered.

Lord Brath surveyed her with satisfaction. "Ah, an unbeliever, practitioner of evil."

Sham glared at him, unable to make the reply she wished because of the gag she wore. The best she could manage was a muffled growl.

The High Priest walked back and forth rubbing his hands together lightly. "I had thought to do that, to have you burned as a dangerous heretic who has bewitched our Reeve, but I have decided not to make a martyr of you."

He turned and faced her. Her eyes widened in horror at what he allowed her to see in his face. She had no doubt that the demon revealed its golem to her deliberately because as soon as it was certain she'd recognized its nature, it became merely the High Priest. She had been wrong, she thought, when she had decided the demon would not dare enter Altis's temple. A creature who would kill Lord Brath was not afraid of Altis—somehow that wasn't reassuring.

"Instead," he said softly, "I have chosen a different fate for you. As the Reeve's mistress, it will be much easier to accomplish my goals."

"You will do nothing in the House of Altis, foul thing," announced a voice from the doorway with a touch of melodrama—not that Sham was in the mood to be critical.

She craned her neck and saw Fykall. He wore his short hair neatly combed and the folds of his linen robes were set with uncommon precision. He carried a rather dusty and battered broom in one hand. The little priest looked calmly at his superior as if he walked in on bound women every other day, something that did not enhance her opinion of Lord Brath.

The golem that wore Brath's semblance turned without haste, and frowned. "Fykall, you have overstepped yourself."

There was nothing in his voice or face to indicate that Fykall had intruded on something secret.

"How so?" inquired Fykall mildly, sweeping the broom back and forth gently on the floor.

Sham noticed that chalky pieces of mortar were breaking off the straw broom and littering the ground.

"I will speak with you later," said the High Priest, in obvious dismissal. "Now, I have business to conduct."

The broom stilled.

"Kidnapping?" queried the little man softly, sounding almost dangerous.

Sham shook her head frantically, but Fykall was looking at the being he must assume was Lord Brath. She wished she could warn Fykall what it was that he faced. She had no wish to see her little broom-wielding defender die.

"She's a heretic, Fykall," explained the High Priest reasonably. "She has been working evil in the Castle. I have reason to suspect she has had a role in the recent killings."

"Ah, but that is for a formal court to decide." As he spoke, the smaller man walked farther into the room, positioning himself between Sham and the High Priest.

Somehow she failed to feel any safer.

"I am afraid she's influenced everyone near the Reeve," expounded the High Priest. "If she hadn't tried her magics on me, I might never have noticed what she was doing. Can you imagine anyone telling the Leopard that his mistress is an evil sorceress? Or anyone going against the Reeve if he refuses to believe? Then she would be free to do her worst unhindered. It is necessary to be rid of her before she can do any more harm.''

It sounded convincing, even to Sham. She hoped that the priest listened and left the room.

''Who are you?'' question Fykall softly.

Sham stiffened in her chair.

The High Priest raised his eyebrows arrogantly. ''I am the High Priest of Southwood, little man. Appointed so by His Grace, The Voice of Altis.''

Fykall shook his head before the other finished speaking. ''No. You are not Brath.''

The High Priest's face went blank, as if all the personality the golem had stolen from the man was gone. Sham wondered if it was some choice on the part of the demon or if there was something that the priest had done.

''You have a little power, priest—I wouldn't let it fool you.'' Like its face, the golem's voice had lost the intonation that made it that of the High Priest.

The priest shook his head and Sham heard a thread of joy in his voice as he said, ''It is not *my* power.''

She speculated that he had been indulging in one of the narcotics that were traded in Purgatory like gold: taverweed maybe, since beggarsblessing didn't generally cause delusions of invulnerability.

''You do not have enough knowledge,'' commented the golem, in much the same voice it might have used to speak about the weather. Sham noticed that it was starting to look less human and more like what it was.

''It is not knowledge,'' said the little man peacefully, ''it is faith, and that I have in abundance.'' He straightened and held out his hand, palm forward. Speaking in a commanding voice that echoed in the dining hall, he said, ''You will give up the essence that you have unrightfully stolen.''

The golem jerked. Its skin blackened and cracked. Its features lost their elasticity and shape, fading into the crude facsimiles that had been formed of clay when it was made. It shrank slightly in size, looking odd in the robes of the High Priest—though certainly no less menacing for all of that.

"Know this," said the priest, without taking down his hand. "You have soiled this temple with your presence and killed Our High Priest. The High Priest had forsaken his calling long ago and so had no right to call upon the power of Altis. Your desecration of this temple, however, will not be so overlooked."

"I am not unarmed, priest," hissed the creature, crouching low and throwing its hand out in a spinning motion.

It was a spell Sham had not seen before and it hit Fykall and forced him to step back. From behind she couldn't see the effect of the spell, but the little priest swayed like a spider in the wind.

The power of the bindings lessened just a bit, but it was a sign that the demon was turning its attention to other things. She tried another spell, a simple fire spell, to burn the bindings and allow her to help. She knew, even as she cast, that there was not enough power to destroy the bonds . . . then something touched her spell and magnified it. The bindings dropped from her hands and feet in ashes.

As she rose the golem began a second spell, one she'd seen before and, almost without thought, she moved to counter it. *Tides*, she thought, the demon was powerful. It was all she could do to keep the spell from touching Fykall or her.

The priest spoke, his voice hoarse, but steady. "We take from you the power given by the death of Our High Priest."

The golem cried out and the hardened clay that formed the bulk of its body began to break and crumble: Whole sections fell off the wooden skeleton. As the chunks hit the stone floor they crumbled into yellow dust, revealing the golem's internal framework. Crudely shaped sticks were bound together by a thin, tarnished silver wire into a mockery of a human skeleton. Its head was a block of wood with a small yellow stone set where a person's left eye would have been.

Sham watched warily for some new spell, but there was none. The wood began to age, turning first grey, then white. As the fragile substance dried to splinters, the High Priest's garments floated down to the ground. The yellow gem broke free of the wooden setting and rolled across the smooth floor until it rested several paces away from the pile of cloth.

The priest rested his broom on the floor and looked at the smallish mound that had been the High Priest. Sham worked to untie the knot holding the gag in her mouth. She must have made some noise because Fykall turned to her and, seeing her trouble, proffered her an eating knife from his belt.

As she cautiously slipped the dull blade between the cloth and her cheek, the sound of a group of men moving briskly through the halls penetrated the room. Fykall moved between Sham and the door, standing with his bedraggled broom as if it were a weapon. Another time, Sham was certain she'd have found something funny in that, but after what she'd seen the priest do to the demon's golem, she wouldn't have been surprised to see Fykall eliminate an army with nothing but that broom.

Even so, Sham wasn't unhappy when Talbot burst into the room followed by the Captain of the Guard, a host of Castle guardsmen, and a rather grim-faced Dickon.

When Talbot raised a hand the Captain barked an order and the guardsmen stopped near the entrance. Talbot peered at the two of them warily. It occurred to her that Talbot had no way of knowing if the demon had killed her and replaced her with the golem or not. Since he couldn't know who the demon looked like now, Talbot must be wondering just who it was he was facing.

Fykall took a step forward, but Sham, watching Talbot's hand tighten on his sword, gripped the priest's shoulder. "Gently, Lord Fykall. These men know something of what we faced here—and have no way of knowing that we are who we appear to be."

Talbot gave her a nod of approval that in no way lessened his alertness and bowed his head quickly toward the priest.

"Why don't ye tell us how ye came to the Temple, Lady Shamera," directed Talbot finally, for he was a Southwoodsman, and Sham knew the sight of Altis' power was almost as doubtful to him as magic had been for Dickon. "—and get rid of that knife while ye talk, would ye?"

Sham grinned and threw the knife so it landed point down on one of the dining tables several yards away, remembering too late that that was a skill the Reeve's Mistress would not possess. *Ah well*, she thought, *maybe no one would remark upon it in the midst of such doings*. Most of the guardsmen, Easterners to a man, were staring uncomfortably at the High Priest's clothing on the floor.

"It was sheer stupidity," Sham admitted, shamefaced. "I've gotten used to being showered with gifts from people who want influence with the Reeve. A messenger brought a ring in a box and insisted I try it on before he left. Someone, probably the demon, spelled the ring so that anyone wearing it would fall asleep. When I awoke, I was here."

She stood and walked to the robes of the High Priest, searching until she found the star-ruby ring, displaying it briefly and tossing it to Talbot. "I wouldn't try it on. It's never smart to fool with magic you're not familiar with."

While Talbot looked at the innocent-seeming ring, Sham glanced at the yellow topaz she'd also picked up.

It was the size of a cherry pit, smallish for a topaz. The style of the stone's cut was ancient: it was carved rather than faceted. The elaborate cuts made the stone seem dull and lifeless; a pretty bauble, but worth less than an uncut stone of equal size would be to a gem dealer now. When the light fell properly on the stone, Sham could see that the carving itself was the rune that had animated the golem.

Sham tossed the topaz in the air and whispered a spell of destruction upon it. When it hit the floor it shattered into powder; that stone would never animate another golem. She looked up to see Fykall's solemn regard.

Sham turned to Talbot. "Fykall destroyed the creature that had taken over Brath, then you came in before we had a chance to catch our breath." She returned her attention to the priest. "Which reminds me that I haven't thanked you yet for your timely intervention."

The small man shook his head, "As Altis's servant, I could do no less."

She hesitated visibly, for the words stuck in her throat—but she remembered the feeling of the strength that had boosted her spell to destroy the demon's bonds. "My thanks, then, to Altis."

Fykall smiled gently. "Praised be His name."

"Would you be interested in dealing with the demon who controlled the golem's actions?" asked Sham. She'd recently discovered how useful Altis could be, as little as she liked Him.

The priest swayed slightly, as if he were listening to someone no one else heard. He smiled and shook his head. "I wish that I could, but there are other forces in this world besides Altis and they all obey certain rules. When the demon attempted to use Altis's temple for its misdeeds, it allowed Altis the freedom to destroy its servant. If Altis were to move against it elsewhere, the path would be open for an equally strong move by a force for evil. I only wish I could be of more service," then he smiled with real humor, "if only to have the Reeve further in my debt."

Sham grinned back, turning to Talbot. "Well, Talbot, I suppose you have a choice. Either one of us is the demon and the other the golem. Or it's just the priest and I."

The Captain reached under his tunic and pulled a chain over his head. At the end of the chain dangled the silver form of Altis' cat, green eyes and all.

"I'm not certain I've followed what's going on," the Captain said, "but if we need to be certain Brother Fykall is who he appears to be, this should work." He handed it to Fykall, saying, "Blessed be the name of Altis."

"Bless those who carry the symbol of His service," returned the priest.

As he spoke the cat's emerald eyes began to glow until they lit the room with a pale green light. When Fykall returned the necklace to Lirn, the glow dissipated.

"Sir," said Lirn to Talbot, "this is proof enough for me."

Talbot nodded his head, though he didn't look entirely happy.

"And for me," agreed Dickon, but he sounded almost as wary as Sham felt at proof of Altis's presence in the room. "We should get back to the Castle. My Lord was tearing the building apart looking for you in case the Captain was mistaken."

"Mistaken?" questioned Sham, looking at Lirn.

He shrugged. "I noticed one of the templemen leaving with one body more than they should have taken. I brought it to the Reeve's attention when we discovered that you were missing, Lady. Lord Kerim thought it would be most expedient to send us here while he organized a discreet search of the Castle."

"You'd best go then, before he works himself into a frenzy," said Fykall.

Sham started through the door after the men, but the priest touched her shoulder to hold her back.

"Lady Shamera, Altis asks that you be very careful not to use his altars for your vengeance. He will not be as lenient in the future as he has been in the past."

Sham nodded her head slowly. "Altis's priest, Brath, caused a friend of mine to be crippled. I exacted payment from those who helped the High Priest do that." She paused, choosing her words so they would sound suitably formal. "By your actions this day, I live. The debt is cancelled and I will not deface his altars again."

Dickon came back through the door. "Are you coming, Lady Shamera?"

She turned impulsively and kissed the priest's cheek before gathering her skirts and pacing decorously forward to take Dickon's arm.

"So THE DEMON HAS LOST ITS GOLEM?" ASKED KERIM.

Upon their arrival at the Castle, Kerim had summoned Sham, Dickon, and Talbot to the meeting room that adjoined his bedchamber for a "discussion." Sham told him what she remembered about the kidnapping. Unlike Talbot, who still gazed warily at her, Kerim had accepted the Captain's proof without question.

Sham ran her hands through her hair in frustration. "As long as that was the only golem it had, yes."

"What are the chances there are more of them?" asked Talbot.

"That golem was old; it was probably made when the demon was summoned." She shrugged. "The only topaz I've seen carved like that was in a necklace reputed to be over eight hundred years old. The demon could animate the golem, and work magic through it without risking the loss of its own body. Finding a proper host for the demon is a great deal more difficult than building golems, for the host must be mage-born. A golem such as the one the priest destroyed—" tides take her if she'd give all the credit to Altis, "—requires both power and time to create."

"So we need to find the demon quickly, before it builds another one," concluded Kerim. "The time has come for speculation. Do you have any guesses who the demon is?"

Sham rubbed her eyes tiredly. "Someone with an odd background—no acquaintances left from his childhood."

"That would be helpful, except there was a war here. There are a fair number of people whose families were killed," commented Talbot. "I, for one. My parents died in the first month of fighting and my three sisters disappeared into the streets. My brother was lost at sea when I was five or six. I can't name a single soul who knew me before I was a man."

"Shamera, can the demon change its appearance?" asked Talbot.

"I don't think so. Maur's book says the demon's host won't age after the demon has taken possession of it. If it could alter the appearance of its host, I think the book would have mentioned that too."

"Can you think of anything else that would help us find it?" questioned Kerim.

She started to shake her head when something occurred to her. "It could be a servant. No one would think to question the background of a servant. Such a person would have the run of the Castle and would not appear out of place somewhere like Purgatory or in one of the noble's residences in the city.''

''What about Lord Halvok?'' Dickon asked.

Sham shook her head. ''If the demon is under the control of a wizard then he is a possibility, but he is not the demon himself. I've just heard from the Whisper that Halvok studied for over a decade with the wizard Cauldehel of Reth. Cauldehel turned down the position of Archmage when the last ae'Magi disappeared. He's several hundred years old and very powerful. I can't imagine a demon being able to fool him for such a long time.''

''I'll begin with the servants then—after I finish going through the court records,'' said Talbot with a sigh. She didn't envy him his task. In the Castle the servants probably numbered several hundred if not a thousand.

''I'll go hide in my room and try to get some sleep,'' she said wearily.

FOURTEEN

As a result of the golem's attack, two guardsmen were stationed outside Sham's door and two more in the passage.

"It's difficult to hunt the demon when I'm confined to my room," complained Sham, sitting on a chair in the Reeve's room. "It's not like they'll be helpful against the demon anyway."

Kerim stopped his slow progress around his room, holding on to a chair for balance, but forcing his legs to bear his weight. "Everyone in the Castle knows that you were abducted, even if they don't know who took you. If I don't take *some* steps to ensure your safety, it will cause talk. Confine your investigations to the court for a while; after a week or so I'll find a reason to reassign the guards."

Sham folded her arms and tapped her foot with disapproval. "I haven't learned anything interesting from the court yet; I can't imagine that will change any time soon."

Kerim gave her a wise look. "I'll come down with you tonight. It will give you a chance to practice staring at me with possessive awe."

She laughed, letting her anger go. "Like that, do you?"

"What do you think?"

She looked for the humor in his face, but Kerim had resumed walking; the pain and concentration necessary to make his legs work again forced everything else out of his expression.

THE DRESS SHAM WORE WAS DARK WINE SILK WITH SILVER and gold embroidery—the Reeve's own colors. Though otherwise modest, it clung with unfashionable tenacity to her well-muscled form.

When she entered the Reeve's chambers, Kerim frowned at the dress in a puzzled fashion. Dickon, who was behind her, laughed—it sounded rusty, but it was a laugh. Sham smiled and turned her back to the Reeve. With her hair up, the delicately embroidered leopard that covered the back of the dress was clearly visible. It was a dress that might have been suitable for a wife, but worn by a mistress it was a blatant flaunting of her power—as long as Kerim would stop chortling before they entered the court.

"Several of my counsellors have been suggesting I have let you gain too much influence over my judgments. I can't wait to see their faces when they see your dress."

Sham let her eyes go vacant and smiled, letting her Southwood accent grow thick, "You like this dress? I like big cats, they're so fierce and splendid, don't you agree?"

"I would never think to argue with you, my dear," snickered the Reeve, pushing his chair through the door Dickon opened.

THE DRESS DREW GRATIFYING FROWNS OF DISAPPROVAL from the more conservative Eastern Lords, thoughtful looks from several women, and speculative smiles from the Southwood delegation—including Halvok. Sham spent her evening straightening imaginary wrinkles from Kerim's tunic and stroking various parts of his anatomy, much to Kerim's amusement.

Late in the evening Lady Tirra approached with Sky in tow. Kerim's mother greeted Sham without her usual venom. To Sham's delight, that caused more of a stir among the gossips than the dress had; even Sky looked somewhat puzzled.

After greeting his mother, Kerim turned to Sky. "You are looking beautiful today."

She smiled graciously, and stepped nearer to the Reeve, dropping to her knees before him. It was an archaic gesture that had been used by Southwood nobles petitioning the king—Lady Sky imbued it with stately grace. The court grew quieter as the nearest people saw her position.

Sham saw a flush rise to Kerim's already dark skin as he said, "Do get up, Lady Sky. There is no need for that."

Obediently, she rose to her feet and looked into the Reeve's face with serious intent. When she spoke, the room was so quiet her words were clearly audible to most of the straining ears. "I wish to thank you, Lord Kerim, for the help you gave me two nights past. I owe you more than I can say."

Kerim shifted uncomfortably. "You made Fahill very happy in his last days, Lady Sky—and my brother as well. You owe me nothing."

Sky smiled and shook her head, her body fairly vibrating with the strength of her intensity. "I owe you everything."

Sham hoped the surge of jealously that tightened her fingers on the back of the Reeve's chair didn't show. Not because such a response was not appropriate for the Reeve's mistress, but because it was something she preferred to keep private. She knew, looking at Sky, that the Southwood lady loved Kerim. She also knew that Sky was a much fitter mate for the Reeve than a thief from Purgatory could ever be.

FOR THE NEXT SEVERAL DAYS, SHAM EXCUSED HERSELF from court, telling Kerim that she was trying to discover how to destroy the demon. She even managed to avoid the High Priest's funeral.

No longer plagued by ill health, though he still used his chair in public, Kerim haunted the court, hoping to drum up support among the Eastern nobles for a series of proposed laws. He told her it was doomed for failure, but it might scare the Easterners into softening their positions on several other hard-fought political battles.

Lady Sky had been glued to his side, at the funeral and at court—both the Whisper and Halvok had seen to it that Sham was aware of it. Halvok had taken it upon himself to scold her for her lack of effort.

She'd continued the pretense of being Kerim's mistress in front of Halvok, for that was the main reason he'd decided to help them. He liked Kerim. At the same time, he hated the Easterners with a fervor that the Shark would be hard-pressed to equal, for all that the wizard hid the hatred very well. Sham's position gave him a way of reconciling both feelings.

"Why do you disapprove?" Sham had asked. "She's just what you need—and she's qualified to be his wife. I'm just a thief who can work a little magic—and if that were well known he'd catch fish bait for putting me in the position of mistress."

Halvok had shaken his head and said, "Lady Sky is a gracious and beautiful lady—which is precisely the problem. She would no more dirty her hands with politics than any other Southwood lady I know. You, on the other hand, would go toe to toe with Altis if you wanted something—and you know what life in Southwood is like for her natives. Kerim cares this much—" he snapped his fingers, "—for what the court says about his private life, and I've seen how he looks at you."

Sham had laughed at him—but her humor left a sour tinge in her mouth. "He's become a good actor. Kerim knows what I am better than you do—I am a thief, Lord Halvok, and have been for half my life. I have very little in common with the daughter of the Captain of the Guards I was before the invasion, and even she would never have aspired as high as the ruler of Southwood. I think you might have underestimated Lady Sky—and you could make her life at court much more bearable than it is."

All he had done was raise his eyebrows and say, "Daughter of the Captain of the Guards—I thought he was nobleborn'' in such a speculative fashion that she shooed him out of her room in exasperation.

SHAM PORED OVER MAUR'S BOOK, TRYING TO FIND ANY-thing of use against the demon. Lord Halvok had been correct, the only spell it contained for permanently getting rid of a demon required a human sacrifice. Without that, she couldn't conceive of a way to produce the power necessary for such a spell.

Talbot, true to his word, was interrogating all the servants in the Castle, ostensibly to find a necklace conveniently missing from Lady Tirra's jewel box. He left Elsic with Sham most of the time.

Whenever Dickon had a spare moment from the Reeve's service he would join them, and Sham began teaching him the basics of magic. She'd spent the better part of the morning trying to show Dickon how to form a magelight. It was a simple spell; Sham could feel the power simmering beneath the man's frowning face, but he couldn't use it.

"You think about it too much," said Sham, exasperated.

"Sorry," he muttered, wiping his forehead.

"Lady Shamera," said Elsic, feathering several cords lightly on the strings of the old harp.

"Hmm?"

"Why were demons taken from where they belonged? What was their purpose?"

She sat back in her chair. "It was an attempt to gain more power, I think. There are stories of demons telling their wizard masters the secrets of various spells and runes—though a man who would take the word of a slave on how to modify a spell deserves the death that he doubtless received. More importantly, the demon could act as a reservoir of power—like the flute you found in the trunk, but safer for the mage. The wizard would send it out to kill and . . ." she hesitated, because he looked so young and innocent, sitting on the end of her bed with the harp nestled in his lap, ". . . do other things that would generate power for the mage to use."

"What other ways?" asked Dickon.

"Sex," answered the young innocent on the bed with a smirk.

"I'm going back to work," Sham muttered, snatching the book from the seat beside her and opening it with a snap that didn't do the ancient binding any good. Elsic launched, pointedly, Sham thought, into a child's ditty, while Dickon began to try again to form light from magic.

It wasn't opened to the section on demonology, but she began reading anyway. The author was expounding on the difference between male and female wizards. Sham tended to think it was nonsense—*she'd* never noticed her powers changing with moon and tide, but she *had* noticed that most such treatises were written by men.

. . . A woman's power is bound to her body more strongly than a man's. Use of strong magics may affect her adversely—so it is better that a woman attend to womanly magics and leave the great spells for her male counterparts . . . There are times when a woman's magic is very strong. When she is breeding her power grows with the child she carries—and childbirth, like death, allows her to perform magics that are far above her normal capabilities.

Sham felt her lip lift in a sneer. "Leave the great spells for her male counterparts" indeed. By the cute little fishes in the tide pools, she'd never heard such nonsense. She threw down the book in disgust and picked up the other one Halvok had given her. She hadn't opened it yet, having concentrated on demonology, so she began with the first page.

Runes fascinated her, being beautiful and functional at the same time. The wizard who had drawn the patternbook had a fine hand, making it easy to picture the runes as they would look put together. Runes drawn for patternbooks were divided in bits and pieces, deliberately kept powerless—otherwise such a book would not be possible. Sham took her time, admiring the precision of each line with the appreciation of having tried to use patterns set less carefully.

Her stomach rumbled, warning of passing time; but she turned one more page—and there it was. The rune that had been marked on Kerim's back. She scanned the page behind it. Bonding magic, yes, she'd known that. Set to draw from the one so bound and give strength to the rune maker. Right, she knew that too—or had a good idea that was its purpose. Then she stopped, with her finger marking the page.

. . . can only be set by invitation of the one bound— although that consent need not be explicit and may take the form of strong friendship, physical intimacy, or emotional indebtedness. Thus the maker can brand his loved ones, servants, or bedpartners with this rune without their knowledge.

Sham rubbed her nose and stopped reading. The demon was someone Kerim was close to; or someone who, at the time the rune was set, had the appearance of such a person. Certainly, from what she'd read, the demon could have used its golem body to place the runes.

Fahill, she remembered, was a close friend. He had died about the time Kerim had fallen ill. Could Fahill have died earlier and the golem have taken his place? Or was it someone else?

What she needed to do before anything else was to question Kerim about what had happened at Fahill keep. It wasn't a task she relished, but it might narrow down the suspects, bringing her closer to the time when she could leave the Castle. Leave him.

It would be best for her if they found the demon soon, then she could go back to Purgatory—or maybe travel a bit.

She stared at the book for several more minutes, before getting restlessly to her feet. Elsic looked up from coaxing harmonic chords from the strings of the harp, but turned his attention back to his music when she didn't say anything. Dickon was concentrating so hard on the small flicker of light he held in his hand that it would have taken much more than the sound of her movement to distract him.

"I'm going to see if I can coax something from the kitchens. Stay here with Dickon and I'll be right back," said Sham. She wanted to talk with Kerim before she discussed her discovery with anyone else.

Elsic smiled and continued playing; Dickon nodded, staring at the lambent spark of magic he held.

Sham went to the door that had replaced the tapestry only the day before. She didn't expect him to be there—these days he was out more than in—but she didn't want to wander the halls with the two guards who were on duty at her hall door.

The newly hung door opened without a sound and Sham shut it behind her. She took a step toward the outer door when the creak of leather drew her attention to the bed.

The first thing she noticed was Kerim's empty chair. She felt an instant of puzzlement before she realized that Kerim was in the bed . . . and he was not alone. If she were not mistaken, the slim, silk-clad back rising out of the bedclothes over Kerim belonged to Lady Sky.

It hurt more than she had thought it would. Sham drew in a deep soundless breath. *Grace*, she cautioned herself as her mother had taught. When life doesn't meet your expectations, it was important to take it with grace. Her father had said the same, but in a different way: lick your wounds in private so your enemies don't see where you are vulnerable.

If only, she thought, stepping silently back to her door; *if only Sky weren't so beautiful, weren't her friend*. It made it harder because Sham understood what Kerim saw in Sky.

She turned to leave them alone, when a short phrase made her catch her breath. "Physical intimacy," the book had read. She hesitated, wondering if her jealousy had affected her thoughts. Lady Sky the demon?

Quickly she found objections to her speculation. Demon hosts were bound with a death rune that could not be removed—killing any offspring of the host body before they develop, and Sky had been pregnant twice in the past two years.

How would a demon counteract a death rune?

—by shielding the child with life-magic. It would require a tremendous amount of power, though the spell itself was not complex. Sky had miscarried after Sham freed Kerim from the demon's rune, a rune that had drawn life from Kerim.

The ease with which she found the answer shocked Sham into looking for reasons why Sky could be the demon rather than why she couldn't.

Sky had been near Kerim when Fahill died. From the expressions she'd caught on Kerim's face, Sham thought that it was possible that there had been some sort of intimacy between them. She was everything a male wizard would want in a demon host, who would be used as a sex partner to raise magic; beautiful, likable and . . . in Kerim's bed. Sham could work out the details later.

She turned to the connecting door, opened it soundlessly, and then slammed it so hard the shiny new hinges protested—the gods knew what Elsic and Dickon would think of that—as if she were entering the room for the first time.

Sham drew in a loud breath, as if in outrage, then shrieked wildly as she ran toward the bed. She was wryly amused that she didn't have to feign her fury. As the noise echoed through the stone walls of the room with almost musical effect, Sky jerked around, revealing the loosened ties of her bodice.

From Lady Sky's relatively decent state, Sham hoped that they had not had time to complete their union. She thanked the powers that they hadn't been alone long, although the dazed look in Kerim's eyes filled her with foreboding. He hadn't even looked away from Sky. All her doubts vanished—he was not a lover, startled by an unwanted interruption, but a man held in thrall by enchantment.

"Slut!" Sham screamed, full into her Lady Shamera role.

She grabbed the ewer of fresh, cold water from where it

sat in lone splendor on a small table conveniently near the
Reeve's bed. Gripping the top with one hand and the bottom by the other, she upended the ewer over the bed,
mostly on Kerim's face, before launching herself to the
waist-high surface.

She balanced on the edge of the bed with the empty
porcelain vessel in her hand. To her relief Kerim sat up
slowly and shook the water from his hair, the dullness of
ensorcellment fading from his eyes. Lady Sky's lips twisted
with rage.

Sham knew she looked like a madwoman, but that was
the effect she wanted. She needed to act like a scorned
woman who had found another in her man's bed—not like
a terrified wizard who had found a demon there instead.
Since she was both, she set terror aside with the hope that
the demon wouldn't want to expose itself.

She hadn't had time for a real plan, but the ewer made
a convenient weapon and she smashed it into one of the
upright posts of the bed. The broken porcelain wasn't sharp
enough to be very effective, but the jagged edge would
certainly tear into soft white skin and leave scars. To a
demon who depended on her beauty to attract her victims,
that might be as effective as a dagger.

Sham launched herself at Lady Sky—who avoided her
by rolling off the bed with a speed that the thief envied.
Sham gathered her feet underneath her and jumped for Sky
again, only to be brought up short by a firm grip on her
free arm.

"Shamera . . ." Kerim's voice was slightly slurred, and
he sounded puzzled.

"Whore!" shrieked Sham, tugging against Kerim's grip
and waving the broken ewer wildly in the air. Lady Sky
took a step back. Sham felt the first touch of relief when
the intent expression on Lady Sky's face was replaced with
a look of fear that Sham was certain the demon did not
feel. What demon would fear a lunatic waving bits of pot-
tery?

"Witch," accused Lady Sky, looking appealingly at
Kerim. "She's cast a spell over you Kerim, everyone

knows it. They're saying that she's controlling you, and you can't see it.''

"Shameless bitch," replied Sham venomously. "I'll see your bones if I catch you in his bed again! Can't you find your own man?'' In contrast to the other woman's ladylike tones, Shamera could have won a shrilling contest with the Purgatory flesh-mongers.

"Go, Sky," said Kerim unexpectedly. "I'll deal with this, but you had better leave for now.''

Lady Sky raised her chin, turned on her heel, and left, shutting the door behind her. Quietly. Sham held her pose for an instant more, before dropping the remains of the ewer to the floor and running a shaking hand over her face.

"You can let go now," she informed Kerim.

He hesitated, but when she didn't make any sudden moves when he loosened his grip, he released her completely.

"What was that all about?'' he asked, his voice still groggy.

Sham spoke without looking at him, "I think I've found the demon.'' She hadn't planned to tell him until she had more facts behind her—or at least had her reasoning straightened well enough that someone else could follow it.

He didn't react at all for a moment, just gathered the bedclothes and used them to wipe the water from his face. "I feel as if I was at the long end of a night of drinking myself under the table. Wait a moment and let me collect my thoughts.''

After a bit, he looked up at Sham, who was still standing on the corner of the bed. "Urgent news or not, I have to thank you for stopping me from doing a very stupid thing. Sky isn't over Fahill's death yet—let alone Ven's. What she doesn't need is to get involved with someone else.''

He shook his head dazedly. "Blessed if I know how I ended up here—last thing I remember clearly is eating in Mother's rooms with her and Lady Sky. Must have had too much to drink, though I haven't done anything like that in years.''

Sham pursed her lips, "It wasn't alcohol, Kerim, it was magic."

He frowned at her. "Like that philter you threatened to feed to my guard?"

"Maybe. Kerim, I don't remember if you ever told me—how did Lady Sky's husband die?"

"The wasting sickness."

Sham held on to one of the tall bedposts as Kerim's shifting weight made the mattress sway beneath her. Her thoughts raced ahead, putting the pieces together. "Tell me, Kerim, could the child that she just miscarried have been yours?"

His face froze, but, after a moment, he nodded. "The night Fahill died, his lady and I sat up far into the night drinking and talking. She was additionally distraught as she'd miscarried only two months earlier. When I awoke, I was in her bed. I don't remember much about that night—but when she came here pregnant, I wondered."

"It was on the way back from Fahill's funeral that your horse stumbled, wrenching your back?"

"Yes," answered Kerim.

"Lady Sky miscarried shortly after I broke the demon's hold on you," said Sham.

"Wait," he said holding up a hand. "You're telling me that Lady Sky is the demon."

She nodded.

He closed his eyes and considered the matter, which was a better reaction that she had thought she'd receive. When he finally opened them, he looked at her perched warily on the corner of his bed and waved impatiently.

"Sit down, you're making me dizzy."

Sham complied, sitting cross-legged—leaving a little distance between the two of them. After she was seated, Kerim said, "I hate to admit it, but she's as likely a candidate as any. Part of me wants to claim that a woman is not capable of such things, but I fought against women in the mercenary troops at Sianim as well as the women warriors at Jetaine—we never managed more than a stand-off with either one."

Sham grinned briefly. "I must admit, if Sky had been a

man, I would have looked at her a lot more closely."

"What makes you so certain now?" he asked.

Sham finger-combed her hair. "It wasn't until I walked in on you that I even considered the possibility. I had come in to talk to you about something I'd just been reading in a . . ." She lost track of what she was saying as a few more pieces fell into place, allowing her to recognize just what the demon was trying to accomplish.

"Book?" suggested Kerim after a moment.

"Books, actually. I've been reading the two that Lord Halvok gave me. I came in here looking for you because I discovered something that indicated that the demon was someone you trusted," she said. "When I saw Sky here, all the pieces fit."

She rubbed her hand across a damp spot on the bedding. "You know that demons are summoned here from someplace else—called by a mage and forced into bondage. They are made slaves to their master's whims. If the master dies, so too does the demon—unless it manages to kill the wizard itself, which is what our demon managed to do. If you were the demon, what would you want?"

"Vengeance?"

Sham shook her head and looked at the bedding. She was tired: too many emotions, too much thinking. "I was once torn from my home, thrown into a strange and dangerous place. I *know* how she feels. I wanted vengeance, yes, but what I desired more than anything was to go home."

He covered her hand with his.

She looked at him then, and gave him a small smile. "I could be wrong, but listen and decide for yourself. I thought at first that the only way for the demon to return to its own world would be to find a black mage who could send it back—but the demon would have to make itself vulnerable to the wizard. It would be easier for the wizard to enslave the demon than send it back. Black wizards, by their very nature, are not honorable; if I were the demon I would be hesitant to trust one with my freedom."

"Wait," Kerim broke in. "This demon is working

magic. Is there a reason that it can't send itself back?''

Sham nodded. ''Black magic is not as easy to control as normal magic because it is stolen by the mage who is using it. To get home, the demon has to open the gate to its world and enter through it. It cannot hold the gate while inside, not with black magic.''

''But you think it has found a way?''

''Yes,'' she said.

''But it can't use black magic to do it.''

''Not black magic alone,'' agreed Sham. ''But there is another magic the demon could use. There is magic involved in death and life.''

''This has something to do with Sky's pregnancies?'' asked Kerim, following what she said far more closely than she'd expected.

''The magic released at a birthing is close to death magic in power, but it is bound to the woman giving birth—a situation encountered by mageborn women only a certain number of times. So it is not really considered a counter to death magic, which is much easier to effect.'' She had known about that magic before, but the old text from Maur's book had reminded her of it. Not pregnancy but birth generated power.

''If the demon uses childbirth to return home, what would happen to the child?''

Sham met his eyes squarely. ''Not being the demon, I don't know. But if she kills it and the man who fathered it, she would have much more power than by killing people who are not tied to her.''

Kerim took a deep breath. ''I seem to remember you saying that demons could not become pregnant.''

She nodded. ''A particularly nasty warding spell was used to prevent the host body from conceiving. Like most warding spells, it conserved energy by remaining passive until its activation conditions are met—in this case the onset of pregnancy. When triggered, the spell begins to extinguish the life-force of the unborn child: death magic.''

''But didn't you say that most spells can only be active for a few weeks without power? Has the power of this spell faded over the hundreds of years the demon has lived?''

"No, that's why this so nasty. It's usually reinforced and maintained by life-energies of the demon. However, to avoid draining the host body, when triggered the spell drains life energy from the unborn child.''

"So Sky can't be the demon?'' He raised his eyebrows.

"Not so,'' Sham replied. "The demon could form a barrier between the child and the rune to protect it from harm.''

"Then why bind the demon at all?''

"Because the barrier requires enough strength that it would kill the demon's host body before the child could be born. I think that our demon discovered another way to power the spell. The rune it used was one that allowed it to drain your strength—killing you slowly as it allowed your child to live.''

"Kerim,'' she said, leaning toward him. "The rune had to have been set by someone who was close to you, intimate with you. It was set near the time of Fahill's death. I believe that it was set by Lady Sky, to protect her baby. When I broke the binding, it killed the child.''

Kerim swallowed and she could tell by his face that he believed her. He clenched his hands in the bedclothes. "Poor little waif.''

"The child was doomed anyway,'' said Sham softly. "If I'm right then it was intended to be the sacrifice she used to get home.''

She let him absorb it for a while before she continued. "That would explain why she frequents the Castle. Here she has the most choice among men who are well-nourished and healthy. But she can't stay here long or she risks detection. My master, Maur, ran into a demon hunting in a village once. The Shark believes it might have been Chen Laut, that it . . . *she* killed Maur because he knew what she looked like.''

Kerim didn't say anything, so Sham continued speaking. "Elsic said that she was closer to her goal than she had ever been. Southwood has always been a refuge for wizards and sorcerers, and the Castle has usually had the King's

Wizard. Nine months is a long time to hide from a powerful mage. She must have been excited when chance filled the Castle with Easterners who didn't believe in magic.''

"You seem to think she was trying to bind me again tonight. Since I'm already weakened, what good would that do her?" asked Kerim.

"Revenge," said Sham softly.

He watched her narrowly for a minute, then said, "What if it isn't Lady Sky? This is all speculation."

"I don't think I'm wrong," replied Sham. "But, we'll have to plan for that contingency as well."

"So what do we do with her?" asked Kerim.

Sham gave a frustrated shrug. "Damned if I know."

A soft creaking noise from the connecting door drew Sham's attention and Elsic stepped tentatively through the resulting opening. "Shamera? Is something wrong?"

Shamera felt her jaw drop as an incredible idea came to her.

While she sat stupefied, Kerim answered for her. "She's fine." He paused, looking at her thunderstruck expression, "—I think."

"Sympathetic magic," muttered Sham, staring pointedly at Elsic. "They use the death of the sacrifice as a source of power—and sympathetic patterning. The sacrifice's soul returns to its origin like the demon they are sending home."

"Shamera?" asked Kerim.

She shook her head, still muttering to herself. "It can't work, it's too absurd. The demon will never cooperate, it has no reason to believe we'd try it."

"Shamera?" asked Elsic.

"Kerim? Do you think you could extend my credit at the dressmaker's?" she asked.

"What?"

"I think I have a plan. I need to find Halvok." Muttering to herself, she stalked to the door.

FIFTEEN

When she came back from speaking with Halvok, Kerim had gathered Elsic, Dickon, and Talbot in his room.

"Lord Halvok doesn't think it will work," she reported blithely, "but he can't come up with anything better, so he said he'll help. Talbot, I'll need you to accompany me to my dressmaker's tomorrow morning, if you would."

"Of course, lassie."

"Elsic, I'll need your help as well."

"Whatever I can do," he offered, though he was obviously surprised to be of use.

"We haven't eliminated entirely the possibility that Sky isn't the demon," said Kerim slowly. "If she isn't, will she be hurt by what you're planning?"

"Not physically," she said, after a moment of thought. "If she is human the most it will do is scare her."

He considered that. "I suppose we really have no choice."

"WHY USE ME AS AN ESCORT?" ASKED TALBOT AS THEY rode through the morning traffic.

"I need you when we go into Purgatory," Sham replied, deftly avoiding a collision with an overloaded wagon.

"Purgatory?"

She grinned. "I need the Shark too."

She shifted her weight and the little mare stopped in front of the dressmaker's. Talbot followed suit, helping her off the awkward sidesaddle. Slipping a coin out of his purse, he handed the copper and the reins of both horses to one of the young boys who haunted the streets looking for odd jobs.

Sham tucked her hand under his arm and allowed him to lead her into the dressmaker's shop.

Buying the thread took her some time. The dressmaker took some convincing before she agreed to sell Sham all her gold thread. It took time to order more from the gold-smith and there were dresses on order. Only Kerim's letter that authorized his mistress's unlimited spending persuaded the dressmaker to relent.

THEY ATTRACTED A LOT OF ATTENTION AS THEY VENTURED into Purgatory. Sham had considered hiding their presence, but decided it was unlikely that Lady Sky bothered hiring spies and the furor was likely to attract the Shark's attention. She could have returned to the Castle and changed herself back into Sham the Thief—but the mottled-silver silk dress (that matched the horse with expensive perfection) might come in useful.

She knew the Shark's haunts and hoped to find him be-fore someone braved Talbot's wrath in hopes of a full purse. Sure enough, as they turned a corner the Shark was waiting in the shadow of a battered awning.

He looked pointedly at a filthy figure that had been fol-lowing Shamera and Talbot for several minutes. Noticing the attention, the skulker abruptly turned on his heel and walked in the opposite direction.

"Business slow, Sham?"

She shook her head. "Actually, I think I've become successful."

The Shark raised his brows. "Oh?"

"They're paying me not to steal. I think it was you who told me that you can tell when you have become a success in your chosen field because then people pay you not to do it."

"Welcome to success," said the Shark, making a gesture that encompassed all of Purgatory.

"I need to talk to Tallow."

The Shark shook his head. "Not unless you want to talk to a corpse. He got his throat slit five, maybe six days ago."

"Then who controls the territory by the cliffs, where the old bell tower used to stand?" she asked.

He scratched his ear and pursed his lips in obvious perplexity. Sham gave an exasperated sigh.

Talbot grinned. "He looks stupider than a codfish out of water. Think a bit of gold would help that mouthbreathing?"

"Nothing," said Sham, "would help that. But it might make him talk."

The Shark bared his white teeth. "Now, Sham, you know you love me—and business is business."

"Like I love the plague," she muttered.

The Shark laughed, effortlessly catching the gold Talbot tossed to him. He dropped the Purgatory dialect, exchanging it for that of a courtier. "A charming runt who calls himself 'Toadstool' has taken over that half of Tallow's territory. You need something from him?"

"I need to talk with him myself."

The Shark shook his head. "He eats little girls like you for breakfast."

"I grind up toadstools for my lunch," she replied. "For dinner I eat shark-steaks."

The Shark sighed, appealing to Talbot for sympathy as he drifted into a rougher dialect. "Always she does this to me. Isn't any way I'm goin' to let her go to Toadstool and talk without me, an' she knows it. Gives a man no room to bargain. She isn't goin' to pay for service I'll give her anyhow.''

Talbot grinned. ''If that's the first time a woman's gotten ye by the short . . .'' he glanced at Shamera, ''er . . . toes, ye can count yourself lucky.''

The Shark gestured to Talbot and fell into the thick accents of a dockworker, ''You see, girl? You're gain' to ruin my reputation. Soon no one will take the Shark seriously. Pretty girl says walk this way, I say how far. Word gain' to get around. Ain't no Shark, but a little Tadpole running the Whisper.''

Sham bent down on the horse until her face was level with his, matching his accent. ''They're gain' to say dead Shark, if you don't start moving. We're all gain' to die of old age right here in this spot wi' the wind a' rattlin' our jaws.''

He laughed and started down the street, letting them follow as they could through the debris that littered the battered cobblestones. Sham drew in a deep breath and coughed. Funny how quickly she'd gotten used to the fresh salt air of the Castle.

The Shark led them to a rough brick and stone building near the old docks, shaking his head when Talbot started to dismount.

''They know we're here. Let them come to us.''

''They'll consider it an insult,'' commented Talbot, familiar with the games of the streets.

The Shark shook his head. ''Tell them you wanted to keep your horses. He won't take it amiss.''

''I hope not,'' said Sham. ''I need his cooperation.''

The Shark smiled sweetly. ''You'll get it.''

She turned to Talbot. ''You know he's not as nice as he'd like to pretend, don't you?''

''Neither am I,'' replied Talbot smugly.

She snorted just as a nattily dressed young man opened the door of the building.

''I beg your pardon,'' he said, in a pure Cybellian Kerim would have been pleased to claim. ''But Toadstool sent me out to inquire as to the nature of your visit.''

The Shark nodded gravely. "These are friends of mine. The pretty little mare here—" he rubbed Sham's horse underneath its cheekstrap and it closed its eyes in ecstasy, "—she's a bit skittish, so we don't want to leave her alone. Could you persuade Toadstool to come out and talk with us a moment?"

"Regarding?"

"I would like to . . . rent some property from him for tonight," answered Shamera.

"I will so inform him." Toadstool's man went back into the house.

They waited. Shamera's "skittish" mare dropped into a three-legged doze, idly switching her tail at the flies.

At last a middle-aged man with a slight potbelly and a round, good-natured face approached them from an alley several buildings away from the one where Toadstool made his office.

"I'd wager he's not as nice as he acts either," commented Talbot softly.

Sham grunted her agreement.

"My friend tells me that you are interested in the rental of a property," said the chubby man congenially.

She nodded. "I need to rent the space near the cliffs, where the old bell used to hang, from now until dawn."

Toadstool pursed his lips. "I know the spot. Tonight's the Spirit Tide, eh? Nice little place for a lover's tryst."

Sham gave him a sly smile. "That's the idea."

He cast an assessing eye on her clothes, just as she had expected he would. It would have been safer to wear her tunic and trousers, but then he might not have dealt with her at all. Purgatory's territorial lords were a fickle lot.

"Ten gold."

"For that price, I want you to make sure that we are not disturbed," said Shamera.

"Eleven gold and I'll supply guards."

"Ten gold," she countered smoothly. "I have my own people. I just need you to put the word out to your folk to stay off the cliffs tonight. For their own safety, you understand. I have a few enemies, and it would be a great tragedy if one of my men killed one of yours by mistake.''

"Ah, quite," he agreed cordially. "Ten gold then."

Sham nodded at Talbot, who opened Kerim's purse and produced ten gold coins.

SHAM WAITED UNTIL THEY HAD RIDDEN OUT OF SIGHT BEfore she reached over and snagged the purse. Stopping her horse near the Shark she tossed him the heavy leather bag.

"Shark, there's another ten pieces of gold here. I know that you usually don't offer protection, but I need people I can trust to keep that area clear."

"Does this have something to do with the demon that killed Maur?"

Sham nodded. "It's not revenge. But it's the best I can do."

"Very well." He put two fingers to his lips and whistled sharply.

A thin man trotted up from somewhere, nodding a grave greeting to Talbot, whom he obviously knew.

"Vawny will escort you to the rental property while I gather a few favors," said the Shark. "I assume that you mean to take up residence immediately?"

"Immediately," she answered.

VAWNY AND TALBOT STAYED WITH THE HORSES WHILE she paced out a design in the sandy soil at the top of the cliffs. The ocean was already lower than usual; even the spray from the breakers didn't come near the top. She'd picked her place carefully. The sandy area was surrounded by large rocks, some as tall as a two-story building, that looked like jagged shark-teeth. Strewn amidst the rocks were small wooden huts cobbled together for shelter. They were currently empty, since the Toadstool had scattered their most recent inhabitants for the night. They would serve as hiding places from the demon until the trap was sprung.

When she had walked the rune through once, she climbed to the top of a convenient rock to inspect her work.

Slithering down to the sand, she made several corrections and checked it once more.

Satisfied, she took a stick and began again, pushing one end deeply into the ground to retrace her footprints. When the pattern was finished, Sham rifled through Talbot's saddlebags until she found the spool of gold thread.

She glanced surreptitiously at Vawny and decided not to push his integrity further than she had to. Before she pulled the thread out of the saddlebag, she turned it black with a softly spoken spell.

She stretched once and started to lay the metal thread in the patterned soil. It took a long time. Her back grew stiff, and the sky began to darken toward evening well before she was through.

"Can I help?" asked Talbot softly, bringing her a flask from his saddle.

Sham accepted the drink gratefully, shrugging her shoulders to loosen her tight muscles. The sea was pulling away from the cliffs now, leaving a widening strip of sand behind. In the distance she could see the top of the sea wall, a dark, ragged, brooding presence on the horizon. The waveless sea between the wall and the beach was smooth as black glass.

Returning the flask, she nodded her head. "Yes, I need you to fetch Elsic and Lord Halvok. They should be waiting for you at your home by now. I'll be through with this before you're back."

AT LONG LAST IT WAS FINISHED. SHAM CLOSED HER EYES and ran a soft pulse of magic through the end of thread she held in her left hand. A brief moment later her right hand tingled faintly where it touched the other end of the thread. The flavor of the magic told her the pattern was correct. Carefully she laid either end in the dirt, making certain that the two did not touch.

With a wave of her hands the sand shifted, burying the rune and the marks her knees had left behind. Standing up, Shamera surveyed the remains of her gown wryly. If this night's work didn't pan out, she was likely to end her life buried in the ragged, dirty silk gown.

She removed the illusion she'd put on the wire. Now that it was covered with sand she didn't need it, and she didn't want any hint of magic to warn the demon. As she set a broken cobblestone in the center of the rune, she heard riders approaching. It was too dark to see them, but it could only be Talbot, Halvok, and Elsic. The Shark would have let no other riders through.

Sham closed her eyes and worked a touch of magic.

IN THE CASTLE KERIM WATCHED THE SMALL RUNE SHAM had traced on his chair arm flare briefly. It was time then.

Despite his formidable self-control and his doubts, a touch of battle fever caused a surge of elation. He wiggled his toes inside his boot, just to prove he could, then he grinned at Dickon.

"Get the horses ready," he said. "It's time."

THE RIDERS DISMOUNTED AND HANDED THEIR HORSE'S reins to the man who had replaced Vawny an hour or so before. As Shark's man led the horses away, they approached Sham.

Elsic cradled Maur's flute in one hand and held fast to Talbot's arm with the other, a reckless grin plastered on his face. "You really think this will work?"

"No," said Sham repressively.

If anything, Elsic's expression brightened. She understood him—it was a good thing to be needed. If the boy were a little older, he wouldn't have half his confidence in the wild scheme she'd come up with.

"Neither do I," added Lord Halvok. "If you want to activate your rune, I can work the spells to force the demon to submit to me, for my lifetime anyway."

"For your *short* lifetime it would be, if the demon had anything to say about it," replied Sham without heat— they'd already had this argument when she'd first approached him for help.

"If Shamera's plan fails, could you try to control it then?" asked Talbot.

Sham shook her head, answering before Halvok could. "No. I have to release the rune that holds the demon in place while I work the spell to send it home. If I fail, it's not going to be contained—nor is it going to be happy with us. Don't worry, though, if my spell doesn't work, the backlash of wild magic will kill us and burn Purgatory to the ground before the demon can do anything to you."

"Thanks," said Talbot, with a wry grin, "that's good to know. I wouldn't want to be killed by a demon."

Sham left Talbot talking with Lord Halvok and walked to the edge of the cliffs. Below her was inky blackness. Though there was no moon to see by, she could tell by the silence that the tide was out. The unnatural quiet seemed expectant.

Elsic seated himself on the ground next to her. His sightless eyes closed, he breathed in the salt air.

KERIM KNOCKED SOFTLY AT THE DOOR, READY TO PLAY his part. Although he was honest by nature, acting was the meat of any politician, and he had no fears about his ability. He worried about hurting Sky, though, and she'd been hurt enough.

"Who is it?" Sky's voice sounded husky with sleep.

"Kerim." There was a pause, and Kerim could almost hear her thinking.

"My Lord?" The door opened partially, and she peered through. Her sleeping gown was sheer and inviting.

Kerim gave her his best boyish grin. "Do you know what day it is?"

"No, My Lord," she smiled with a hint of shyness.

Looking at her, he found it even harder to believe that Sham was right. He had a feeling that he was going to be apologizing to Sky before the night was over.

"It's the day the Spirit Tide breaks. Have you ever seen it at night?"

"No, My Lord."

"Well, get dressed then. You have to see this. I know

you're not up to a strenuous ride yet, but we'll take a gentle horse for you—I have one with paces as smooth as cream . . . and I believe I owe you an apology for last night.''

She drew herself up. ''What about Lady Shamera?''

Kerim allowed a sad smile to cross his face. ''Ah, Lady Shamera . . . Perhaps you could put on a dressing robe and I'll come in and tell you about her. The hall is not the place for it—I promise I'll keep my hands to myself.''

The door shut momentarily; when Sky opened it again, she was decently covered in an ivory silk bedrobe. ''Come in, my lord.''

He slipped by her, a difficult thing to do gracefully with his crutches but much easier than the wheeled chair, and took up residence on a uncomfortable wooden stool. She looked from him to the only other seat in the room, a padded loveseat, and smiled before she sat in it.

''You were going to tell me about Lady Shamera?''

''Yes,'' he sighed and looked at his feet before turning his gaze to hers. ''I am not her first protector, you know. She enjoys men. I met her soon after you came here, and I think that it was knowing that I had to leave you alone that drew me to her.''

''But I was crippled and it was getting worse.'' He swallowed heavily and continued in almost a whisper. ''I knew that Ven loved you, and would make an admirable husband and father. The child . . . the child was mine, wasn't it?'' He didn't have to feign the sadness in his voice: the poor babe, doomed by demons and wizards long dead or by mischance, he supposed it didn't matter which.

''I thought I was dying. I could see no good in making you a widow a second time, so I went looking for something to put between us—and I found Shamera.'' He played with the top of his left crutch. ''Then I began to recover.''

''I noticed that you have been getting better, my lord. Can you tell me why?''

He hesitated and managed to look frustrated and slightly guilty. ''That's the truly odd part, and I'm not certain it is my secret to tell.''

"My lord," she said meeting his eyes squarely. "Anything you say will stay with me."

He gave her a measuring glance, then nodded as if in sudden decision. "Late one night, when one of the cramping spells began, Shamera came in and . . . worked magic." He let some of the wonder he had felt creep into his voice. "I would not have believed it if I hadn't seen it myself. Shamera has told me that the wizards are largely fled from here, though there are a few, like her, who hide what they are."

"Did she find out who did that to you?"

Kerim nodded his head, even while the meaning of the mistake she'd just made washed over him. He'd never told Sky that Sham had been undoing a spell laid upon him— just that she'd worked magic. "She seems to think so," he said smoothly. "After the High Priest died—and this is the strangest part, I'm not sure I'd believe it if Shamera hadn't had Brother Fykall to back her up—something took over his body, or wore his shape. Shamera says that it was a demon. It made the mistake of going to the Temple of Altis, and brother Fykall destroyed it."

Sky's mouth tightened with anger momentarily. If he hadn't been watching her closely, he would have missed it. The guilt that he'd been feeling for misleading Sky all but melted away.

"I owe Shamera a great deal—my health, and even my life. But—" he looked down, as if caught by shyness. "—I don't love her. Last night made me realize that I had to talk to her, and tell her how I felt. I'd already left it too long; I was afraid I would hurt her."

He grinned suddenly. "I almost wish you'd have been there. I was expecting to face down the virago who leapt on my bed with a broken pitcher and faced a merchant instead. She let me say what I had to say, then smiled and laid down terms she thought were fair for services rendered."

Kerim smiled coaxingly. "Come with me tonight, Sky. I haven't been to the sea for a long time. The Spirit Tide is something you will remember for the rest of your life."

"I . . ." she gave him a look filled with desire and fear. "I don't know if I should . . ."

"Come with me," he lowered his voice into a purr. Practicing with Shamera had improved his seduction technique.

She drew in a breath, and recklessly said, "Yes, I would like that. If you'll wait a moment in the hall, I'll put on riding clothes."

"For you, I'll wait," replied Kerim softly, rising to his feet and crossing the distance to the hall as lightly as someone on crutches could be expected to.

Lady Sky gave him a quick, bright smile before she shut the door.

LANTERN IN HAND, DICKON WAITED OUTSIDE THE WALLS of the Castle with three horses: A sweet-faced bay mare, his own sturdy gelding, and Kerim's war stallion, Scorch.

The stallion looked rather odd with the crutches attached to the shoulder of either side of the saddle, but he was used to carrying stranger things than crutches. Kerim rubbed the black muzzle affectionately.

Cautiously, with Dickon holding the opposite stirrup so the saddle wouldn't slip, Kerim gripped the saddle at pommel and cantle and powered the rest of his body up and into position. Not graceful, but it was effective. Dickon handed Kerim the lantern, and helped Lady Sky on her mare before mounting himself.

"We are not to go alone, my Lord?" questioned Lady Sky softly, with a pointed look at Dickon.

Kerim shifted his weight until the stallion sidestepped next to Lady Sky's mount. Reaching over he took one gloved hand into his free hand and brought it to his lips. "Alas, no, Lady. The best place to view the Spirit Tide is on the other side of a bad section of town. Despite the fact that I've paid off the proper people to ensure a quiet ride, it would be sheerest folly to go into such a place with only a crippled warrior such as myself to guard you. Dickon is quite a hand with that sword he carries."

Lady Sky smiled. "So this is not such an impulsive trip after all—you could have given me more notice."

Behind her, Kerim noticed that Dickon was frowning his disapproval. He'd cautioned Kerim about flirting too hard and hurting Sky.

"Ah, me." Kerim grinned. "I have betrayed myself. No, Lady, I've been planning this for most of the day." He gave her a convincing leer. "But if I had given you notice, you'd not have met me in your sleeping gown."

Lady Sky laughed and followed him as he nudged his mount into a swinging walk.

IN SPITE OF HIS SPOKEN PESSIMISM, KERIM'S RIDE through Purgatory was without incident. He could feel the eyes peering at them from the inky blackness, but they stayed there. Apparently Shamera had greased the right fists with his gold. He took his time, flirting and delaying. By the time they reached the broken timbers of the old bell tower, he calculated that they only had a short time before the tide returned.

Kerim stopped the stallion near a clump of scrub a fair distance from the cliffs. Returning the lantern to Dickon's care, he dismounted with more expediency than skill, but ended up on his feet, which was something of a salve to his pride.

While Dickon saw to Lady Sky's dismounting, Kerim untied the leather strings that kept the crutches in place. He was still unsteady on his feet, but with the crutches he had a fair bit of mobility on the rough ground.

"Come," he said, leading Lady Sky away from the horses and Dickon. "You'll have to take the lantern."

The nearby buildings were nearly rotted through from the salt-sea air. Kerim ignored them as he made his way to a small area of sandy dirt near the cliffs. He stopped with the base of one crutch resting near a solitary piece of broken cobblestone. Sometime during the ride the stars had come into their full glory. Even without the moon's light, it was possible to see the beach far below.

Sky drew in her breath as she gazed beyond the cliff. "How fascinating."

"Beautiful," he agreed, "an unexpected act of nature—

like you." He reached into his belt pouch and looked for something that wasn't there.

"Plague it," he said, with boyish embarrassment, "I brought you something, but I forgot to get it from Dickon. Wait here, I won't be but a moment."

She gave him the lantern. Holding it awkwardly, he turned and rapidly made his way back to the horses while Lady Sky waited, her beautiful profile turned to the sea and a faint smile on her face.

As soon as Kerim was far enough away, Lord Halvok sneaked soundlessly around the remains of the building he had been hiding behind, giving Sham a hint at the reason his guerrilla campaign had been able to hold out against the Easterners. He stopped at the place she had hidden the break in the wire.

Quickly he brought the ends together, fusing them with a touch of magic that caught Lady Sky's attention. Hidden in the shadows of another building, Sham bit her lip. Halvok's fate rested on her rune skills, and she'd never had to make a rune of this size before.

As the magic built, the golden thread began to glow, burning brightly beneath the covering sand. Under other circumstances the rune would have been enough to hold its prisoner indefinitely; a demon was as capable of unmaking a rune as Sham or Halvok was, so Halvok knelt where he was and continued to imbue the rune with magic.

"What are you doing?" asked Lady Sky staring at Lord Halvok in surprise and taking a step back. "Kerim?" her voice rose in fright, "what is he doing to me?"

Coming out of her hiding place, Sham flinched at the fear in Sky's voice. Looking at her standing alone on the cliff edge it was difficult to remember the reasoning Sham had used to convict her. Instinctively Sham glanced at Kerim, knowing that he'd had his doubts as well. Kerim was frowning as he gripped Dickon's arm. He gestured as he talked—though Sham couldn't hear what he said.

Elsic stepped out around a rock, the flute in one hand and his other resting lightly on Talbot's shoulder. "I know you, demon," he said, his face turned to Lady Sky. "I've felt you in my dreams."

"What are you talking about? Kerim said the priest killed the demon," said Lady Sky, looking more frightened than ever. "Kerim?"

"She's going to send you back," said Kerim gently, as he approached with Dickon. "Isn't that where you've been trying to go all this time? It's time for you to go home."

"No . . ." Lady Sky's voice lost its cultured softness as she wailed despairingly. "You don't know what she's trying to do!"

"Nor does she," said the Shark from just behind Sham, causing her to jump. "But that never stopped her before."

"What are you doing here?" asked Sham in a voice designed to carry only to the Shark's ears.

He grinned. "You think I'd miss the most exciting bit of news to happen around here since the Eastern Invasion?"

"Stay back with Kerim," she warned him. "This could get nasty."

"Shamera?" asked Lady Sky. "Why are you doing this? I thought you were my friend."

Sham walked forward until she stood just outside the barrier Halvok held. "Chen Laut," she said, and gestured.

It was unnecessary to call the demon's true form in order to send it back to its world, but Sham needed the reassurance of knowing she was right. So she call the demon by a name it had held for centuries. It was not its true name, but it had power all the same.

The sand at Sky's feet shifted, as if at a strong wind. Sky herself jerked like a marionette in the hands of a toddler, shifting . . . The body fell limply to the ground, and over it stood the demon.

Larger than a horse it was, a creature of flames the color of magic. Eight fragile limbs held its apparent bulk off the wet sand, but there was nothing arachnoid about the rest of the demon. A tail of gold and red ever-changing flames hit the edge of the rune with a crack, driving Lord Halvok to the ground at the unexpected pain.

But there was no question who was hurt worse. The demon screamed, an unearthly trill that covered the spectrum of sound, as a blue-green light flashed from the rune to its tail. When it was through, the demon crouched in the center of the rune, swaying back and forth.

"Halvok?" called Sham.

"Fine," he said, though he sounded hoarse. "The rune will hold her."

"Three times bound was I," said the creature using Lady Sky's voice. "Three dead wizards litter the cold earth. Your binding too, I shall come through in better condition than you, wizard. Get what power you can while you may, you will be dead soon enough."

"I will die," Sham agreed readily, "as all mortal things do. But before then I will see you home again. Talbot, what's the tide like?"

"If you destroy me," continued the demon, "I will haunt you and your children until there is one born I might use, witch. I will take that one's body and hunt until your descendants walk not upon this earth."

"Not yet," answered Elsic, listening to the sea as he fingered the flute, "but soon."

Talbot gave the blind boy a sharp-eyed look. "It's still out."

"Jetsam," purred the demon, shifting its graceful neck so it was peering at Elsic, "—cast-off selkie garbage. If you aid in my binding, I will seek you out when I am free, and throw you back to the sea where your own people will rend you and feed you to the fish as tribute."

Elsic smiled sweetly. "I aid in no binding."

The demon paced sinuously within the outer bonds of the hold-rune. It was careful not to touch the edges.

"Now," said Elsic.

Dimly Sham heard the muted roar of the returning waves begin. Elsic put the flute to his lips and blew a single pure note that pierced the night as cleanly as a fair-spent arrow. After a few experimental scales, he slipped into an unfamiliar song in a minor key.

Sham felt the magic begin to gather. She took a deep

breath, and silently reminded herself that most of the magic she would work were spells she already knew. She'd spent half the night memorizing the only one that was new until she could recite the steps backwards in her sleep. If her concentration or confidence faltered, it would release all the power of the Spirit Tide into flames that would swallow them and Purgatory as well—inspiration for the poorest of students, and she had never been that.

In the original version the death of the sacrifice gave power to the spell. The sympathetic magic of death sent the demon to where it belonged as the soul of the sacrifice traveled home. She intended to replace both functions with the Spirit Tide as it came home to the cliffs.

The magic that the tide generated was formed by the sea, and humans worked only with unformed magic. Like limestone and marble, the two kinds of magic were formed by the same materials with tremendously different results.

Elsic gathered the green magic of the sea, and the flute transformed it into its raw form. Sham had to hold the gathering forces until the last moment before she worked the final spell. There would be no second chances.

Sweat ran off her forehead and she swayed with the effort as the magic grew exponentially with the progress of the monumental wave of water that had begun to swallow the sand. Someone gripped her shoulders briefly and steadied her.

Still the magic grew. The first two spells were easy, nothing that she hadn't cast a hundred times before. She began to draw on the magic.

First to set the subject.

The demon screamed as she worked the spell, weaving it around the creature.

Second to name its true name.

Demon, Chen Laut, bringer of death, stealthy breaker of bonding spells laid upon it by greedy men. Avenger, killer, lonely exile. Sham understood the demon, and wove her knowledge into the spell. It was enough—she knew it. She could feel the demon trying to break the naming, but it was futile.

"Southwood lord," called the demon, "Bind me to you and I will help you drive the Easterners from Purgatory. If you allow her to destroy me, they will never go."

Halvok stiffened, like a hound scenting fox.

"If she chooses to bind rather than destroy, Shamera will not drive them away," continued the demon persuasively. Sky's voice rang clear through the growing roar of sea and wind. "She's in love with the Reeve. She's too young to really remember how it was, what it felt like to hold your loved ones as they die. But you do, don't you? You remember your wife. She wasn't beautiful, was she? Not until she smiled. She was wonderfully kind. Do you remember how much she loved your children? Then the Easterners came, while you were fighting elsewhere. You returned home and found only what the soldiers had left. She fought to protect the children, your wife, even after what they had done to her."

"Halvok," said Sham, her voice trembling with the effort of speaking while she tried to hold both the magic and the demon. If Halvok dropped the rune at the wrong time, it could spell disaster. "Halvok, that world is gone. Driving the Easterners out of Southwood will not set time back. It won't restore your wife, nor even the person you were before they came."

She had told Kerim that what the demon wanted most was to go home—she knew how the creature felt. As she exacted vengeance from those men who had crippled Maur, she had known that it was only a substitute for what she really wanted: to return to what once was, to go home. "Only death will come from seeking it, Halvok. Not just nameless Easterners will die—but your friends and colleagues. People you've come to know and care for. And once the killing starts, it won't be Eastern blood alone that feeds the soil. Hasn't there been enough death?"

"Yes," said Halvok. "I am sick of—"

The demon struck the rune.

Halvok fell limply to the sand and the steady glow the rune had been emitting flickered wildly.

No time to question. Running to the place where Halvok

lay, Sham drew her knife, nicked her palms, and placed both hands on the gold thread. Power surged through her from that contact and she cried out. The magic from the waves buckled and the skin of her hands turned red and blistered from the wild magic that seeped out of her control, but the blood made the difference as she had known it would. It made the rune hers again, no matter how the magic surged and fought it.

She couldn't let the rune fail until just before the wave hit the cliff, or she wouldn't be able to open the gateway to the demon's realm no matter how much power she had. She would have to break it, symbolizing the breakage of the bonds that held the demon to this world. It shouldn't have been difficult. Halvok could have done it by dropping the two ends of the wire separately, but Sham was tied to the rune by blood.

She needed Halvok, but he lay silently on the ground, Talbot kneeling at his side. She hoped he was alive.

Still the magic grew. She couldn't see the Spirit Tide, but the sound of the water rushing over the sand had become deafening. Ignoring the smell of singed flesh she continued to gather the magic.

"Now," shouted Kerim and Talbot together.

She broke the rune. Bound to her by blood, the rune's death hurt her, making her hands cramp until she had to force herself to her feet so that the tension of the wire would pull it from her grasp. Pain wasn't the real problem, or rather not the whole of the problem: It was what the pain did to her concentration that mattered.

It took a long moment for her to regain control of the forces she held.

Just as she began the final spell, before the demon realized that it was no longer held by the rune, the great wave struck and the cliffs shook. Water coated everything, spraying in great heavy sheets. Elsic faltered and the magic flared wildly until she couldn't tell hers from the magic that sang in the waves. Sham knew Elsic had resumed playing only from the feel of the magic flowing into her; she couldn't hear the music over the pounding water.

Crying out in a voice that was nothing against the roar that shook Purgatory, she continued working the last spell.

The first of her spells gave her an awareness of the demon, so she knew when it sprang. She spoke faster, finishing as the demon's hot, sharp tail raked her side.

Something *rippled* in the night and the demon stilled as the rift grew. In that bare instant Sham realized the place she was sending the demon didn't exist, not as she understood the term. For a brief moment that might have been an eternity, she stood at the gate and understood things about magic she'd never realized before, small things . . .

A second wave hit. Smaller than the first, bringing with it more water, more noise, and more flute-born magic.

Buffeted by pain, awe, and a new surge of magic, Sham lost control, consumed by the torment of the demon's touch and the fire of wild magic. The gate flickered, then steadied, held by someone else.

Give me the power, witch, said Sky's voice, slipping beneath and between the waves of pain as Sham regained a tenuous hold on the magic. *You have my name, give me the power. If you do not, it will kill you and all those here this night.*

Sham struggled to think. With the power she held, the demon could destroy Landsend. She didn't think even the ae'Magi would be able to stop it. Now that Sham had shown it how, it could go home any time it wanted to. Demons were creatures of magic; they were not bound to use unformed magic as she was.

Elsic played, and the magic continued to grow as a third wave hit. Sham couldn't even divert enough attention from her tasks to tell him to stop.

Silly witch, hatred of your kind does not mean so much to me that I would stay here another moment. Give me the magic and let me go home.

"Take it," said Shamera, knowing that she could not hold it for much longer.

Power flowed out of her faster than it had come, and the demon accepted it with a capacity that seemed limitless. When it held all she could give, Sham collapsed on the sandy cliff top curling around the pain in her side. She watched the demon as it steadied the gate to its home.

The demon turned toward the rift Sham had opened, then hesitated.

Sham had a moment to wonder what she was going to do if the pox-ridden thing decided it didn't want to go back when, feather-light, its tail brushed her side again. The pain that had resided there was replaced by cool numbness.

Sorry, said the demon in a voice as soft as the wind.

Then it was gone.

The gate hung open above the broken bits of golden thread. Sham struggled to her knees. She had given all her magic to the demon; there was nothing left. If it didn't close . . .

It snapped shut with a cracking sound that rose above the thunder of yet another wave of water. For a moment the night was still—then the fires began.

They lit up the night like a thousand candles, burning the saltgrass where the gate had been first, then spreading faster than even a natural wildfire through the damp foliage. When the next wave hit the cliff and sent fine spray high into the air, flame touched the algae that lived in the water, making the droplets of spray spark gold and orange in the night.

"Back," yelled Shamera, stumbling to her feet as best she could. "Damn it, get back."

The magic that she'd given the demon was from this world. What the demon hadn't used had returned when the gate closed. A clump of driftwood burst into ashes as the magic passed near.

"Shamera, get away from there." She thought it was Kerim who called, but she was too busy drawing upon what little magic she had left to be certain.

Cold hands closed on her shoulders. "What can I do?" asked Dickon.

"Support me," she said, her voice thin even to her ears. "Release your magic to me."

Like his magelight, the power he fed to her flickered randomly, but it helped. The old bell tower went up in a blaze of glory, but Sham managed to keep the wild magic from raging where it would. Like a sheepdog, the threads of her mastery nipped here and there, cornering the worst of it against the cliff where the water would control the damage.

Kerim stood back with the rest, wishing futilely for the means to help. The Shark stood on his right, looking much like Kerim felt. Talbot knelt on the ground with the unconscious Halvok's head resting on his knee. The sailor's eyes were focused on Shamera and Dickon. Elsic sat beside them, his lips tight with anxiety—Kerim thought perhaps that Elsic, blind as he was, had a better idea of the struggle than any of the rest of the audience.

Shamera was lit by an eerie brilliance like the phosphorescent plankton that floated on the sea, only many times brighter. Foxfire flitted here and there in Dickon's hair and on his back, dripping from his fingers to the ground where it shimmered at his feet. The air carried a scorched scent and a feeling of energy like it had just before lightning struck.

Another wave hit the cliff, but this one was only dimly lit by the odd little flickers that had covered the ones before. When the water ran back to the sea it left only darkness behind it. Dickon swayed where he stood, as if it took all of his strength to remain on his feet. Sham fell into an untidy heap on the ground.

The Shark beat Kerim there only because his crutches hindered his movement. Kerim hesitated by Dickon's side, touching him lightly on the shoulder.

"I'm all right, sir," said Dickon, "just tired."

Kerim nodded, dropping his crutches. He fell to his knees next to Sham where she lay face down in the wet sand. The Shark, kneeling on the far side, held his hand against her neck.

"She's alive," he said.

Remembering the fires that had flickered over her, Kerim reached out carefully, and with the Shark's help, turned her face out of the sand. Elsic and Talbot joined the quiet gathering with Halvok braced between them.

Halvok made a gesture and a dim circle of light appeared in his hand. The Southwood noble looked tired, and he moved with the painful slowness of an old, old man.

By his light it was possible to see that Sham was breathing in the soft panting rhythm of a tired child, and some of the tightness in Kerim's chest slackened. He began to examine her with battle-learned thoroughness for wounds, but found only blisters. They clustered tightly on her hands, then scattered here and there. Her side was covered with blood, but all that Kerim could find was a growing bruise.

He had expected much worse.

Carefully, he gathered her into his lap and wrapped her with his cloak to keep her from getting chilled. As he worked, he thought it didn't seem possible that this bedraggled and dirty thief was the wizard whose blazing figure had recently lit the night. The Shark watched him coolly.

"It's gone," said Halvok, breaking the silence. He shook his head in private amusement. "Not too badly done, for an apprentice. I'll speak to the wizard's council and see if we can get her raised to master. Sending a demon to hell should count as a masterwork."

"Not hell," corrected Elsic with a dream-touched smile. "It was beautiful—didn't you see it?"

FINIS

When Sham woke, she was in her room at the Castle. With her eyes closed she could hear Jenli arguing with someone. A door closed and the sound was muffled. Sham began to drift off again.

"Shamera," hissed Kerim softly and her bed dipped under his weight.

With an effort she forced her eyes open.

"I had Dickon distract your maid so I could come in here and talk to you. She's been as bad as a cat with one kitten since we brought you back, although," he added with a twinkle, "I think she was more upset about your dress."

Sham started to grin in response, but stopped when she felt her lips begin to crack.

"I feel—" she said carefully, so she didn't cause more damage, "—as if I need an apple."

He looked blank. "An apple?"

"Hmm," she nodded. "Don't you Easterners roast your pigs with apples in their mouths?"

Kerim surveyed her and laughed. "Except for your hands

it's little more than a sunburn, and Dickon says even your hands won't scar."

The outer door opened a crack, then snapped shut again.

"I needed to ask you something before Halvok talks to you. I don't want you to agree to his proposal before you listen to mine," said Kerim hurriedly. "There's not much time. I'm not sure how long Dickon can keep Jenli occupied. I would like you to consider taking Maur's post. I..." he said softly, then hesitated and adopted a more businesslike tone. "We need you—just today I've gotten word that there's something odd at the hot springs just outside of Landsend. There's no king of course, so we'd have to change the title."

Sham carefully kept all expression out of her face, mostly because moving her face hurt. "You want me to be your wizard?"

He nodded. "I've talked to Fykall and he's agreed to give you Altis's blessing, so you'll have that as well as the state's endorsement."

"A powerful position," said Sham slowly, uncertain how she felt about having Altis's blessing.

Kerim leaned back against the headboard of her bed. When he spoke his voice could have melted ice. "I trust you."

To give herself time to think about what that tone meant she asked, "What's Halvok's offer?"

"The Wizard's Council has agreed to raise your status to master."

Sham shrugged. "It's a formality."

He nodded. "That's what he said. Additionally, he was able to arrange a position for you with the ae'Magi." His tongue stumbled over the unfamiliar term.

Impressed, she said, "That's quite an honor."

"It would allow you to work with other mages. You would have access to the Archmage's libraries." He softened his voice and leaned nearer. "You would be safe there: no mobs, no demons."

He knew her too well. Sham cocked her head at him, then leaned forward and touched his lips with hers. Considering the blistered state of her mouth, it was quite a respectable kiss—for which she gave Kerim full credit.

She pulled away, the corner of her mouth tilted up, and she answered in the thick accents of his mistress. "No mobs? No demons? How utterly boring."

ABOUT THE AUTHOR

Patricia Briggs lived a fairly normal life until she learned to read. After that she spent lazy afternoons flying dragonback and looking for magic swords when she wasn't horseback riding in the Rocky Mountains.

Once she graduated from Montana State University with degrees in history and German, she spent her time substitute teaching and writing. She and her family live in the Pacific Northwest, where she is hard at work on her newest project.

Visit her website at www.hurog.com.

From national bestselling author

Patricia Briggs

DRAGON BONES

0-441-00916-6

Ward of Hurog has tried all his life to convince
people he is just a simple, harmless fool...And it's
worked. But now, to regain his kingdom, he must
ride into war—and convince them otherwise.

DRAGON BLOOD

0-441-01008-3

Ward, ruler of Hurog, joins the rebels against
the tyrannical High King Jakoven. But Jakoven
has a secret weapon. One that requires
dragon's blood—the very blood that courses
through Ward's veins.

Available wherever books are sold or at
penguin.com

B054

From "a natural born storyteller" *

PATRICIA BRIGGS

The Hob's Bargain

0-441-00813-5

Hated and feared, magic was banished from the land.
But now, freed from spells of the wicked bloodmages,
magic—both good and evil—returns.
And Aren of Fallbrook feels her own power of sight
strengthen and grow.

Overcome by visions of mayhem and murder, Aren vows to save
her village from the ruthless raiders who have descended upon
it—and killed her family. She strikes a bargain with the Hob, a
magical, humanlike creature who will exact a heavy price to
defend the village—a price Aren herself must pay.

Available wherever books are sold or at
penguin.com

* *Midwest Book Review*

From national bestselling author

Patricia Briggs

RAVEN'S SHADOW
0-441-01187-X

The Raven mage Seraph must protect the world
from the terror that threatens to reemerge after
generations of imprisonment.

"A TALENTED STORYTELLER WHO
ENCHANTS HER AUDIENCE."
—*MIDWEST BOOK REVIEW*

Available wherever books are sold or at
penguin.com

B055

Coming September 2005 from Ace

Rakkety Tam
by Brian Jacques
0-441-01318-X
Rakkety Tam MacBurl, the mercenary warrior from the borderlands, and the brave squirrel Wild Doogy Plum embark on a quest in this latest *New York Times* bestseller in the *Redwall* series.

Path Not Taken
by Simon R. Green
0-441-01319-8
John Taylor has just discovered that his long-gone mother created the Nightside, the dark heart of London. To save his birthplace, he will have to travel back to a distant—and probably deadly—past.

Also new in paperback this month:

War Surf
by M.M. Buckner
0-441-01320-1

Robots
edited by Jack Dann and Gardner Dozois
0-441-01321-X

Available wherever books are sold or at penguin.com